THE WRECK

Norway, 1940: On the run from invading Nazis, eleven-year-old Ivar is trained as a spy by the Norwegian resistance and sent on a mission that could alter the path of the war — but when he comes face to face with the man who killed his family, revenge becomes the only mission possible . . . Norway, present day: Henrik Bonde, a far-right politician, is poised to seize power with an audacious move that depends on a haul of Nazi gold aboard a sunken German battleship. Determined to stop him are an ancient convict and a down-and-out former Royal Engineer, desperate to outwit the Oslo Police who are pursuing a case that will uncover Norway's shadowy wartime past. One thing is certain: more bodies will be sinking into the Oslofjord . . .

BRUNO HARE

THE WRECK

Complete and Unabridged

CHARNWOOD
Leicester

First published in Great Britain in 2012 by
Simon & Schuster UK Ltd.
London

First Charnwood Edition
published 2013
by arrangement with
Simon & Schuster UK Ltd.
A CBS Company
London

A catalogue record for this book is available
from the British Library.

ISBN 978–1–4448–1697–6

Published by
F. A. Thorpe (Publishing)
Anstey, Leicestershire

Set by Words & Graphics Ltd.
Anstey, Leicestershire
Printed and bound in Great Britain by
T. J. International Ltd., Padstow, Cornwall

This book is printed on acid-free paper

For Mona

If there is one thing for which Man will go to the ends of the earth, it is a dream. If there are two, the second is the man promising to make that dream reality. Thus, while the recipes for the manipulation of one's fellow man are manifold, at heart all share the same three ingredients:

1. Find out what truly he wants.
2. Tell him you will give it to him.
3. Never concede that he is a victim of deception.

— Dr Walther Ziegler,
Die Ränge der Mensch, 1935

Prologue

Nazi ideology stated that the Third Reich was destined to last for a thousand years. To achieve this, it was calculated that the German people would have to be at least two hundred million strong. They had a problem. The population of Germany was somewhere between sixty-five and seventy million and the birth rate among 'superior' Germans was in decline.

To remedy this issue, Reichsführer-SS Heinrich Himmler established the *Lebensborn* programme in 1935. Initially, the programme was enacted as a form of encouragement, aimed solely at Himmler's elite *Schutzstaffel* military corps. Incentives for stocking the core gene-pool of the Fatherland with 'racially ideal' progeny included exclusive maternity homes at which burgeoning families would receive the very best in pre-and post-natal care and money to ensure that their offspring would want for nothing. Even so, the population did not grow as fast as prolonged world domination would require, and soon enough Himmler widened the parameters of the programme. So long as mothers-to-be could prove their unborn child hailed from a minimum of three generations of racial purity, and provided it showed no signs of inferiority following birth (physical, genetic or racial) all the benefits of *Lebensborn* would be forthcoming.

But two hundred million still lay way off on

the horizon, and when the war really got going, the military was losing men faster than children were being born. With numbers dropping instead of rising, Himmler kicked *Lebensborn* up another couple of gears. It became a full-blown breeding programme. The facilities operating in Germany were no longer the straightforward maternity homes the programme had started with, nor even drop-shops for women who found themselves compromised by unwed but racially pure pregnancies.

Under *Lebensborn*, some 250,000 'biologically fit' children were kidnapped from occupied territories and brought to the Fatherland for Germanization. Facilities were also established in Austria, Belgium, Denmark, France, Holland, Luxembourg and Poland, but the only country that could match Germany for the number of premises opened, and the number of births recorded, was Norway.

Himmler revered the Norwegian as the ultimate living manifestation of the Aryan race, and encouraged German soldiers to couple and procreate with Norwegian women. In return, the women and their children would receive care and attention and a healthy diet, with meat and vitamin-rich fresh vegetables.

Norway's population was three million at the time of invasion, while the German occupying force reached close to four hundred thousand before liberation. That's a German soldier for every other woman of childbearing age.

1

1

2009

Oslo Prison was a gothic-looking building, all high brown stone walls and turrets, sandwiched between the main police station and the city's only mosque, in an area called Grønland, just east of the centre. Most of the cells on the prison's C Block were eight square metres. The longer a man was incarcerated there, the more his room grew to resemble a physical representation of his mind. Photographs, letters, drawings, newspaper clippings, all pinned to the walls, layer upon layer — each one a thought, a memory, a fantasy. Then one day — release day — it was all gone. A network of black pinholes was all that was left on the white gloss walls, like an unintelligible version of a child's dot-to-dot puzzle: patternless. And the cell was stripped back to the stainless-steel sink and toilet and the pine bed bolted to the wall under the barred window. On those days, it was like a brain had suddenly been wiped clear of all it had learned and yearned for, scrunched up and stuffed into a single manila envelope, like the one lying on the stained ticking of the mattress next to the man in cell 236. He was perched there like a sagging finch, skinny, lank, his straggled, grey head bowed. How many years? And just one envelope, barely an inch thick.

Olavsen swung the four-inch plate steel hatch shut and pulled open the door. The cell's occupant looked up, his ancient, clouded eyes expectant, hesitant, his skin latticed with wrinkles, the lower half of his face so wizened that the fibrous tobacco-yellow hair looked less like a beard than simply what was left once age had worn away skin and tissue.

'Hey,' Olavsen said to him, struggling to inject his voice with any enthusiasm. 'Remember: today is the first day of the rest of your life.'

The man rose, leaving his envelope on the bed.

'Don't you want that?' Olavsen asked him.

'Bin it,' the man said.

★ ★ ★

'Well, Mr — '

Warden Eide stopped and glanced at the name on the file in his hands. 'Lars Borgerud. It seems you've done your time here with us. And apparently we're satisfied you've made a full rehabilitation during your stay. How about that?'

There was a sting in the warden's tone and the amused shine in his eyes told Morten Damberg he was missing something here. Damberg looked at the old prisoner sitting next to him on the visitors' side of Eide's desk. The man did not respond to Eide. He just stared at the green leather desk top.

'It's time to forget about the past and look to the future, Mr Borgerud,' Eide continued, his scorn still evident. 'And to start you off, you've

6

been assigned a new parole officer. This is Morten Damberg.'

Apparently bored now, Eide dropped the file onto the desk and nodded at Damberg. Then, sinking into his chair, and swivelling to face the window, he folded his hands over his potbelly and gazed out at the cloudless sky.

'Mr Borgerud?' Damberg said, and waited a moment for a reaction from the old man. When none came, he glanced at Eide, who lifted a hand and lazily wound his forefinger in the air — *get on with it.*

'Mr Borgerud, my name is Morten Damberg. As Warden Eide said, you've done your time here. Now you can get on with your life.'

Damberg opened his own file and placed a piece of paper on the desk in front of the old man.

'To help you with this you've been set up with an address, here. It's a nice place, by the river, people your own age. You'll have a room to yourself, with full amenities, meals. And of course it's staffed, for your own health and safety.'

'You'll be right at home,' Eide shot over the desk at them, entertaining himself.

Ignoring him, Damberg pulled out another sheet of paper from his file, placed it on the desk in front of the man's eyes and ploughed on.

'The credits you've earned during your incarceration have been deposited every month into an account set up in your name with DNB, Mr Borgerud — these are the details. Your pension's also being placed in this account. Now, this piece of plastic here is called a debit card.

7

You can use it to get cash out of an automated teller machine.'

Damberg explained how to use the card, then placed it on the piece of paper.

'At your age, Mr Borgerud, there's no need for you to work. But we don't want you getting isolated.' Damberg closed his file and leaned forward. 'Some people find it difficult to adjust to the outside world, Mr Borgerud, and you've been in here a long time. The world has changed. 2009 can be a daunting place for a person in your position.'

Still the old man didn't move or react in any way.

'I can understand if you don't want anyone to know where you've come from, where you've been, and no one needs to know if you don't want them to. I'll be around to see you often enough, but it's important for you to reintegrate, and that'll take effort. Start with small, brief conversations, with your neighbours, staff at the home. Then build it up. And remember — you can always call me. If you have any problems, any questions, you can reach me on this number.'

Damberg flicked the business card he was holding, then placed it back in the file and lifted the rest of the contents from the table, placing them back in the file too, before holding it out to the old man.

'There you go, Mr Borgerud. Good luck to you.'

But the old man didn't take the file. He looked up at Eide. He was scared of his master, Damberg could see it now, like an injured creature found by a cruel kid. He didn't want to give Eide any excuse to dish out more punishment. But blended with that fear was something else. A steeliness, a belief.

'Take it,' Eide said, realizing he was being asked permission. 'We're done here.'

But the old man still didn't take the file.

Damberg got to his feet. He hooked his hand under the old man's armpit and helped him up, then led him to the door. Before he opened it, Eide spoke from his desk again.

'Borgerud?' he said, the sarcasm gone. The old man looked back at him. 'You be sure to remember what Damberg said. Wise words. Do you understand me?'

The old man opened his mouth, as though he might say something, but then closed it again without speaking a word.

'He's right, Mr Borgerud,' Damberg said, sliding the file into the old man's hand. Then he opened the door and the old man shuffled out.

★　★　★

'You're a parole officer, Damberg,' the warden said as soon as the door was closed again. 'Not a social worker.'

'A parole and *acclimatization* officer, sir.'

Eide leaned back in his chair and joined his hands behind his head, revealing dark sweat patches under each arm. He smiled. 'You want to make your mark, junior, to touch a life? I suggest you try someone else. We've got plenty of candidates here.'

9

'He's in here for putting his wife out of her misery, sir,' Damberg said.

'Pass the fucking Kleenex. So what?'

'So he sacrificed himself,' Damberg said. 'I think he deserves our pity.'

'Just take my word for it, Damberg. You don't know him like I do. Now who's next?'

★ ★ ★

Olavsen walked across the courtyard towards the sheet-steel exit gate, arm in arm with the old man, who was still holding the file Damberg had given him. It took three times longer than usual to get there, the old man limping like a lame horse. Olavsen let go of him at the gate and found a key on his chain. When he had the gate open, they both stood there looking down the tree-lined drive, the parched leaves and grass and shimmering asphalt leading up to civilization, the traffic growling along the main street at the end. A black Mercedes C-class was parked a little way up the drive.

'Better than snow and ice, I guess,' Olavsen said. 'That your ride?' The old man just stared at the car.

'You got anything planned?' Olavsen tried again. This time the old man turned to him. The expression in his old eyes was the same one Damberg had seen: a mix of determination and fear. But still he didn't say anything, so Olavsen put out his hand for the old man to shake. The hand stayed empty. The old man stepped through the gate and hobbled away towards the car.

Watching from the gate, Olavsen tried to see the Oslo of 2009 through the old man's eyes: cars the size of tanks, motorcycles that looked like they might sprout wings and fly into the sky, the riders kitted out like astronauts. The trams were the new, modern kind, and most of the buildings would be new to him too, probably. And people, people everywhere — men, women, children, their faces white, black and everything in between.

Olavsen said, 'Good luck, old man,' to himself, then closed the gate.

Down the drive, the old man stopped at the Mercedes, but he didn't get in. The driver's window was open six inches. The driver was youngish, fair, wearing black-lensed Aviators. The old man produced a folded A4 envelope from his inside jacket pocket. Another piece of paper came out with it, folded many times until it was a thick wad only an inch square, and fell to the ground. The old man dropped awkwardly to his knees and scooped it up again.

'What've you got there?' the driver said when the old man came back into view. 'The secret to the meaning of life?'

The old man didn't reply. Instead he pocketed the wad and fed the envelope through the window. The driver took it.

'You don't look like much, you know?'

The old man didn't respond.

'I suppose it's a long time ago. You understand what will happen if the information proves inaccurate?'

The old man didn't respond.

11

'I'll take that as a yes,' the driver said, and drove away, leaving the old man standing there.

Just then a young couple turned in to the drive right next to the old man, the first of the day's sunbathers, Olavsen figured, arriving early to stake a spot on the crunchy brown lawn beyond the trees outside the police station. The young woman was all slim brown limbs, electric-green bikini top, hotpants and flip-flops. The old man stared at her so long and so hard that her man glared back at him, frowning: *eyes off, pervert*. Then he laughed something to the girl and pulled her by the hand towards the trees. As she was led onwards, the girl looked back too, but the old man had already turned away, heading for the main street.

★ ★ ★

Along the road, the old man entered a hardware store. He spent a good couple of minutes looking for the correct aisle, then another minute selecting the right pair of pliers. When he was happy, he tore the pincers from their card and plastic packaging right there in the shop. Then he shuffled up the aisle and found a stainless-steel float used for carrying wet plaster. He propped the float upright on a shelf, flat steel side out. It gave a pretty good reflection of his old face. The old man looked at himself a moment, then opened his mouth wide and stuck the pliers in.

2

1940

Sixty-nine and a half years earlier, on the night of 8 April 1940, the sun's warmth was a distant memory on the Oslofjord. Spring had started to make its first moves against an extreme winter — the daylight hours had started to stretch out and the thick blanket of snow whitening the evergreen pine forest had begun to melt a little — but at night the temperature plunged. A thermometer would have claimed the temperature was a little above zero, but with the damp of the fog and the wind, it felt a lot lower. If you happened to be coming in from out of town, as some people were doing that night, you could be forgiven for assuming that the people of the fjord would be holed up in the homes that trailed along the sixty-kilometre waterway; sitting in front of their fires or snuggled up in bed under blankets. And that is exactly where most were — but not all.

At 11.30 p.m., the telephone rang in one of the traditional Nordic wooden houses in Drøbak, a small town perched on the east side of the fjord some thirty kilometres down from Oslo city, right where the channel is at its narrowest, less than a kilometre wide. The house belonged to Andreas Anderssen. Anderssen was in bed asleep when the phone rang. On hearing the bell

13

he forced open his eyes, but saw only darkness.

He reached out a hand and groped the receiver from its cradle.

'Anderssen,' he said into it when the cold plastic touched his cheek. His voice was a croak. He'd been sleeping with his mouth open again. Snoring probably. He closed his mouth and worked up some spit.

'Kommandørkaptein Anderssen?'

'Used to be,' he said, swallowing. 'I retired. In twenty-seven.' He pushed himself up onto an elbow. The luminous hands of his alarm clock told him he had been down for an hour. At his age you needed more sleep than that. His bones felt even heavier under his skin than they usually did. 'That's thirteen years ago,' he said.

At least his voice was normal again.

'With Kommandør Madsen on sick leave you're all the reserves I've got, and what with the current international situation being so . . . ' The voice paused, then concluded, 'twitchy.'

'Birger?' Anderssen said with a sigh, recognizing the voice now. 'It's nearly midnight.'

'You can sleep tomorrow, old man. We need you here. Get down to the marina. I've sent someone. One of the fresh recruits, so try not to scare him, all right?'

'What about?' Anderssen said, taking his spectacles off the nightstand. 'What's going on over there?'

'Could be it's more than a twitch.'

Anderssen nodded. He used to wake up in the middle of the night all the time. If a sound or movement came from his wife next to him he

14

had awoken immediately to interrupt the terror that took hold of her almost every night towards the end, covering up her perspiring body with the blanket she had kicked off, stroking her forehead, chatting to her. What he actually said didn't matter. She hadn't been able to grasp the meaning of his words. She just needed to hear his voice. It wasn't a soothing one, particularly, but it was familiar and safe, he supposed. Her breathing would grow calmer, and she'd drift off again.

Then one morning he woke up and the sun was shining through the window and he realized that he'd slept all night through. Not a single noise had roused him. Not once had he felt the sudden, jerking movement as every muscle in her body tensed with pain. Lying there next to her, facing the bedside, staring at the alarm clock, not daring to look round, he had tried to convince himself that he could hear the sound of her breathing over the ticking of the clock. But he couldn't, and suddenly he was sucking in mouthfuls of air in short sharp gulps, as though his trachea was too narrow. But still he hadn't moved. For nearly an hour he just lay there, crying in silence.

Since that day, Anderssen's sleep had not been interrupted by anything but dreams. In those dreams the fog of despair was blown away, and she was standing there, waiting for him, night after night, sometimes young, sometimes old, always beautiful.

'I'm coming,' he said, and hung up.

He kneaded his palms into his eyes, then slid his spectacles into place and pushed himself up

15

from the warmth of his bed into the cold of his bedroom. He ran a business now; he was a pilot, too, but it wasn't the same. Nothing seemed to occupy him any more. He stretched, shoving his fists into the small of his back, then looked over to the corner of the room.

His old uniform was ready and waiting, laid out on the chair, just as it had been ever since Birger had called, all those weeks ago, and put him on alert. Anderssen didn't like having his dreams interrupted, but now he was awake, and at last Birger's promise had come good. He was going back in.

★ ★ ★

Most of the activity on the Oslofjord was of a military nature that night, but there was some civilian traffic, too. Håvard Langeland's 11-year-old sister, Eva, woke up when he went into their shared room to collect his fishing flies from under his bed. Her wild, electric-red curls rose into the vague light, bouncing around like a fistful of uncontrollable ginger springs, and, rubbing her sleep-filled eyes, she asked her big brother where he was going.

'Fishing,' Håvard said. He moved to her bed and tucked her in. 'You go back to sleep, sis.'

Eva returned his gaze as he pulled her quilt up under her chin, her large, deep-blue eyes already more than halfway back to dreamland.

'Catch a big one, won't you?' she said, her warm freckled face smiling as she closed her eyes again.

'I'll try,' Håvard said, and kissed her forehead.

Downstairs, he put on his winter outer clothes, then left the house, and trudged through the snow. He arrived at the Petersen house ten minutes later. He left it again, together with Britt Petersen, at pretty much the same time that Andreas Anderssen was setting out from his home.

Britt was eighteen, gangly, and still a tomboy. If you asked her mother, Sigrid, she'd tell you Britt was spoiling her God-given beauty with the dungarees and the hair always pushed into a fisherman's cap, and that she put Britt's complete lack of interest in anything traditionally feminine down to the death of her father; that the whole tragedy threw her daughter off the normal female trajectory. Sigrid thought perhaps Britt blamed her for Håkon's death, or for some reason saw it as her duty to take on her father's role. On the other hand, put the same question to Håvard — who was seventeen and also gangly, with a crop of electric orange hair, a large nose, receded chin and the general uncoordinated gawkiness of a boy still fighting his way through adolescence — and if Britt wasn't anywhere around to hear, he'd tell you she was pretty much perfect in every conceivable way just as she was. To his mind, the only thing wrong with her was the fact that she showed no interest in him whatsoever, romantically speaking. But he was her best friend, and constantly in her presence, and while sometimes this role was a painful one, it was better than nothing.

While Andreas Anderssen was out wearing his

thick military-issue greatcoat, the two teenagers were dressed in so many layers of civilian wool that they struggled to make their way through the snow with their backpacks and fishing rods. Humans might not like the cold much, but fish do, including cod and sea trout, and the night was the best time to catch them, which, ostensibly, is what Britt and Håvard were on their way to do. The idea was that the fish rose as the temperatures nearer the surface lowered to suit them, and late at night there weren't so many boats around, which was an advantage, because their engines scared the fish back to the depths. It was definitely cold enough to tempt the fish up — Britt and Håvard could feel it creeping in through their boots and doubled wool socks and the pre-expedition aquavit they had downed to keep themselves warm. By the time they arrived, fifteen minutes later, at the craggy cove just outside town, the warmth had slipped out of them altogether, though, so Håvard pulled a bottle out of his pack. As he took a slug, the whine of a small engine came through the fog.

'I guess that's the fish gone,' Britt said, taking the bottle. She didn't sound too disappointed.

'I guess so,' Håvard replied, similarly unbothered. 'It sounds like there's some action at the fort, too.'

He nodded out in the direction of the Kaholmen islands, only a couple of hundred metres across the water from where they were, but shrouded in the bitter fog, with only the faint blur of lights visible. The islands were small, but big enough to house Oscarsborg fortress. It had been there since the dark ages, and hadn't been modernized since the 1800s, but it was still an operational, if antiquated, military base, and the sound of voices slinging out unintelligible orders indicated something was going on there.

'Drilling at this time of night,' Håvard said. 'I don't envy those guys.'

'Still,' said Britt. 'We might as well set up now we're here.'

They had expected a silent night to greet them, but neither was particularly upset by how the situation was panning out. The fishing got them out there, and it'd be nice to return with a couple of kilos of cod meat. It would help Håvard's self-image as he edged towards manhood — a hunter-gatherer Alpha male providing for his family; and Britt's mother wasn't going to complain about a free cod supper, either. But really the activity itself was peripheral.

Britt dropped her rod and pack, unfolded her stool and took a hit of aquavit. It made her shiver, but she felt the warmth travel to her extremities immediately. Then she looked at her watch. They had nearly three hours before Ivar's alarm was due to go off. 3 a.m. had not been a time she had plucked just at random. She chose it because it was perfect for everyone. It gave them plenty of time.

Last summer, when she was fucking Kristian Helstrup in the woods north of Drøbak, Britt had chanced to look up through the web of trunks and branches and spotted her little brother watching them. In the brief moment before Kristian pulled her head back down to him, Britt saw a mix of fascination, confusion and fear in Ivar's eyes. The next time she looked up, a minute or two later, he was gone.

Britt did not bemoan this loss of innocence, or think it unnatural or strange that her brother should have been secretly watching her with Kristian Helstrup. Had she an older brother to learn from, she would probably have done the same thing; most would, she thought. Curiosity was a natural instinct. Put it together with another natural instinct — the desire to fuck — and the whole situation looked pretty normal to her. In fact, when she recalled being eleven years old herself, she realized that Ivar was probably hungry for knowledge.

Britt knew that, after seeing her riding Kristian up there in the woods, it would not just be Ivar's view of his sister that changed. The scene would have completely and permanently altered his idea of women, and he would require clarification on the concept of sex. This Britt would happily have offered, but for one event.

Every now and then, Ivar saw red. The world was unjust. It never seemed to favour him. And it wasn't only the fishing that Britt got to do. She had left school. She was earning money. She was going out when she liked, screwing men and drinking booze. In short, she could do what she wanted, she was suddenly a grown-up, and their mother didn't look at her like she was a kid any more. But Ivar was Sigrid's baby, and to Ivar, Britt thought, it probably felt like he always would be, never to gain the senior rights he saw his sister enjoying, and Britt was pretty sure that was why one day, in a rage over something else entirely, through the streaming tears, Ivar had blurted out to his mother what he had seen in the woods that summer.

Later on, when Britt still hadn't returned after storming out, and Ivar was asleep in bed, their mother Sigrid had had a chance to think about the whole situation, and she realized that she was, in fact, relieved to hear Britt had been getting with boys. She was eighteen years of age, for God's sake. It would be strange if she wasn't experimenting. Her daughter was a normal girl, after all. It was one less thing to worry about.

Of course, at the time, the accusations had flown. Sigrid worked ten-hour days in three part-time jobs, and looked after Ivar the rest of the time. She was exhausted and still broken by Håkon's sudden death. The chidings, and words like slut and whore, and finally the tears — they were just a release. But that didn't make much difference to Britt, who had upped and walked out, and from that moment on she knew that neither her mother nor her brother needed to know about her adventures. But she had to discuss this rollercoaster ride of sex and emotion with someone, because she was struggling to understand what the hell was going on herself. That was where Håvard came in. And the fishing. Britt didn't have any girlfriends there in Drøbak. Since they'd moved back in thirty-eight, somehow the connections had never come. Maybe the local girls had a mistrust of a tomboy, or of a new girl, or of a tomboy-new-girl who fraternized with men ten, fifteen years her senior;

or maybe their friendship slots were simply all filled up. Whatever, Håvard gladly stepped into the vacancy, and was now the nearest Britt had to a girlfriend. They were both fatherless, both outcasts, and if anything, he was better than a girlfriend, because maybe he had some idea of how men actually thought. But he didn't. His heart was filled by romantic love — by adoration, not lust — and tonight, when Britt told him about Tor from Husvik — a 39-year-old miller who liked to hold her hands behind her back with one hand while slapping her behind with the other — 'You're a man. What's that about?' — Håvard listened and sympathized, but couldn't answer her. And with every new detail, though she remained unaware of it, his heart broke a little more.

3 a.m. gave her plenty of time to spill news of this latest adventure to Håvard.

And 3 a.m. would also be exciting for Ivar. If he had started out with them, he'd have been whining about the cold by half past midnight and refused to leave for bed until they all did. He had been convinced to join them later because it was the middle of the night and involved the clandestine activity of leaving the house without detection. This appealed to a kid who spent most of his time pretending to be a spy or elite soldier, even more so because it was a conspiracy hatched with his sister. Britt figured Ivar felt like he was losing her to adult life, and she knew what it was to lose the attention of a revered elder. Six or seven years ago she had grown disillusioned when it became clear to her that her father wasn't solely her personal playmate. She knew that, in those circumstances, you cling to the moments you get, and the laying of the plan for Ivar to join her down at the cove was as much one of those moments as the expedition itself. On top of the anticipation, he would also still get six hours sleep — enough for any eleven-year-old. Sigrid couldn't complain about that. If she did, they'd just tell her that he had been woken up. By a boat or something.

★ ★ ★

It was the engine of a twelve-foot skiff that Britt and Håvard had heard. Andreas Anderssen found it and its single occupant — the fresh recruit Birger had promised — waiting for him in the marina. The boy, still in his teenage years, was a *menig*, or private, and saluted before helping Anderssen aboard. He then set about guiding the boat through the fog.

Soon enough, the Kaholmen islands became apparent, two hillocks rising out of the water between the hills of the mainland on one side and a much larger island beyond, Håøya, on the other. Cresting the top of the southern island, like a dour stone tiara, was a low, thick, horseshoe-shaped building, curving round the rise, the faint lights in the windows twinkling like cheap yellow jewels. Oscarsborg fortress. In front of it, pointing southwards along the waterway, Anderssen could just about make out the main battery. Three 28cm guns, their great ten-metre barrels sticking out like the antennae of an insect, feeling for threat in the darkness.

Between the guns and the main building, lights were moving back and forth like fireflies. But as the boat drew closer and the fog thinned, Anderssen saw what he already knew. They were not fireflies. It was too cold for that. These were men holding blinkered lanterns, moving with intent. They were soldiers, and they weren't drilling. They were preparing.

'Do you know what's going on, Menig?' Anderssen asked.

'No, sir,' he answered.

'But something is?'

'I think so, sir.'

'There'd better be. It's cold out here, and you need your sleep at my age.'

The private glanced at him. He was nervous and did not know how to respond.

'How long have you been here now, Menig? A week?' Anderssen said, turning to look at the soldier on the tiller. He saw now that the boy still wore the wispy hair of puberty on his cheeks. Anderssen was aware the new recruits had only just come in, but he didn't know some of them had just been born.

'Yes, sir. A week,' the private answered.

'And you've been in training since you arrived?'

'Yes, sir.'

'So the mines are laid?' Putting down a barrage across the main channel was to be part of their training, Anderssen knew. The international situation was 'twitchy', after all.

'I understand we're putting them down next week, sir.'

With Anderssen looking back at him, not knowing what else to do, the private smiled. Anderssen did not. No mines meant that the way to Oslo was clear.

At a small dock next to a short, broad bridge that connected the two islands, North and South Kaholmen, another private helped Anderssen out of the boat. Straightening, the senior man watched a group of soldiers rushing across the bridge, their boots thumping on the timber.

'Find Løytnant Karlsen, Menig. And Minør Bexrud,' Anderssen said to the lad in the boat. 'Tell them to start moving the torpedoes into the battery. Tell them to load up. I'll meet them there. Set to run at three metres depth.'

'Yes, sir.'

The private ran over the bridge to the north island and Anderssen and his escort headed onto the south, up the hill and into the main building. The two of them climbed the flight of stone steps in silence, the noise of activity growing as they ascended, until the private opened a door into a room full of men in uniform, every one of them busy, talking into radio receivers and to each other.

Standing in the middle of the room was a grey-haired man wearing an expression as stony as the building they were in. He was not much younger than Anderssen, but Colonel Birger Eriksen was not the retiring kind. He was clearly in charge here, conducting the chaos.

'When I said everyone, Løytnant, I meant everyone. All the way down to the cooks and the dishwashers. Get them out of their beds and

25

deploy them to their secondary positions immediately. And do it yourself this time. We don't know how long we've got here.'

The lieutenant saluted his senior officer and departed without saying a word, brushing past Anderssen as he went.

Eriksen jerked his head round a degree.

'Breland!' he barked. 'Report.'

Another man came running to the colonel from across the room.

'The main battery is being manned and loaded as we speak, Oberst Eriksen. Likewise Husvik and Kopås.'

'And Nesset?'

'That's all so far, sir.'

'That's all?'

'We're moving as fast as we can, sir.'

'What about support?'

'The request has been dispatched.'

'And the order for civilians to remain in their homes?'

'Also dispatched.'

'Torpedoes?'

'The boat was sent for Kommandørkaptein Anderssen, sir.'

'Then where in — '

On hearing his name, Anderssen stepped into the colonel's line of vision and saluted.

'Oberst Eriksen.'

Eriksen considered Anderssen's ruffled form for a moment, controlling a smirk.

'I hope I didn't wake you, Kommandørkaptein.'

'You certainly did.'

Eriksen tutted.

'And at your age you need your sleep, I suppose.'

'I do,' Anderssen answered. 'Not only that, I enjoy it, too.'

'Too much sleep dulls the senses, Kommandørkaptein.'

'Then I fear sharpness must be overrated, Oberst.'

Eriksen released the smile, allowing it to spread over his face, and the two men shook hands.

'So what is it that has you — and therefore the rest of us — out of bed at this ungodly hour, Oberst?'

Eriksen looked at Anderssen for another moment, and his smile did not change, but his eyes did. Anderssen recognized the strain of concern that entered them. Eriksen then stood to one side and pointed through the window, far beyond the barrels of the main battery, into the bank of fog.

'That,' he said, taking the pair of binoculars Breland proffered and handing them to Anderssen. Anderssen took them, and stepped forward as he placed them to his eyes. All he saw was thick fog, glowing in the moonlight.

'What?' he asked, lowering the binoculars and looking at Eriksen.

'Precisely the question, Kommandørkaptein.' The colonel was not smiling any more. 'What? Horten has reported foreign vessels entering the Oslofjord. They refused communication and could not be identified before disappearing into the fog, so we don't know who they belong to.

The only thing of which we can be absolutely certain is they're not ours. I've therefore ordered the fortress to a state of readiness — hence your being here.' He wiped his lips before adding, 'It seems we are being invaded, Kommandørkaptein.'

The two older men held one another's gaze for a moment. Anderssen broke the stare and glanced around at all the junior men bustling around them.

'Oberst,' he said, returning his gaze to the colonel. 'A word, if I may?'

'Of course,' Eriksen said, putting his hand on Anderssen's shoulder and guiding him to one side of the room.

'What is it, Andreas?'

'What are you going to do, Birger?'

'Warning shots were fired from a patrol ship, and then from Rauøy. They were ignored.' Eriksen moved his face closer to the shorter man's. 'Their intentions can't be honourable, Andreas, arriving in the middle of the night and creeping around in the shadows like this.'

Anderssen was nodding, as though making a calculation in his head.

'How many?' he said.

'Horten says it was a flotilla, consisting of at least seven craft.'

'What class?'

'Rauøy identified at least two cruisers before they all disappeared.'

'And the rest?'

'Smaller — corvettes and destroyers, probably.'

'May I speak candidly, sir?'

28

'Of course you may,' Eriksen said, as though offended by the request. 'You know I value your opinion. Speak your mind, please.'

Anderssen nodded again, and said, 'You do see that there is nothing we can do, don't you?'

The senior officer smiled at the earnest face looking up at him.

'We are the last line of defence before they reach the city, Andreas. Our capital city.'

Anderssen jabbed a thumb over his shoulder at the men in the room.

'How many officers do you have here? A handful? The rest have only been here a week.' Anderssen placed a hand on Eriksen's forearm. 'Our defences are manned by old men and boys, Birger, and armed with weapons built in the last century. If we make an aggressive stand, we'll take a battering.'

'We must all be prepared to do what we can, Andreas. No matter our age. And what we are capable of is not nothing — if we are ready.'

'And what if it's the British?'

Worry slipped into Eriksen's expression.

'In the current situation we remain a neutral nation, Andreas.'

'Maybe it's a secret landing.'

'There's been no word.'

'Perhaps the communiqué hasn't arrived yet. Or perhaps something has happened upstream and they can't send word, and these ships are here to help defend us. Maybe — '

'I am aware of all the possibilities, Kommandørkaptein.' He wasn't Andreas any more. The colonel was pulling rank. Anderssen had

had his say, and it had been duly noted. Now it was time to follow orders.

Anderssen remained silent, but Eriksen could tell he had offended the old soldier.

'I promise you I will wait for as long as I can, Andreas. But if they continue to refuse to respond . . . '

'You will risk entering our country into war.'

The words hung between them for a second as they stared at one another. Eriksen was the one to break the silence this time.

'There's no choice on that count, I fear, Andreas. The war has come to us. The only choice left to us now is *how* we enter it.'

'Very well, Oberst.'

Eriksen smiled again, the bonhomie returning to his eyes.

'I'm glad we see things the same way.'

Anderssen stuck out his hand and Eriksen took it.

'Oberst.'

'Andreas.'

'The very best of luck to us, sir.'

'We may well need all we can get, my friend.'

3

A drop of sweat dropped off Curt's forehead onto the page in his hands. The grid of numbers printed on the paper showed the times of trains coming into Oslo S, the city's central station, and when they left. His was the 8:19 — thirteen minutes away.

He smeared the rest of the beading perspiration from his brow onto the sleeve of his shirt. Straight away his pores replaced it. It wasn't meant to get this hot in Oslo, not in September. By now winter should have been creeping back over the horizon. But it wasn't. It just kept getting hotter and hotter. On his way there he'd seen a viper coiled up on a rock on the verge at the side of the road, the vicious, poisonous, camouflaged little serpent taking in the rays while it waited for passing victims.

Climate change, he supposed. He wasn't alone on the platform. At the other end, not twenty metres away, overlooking the rails, stood a skinny old man in threadbare khakis and a scummy houndstooth, his white shirt a patchwork of orange sweat stains. His bearded face was pointed skywards, his eyes shut, and he was muttering to himself. Praying. He must have heard the scrape of Curt's feet or something, because before Curt managed to move his eyes away, the old man

31

opened his and their gazes met. On seeing Curt, the old man's eyes grew, like a lost kid just found by his mother.

Curt had lived in foreign countries long enough to have a drill for situations like this. You keep silent for as long as possible. If your luck held there would be some gabble but the stranger would move on. If your luck didn't hold, then you told the person where to go in no uncertain terms: if taciturnity didn't work, a little abrupt aggression usually did the trick. Especially here, where he'd gleaned from firsthand experience that the black man was a relatively unknown, and therefore feared, quantity. Survival instinct takes over and they get out of there. But that was a last resort, and when the old man arrived at Curt's spot and spoke, Curt was staring up the railway track as though he hadn't seen him.

But Curt heard him, sucking in air, and sensed him looking him up and down — his face, his clothes. Then the old man spoke again, in English this time, a croaky, hollow, accented voice, like he hadn't spoken or drunk anything in days.

'So what are you, boy?' he said.

Curt whipped round to face him.

'The hell did you — '

Curt silenced himself. The eyes sitting behind that old face were just as used-up as the rest of him, as you'd expect them to be, yellowing and clouded, but still they managed to be full of some kind of life.

Curt turned back to the rails, silently cursing his lack of self-control.

32

You didn't speak. Especially not in English. Because now there it was — half a sentence that made up a whole tank of fuel for conversation, and just because the old man had referred to him as 'boy'. Jesus. He knew better than that.

'An Englishman,' the old man said. It sounded like this was exciting to him. Probably any answer would have been. 'The 8.19 Flytoget into Sentralstasjonen is next, I believe.'

Curt kept looking upline, letting the man's observation hang in the air.

Then the old man said, 'So what is it that brings you here?'

He must have seen Curt wasn't going to answer because he didn't pause long.

'I mean to the country, not to this very spot. Usually it's one of three things. First: tourism. The fjords, the snow, the fresh mountain air. But you are here. Number two is the oil, of course, but no, I believe what brings you here is number three: the women. And in this heat. In all my days, I have not . . . ' He was shaking his head in wonderment. 'They are like mayflies, their bodies hidden from view through the long winter months, waiting for their moment. Then suddenly it arrives, the sun appears and their clothes come off, and they are everywhere, flocking — a visual symphony of beauty, a ballet of near-naked feminine perfection.' He pictured it all for a moment, then shook it out of his head, focusing on Curt again.

'It cannot be women that bring you *here*, though.' He pointed at the tracks. 'Perhaps *a* woman?'

33

'When life is done with you, you do well to be done with life, that's all,' Curt said. 'You ought to take heed of that. Now, my train'll be coming through here in a few minutes, so I'd appreciate it if — '

'A few minutes?' The old man tutted. 'It arrives at Sentralstasjonen at 8.19, and that is two, maybe three minutes down the line. It will pass under this bridge we are on at any second now.'

Just as the old man spoke, Curt heard the buzz of electricity surging through power lines. The power lines were located directly below him, suspended in midair over the rails. The rails were forty feet below the maintenance platform they stood on. The maintenance platform was attached to a road bridge that carried traffic over the train line.

Curt looked up and saw the train now, still a way off, snaking its way through the city's buildings.

'Then all the more reason for you to leave me alone,' he said.

'No,' the old man said.

'Then maybe we should do it together,' Curt said. From the old man's pleasure at seeing another person, Curt had supposed that he wasn't ready, and hoped the offer would scare him off. 'I won't let you ruin this for me.'

The old man didn't move, so Curt grabbed his wrist, tiny beneath the material of the jacket, just thin brittle bone, and pulled him closer.

'I have not come here to ruin anything, simply to make a proposition,' the old man said, looking up from Curt's grip on him.

Curt looked upline again. The train had disappeared from sight, but he could hear it thumping over the sleepers. It was closing in. Not far away at all now.

'What is your name, soldier?' the old man said.

Curt raised his hand to where his opened shirt revealed his bare chest. At the end of their chain his tags were lying against his skin for all to see.

'Curt,' he said.

The cables gave off a noise like laser shots in a sci-fi film, and the train reappeared, up the tracks a way, on the home straight now, shooting towards them. They'd have to time it just right. The drop from the maintenance deck would probably do the job. Curt figured that was why so many chose the spot, but he wasn't about to take that risk. If the fall wasn't enough, he didn't want to have to lie there, broken and hurting, and have time to look up and see the train coming at him and have to wait for it to hit. Worse, he didn't want to give the driver a chance to pull up. But skimming off the roof and bouncing away like a roulette ball dropped in the pot wouldn't be too much fun either. Nor would it necessarily do the job. Then he'd be lifted into an ambulance a mangled mess, and come out too crippled to get it right next time. But hitting the track a split second before the train came through — no one was coming back from that.

'Well Curt,' the old man said, wriggling free of his grip. 'I need your help.'

'Don't worry, old man,' Curt said. Maybe the old man *was* serious, after all, and just needed some kind of companionship to get it done. 'I'll see you through. All we have to do is step off. I'll make sure you get there. And don't worry.' He moved the old man to the edge of the platform, looking at him now, all trace of amusement gone from his expression. 'You won't feel a thing. I promise. Get ready now.'

Curt turned back to the train line, watching the locomotive come, one, two, three, four carriages backing it up.

'And maybe *I* can help *you*, Curt,' the old man said, raising his voice over the rattle of the train. 'Maybe together we can help each other.'

Curt edged forward to the edge of the deck himself now, until the toes of his All Stars extended over the lip. The train was seconds away. He could make out the letters on the roof. OCX, whatever that meant. So meaningless, and yet this was it. That momentous occasion. The end of his life. Adios world.

He closed his eyes and stretched his arms out like wings. All he had to do was step forward, *lean* forward, and then he'd feel the rush of air, like he was flying in a dream, then a moment of pain so fractional it would hardly exist, and then nothing: no desert, no mountains, no caves, no war. No nothing. No Freia.

He let his weight shift forward. But before he reached tipping point he felt cold fingers encircling his wrist and opened his eyes. The old man was clinging to him with one hand, squeezing, probably as hard as the adjoining muscles and sinews could manage. In his other hand, between his arthritic thumb and forefinger, was a small object, no more than a centimetre cubed, shiny, yellow and irregular.

'The fuck's that?' Curt said, angry.

'A reason to live,' the old man called as the train rattled through beneath them.

★   ★   ★

The old man was light and fragile in Curt's hands, like he was nothing more than hollow bones held together by cotton wool. Shaking him, it felt like he might just come to pieces, that his limbs and torn-crêpe-paper skin might just fly out of his flailing clothes. Curt stopped shaking when the last carriage had passed beneath them.

'A man comes here to die, and you do this? Old man, I ought to throw *you* off this bridge,' he said. 'Start talking. Beginning with that thing in your hand. What is it?'

'It's gold, 18 carat. At today's prices that's three thousand kroner at least. And you can have it.'

'Just like that?'

'Just like that.'

Curt let him go.

'What's the catch?'

The old man opened his hand to reveal the small nugget. Curt took it. It was heavy. It *was* gold. Unquestionably.

'Catch?' the old man said, taking the nugget back.

'You said this was a proposition. What do I have to do in return?'

'Steal something.'

37

'What?'

'A briefcase. More specifically, an envelope in a briefcase.'

Curt thought for a second, then said, 'Do it yourself.'

'If it came to a chase, I'm afraid my legs would fail me.' He bent and rapped his left calf. It gave off the hollow sound of a moulded plastic prosthesis. 'But you're young. Fit. You will easily get away.'

Curt looked at him, trying to discern if he was serious or just winding him up. He couldn't tell either way.

'Three thousand kroner doesn't buy anything these days.'

'It would buy you a ticket home.'

'So?'

'A ticket out of here.'

'I've already got one of those,' Curt said, nodding down at the rails.

'Then there must be someone you know who could use the extra money.'

'Three thousand kroner isn't going to buy her a month's groceries.'

The old man paused, then said, 'There's more.'

It worked.

'Where?' Curt said.

'Take the briefcase, deliver it to me, and when you have earned this piece, I will show you where the rest is.'

'You better not be fucking me around, old man.'

He levelled Curt's gaze.

'I'm not,' he said. 'But even if I were, what have you got to lose?'

His expression persuaded Curt that he was serious. Curt couldn't tell if he was crazy or not, though. But he was right about one thing — Curt didn't have anything to lose.

'Who's the mark?'

The old man leaned in towards him, and enunciating each one deliberately, spoke two words.

'Henrik. Bonde.'

'Who?' Curt said.

4

At the head of the flotilla stealing through the fog-laden Oslofjord on that April evening in 1940 was the Admiral Hipper-class cruiser, *Blücher*. Its captain, Heinrich Woldag, had passed the order for silence and minimum illumination following entry into the fog bank, and though his ship was a behemoth of battle filled with the tools of war, and the size of a city block, all he could now hear was the sound of her hull cutting through the water and the deep, regular chug of the engines.

Woldag glanced at the man next to him, a thickset, bald-headed rear admiral named Oskar Kummetz. The commanding officer of the invading flotilla looked calm, standing there staring through the window into the fog, his hands clasped behind his back. Woldag knew why.

Intelligence said the Norwegians were woefully underarmed and underprepared. They were no match for a German invasion on this scale, and more importantly, they knew it. For this reason the warning shots fired across the bow some hours earlier had not concerned Kummetz. The whole show was little more than a charade. No proud nation wanted its people to think it had just bent over and let invaders in, but there was

40

no question of the outcome here today, and the fact was the Norwegian politician Vidkun Quisling had assured Berlin that their cause had support in Norway. He had told them that, for a few carefully distributed payoffs, he could guarantee their way to a smooth takeover of the entire country. Everything had been arranged. The payoffs were in a cabin somewhere in the bowels of the ship, along with most of the 163rd Infantry Division. That was the sort of knowledge that could make a man confident.

Too confident, and that was why Captain Woldag was now sweating. The way Kummetz and others had talked when they came on board at Swinemünde in the Baltic, he thought they were going to be little more than transport for the 163rd. Certainly there had been nothing to suggest they would require full speed or heavy artillery, and his orders regarding the state of readiness of the *Blücher* reflected this. Not all the boilers were burning, and the heavy guns were inactive.

On hearing the warning shots whistle past, Woldag had begun to suspect his orders were a mistake. Whatever the guarantees, what sort of captain does not raise his ship to a state of full battle readiness when entering uncertain waters? When entering uncertain *foreign* waters? When *invading* uncertain foreign waters?

That was precisely the question Woldag didn't want Kummetz to ask himself, and why, since the shots had been fired, rather than acting decisively, the captain had instead been wrestling with a decision: show his hand and lose face, perhaps his rank, but strengthen the invasion; or hide his mistake and pray it would not be exposed.

Woldag still hadn't made up his mind, and that was why he was sweating.

He looked back out the window. The fog was beginning to thin. He could just make out the shorelines. Not far away.

Then the navigator, Lieutenant Bohm, said from the rear of the bridge, 'Kapitän, we are approaching the Narrows.'

And Captain Woldag knew it was too late. Time had made the decision for him.

* * *

As these words were spoken, the alarm clock on Ivar Petersen's bedside table began to ring. He woke up immediately, grabbed the clock and wrapped it in his blanket like it was a cat that needed strangling, stifling the noise of the bell to a dull rattle. As he waited for it to die, the 11-year-old looked across the room to the second bed. Even though she had turned eighteen in November and had been holding down a job at Bergstrom's boatyard for the best part of two years, Britt still shared a room with her kid brother. She didn't have any choice. The house only had two, and God knows she preferred Ivar to their mother. The bed was empty, tonight like many other nights, but this time Britt wasn't out rolling with some man; she wasn't having a hairy male hunting and scrabbling and rubbing in the hair between her legs like Ivar had seen last summer.

She was down at the water fishing for sea trout with Håvard Langeland. Of course, Ivar had wanted to be there from the beginning and his attempts to get permission to join his sister for the whole night had led him to unsheathe three of the big guns in his arsenal of persuasion — reason, then anger, and lastly begging — but Sigrid had not wavered in her insistence that a boy his age needed his sleep. Ivar stopped just short of arming the biggest gun of all. He was loaded and ready to go, but the second before he was going to let rip with the tears, his mother had turned away from him, and as she went he saw *her* eyes welling up, so he held his back. Sigrid's tears had been making regular appearances in the two years since Ivar's father had dropped dead back in Oslo. They came on like a tropical rainstorm — suddenly and without warning, in the middle of making a bed, or washing the dishes, whatever she happened to be doing, and whenever Ivar was witness to them, they sliced like a razor inside his chest.

So Ivar had gone to Britt instead. She'd been sitting on her bed, pre-rolling cigarettes for the night ahead. Ivar laid out the latest developments. After thinking and rolling tobacco for a minute, Britt told him to get to bed as soon as he could. When Ivar began to protest, Britt threw her alarm clock at him, telling him to set it for 3 a.m. She even threw a wink with it. That wink was what had ignited Ivar's heart, what lit it up like a fireball, and after that, the fishing didn't matter any more. It had been subverted by the

Plan. The planning. If the two of them were hatching plans together, it meant that he was Britt's Most Important Person again, like he used to be. Not the Men, with their grunting and the words Ivar didn't understand, or even Håvard, the Impostor. They were siblings again, and he hadn't felt that since their father's heart had given out at the mill.

The alarm finally dead, Ivar climbed out of bed, laying down first one foot, then the other. Then he stood, slowly, easing the creak of the floorboards beneath his feet. Doing things this methodically wasn't easy — the excitement was making his legs wobbly — but stealth, he reminded himself, was in the training of the crack troops of the Drøbak Brigade. As was preparation for environment, so he put on a second pair of long johns, a second thermal long-sleeve, three pairs of wool socks, canvas britches, a cotton shirt, and two thick jumpers, then he crept out of the room, as slowly as he'd stood up, moved past his mother's bedroom door like a ghost and went down the stairs. In the back room that counted as kitchen, and sitting- and dining-rooms when it was just the three of them, he pulled on a rabbit-fur deer-stalker and a pair of boots, grabbed his gloves and eased the bolt on the back door out of its shaft. In the cold weather, the door stuck and he had to yank it open. That made a sudden noise, and he stood for a moment, listening out for movement from above. When nothing came, he stepped outside and shut the door again as quietly as possible. Leaning on the outer wall of their house were three pairs of skis and poles. Ivar laid a couple flat — silently — hooked his feet in, took up the poles and pushed off. Skiing in the dark was no joke, but Ivar considered his ability to do so his greatest talent — what got him his job on the Brigade in the first place — and he was off into the cold darkness laughing his excitement out into the icy air.

At that time (3.11 a.m.), Constable Mathisen — Drøbak's local law-enforcement officer — was working his way through town, following the orders that had awoken him: anyone out, get them back inside. But he came across no one, either in town or at the harbour. He did not see Ivar, because Ivar, the more alert of the two, saw him first and hid; and at no point did Mathisen consider stretching the boundaries of his rounds to include the cove to which Ivar was heading, where Britt and Håvard were three-quarters of the way through their first bottle of aquavit. After all, who would choose to be out in this cold?

At 3.50 a.m., Mathisen turned homewards, his mind on his own supply of warming liquor.

★   ★   ★

'A final check, please, gentlemen.'

Colonel Eriksen was now outside, standing at the main battery of guns on the south side of South Kaholmen. Each one required eleven men. There was the aiming and the firing, but also the reloading and that required cranes and carts to shift the weighty shells.

'Ready, sir,' the gunner replied.

45

'Good.' Eriksen turned to the dugout behind the guns, where the radio operator sat.

'Any word from High Command, Løytnant?'

'None, sir. We have failed to re-establish contact.'

'And from the aggressors?'

'Nothing, sir.'

'Insignias? Markings?'

'No, sir. Visibility is still too low.'

Eriksen stared out, towards the white glow of fog. The flotilla was entering Norwegian waters, secretly, in the middle of the night. As he had said to Anderssen, whether or not Norway entered the war was no longer the question. The question was more difficult. He should have received orders from Command HQ at Akershus Festning in Oslo, but they had not received any communication of any kind for several hours. The Oslofjord was not the only point of entry for an invading force, of course. So what if Oslo had already been taken? What if Norway had already capitulated? Nazis or British, it was inevitable. The army was the same the whole country over — undermanned and underfunded. Any resistance here would be a waste of lives, just as Anderssen had said. But this was an invasion. What was he meant to do? What was he supposed to tell these boys looking to him for leadership? That they should just lie down and take it?

★ ★ ★

Small pockets in the fog were beginning to open up. Through the windows on the bridge of the

Blücher, Captain Woldag could make out land rising from the water on either side of the ship, high and monochrome, lights from homes twinkling through. They looked close enough to reach out and pluck, like edelweiss.

'We enter the Narrows,' Rear Admiral Kummetz announced.

Captain Woldag stared at him. The senior man's face was alight with anticipation. Woldag's was now drenched with sweat, and he could feel the eyes of everybody on the bridge boring into him.

His was the order to give, but instead of repeating the rear admiral's words, he said, 'Forgive me, Herr Konteradmiral. But would it not be wise to send another ship ahead of us?'

Kummetz turned to Woldag. He inspected his inferior officer's wet face in disgusted silence. Back-up finally arrived for the captain in the shape of General Engelbrecht, the 163rd's commanding officer and senior *Wehrmacht* man on board.

'I must agree with the Kapitän, Herr Konteradmiral,' he said. 'The *Blücher* is full of men. Indeed, she herself is too valuable a prize to risk. The *Lutzow*, or *Emden*, or *Möwe* are all large enough to prompt reaction if the Norwegians intend to engage.'

Kummetz turned his glare on both men before speaking again.

'Tell me, gentlemen,' he said. 'What do you think would be the reaction of our Führer if he were to hear that his forces entered into the waters of invasion by first testing its temperature with a toe?'

He received no response and the thick silence was only broken when the door to the bridge was pulled open, the scrape of metal jarring into the void. All eyes turned to see a small, wide man in a greatcoat enter. He pulled the door shut, then turned. His face was fleshy and pale, his lips thick and wet, his posture slightly stooped. The peaked cap on his head was black where the other men's were grey. It bore the party eagle, as all officers' caps did, but also the *Totenkopf* — the death's-head emblem of the *Schutzstaffel*. He did not appear at all perturbed to have so many greet his arrival. Indeed, it seemed almost as though he might have expected such high regard. He raised his right hand to his audience and, standing closest to him, Woldag saw the image of the skull repeated on the third finger of his gloved hand. Its grinning teeth glinted from a silver ring. Woldag knew what it was. An SS Honour Ring, of the kind awarded by Reichsführer Himmler personally.

'*Heil* Hitler,' the man said.

In unison, every person on the bridge duplicated his action and words like a classroom of children. This included Kummetz, who, following the greeting, addressed the man personally.

'Oberführer von Westarp,' the rear admiral said, bowing his head in respect as he spoke the man's name. 'Your timing is impeccable.'

'It is, Herr Konteradmiral?' the SS man said, unbuttoning and removing his coat, revealing an immaculate black uniform amply filled by a stout, pudgy little body.

'It is,' replied Kummetz. 'For I believe you

48

have met our great leader, have you not, Herr Oberführer?'

Von Westarp nodded. 'That is correct. I have had that privilege on a number of occasions.'

'Then of all of us here you are the most likely to be capable of predicting how he would expect an invasion force of the Third Reich to conduct itself.'

'Of course, Konteradmiral,' von Westarp replied, 'I would never assume to know the thoughts of the Führer, but on this we do not have to fall to presumptions, for on matters such as this he is very clear. We must dive in headfirst. With strength and confidence. The *Blücher*, you see, is not merely a ship, gentlemen. She is a symbol. She represents the power of Germany and our fight for the Aryan race. To hesitate or cower behind others would be to exhibit weakness, a weakness from which we do not suffer.' He stopped, and passed his eyes across every person on the bridge. 'A weakness from which no true German suffers.'

'Thank you, Herr Oberführer,' Kummetz said, turning to Woldag. 'Besides, Kapitän. The *Luftwaffe* is already in the air, and heading for Oslo. Do you really want them to get there first? We are *Kriegsmarine*, Kapitän.'

Woldag felt the rivalry between the branches of the military as keenly as anyone, and the rear admiral's remark smarted as much as it was meant to.

Meanwhile, the SS man, von Westarp, had turned to the window, little interested in or even aware of the tensions playing out between the commanders on the bridge. The fog was thinning further and he followed the line of lights trailing northwards, up the water's edge to where the dots culminated in a disorderly and diffused concentration, like an image of a galaxy.

Despite Kummetz's words, and the SS man's, Woldag was still resisting giving the order, so Kummetz nudged him a little more.

'Now, if you will, Kapitän. The Oberführer was quite clear, I believe.'

'Very well, Herr Konteradmiral,' Woldag said.

Von Westarp turned to the man next to him.

'Oslo?' he said.

Woldag's face whipped round to see who was breaking the silence. Von Westarp met his gaze. Woldag's eyes were burning with resentment, but he said nothing to the SS man.

'Leutnant Lund,' he said instead, still glaring at von Westarp, and speaking with a forced calm. 'Pass the order. We enter the Narrows.'

Von Westarp's neighbour rose from the chart that he'd been inspecting.

'No, not Oslo, Oberführer,' he whispered, and moved his light to show von Westarp the name of the town.

'Drøbak.'

* * *

'So what have you caught so far?' Ivar asked, removing his skis and sitting down on Britt's stool. His sister was standing a few metres away, by the edge of the rocks, looking out at the water.

Håvard nodded at the rock by his stool, where two small trout lay inert. 'Only those two. It's too noisy out there.'

'Why? What's going on?' Ivar said.

'Some kind of training exercise, we think, right Britt? You want to try some of this, Ivar?'

Håvard passed the bottle of aquavit over to Ivar.

Ivar's eyes widened in awe at the possibility of his first proper taste of aquavit.

'Thanks,' he said, taking the bottle, but as he was raising it to his mouth, Britt strode over and grabbed it.

'She'll smell it on you,' she said. 'And the same goes for cigarettes, Håvard.'

'But it's cold,' Ivar said.

'There's a thermos in my pack. No liquor.'

Fucking was one thing — a natural instinct — but she didn't want her kid brother smoking and drinking. Fucking didn't mess you up. You just had to meet her boss Bergstrom to know that alcohol and tobacco could. You didn't want to start too young with that stuff.

'You want to be useful,' she said. 'Take this and get gutting.' Britt put a knife in Ivar's hand. Her coronation knife. A prized possession. Their father, Håkon, had been given it by his father in 1906, the year the Danish prince Carl was installed on the Norwegian throne and became King Haakon VII. Engraved on the hilt was an 'H' with a '7' through the middle of it, the King's monogram, but for both Britt and Ivar, growing up with Håkon showing them how to tie knots and flies, and whittling with the knife, the emblem was synonymous with their father, more familiar to them than his actual signature. H for Håkon, not Haakon. Ivar took the knife, but before he could move to the fish, the high pitch of a fishing rod reel whining made all of them start. Håvard was the first to react, jumping out of his seat and grabbing the arcing rod. Ivar and Britt were right behind him. Håvard put his hand on the reel handle, slowing it, pulling back, allowing the rod to bow.

'Let it run,' Britt said. 'You've got to work him.'

'I know,' Håvard said, feeling Britt's hand on his shoulder all the way through his body. 'I am. I know what I'm doing, okay?'

'What do you reckon?' Ivar said, trying to squeeze between them and see the action. Britt moved aside and Ivar managed to squirm through and stand right next to Håvard. 'A cod?'

Britt had moved because she wasn't looking at the rod any more. Or at the line shooting into the black water. In fact, she wasn't interested in the fish at all. She'd been distracted. By a deep growl coming across the water, through the thinning fog.

'How big?' Ivar asked Håvard, not even noticing his sister moving still further away.

'Do you hear that?' Britt whispered, but neither boy responded or took his eyes off the fishing line.

Britt took another step forward, straining her ears.

'I don't know,' Håvard replied to Ivar.

'Shhht!' Britt hissed back at them, waving a hand.

52

'But one thing's for sure . . . ' Håvard continued.

'That's no outboard,' Britt said. 'It sounds like . . . '

'It's no tiddler,' Håvard said, grinning and yanking back on the rod a final time. A cod, two kilos at least, came thrashing into the air.

At that moment, a Norwegian military auxiliary craft lying in wait not far south of the cove switched on its searchlight. The beam shot out through what remained of the fog.

Britt continued, 'some kind of . . . '

Håvard and Ivar's eyes moved up from the cod. The fish plunged back into the water and the reel began to whine again as it bolted to the depths.

' . . . ferry,' Britt concluded, but she wasn't looking at a ferry. She was looking at the *Blücher*, towering above her, wreathed in the fog, like an iron mountain silently sliding through the water.

★　★　★

On board the *Blücher* the searchlight had burst into the bridge with all the brilliance of an explosion. Every man covered his eyes and ducked as though under fire. But the noise of an explosion did not come. At least not immediately. Rather, the beam raked the ship from front to back, flashing across the faces of the men as it went. Then it was directed above the ship, into the remaining fog. This acted like a zap of electricity entering a gas-filled bulb. The precipitation in the air was suddenly alight, a bright, glowing

53

soup, and on the *Blücher* visibility was instantly reduced to nil once more.

Woldag glanced at Kummetz. The rear admiral was smiling, as though pleased that the subterfuge was now over.

He turned to Woldag.

'Full speed ahead, Kapitän,' he said.

★   ★   ★

'Oberst Eriksen!'

It was Breland, just a few metres away, his binoculars glued to his eyes. When Eriksen didn't respond, Breland lowered his binoculars.

'Oberst Eriksen!'

This time he broke through Eriksen's thoughts.

'What is it, Breland?' he said.

Breland raised a hand and pointed south.

'They're here.'

Eriksen raised his own binoculars to his eyes and saw an unmistakable shape creeping from the mist. The bow of a warship, a heavy cruiser, it looked like, high, dark and angled, like the nose of a black shark driving through the freezing waters. He lowered his binoculars. Every single man around him was completely silent and completely still, every pair of eyes directed at him.

He could just hear the low hum of the ship's giant engines.

Eriksen nodded once.

'It's time, gentlemen,' he said. 'First gun?'

'Yes, sir!' all eleven manning the weapon replied in unison.

Eriksen looked through his binoculars again.

54

'Set a range of 1,400 metres,' Eriksen said, his voice steadier than he thought possible.

He heard the ratcheting of gears to his left.

'Range set, sir.'

'Good,' he said. He lowered his binoculars and turned to the dugout.

'Pass the order, Løytnant: we are being invaded. And we shall engage. Following the signal of primary fire, secondary batteries are to engage as soon as they have range.'

The operator repeated his words into his radio.

Eriksen could see the ship with his bare eye now, creeping towards them. Nearly there. Nearly.

'Fifteen seconds, sir,' someone said to his left. 'Ten seconds. Nine. Eight. Seven . . . '

'Well, Andreas,' Breland heard Eriksen mutter under his breath. 'Either I'll be decorated — '

'Two.'

' — or I'll be court-martialled.'

'One.'

Eriksen dropped the binoculars from his eyes. 'Zero.'

'Fire,' he said.

★ ★ ★

'Leutnant Lang!'

Knowing what he did about the *Blücher*'s lack of battle-readiness, Woldag could not share Kummetz's relief, but nor did he now fear for his rank.

'Ready — '

Woldag did not succeed in barking out his

55

order to ready the main guns and light the remaining boilers. At that moment Officer-of-the-Watch Löw said,

'A large-calibre muzzle flash, Kapitän. Two points off the starboard bow.'

Woldag whipped his face back round just in time to see the light from the Oscarsborg gun die, and a few seconds later he heard the almighty boom of the explosion that accompanied it.

The whistle of the shell escalated in volume. A moment before impact, he saw it arching in, a black blur flying through the remains of the mist.

The sound of the impact swallowed him, and the metal beneath his feet seemed to vanish as he was thrown against the wall. The whole ship shook and rolled in the water, and did not stop shaking and rolling before, from somewhere, he heard the warning come again.

'Kapitän, a second inbound.'

Woldag flailed around until his hand met something metal and solid. He grabbed hold of it and wound his other arm around his head for protection.

Same again: the whistle of the shell growing until it eclipsed all sound of the yelling and screaming and squealing metal and then, when the whistle reached an unbearable pitch, it was replaced by the almighty explosion of the second impact. The whole ship seemed to lift out of the water and flip round, while he went the other way.

Somehow he managed to hold on, and he uncovered his face.

The boat was still rocking, in great, rolling

lists. The bridge was filling with a thick black smoke. It was coming through the broken windows, as was the sound of chaos from the deck below, and fluttering, spasmodic light. Not the white light of the search beam. This was yellow. The yellow of flames.

Woldag climbed to his knees, grasping for balance, and when he rose to his feet, the heat coming through the smashed windows hit him instantly. The first shell had hit the lower part of the command tower. Through the black smoke he could see that the main fire-control platform had been destroyed; the same went for the men stationed there. The second shell had hit the port side of the ship, just behind the funnel. The aircraft hangar was burning, wrecked. He could just about see the bodies of personnel there in the flames, along with both Arado reconnaissance planes. The turret of the mid-battery was a mangled mess of iron, bent and melted like some dying mechanoid space creature. Around it, splayed out like petals on a hell-flower, a dozen men lay charred and inert. Beside them, those still living were scrambling to kill the fires. And now the rest of the Norwegian artillery had started, strafing in from both the fort and the mainland.

And the *Blücher* was a floating beacon for those to aim at.

Woldag looked back into the bridge. The radio operators were coughing and shouting into the receivers at their stations. His fellow officers were climbing to their feet around him. Their faces were lit only by the flames, illuminating expressions of fear, panic, outrage.

It was outrage that Kummetz felt, as he wiped his hairless head with a handkerchief, then replaced it in his pocket.

'Their intentions are clear, I think, gentlemen,' he said. 'So let us now make ours clear to them, Kapitän. Full ahead and prepare to engage. Let them feel the full might of a German invading force.'

Woldag did not argue this time.

'Lang?' he said, trying to see ahead through the flames and smoke, as he addressed the radio operator.

No one responded.

'Lang?'

A clicking sound, like someone turning a light switch on and off, was coming from the rear of the bridge, discernible over the chaos on the deck, but again there was no reply.

Woldag placed his cap back on his head and turned. Others, all on their feet again now, looked towards the sound, too.

'Leutnant Lang!' Woldag spat. 'We do not have time — '

He stopped. Lang was not even looking his way. He was frantically flicking switches, twisting knobs, pressing buttons.

'What is it, Lang?'

Lang stopped and looked back at his captain.

'Herr Kapitän, our primary electrics were lost on the second impact.' His anxiety was unmistakable to everyone on the bridge. 'It hit — '

'My God,' Woldag cut him off, throwing a

58

hand over his mouth and turning back to look at his burning boat once again.

'Yes, sir,' Lang said.

'What is it?' General Engelbrecht demanded.

'The heavy artillery is not prepared for battle,' Lang said, more to Kummetz than Engelbrecht. 'And no electricity means no power to the medium calibres, which means they can't be fired. We are left with only the anti-aircraft rounds. Which means — '

'We're completely exposed,' Engelbrecht said.

Woldag turned to Lang.

'What about the steering?'

'With no electrics, there are no hydraulics, Herr Kapitän. With no hydraulics, there is no steering.'

Kummetz smiled.

'Then we have no choice,' he announced, ecstatic. 'The way is too narrow here for us to turn using only the engines and propellers. We must continue.'

'What about the radios, Lang?' Woldag said.

'Operational.'

'And the fires?'

'Being brought under control as we speak, sir.'

'Additional damage?'

'Some dead, and more injured, both ours and yours, Herr Generalmajor.'

'The ship, Leutnant,' Woldag said.

'We've two bulkheads blown, sir. We're taking on water, but slowly.'

Woldag turned to Kummetz, as did the rest.

'We are fine, Herr Konteradmiral,' he said to his commanding officer. 'For now. But Herr

Generalmajor Engelbrecht is correct, sir. We are exposed.'

'The main battery that just hit us holds the largest guns they have,' Kummetz said, apparently experiencing only euphoria, and entirely unconcerned by developments. 'German. Made by Krups, I believe, weapons for fighting at distance. They cannot be employed at close range, and other than those, the fortress is an antique, whilst we are aboard the most technologically advanced military cruiser of the greatest military force in the world. Remember the Oberführer's words. Full speed ahead, Kapitän.'

'You heard Konteradmiral Kummetz, Leutnant,' Woldag said, holding Kummetz's gaze. 'Full speed ahead. Ring it down.'

'But sir — '

Woldag whipped his head round to face Lang. Woldag knew what his concern was. Without all boilers burning, full speed could not be attained, but he considered it pointless to reveal *that* shortcoming in his preparations as well. The ship was damaged, after all. No one could guess what speed she could achieve, regardless of the number of boilers burning.

'Do not question me, Leutnant,' he growled.

In an attempt to ease the tension, Kummetz lifted a conciliatory hand.

'Come, gentlemen. Now is not the time. We must be efficient. Now is when we prove our mettle. We need only to get beyond these islands. It is their last line of defence. Make sure the men know it. We must keep up morale. Generalmajor, pass word to your officers — your men will be

60

eating breakfast in Oslo.' He turned to Woldag. 'Kapitän — pass the order to return what fire we can. And tell them to start with that searchlight.'

★ ★ ★

Håvard and Ivar had joined Britt at the edge of the rocks. They were standing in a row, height ordered, staring out, any thought of fish or sex gone in the flashing light of the massive fire fight that was taking place just a few hundred metres away.

'Ivar?' Britt said, without moving an inch.

'Yeah?' Ivar responded, without a glimmer of interest in what his sister might have to say.

'Go wake Mamma.'

Ivar's head moved in a tiny nod.

'Okay.'

But his body didn't move at all. He was rapt. War was happening right in front of him — cannons firing, a flaming battleship cruising up the water, all of it right on his doorstep — and yet he felt completely safe. It was like he was watching it at the picture house. Only this was better. In this theatre he didn't only watch the action. He could smell it. He could *feel* it — the heat, the earth-shaking thunder of explosions — and it made him tingle with excitement.

The spell was broken when the first tracers came off the ship. They flew like laser darts in the night towards the mainland. Britt threw the bottle of aquavit at Håvard. He caught it. Ivar was watching the tracers go, his eyes open nearly as wide as his mouth, when suddenly the ground

61

vanished from beneath him.

Britt threw Ivar to the floor and dived on top of him. Then she waited. When she didn't feel anything, she looked up. It had looked like the streaks of fire were coming straight for them, but in fact they were going up and over, towards Kopås, and downstream in the direction of the searchlight. Britt grabbed Ivar by his lapels and stood him up. Her brother's eyes were still wide, but with fear now.

'Get home,' she said.

'Aren't you coming?'

'No. Tell Mamma we're fine. We have to see if there's anything we can do down here.'

'But I want to stay with you,' Ivar said, still watching the tracers.

'You can't, Ivar. You're ten years old.'

'I'm eleven,' he protested.

'You'll slow us down. You've got to get back to Mamma. She'll already be tearing her hair out wondering where you are.' But he wasn't budging. 'Listen, Ivar. You've got to make sure she's all right, okay? That's the Drøbak Brigade's job in this. Get to her and tell her to grab the kitty and the two of you get over the hill, okay? I'll meet you at Auntie Laila's. Now get moving!'

Britt gave Ivar's behind a slap and the kid broke into a run. He left his skis behind, and she watched him move out on foot, until he was gone behind the pine trees. She didn't know what the hell she and Håvard were going to do to help, or if there was anything they *could* do. She hadn't thought about it all. They'd just been words to get Ivar away. Her first thought was that

Sigrid would be furious if Britt had let Ivar stay there. Her second was that she wanted to watch the action.

'Over there,' she said to Håvard, pointing to where the rock opened up, offering a little cover.

Håvard was wearing exactly the same expression as Ivar. Fear. He shook his head.

'I'm going back,' he said.

'Wimp,' Britt smiled.

Håvard grabbed his pack and threw it over his shoulder.

'History's happening right in front of our eyes and you're scared of a few bullets.'

'That's not it, Britt,' he scrambled, trying to save face in front of the girl he loved. 'I'm scared for my sister and my ma.'

'Sure you are.'

'It's the truth,' he said, suddenly angry and indignant.

'Fine,' Britt said after him as he walked away. 'At least leave me the rest of that bottle.'

He paused to glare at her, but she wasn't looking his way any more so he set the bottle down and left.

5

Mr Bonde,

I become eligible for parole in three months. You know who I am. Parole is unlikely to be granted without exterior influence. I therefore have a proposition to make.

There is gold in the *Blücher*. I know where it is. Precisely. In exchange for my release, I will give you that information.

Snorre Nilsen

* * *

Henrik Bonde had received the letter nearly a year ago.

At first he thought it was a prank. But his life as a politician hadn't been keeping him busy a year ago and he started doing a little research. The stationery was prison stationery. The postmark was not the prison's, though. It had been posted at the post office on Grønland-sleiret, just around the corner from the prison. Perhaps he had persuaded a guard to smuggle it out, so it wouldn't be read. He started digging a little more. When it turned out that the handwriting matched an example he found in the National Archives, he started researching the gold.

There were rumours about gold being hidden in the heart of the wreck. Nothing concrete, just word-of-mouth stuff. But the *Blücher* had been an enormous warship with a thousand different chambers. If you didn't know where to look, it would take you a year to find anything, even if she was still floating. Ninety metres down in pitch-black water, crumbling away, the task would be impossible, and the rumours had passed into being myth. But rumours always started somewhere. So Bonde had started to look into how difficult it would be to find something down there if you knew where to look.

An acquaintance of his, a StatOil lobbyist by the name of Himberg, had put him onto Georges Broussard. Broussard was a private dive coordinator. Bonde gave him the dive stats. Broussard said with the right divers and the right equipment it would be possible. That was when Bonde had gone to work on the parole board.

He'd been a member of the Advance Party for the best part of three decades. He knew judges who knew people, all of whom were ambitious and prone to work for promises and banked favours. But it had still all taken time. Nilsen wasn't the sort of prisoner they could just let walk out into the cold light of day. But finally it was happening. That the day of his release was the day before elections was bad luck. That Bonde had been sent on a countrywide tour in the build-up to the election was worse luck. He'd had to send a driver to pick up the file from Nilsen. All this made time tight, because since

Nilsen's release date had been set, Bonde had been making some additional arrangements.

He was sixty-six years old and his political career was on the wane. A new breed of bright, slick young things had taken over, led, in the Advance Party, by its leader of three years, Karl Nygard. But Bonde didn't want to be on the wane. He wanted to be on top. And the additional arrangements were going to make that happen.

Bonde had made contact with the Organization through a string of increasingly disreputable associates. He hadn't set out to make the deal with them specifically, but it was they who had said they could supply Bonde with what he needed for the lowest price. They met at a kids' fair at the Holmenkollen ski jump.

When he'd arrived, he spotted the man immediately: in his thirties, grim-faced and skinny, hatted and sharply dressed, he stuck out like a sore thumb amongst the parents and kids. They walked, and in heavily accented English the arrangements were made: fifty million kroner in cash, or gold amounting to that much, 5 per cent in advance within the next twenty-four hours, the rest to be paid in full at Bonde's leisure, but before election day. For this amount Bonde would receive five hundred thousand ballot papers with a cross next to the Advance Party, distributed according to his needs throughout the country. Then he'd told Broussard to get a team together.

It was a good price. They kept it low, because by supplying Bonde, the Organization would be gaining something better than money. They'd have the leader of the country over a barrel. But *that* was a price Bonde was willing to pay. They knew he could make trouble for them, too, once in power. With a click of his fingers he could start a commission to look into organized crime in Norway, and they'd be right at the top of the list. They had nonetheless made it clear what the consequences of non-payment would be. But he had, what? Ten years left, if he was lucky? He wanted to taste power before he stepped off. He was willing to risk those ten years on the word of a convict.

There had been some anxious times in the lead-up to Nilsen being released. Bonde had missed the payment deadline a number of times. But he'd told them to be patient. And they had been. And now it was on. Nilsen was out today.

All Bonde now needed was to become leader of the party, and for that too he had a plan.

★ ★ ★

'Mr Bonde?' Iversen said, opening the door to cabin 237.

Henrik Bonde, the man inside 237, was staring at himself in the mirror — neat grey hair, hollow, lined cheeks, deep-set crystal-blue eyes. They didn't look up.

'It's past eight, Mr Bonde,' Iversen said, leaning further in. 'We're late.'

Two weeks ago Iversen had received a memo from his boss, the Advance Party leader, Karl Nygard. He was to fly north with Bonde and a small team — all the way north — then travel south by chartered ferry, stopping off at prearranged meeting houses, drumming up support for the elections. The ferry could itself act as a mode of canvassing. People could get on at one stop, hear Bonde give his speech in the auditorium, get off at the next. Travelling by water had made it slow, but numbers hadn't been bad. Bonde had been around a long while. The old guard knew who he was, and that was what irritated Iversen. The election was tomorrow, and he'd spent the last two weeks overseeing an 'eighties reunion. And just as with pop bands getting back together twenty years after their prime, there had been something a little sad about the whole trip; Bonde was certainly no longer at the forefront. Which is where Iversen thought he should be.

Magnus Iversen regarded himself as one of the New Breed — he was not yet thirty and senior advisor to Nygard, the leader of the nation's second party — a position they were hoping to better at the upcoming elections. Yet here he was, stuck on a floating tin bucket keeping an eye on a political has-been. And now, to add insult to injury, just as he thought it was all over, last night Bonde had announced over the tannoy that he was going to be giving his speech one last time the next morning. That was now. Or rather, five minutes ago.

'Mr Bonde?' Iversen said.

Finally Bonde stood and without saying a word, walked past him out of the cabin. The width of the corridor only allowed for single file.

Iversen followed him a couple of paces behind.

'You know, it's game of you, Mr Bonde, but I feel I should reiterate what I said last night. Good speech though it is, everyone on this ferry has already heard it. More than once. What I'm trying to say is, it's done its job. I don't think this is necessary.'

'It's necessary,' Bonde grunted over his shoulder.

'Then do you mind me asking why?' Iversen said as they walked past the last few cabins and came out into the bar with the cubist-vomit-design carpet common to all ferries. The place was empty at that time of the morning. No customers, no barmen, just the whiff of cleaning product mixed with stale alcohol. Through the portholes Iversen could see land growing out of the water either side of the Oslofjord.

They made their way through the chrome-and-black-plastic tables to the orange fire doors. They led through to the auditorium, a wide, low, windowless room, sloping towards a lectern like a subterranean lecture theatre. It was hot in there, airless, and three-quarters full — Iversen didn't know how. He hadn't realized there were even that many people on the ferry. Every one of them turned to see the two men come in and a ripple of applause began.

Bonde started making his way down, shaking hands, Iversen standing third-wheel at his side.

At first glance, this audience appeared wholly typical of those they'd been attracting over the last two weeks. These people weren't of the New Breed; they weren't young professionals being wooed by Nygard's generous tax-and-growth policies, or even the middle classes naturally concerned with the way their country was going, and attracted by his tough stance on immigration. These were more of the same: old-school, working-class, dyed-in-the-wool Norwegians. Norway for Norwegians. A few millennia stuck in a coastal mountain valley will breed that sort of isolationist mentality. And a vote's a vote.

Iversen watched Bonde delivering the empty pleasantries as he moved along the aisle. About three-quarters of the way along, he noticed that the woman vigorously shaking Bonde's hand was wearing a name tag. The tag bore the woman's name — Asta Bredesen. Another word was printed beneath it: *Partimedlem*. Party member. Iversen smiled at the woman when she looked his way — middle-aged, brassy, dyed blonde hair, too much makeup, bad teeth. Another old-schooler.

Bonde moved on to the next row. Iversen moved on with him. The man sitting by the aisle also had a name tag, which also had that word printed on it: *Partimedlem*. That was when the strange feeling started bubbling in Iversen's stomach. He started looking around the audience, from person to person, not at their faces, but at their shirts and blouses and t-shirts and jackets. Every one of them had a name tag, and underneath every name was that word: *Partimedlem*. It wasn't rare for members to come to this sort of thing — a decent speech was a morale-booster — but an audience containing *only* members? At a gathering only announced the night before? What were the chances?

'Mr Bonde?' he said. They'd come to the penultimate row. The applause had been growing all the way along and Bonde shook a couple of hands there before moving on to the people in the front row.

'Mr *Bonde*,' Iversen repeated, a little more urgently.

Bonde looked round at Iversen as he was receiving a double-handed wringing from an ageing man plainly excited to be in his presence. Seeing Iversen's puzzled expression, Bonde smiled, and breaking away from the audience member, he put his arm around the younger man's shoulders, and leaned in.

'They may not be slick and pretty, Iversen,' he said over the applause, which was growing a little over-excited now — the man in the front row was clapping with his hands over his head. 'But take a good look at them, because these people — they're my army.'

Bonde hopped up the couple of steps to the stage in one go, like a young man, and took his place behind the lectern, grinning, lapping up the applause.

Iversen was stunned. His army? He'd never heard Bonde speak like that before. It was only twenty-four hours until the election. For the first time in their history, the Advance Party had a real chance of winning, of leading a coalition into parliament. They didn't need any controversies. They didn't need any talk of armies. They just needed to hook as many floating votes as humanly possible, and that was what Iversen's speech that Bonde had been giving on this tour was geared to do.

But these people weren't floaters. They were members. Long-standing, paid-up party members. Nygard already had their votes. What was Bonde doing here?

Above him, Bonde raised both his hands and the volume lowered.

'My friends,' he said. 'The time for change has arrived.'

Iversen suddenly identified the feeling he'd had in his belly when he saw the name tags. It had been unease. But now, with those words, Bonde had shot a dose of something else through him, and the ice water of panic was suddenly rushing through his veins.

He had heard Bonde give his speech what, thirty, forty times on this trip? That was not the opening line.

★　★　★

Less than two minutes later, Iversen was pushing his way back through the fire doors, his phone rammed to his ear. His skin, usually tanned, was pale. Sweat beaded his brow, and his shirt was translucent-wet and sticking to his chest and back. The air conditioning in the bar hit him like a wall of relief, but he didn't break his stride, not until he was halfway to the bar itself, when the ringing stopped.

'Mr Nygard's office,' the voice at the other end said.

'Hanne,' Iversen said. 'Get me Karl, straight away.'

'One moment, Mr Iversen.'

72

The line beeped and Iversen looked back towards the orange fire doors. The muffled sound of a booming voice made its way through.

'Iversen?'

Iversen turned away from the doors.

'Mr Nygard. I — I — It's not my fault.'

'What're you talking about, Iversen?'

'He's — He's — '

'He who? Spit it out, man. What's going on? The elections are tomorrow. I'm a busy man.'

'I — '

But he couldn't spit it out, so he just marched back to the fire doors, opened one of them and held out his phone. Cheering had broken out in the auditorium. Opening the door was like switching on an amplifier. But only for a second, because the noise was fast silenced, and the voice boomed again.

'The future of our country is at stake, my friends . . . '

Every person in the room was on their feet. The words pushed them onto their toes as they tried to stifle a surge of excitement.

' . . . It is *our* country . . . '

But they couldn't control themselves. The cork was out, chaos unleashed. On the stage, raised up at the other end of the room, visible over the crowd's heads, Bonde had a fist balled midair in front of him, and his eyes were burning.

' . . . Let us reclaim it!'

His final word was inaudible over the noise, but Iversen saw Bonde's lips moving:

'*Together!*'

Iversen watched him for a second longer,

through arms waving and fists pumping, standing up there on the stage, his chest and armpits dark with sweat, his arms out wide, his face shining with perspiration, glee, the thrill of adulation. Of power.

Iversen released the door. But it didn't close fast enough to cloak the chant of 'Bon-de! Bon-de! Bon-de!' that started up.

His phone back at his ear, Iversen heard:

'I said what the *fuck* is going on over there, Iversen?'

'He — I — ' Iversen was shaking his head. In despair. In amazement. Then he laughed, incredulous. 'They're chanting his fucking name, Karl!'

'You think I can't hear that?' Iversen could hear panic in Nygard's voice. But he was controlling it. 'Now pull yourself together, boy, and tell me why I'm getting the feeling this is a bad thing.'

Iversen felt the sting of Nygard's patronizing words, and recoiled.

'He's rallied them, Karl,' he said. Then his tone dropped half an octave, and finding some bite, he added, 'and they're coming for you.'

'What do you mean, coming for me?' Nygard said.

'He's challenging. For leadership. He wants to take us further to the right.'

'What the *hell*? He'll ruin us!'

'He doesn't think so. And neither do they. You heard them in there. They're baying for it.'

Iversen wiped his forehead with his fingers and looked at the moisture that came off, rubbing it with his thumb.

74

'He even got them to turn the air con off in the auditorium. In this heat. So he could get them all worked up. He's convinced them you let them down, Karl, that you represent compromise, and they're spitting blood in there. It's a frenzy.'

'But he'll destroy everything we've built.'

'If he loses, but then what would he care anyway? There's no way you could let him stay after this,' Iversen said. 'Think about it. If he's going to challenge, this is the perfect time. If he'd announced it a month ago and won, but the votes didn't come in tomorrow, he'd be out. Blamed for the failure, for dismantling all you've built. He can't risk that. He knows he needs your votes. But he can't wait until after the election, because what if you take us into government? People won't want to replace you then.'

'They don't want to replace me now.'

Iversen ignored him.

'But if he announces his challenge immediately, Karl, as soon as he gets off this boat, just before the elections, and we win, when the leadership ballots go out in a few days, he can take the credit for the result. You heard them. The core membership's already on his wavelength. He won't need to convince them the nation was voting on the promise of *his* leadership rather than yours. And victory could help convince the rest. If we flop, so be it, but if we don't and subsequently he wins leadership, and walks fresh into government, shit, Karl — it'll be seen as the most audacious political move the country's ever seen. He'll be flying.'

There was a silence at the end of the phone.

All Iversen could hear was the muffled 'Bon-de! Bon-de! Bon-de!' But Iversen's little speech had given Nygard a chance to compose himself, to assess the situation.

'Iversen?' he said. 'You listen to me now. I can take care of this. But I need you to contain the situation on that rig. Get up to the bridge. Slow the boat down. Whatever it takes. Bribe the fucking captain if you have to. Just keep him on the water. For as long as you can. When you do arrive, appeal to his sportsmanship. Tell him, as a gentleman, he should inform me in person that he's challenging before he announces. I'll send a car. Ensure he comes straight here. Do you understand me, Iversen? No fucking press.'

★ ★ ★

Nygard dropped the phone into its cradle.

He hadn't seen this coming. Henrik Bonde had been a member of the party since it was formed back in the seventies. He was an old man now, in his sixties: a grandee if you were kind, a has-been if you weren't. Certainly not a part of the youthful new-look party Nygard had fashioned, of which he himself was the guiding light and poster boy: forty-three, handsome, well-groomed, elegant, intelligent. That was the look that had taken them from being a political sideshow to the country's second party in the last general and local elections. The polls said they could be the first this time. He was damned if he was going to let that old man ruin it all with a misguided shot at personal glory.

Nygard picked up the phone again and punched in a number from memory.

His predecessor and mentor, Steinar Akse, a contemporary of Bonde's who had known when the time had come to stand gracefully aside for the younger generation, had given him the number, along with a key. Akse had taken Nygard aside at his retirement party, just before he headed for his native Southlands, and recited the digits, demanding Nygard memorize them, assuring him that they constituted a useful number for a senior politician to have at his secret disposal, and explaining what to do if ever he had call to dial them.

From political problems to personal, you could call it any time, and the result? Those problems would be solved, with no questions asked. But it was to be used only when very, very special measures were called for. When no other solution could be thought of. When everything was at stake.

At the time, Nygard had considered that sort of shadowy deal a remnant of the old guard; old tricks for old dogs brought up during the Cold War, not something the new guard would be needing. He had only memorized the number and taken the key for the old man's peace of mind. It never occurred to Nygard that he would ever need either of them.

But it turned out Old Man Akse had been right: a new look didn't necessarily mean abandoning old tricks. Everything was at stake, and the number was the only solution Nygard could think of.

The man at the other end of the line was the last-ditch solution because he was a man who fixed situations that could not be fixed on the level. Once the situation was dealt with — which, seeing as the 'fixer' was unrestricted by such niceties as morals and laws, it soon would be — a case containing 500,000 kroner was to be left in locker D91 at Oslo Central station.

The fixer had one key, and Akse (and now Nygard) had the other. And that was the end of it, until such time as you needed the man's services again.

'Yes?' a foreign-accented voice answered.

'You know who this is?' Nygard said.

'Of course.'

'Your rates and method of payment remain the same as for, ah — ?'

'Your predecessor? Some things never change,' the man said, amused. 'The name?'

Nygard swallowed. Another thing Akse had impressed upon him was that, once a fixer had been deployed, it wasn't easy to extract him.

'Who is it you want taken out?' the man said.

'Henrik Bonde,' Nygard said.

* * *

Hanne Olsen, the secretary who had taken Iversen's spluttering call, had worked for the Advance Party since 1981. As a young woman she had been beautiful. Now fifty-three, she wouldn't be winning any beauty contests, but she still fit Nygard's new look: not young, but slim, well-dressed, efficient; plus she knew the party backwards,

78

not to mention the political world as a whole. That was why Nygard had chosen to keep her on once Akse had retired. The youthful Nygard had needed experience backing him up. Besides, Hanne had been unquestioningly loyal to Akse, and had received the old man's stamp of approval, and to Nygard it went without saying that he would receive that same brand of loyalty. He was wrong.

Hanne was of the old school, politically speaking. She had been in tune with her former boss, and the loyalty she had shown him was rooted in their shared views. Despite her outward appearance and her helpful manner, despite Nygard's success and rising popularity, Olsen could not like her new leader. He was too slick, too slippery and therefore, in her opinion, untrustworthy.

Henrik Bonde, on the other hand, she could identify with. What you saw was what you got with the old guard. And she had known him since the old days. For a couple of months, they had secretly been an item. It was the mid-eighties. He was party powerful, handsome, going places. Those were the days when secretaries slipped into offices and closed the door and dropped the Venetians.

When Iversen had called from the ferry sounding so desperate and she had patched his call through to Nygard, Olsen had kept listening. This was a habit of hers. On hearing the news that Bonde was challenging, she knew immediately for whom she would be casting her vote. The news excited her, it took her back to the featureless hotel rooms, their sweating bodies flailing around on the bed; it reminded her of the carpet burns on her knees and back, the excitement of the sheer recklessness of it all. He had been strong back then; he had known what he wanted. More importantly, he'd seemed to know what she wanted, too. Maybe he still did.

Floating in her fantasy world of memories, Olsen had neglected to hang up the phone when Iversen did, and had been just sitting there, the receiver to her ear, reminiscing, when she heard Nygard come on the line again. It jerked her out of her thoughts, and she was about to silently hang up when the foreign-sounding man picked up.

Now, the call over, she wasn't getting hot under the collar any more, but scared. She knew that voice from eavesdropping on Akse's calls. But short of calling the police, she didn't know what she could do.

★   ★   ★

'I told you yesterday it's coming. And the day before that. It's all under control.'

Bonde and Iversen were at the front of the queue to come off the ferry, waiting for the gangway to be opened by the uniformed attendant, who kept looking at his watch.

'I'll let you know.'

Iversen didn't know who Bonde was talking to, but when he ended the call, Bonde couldn't keep still. He was twitching, hyper-alert, sweeping his hair back, his forehead sheened with perspiration, his shirt still two-tone with

80

sweat, his suit jacket folded over his forearm, his briefcase in his hand. He was surging with adrenalin.

Iversen himself was in a more thoughtful state of mind.

This was a chance for him. He just had to be careful, and make sure that, whatever happened in the next seventy-two hours or so, he ended up standing next to the winner, a beacon of strength and support. Indispensable.

If he took extreme measures to prevent Bonde from announcing his candidature, but then the old man ended up winning anyway, there was no way Bonde would want anything to do with him. On the other hand, nor could Iversen overtly disobey Nygard's orders.

Information was key. He needed to know what each man planned to do and when. He'd decided that the best course of action was to try and delay Bonde, in the interests of pleasing Nygard, while in person to Bonde he had to appear to be the challenger's closest ally and right-hand man. He'd already slipped the attendant a small fortune to delay disembarkation for as long as possible. The next thing was to neutralize the phone Bonde was spinning restlessly between his fingers.

'What's going on here?' a voice called from behind.

Iversen looked over his shoulder. Everyone else on the ferry was gathered behind them, trying to see what was delaying their onward journey. Next to him, Bonde was starting to mutter about being kept waiting. His restlessness was turning to irritation. If he had to wait any longer, irritation might turn to suspicion.

'Come on,' Iversen said to the attendant. 'Release us. We've all got places to be.'

The attendant looked at Iversen, confused. Iversen gave him the smallest of nods. The kid shrugged, then pushed open the door.

'About time,' Bonde said, shoving his phone into the pocket of his jacket pocket and marching through. Iversen was on his heels. The airless, covered ramp smelled of stale salt and plastic.

'Mr Bonde,' he said as they moved down the slope. 'I've been thinking.'

'What have you been thinking, Iversen?'

'That you can win this.'

'Thanks for the vote of confidence,' Bonde said. He was confident, amused, and didn't hide his sarcasm.

'I think there are a couple of things to consider, though.'

'I'm listening.'

'We want to avoid accusations of opportunism. This needs to look considered, planned, like what you're doing, you're doing for the good of the party, for the good of the country.'

'Which of course I am.'

'Of course. So the first thing to do is head over to HQ. There'll be a car waiting for us. You call a press conference en route. It'll make it clear you've done the right thing by Karl. That you informed him of your intentions before announcing. Then if he starts whining, he'll come out looking panicky, already a sore loser.'

They reached the bottom of the ramp. At the

end was a door that hadn't yet been opened by an attendant. Iversen reached round Bonde for the door handle with his left hand, while slipping his right hand into the folds of Bonde's jacket.

'Plus,' Iversen said, almost with a sigh of relief as the air and light from outside streamed through the doorway, 'if you wait until this evening, or even late this afternoon, you'll avoid the print headlines and considered analysis. They won't have time to accuse you of opportunism. It'll just be the announcement — *bang!* — and you'll be on every TV in the country. People will go to bed with Henrik Bonde on their minds, thinking *he's got some balls, maybe he can just do what he says he will.*'

The clean and modern shape of the ferry stood right next to the ancient one of the medieval fortress, each towering on either side of them. He and Bonde were sandwiched between the two, ants in a tarmac canyon.

Bonde stopped on the quay, Iversen too. Their fellow passengers swarmed out around them. A few came up to Bonde and congratulated him, shaking him by the hand, including the guy from the front row.

Iversen waited for him to move on, looking for the car. He spotted a black BMW on the road, and also a gathering of people, beyond the barrier, maybe twenty of them. They were holding cameras, boom mics, notepads.

'You called them already,' Iversen said as the man walked away.

'We can't stop the people on this ferry spreading the word, Iversen. And the public votes will come. Don't you worry about that. The country is ready for Henrik Bonde. It's ready to reclaim itself, for its own people. That I can guarantee. All we have to do is tell them. What I need you to worry about is Nygard. If you want in with me, I've got a place for you, but first you have to prove your worth. I need to know everything he does, and I mean everything. You take the car, and get on him. We can't be seen together after I've spoken to them, not until this is done with. I'll get a cab.' Then he added: 'Keep your phone close. I'll be calling you.'

Bonde turned, made his way through the barrier and stopped in front of the journalists, shaking their hands one by one. One of them, a man in a suit and a pair of Aviator sunglasses, handed him an A4 manila envelope. Bonde put it in his briefcase, then stared into the cameras and gave it his all. The man in the Aviators did not wait to hear the speech, but returned to his Mercedes C-class and drove away.

All through this, Iversen didn't move. He just stood there, his head pounding with the heat. Then a phone started ringing in his pocket and he pulled it out.

Bonde wouldn't be able to call him, not in the near future, because he didn't have a phone, not any more. Iversen had taken it from his jacket as they came out onto the quay, and now it was ringing in his hand. Iversen switched it off, his heart joining his head in the drumming.

If Bonde found out he had his phone, he would know he couldn't trust him, and that was an eventuality Iversen couldn't allow. Because from what Bonde had said, from the sheer unequivocal confidence seeping from his guarantee, Iversen knew: somehow, before even a single ballot paper had been posted, Bonde had secured himself the public vote.

6

'You hear that?' Private Fredriksen whispered to Private Borg, the other man sitting with him in the pillbox on South Kaholmen.

'Hear what?' Borg said.

'Voices,' Fredriksen said.

Borg leaned forward towards the concrete slit they were both facing, the light of fire and the flashes of explosions flickering across his face.

The front boat of the invading flotilla couldn't have been more than two hundred metres away, but the glaring inferno eating up the deck made it impossible to identify its nationality. Norwegian guns were pelting it from the mainland now, too. Return fire was weak, just the AA rounds, coming at Kaholmen and towards the Kopås battery over near Drøbak. It looked like the beast was all teeth and no bite, and as she came in line with the islands she was burning like a giant Viking funeral pyre. But Fredriksen knew the men on board were no Vikings. They weren't dead either. Between the noise of the shelling and the wind whipping from the sea, Borg heard voices now, and plenty of them, singing in unison, snippets echoing out of the ship's hull.

Deutschland, Deutschland, über alles. Über alles in der welt.

'Nazis,' Borg said, not taking his eyes off the scene or moving an inch. 'Ring it through.'

Fredriksen was already holding the radio receiver.

86

'Not that it matters now, though,' he said to Borg. Then, into the receiver: 'Control? This is Fredriksen.'

★ ★ ★

Despite the words' meaning, the singing aboard the *Blücher* was not victorious. It was defiant. The antiaircraft gunners were doing what they could, and the main battery of the fortress was alight, but the ship was in bad shape and the thousand-plus men waiting below deck to be offloaded at Oslo knew it just as well as those above, only they were stuck in the 'tween decks and singing was all they had. At least thirty had been killed when the second shell had breached the deck, and now flames were swirling up out of the resulting black hole; where the fire stopped, thick black suffocating smoke took over. All lights had gone out, too, and one of the kerosene stores had ignited. The emergency fans had come on, but they only sucked in more smoke from outside. Still the men below deck were ordered to dig in and stay put. The deck crew had formed chains and were throwing buckets of water on the flames where they could, but it was like spitting at the sun, and every new shell brought a new fire to fight and fewer men to fight it.

Up on the bridge, each impact threw the senior officers off balance. Every one of them was holding on to something, and as Woldag rose from the last impact, he caught sight of someone moving towards the exit, swinging from hand-hold to handhold like a black-uniformed ape

87

moving through a metal canopy.

'Von Westarp!' Woldag shouted and the small man turned, his face blackened, sweating. Woldag instantly regretted the aggression in his voice, and the lack of respect. 'Herr Oberführer, I must insist that you remain on the bridge. You will be safest here, sir.'

Von Westarp looked back at him, struggling to keep his footing as another shell hit. Kummetz was next to Woldag.

'The Kapitän is right, Oberführer,' the rear admiral said. 'This will only last a couple of minutes.'

Von Westarp pulled open the door. More smoke billowed through, hunting for new space to fill, faces to blacken. He turned back to Woldag and Kummetz.

'This is your boat, Herr Kapitän,' he shouted. 'And your fleet, Konteradmiral. I am not a part of your *Kriegsmarine*.'

'Then perhaps you do not know that there is nowhere to hide on a ship of war, Oberführer,' Woldag spat. 'And nowhere to run.'

'Remember your own words, Oberführer,' Kummetz called to the SS man.

'Herren Kummetz, Woldag,' von Westarp said. 'Do not for an instant think I shy from battle. In this war we each have a job, gentlemen. Do yours. Finish this and get us to Oslo so I can do mine.'

Von Westarp slammed the door and was gone.

★   ★   ★

Sigrid had woken up as soon as the firing had started. When she looked out of the window and, seeing the fire through the trees, formed an idea of what all the noise was about, her first thought was for the children. She went straight to their room. It was empty. It didn't take her long to check the rest of the house. The whole building was empty. She yanked the back door open and made straight for the outhouse. Also empty. Others were out of their houses by now, and she ran up to her neighbours, Rolf and Tone Torgersen.

Tone was holding their baby, Lisbeth, who was crying. Rolf was holding on to both of them tight, trying to make out what was happening down on the water.

'Tone. The children,' Sigrid tried. 'They're — they're — have you seen them?'

The Torgersens only managed a concerned 'no' before the tracers from the flak battery on the *Blücher* started flying overhead towards Kopås and scared them back into their house. Sigrid remained outside, continuing her search, worry turning to fear, approaching other neighbours as they made for cover, but none had seen her kids. Then she remembered, and stopped dead in the middle of the street.

Britt was fishing down in the cove with Håvard. Ivar must've woken up and gone down to join them. They were down by the water.

Fear shot up to panic, and in an instant panic turned to anger, and Sigrid was moving again, sprinting, pushing aside anyone who got in her way.

No way was this going to happen. It couldn't.

She wouldn't *allow* it to happen.

Not all the tracers were making it to Kopås. One had hit a house ahead of her, near the church, and it was burning; the family had escaped but did not know what to do — fight the fire, run to their neighbours, or into the church or the woods, or just watch. And that's what they were doing, watching, agape. Sigrid screamed as she ploughed through them.

Not today. Not any day. She was *not* about to lose more of her family.

But then something hit her, like a scorching docker's hook had just swung out of the air and slammed into her chest. It took her clean off her feet.

★ ★ ★

The torpedo battery was built into the rock of North Kaholmen island. Lieutenant Karlsen and a crew of ratings were manning the three tubes, ready to reload as soon as they were emptied. They had nine torpedoes total and each took about two minutes to load. Ten metres above them at the top of the hill, Commander Anderssen and his NCO, Bexrud, were sitting in the cupola, a stone pillbox accessed via a series of ladders from the loading bay, waiting for the *Blücher* to come into view through their 70-degree horizontal slit sight. Suddenly, a round hit the pillbox and rang out like a bell. Both men ducked instinctively.

'They get any bigger, and we won't be here to do this,' Bexrud said.

'They sound bigger than they are,' Anderssen

said — unconvincingly, Bexrud thought. 'The shape of this structure amplifies it. We're fine. Just try to ignore it.'

Bexrud shook his head and they fell silent, listening to the cacophony of battle. Twenty seconds later, a massive ship edged into view, half a kilometre out, flames licking from it and smoke billowing. Unlike Fredriksen and Borg, Anderssen didn't hear any voices coming from it. All he heard was the constant, hypnotic boom of the artillery fire. Which was fine, because he was trying to ignore everything — the noise, the cold, his nerves. Everything but the ship, its relation to his torpedoes and the aiming mechanism he was tweaking.

'Karlsen,' he said into the radio. 'Adjust to seven knots.'

'Seven knots,' Karlsen's voice came back. 'Torpedo ready.'

Anderssen moved his hand from the adjustment wheel and wrapped it around the handle to his right, and felt for the firing pin.

Watching the *Blücher*, he turned a fraction towards Bexrud.

'Cross everything you've got,' he said.

Bexrud frowned.

'But you've practice-fired these torpedoes hundreds of times,' he said.

'So we know the mechanics work. But every one of the missiles is fifty years old, and we've never tested the explosive heads.'

'And this is the moment you choose to inform me of this?'

'It seemed like the time.' Anderssen shrugged.

'That's why I'm saying cross everything. And we're coming into range in five, and four, and three, and two, and one, and firing number-one tube.'

He pulled the firing mechanism and after the mechanical click, for half a second nothing happened. Anderssen looked at Bexrud and was about to speak when a loud *ppffttt* came from the machinery below them, like an oversized bottle of beer was being opened somewhere deep inside the rock, and that was rapidly followed by a *phunngg* as the torpedo accelerated out of its tube and into the water.

Anderssen exhaled in relief.

'Okay, Karlsen,' he said into the radio. 'Adjust sight to five knots for number two.'

'Five knots,' Karlsen said. And a second later: 'Torpedo ready.'

'Firing number-two tube.'

Anderssen pulled the firing mechanism again and the same thing happened: briefly nothing, then the *ppffttt* followed by the *phunngg*.

'Number-three tube, five knots.'

Anderssen was about to pull for the third, but then an explosion hit the front of the already burning ship. It was a hit — inconsequential, and the ship kept moving, but a smile spread across Anderssen's face.

'They work,' he whispered. 'These antiques actually blow.'

'Torpedo ready, sir,' Karlsen came over the radio.

'No,' Anderssen said. 'There are more ships following this one. That'll do it. Reload, and wait.'

As he spoke, the second torpedo hit.

By then von Westarp was down from the bridge and on the deck of the *Blücher*. The explosion of the second torpedo threw him into the air. He landed on his front and began to skid along the steel deck headfirst. Then his shoulder hit something, the impact flipping him round. He kept on sliding, on his back, now, and feet-first, flailing, grabbing at anything that flew by in the firelit dark. Five metres from the flaming hole to the 'tween deck, he slapped his palm around the bottom rung of a gangway ladder and felt his body grind to a halt. He looked down at his feet. They were hanging above the flames.

The torpedo hits had come on the port side. The impact of the second made the whole ship roll 45 degrees onto its starboard side, which was what had caused von Westarp to shoot along the deck. The *Blücher* was now rolling back portways, trying to correct herself. Von Westarp started sliding back round the other way, pivoting from his handhold. He grabbed the ladder with his other hand, but the weight of his body and the leather of his gloves conspired to make gripping the tubular metal impossible and he went careering back the way he'd come, his body thumping and spinning down to the wall of the ship. He grabbed at the chain above his head as the roll began to reverse yet again, hooked his arm around it and held on and hung there, secure, as men all around him slipped back down towards the fires — roaring now, higher and hotter than ever — screaming as they plunged into the flames.

Von Westarp waited for the roll to ease, then pulled himself to his feet, found his balance and looked over the side of the ship. The black water swirled fifteen metres below him. The *Blücher* was still moving onwards, but she was listing badly, her hull dipping 25 degrees to portside. Von Westarp was no sailor, but he knew that meant the ship had been breached below the water line.

Soldiers were still fighting the fires, but if it had been hopeless before, now it was plain futile. The flames were spreading faster than ever, forming a wall of fire that divided the deck in two, fore and aft. And it wasn't only the ship that was burning. Flames were dancing on the surface of the water, too, running across the oil leaking out of the ship. Men, swimming for their lives, were screeching like hell as their wet uniforms burned, and the skin beneath was flayed from their flesh. And the dance was on the move. The oil was slicking all around the boat to the starboard side. To von Westarp's side.

He turned and hooked a leg over the side of the boat. He was about to throw himself over when another sound caught his attention, a voice. He turned and coming out of the black smoke he saw a figure, groping along the chain towards him.

'Oberführer . . . please . . . help me . . . ' the man said.

Von Westarp did not recognize him, but he might have known him once. His uniform was charred, his face black. He could hardly walk

94

and was clutching one of his shoulders where it had been opened up by shrapnel. He crawled on, pulling himself towards von Westarp.

Von Westarp glanced over the side again. The flames were coming. Other men were already clambering up and away from the main fire, to the high starboard side, and jumping overboard. Von Westarp had been a strong swimmer in his day, but that was in the gymnasia and lakes of Bavaria, and as a youth, not as a middle-aged man in the seas of Scandinavia at the tail-end of winter.

He switched his head 180 degrees. There were islands coming up on the west side. They'd pass right by them if only the ship made it that far. But to get to them he would have to cross the boat, or else swim round it, and that meant either passing over the deck or cutting through the oil. Neither was an attractive option. He would have to swim east, to the mainland. And soon. The drive of the boat was whipping the burning oil round the hull faster and faster. It looked a hundred metres to shore, more — two, maybe three. He didn't want to carry any excess weight over that sort of distance, so he pulled his Luger out of its holster and pushed it into the pocket of his trousers. He then started to unbuckle his Sam Browne from his shoulder.

'Herr von . . . ' the man cried, getting close now. 'My shoulder . . . I can't swim. Oberführer von Westarp. Please. Take me over. *Help* me.'

Von Westarp looked back at the man. He could see his eyes now, the whites glowing out of the black of his skin and the night, catching the flames. Terror, that's what von Westarp saw in them.

The soldier let go of his shoulder and reached out his hand.

And he was begging. The true Aryan does not beg. He does not feel fear. His mind and body are too strong for that. Besides, this was a beggar that would weigh 80 kilos at least — more, with a sodden uniform.

Von Westarp looked down. The flames had arrived on the water below him already. The coward had delayed him. Von Westarp threw his Sam Browne overboard and bent to pull off his boots.

'What is your name and rank, soldier?'

'I am Oberfähnrich Werner Hoch, sir. You are my saviour, Oberführer. A true — '

When von Westarp straightened, bootless now, Hoch saw the disgust in his eyes and stopped speaking.

'You are exhibiting cowardice, Oberfähnrich,' von Westarp announced. 'And as you know, this world has no room for cowards. You are lucky enough to be a member of an Aryan race. Prove yourself worthy of your birth. Earn it. If you survive today, you will have deserved to live and call yourself a son of Germany. If not, you can die knowing your loss was to the benefit of humanity.'

'No,' Hoch said. 'I beg of you. In the name of all that is great and kind. Please. Do not leave me here.'

Hoch fell to his knees now. His *knees*.

Von Westarp removed his SS-Oberführer's cap

and considered it for a moment, the Reich's eagle and the *Totenkopf* below it.

'Stand up, Hoch,' von Westarp said, extending his hand to the stricken soldier. Hoch took it and rose. Face to face now, von Westarp said, 'The weak shall not survive, Oberfähnrich. Not today, and not tomorrow. You should consider your position fortunate. Soon you will know absolutely of what you are made and whether you are deserving of life. Come. I will see you on the other side.'

With that, von Westarp shoved the soldier away, towards the edge of the boat. As Hoch fought inertia, the two men's eyes locked — Hoch's fear-filled, von Westarp's curious. Then, just as the injured man lost the battle and fell backwards off the ship, von Westarp saluted him.

He then moved to where the man had stood and looked down. Hoch was already lost from sight.

'Good luck to you, soldier,' he said, and after throwing his cap overboard he hoisted a leg over the side and followed it down.

The cold of the rushing air was replaced by the heat of the flames on the water's surface, but only for a fraction of a second before the iciness of the water engulfed him and the terrible sounds were doused.

His muscles seized instantly, but he stretched his limbs and forced himself to swim. He felt his Luger slip from his pocket and groped for it, but the water below him was black, and feeling was receding from his limbs like a snail retreating into its shell, and the pistol was lost.

Above him, blurred figures were silhouetted by the firelight, men being burned, drowned, frozen — men being *tested* — but von Westarp conquered, and he swam, he swam until his lungs felt they were being squeezed in two giant fists and then, just as he was about to pass out, he felt rock beneath him. The seabed. The shallows. He pushed upward, but obstacles had him trapped beneath the surface. Bodies: sopping, slippery, dozens of them, their burned flesh and uniforms pushing against him. It was like a scene from hell. With all his remaining strength, von Westarp battled his way through, scrambling over the moonlit bodies, slipping between them, but lifting himself, emerging again like a monster from the deep, gasping the air poisoned with the odour of burned flesh into his lungs, pulling at whatever met his grasping hands, dragging himself onwards by belts, arms, hair, onwards, and onwards, to survival.

★ ★ ★

From where Britt had been lying beneath the overhang, it looked as though the *Blücher* had erupted like a volcano. The oil fires on the water were flowing like lava, and, upended, the ship itself looked something like a mountain as it sank.

But the flashes of fire flying off the side of the ship into the burning water were not magma rocks or red-hot ash. They were men. Suddenly history was making her stomach squirm like she had swallowed a live snake.

The firing both ways stopped. The rest of the boats had halted. They were hanging back in the smoke and fog, out of range, watching their leader die.

Britt came out from her cover and was still watching the lead boat edge further and further beneath the surface of the water when something sloshed up onto the rocks below her. Then another came. She focused, her eyes adjusting to the darkness after the flames. The water was full of human flotsam, the cove packed with bodies bobbing in the waves. She clambered down to the shore and took hold of the first man she came to. He was floating face-down in the water. She rolled him over, and the snake in her stomach momentarily froze. Britt was not even sure this could be considered a man any more. Fire had stripped him of his hair. His scalp was a sticky wet dome glinting red and black, and his face was barely recognizable as human, a dark mask made of that same viscous black-and-red substance. All the usual features — the chin, the mouth, the nose, the ears — were still there, but somehow, in the dark, with the water and blood, and remnants of skin breaking the lines, they were more like impressions — almost there, but not quite. That wasn't true of the eyes, though. They were open, the eyelids burned away, the pupils staring beyond her, up into the smoke-filled night, still human and lucid.

Claustrophobia seized her. The snake in her gut reanimated, wriggling and constricting. It moved up to her chest and she was struggling to take in air, and when she managed to pull in just a little bit she knew immediately what the result was going to be. Britt let go of the body and the snake shot out of her mouth, the vomit splashing into the water, onto the bodies. Bent double, she tried to suck in deep lungfuls of air, but the taste was foul — sick and death and smoke combined.

She scrambled back up and grabbed the bottle of aquavit.

Wiping her lips, she said, 'Holy fucking shit,' and took a drink, looking down at the bodies. So many lives gone. Finished.

Suddenly an arm rose from the stack of dead.

'Holy fucking shit,' she said again.

'You,' came a voice, in Norwegian but carrying a German accent.

Its owner was dragging himself through the bodies towards Britt, clambering up the rocks, like a sea creature. He stood up, a couple of metres in front of Britt, plump, soaking, shivering, wearing just a grandpa shirt and black knee-length pantaloons opened around his knees. Unarmed, so far as she could see.

'Please,' he said, in Norwegian again. 'Take me to your home. Feed me and clothe me. I will see to it that you are handsomely compensated.'

He was talking as though she would automatically comply.

'Your boat's gone,' she said. 'And the rest of the fleet has turned around.'

The German looked towards the water and saw she was right. The *Blücher* had completely capsized, and the bow had sunk beneath the surface of the water now. The stern was sticking up in the air, the massive bronze propellers shining.

'They will return tomorrow,' he said, looking back at Britt. 'Stronger, more forceful. Less gracious. If you help me I will see to it that you are not one of those punished for resistance.'

'Head south,' Britt said. 'Maybe you can catch them, go back where you came from. Just stay out of my fucking country.'

* * *

Von Westarp had no strength to force the issue. He stood there a moment, examining her, memorizing her fine, strong features — the blue eyes, the handsome nose, the high brow, the pronounced, round cheekbones, the jutting chin, the mole at the corner of her left eye. Then he turned and waddled into the forest as fast as his frozen limbs could carry him, thinking as fast as his frozen brain would allow.

Oslo was too far. Attempting to walk there at night, in wet clothes, in the bone-chilling cold that had him shaking as he moved, would be suicide. He could head south to where the other ships would regroup, but that was too far as well. If he was going to survive, he needed to get dry and warm immediately.

* * *

Håvard had been back to town, but now he was racing back down to the cove again, calling, 'Britt!' at the top of his voice. 'Britt! Britt!'

When he arrived, Britt was sitting on the rocks looking out at the water, at the bodies, at Oscarsborg. The *Blücher* was gone.

'Britt!' Håvard heaved.

Britt turned, held out the bottle.

'You missed the show,' she said. 'And you'll never guess what just happened. I was — '

Håvard pushed the bottle away.

'You've got to come, Britt.'

Britt saw the concern on Håvard's face.

'Why? What's happened, Håvard? Are the girls all right? Your mother?'

'They're fine. It's not *my* family, Britt. It's yours. It's Sigrid. And Ivar.'

★ ★ ★

Von Westarp spotted a light up ahead and headed through the forest towards it. As he drew closer, he made out a house, standing on its own. He would make sure its residents saw more clearly what they had to lose if they did not comply, and what they had to gain if they did. Hopefully they would not be so admirably foolhardy as the young woman.

He paused at the edge of the tree line. The building was fifty metres away. The light was coming from a window. An old woman and an old man were standing at it, looking out, curious as hell, and not a little frightened. Von Westarp stepped out from the trees, thinking so long as they didn't have a son or grandson about the place, this would be simple. He'd just —

The sudden sound of tyres skidding on mud

102

and gravel was right by his ear. He froze, hoping he hadn't been seen, but a second later he knew it was the wrong thing to have done. A pair of dazzling white lights suddenly came on. He was standing in their beam in the middle of a rough road, half-dirt, half-snow.

'Turn those lights off,' he said, in Norwegian, raising a hand to shade his eyes from the light and making to move forward. A voice came from the darkness beyond the lights. It said only, 'Uh-uh!', but it was accompanied by the sound of the cocking of a gun, and that stopped von Westarp in his tracks.

'I know you must be scared,' von Westarp said calmly. 'But I urge you not to be unreasonable. I am not your enemy. The National Socialists are friends of the Norwegian people.'

The metal creak of a car door opening came next, then feet crunching into the snow.

'Take me to your home, give me clothes and a bath and food and use of your vehicle and I will make sure you are well taken care of. Drive me to Oslo, and on arrival you will be handsomely rewarded. Our orders from the Führer are clear. Life for Norwegians need not change for the worse upon our arrival. But there is no reason why it cannot improve.'

The sound of footsteps ceased just as a figure emerged from the darkness, but still it was little more than an apparition.

'You are SS?' its voice came. In English.

'I — ' but von Westarp was too cold, and now confused, to manage a coherent sentence. 'But — '

'I am told the SS is not to be trusted. That you are not soldiers. That you have no honour.'

'Then those that tell you this do not know Oberführer von Westarp, my friend,' von Westarp said, effortlessly switching to English. 'My word — '

'And you cannot identify the sound of a Luger when you hear it.'

The language was German now, and the man began to laugh. He was joined by others, still in the vehicle.

Von Westarp's body did not relax even a fraction. Tension had turned to irritation.

'Woldag,' he said.

'None other, Herr Oberführer,' the *Blücher's* captain said, stepping forward.

'And you have found a vehicle, I see. I congratulate you on your resourcefulness. It is ... most unexpected,' von Westarp said, also stepping forward. 'I hope she doesn't sink.'

'And this would concern you, Oberführer? We all have roles in this war, after all, and yours, I believe, involves abandoning a ship at the first sign of resistance.'

'And yours, Kapitän Woldag, was to carry Engelbrecht and his men to Oslo, destroying all that stood in your path. Congratulations. You have succeeded in failing even in tasks so simple as carriage and demolition. But fear not — ' von Westarp pointed a finger skywards and cocked his ear. 'Do you hear that?' A deep and distant hum had begun to resonate through the air. 'The *Luftwaffe* to the rescue, Kapitän?'

Woldag looked at the man. He resembled a

giant, milky-white toad that had been squeezed into an undershirt and plus-fours. And still wearing his black leather gloves and proudly bearing the *Totenkopf* ring on his finger. With the shock of black hair slick across his head, he looked like a pathetic caricature of the Führer or Reichsführer, and yet he still managed to behave in so superior a manner. Woldag resisted further antagonizing von Westarp and, in fear of the SS man actually surviving, fast rejected the idea of leaving him to fend for himself.

'You are in luck, Herr Oberführer,' he said. 'All one hears of the honourable *Kriegsmarine* is true. And so, delightful though it is, let us cut short our little chat. You are shivering, after all.' Woldag took a step aside, not allowing even a smirk to reach his mouth. He clicked his heels and pointed an arm at the vehicle. 'After you, Herr von Westarp. I insist. You have work to do, I understand. And nothing so elementary as demolition, I am sure.'

Von Westarp moved to the car, but before he got in he stopped in front of Woldag, a few drops of fjord water still on his chin. He spoke his cryptic message quietly.

'You are quite wrong, Kapitän. My role here is to be quite as elementary as yours. We are merely at opposite ends of the spectrum. You come to destroy. I come to *create*.'

★   ★   ★

If she had stopped to listen, Britt would have heard the drone of aircraft, too, but she and

105

Håvard were running, as fast as they could, up towards the town. They burst out of the trees and headed for the main street.

'Over there.'

Håvard pointed at the gathering of people outside the church. Britt slammed into them and started peeling people away.

She could hear a single voice coming from the centre. High, aggressive, hysterical. 'Leave her alone,' it cried.

People complained when they felt her shoving them aside, but when they realized who was manhandling them, word rippled through and the crowd eased open.

In the middle of the ring, sitting on blood-soaked snow, was Ivar. He was wielding their father's coronation knife. His hands were covered in blood, his clothes too. Tears were streaming from his eyes. In his arms was their mother. But for the splatters of blood across it, her face could have been that of someone asleep. Not so the rest of her. Her chest was simply no longer there, just a bloody mess of clothing, bone, flesh and innards slipping out over Ivar's lap.

'Leave her alone,' the boy was spitting at the crowd, swinging the knife from side to side, like he was guarding her. 'She's my mamma. *My* mamma.'

★　★　★

At the same moment that Ivar saw Britt standing there staring at him, crying, the *Blücher* hit the

106

bottom of the fjord, just 300 metres off the Askholmen islands, two kilometres to the north of Oscarsborg fortress. The impact with the seabed resulted in a massive underwater explosion, which in turn caused a huge burning bubble to rise. When this fireball reached the surface, it ignited the remaining oil that had spilled onto the water. The Drøbak Narrows became a furnace, burning many more men as they swam for safety. This was the final death cry of the ship, and occurred a little more than two hours after Colonel Eriksen had given the order to engage.

Believing the *Blücher* to have run into a mine barrage, the rest of her flotilla retreated. Soon afterwards, the *Luftwaffe* began to drop bombs on the fortress and surrounding area, and continued to do so for many hours without pause.

In terms of the invasion, the loss of the *Blücher* was only a minor setback for the Nazis. By 10 April, it was plain that elsewhere in the country the invasion had been a success and, seeing that further resistance would do no good, Colonel Eriksen ordered his men to lay down their arms. In terms of future resistance to their occupation, however, the delay in occupying Norway's capital city was catastrophic for the Nazis. By the time planes and paratroopers started landing at Oslo's Fornebu airport, the Norwegian royal family and governing cabinet had escaped with the nation's gold reserve. They refused to cooperate with the Germans as they moved over the country, instead urging the Norwegian people to continue their opposition to occupation. Eventually they made it into exile in Britain, and then on to Canada, from where they could direct and fund the emerging resistance movement that fought against the iron-fisted Reichskommissar, Josef Antonius Heinrich Terboven.

★ ★ ★

Despite the events at Drøbak on 8–9 April 1940, the Norwegians did not suffer a single military casualty there (although two civilians — both women — lost their lives). German losses on the other hand numbered between 800 and one thousand.

In the days that followed the invasion, in the chaos before order was restored, reports were made of another German casualty worthy of note. Following the sinking of the *Blücher*, Captain Heinrich Woldag was sent to Berlin under a cloud of shame to make his report. Having done so, he was ordered to return to Norway for the funeral of the fallen *Blücher* men. His Junker 52 aircraft departed Kiel Holtenau on 16 April 1940. Plane, pilot and passenger were never seen again. The report filed stated that technical faults had caused the aircraft to crash into the Oslofjord. This report was filed the very day of the crash. The report was signed by Oberführer Gerhard von Westarp.

2

7

Born in the east of Oslo to an electrician father who died of an aneurism when she was seven, Ingrid Hansen grew up with her nursery-teacher mother in a small apartment off Vogts Gate, watching reruns of Angie Dickinson in *Police Woman*. She knew from an early age that, grades permitting, when she had finished school she would attend the Norwegian Police University College and join the force. The grades did permit, and she bagged herself a degree in psychology as well.

It was surprising that the post of Junior Sergeant in Crime Squad should be advertised in the college newsletter. Crime Squad was a senior department dealing with serious crime in the capital, after all, but when she saw it, Hansen knew she had to give it a shot. Others in her graduation year had better grades, and of course other applicants still would come from the qualified force and have genuine experience. On paper, then, it was difficult to explain why Ingrid Hansen was selected for the newly available position.

But that was on paper. In the printed word. But each application for the job was also accompanied by a photograph, and of course the process of elimination included interviews with the chief, Superintendent Lars Egeland, and in her picture, as in the flesh, Ingrid Hansen was a beautiful young woman. When a woman is that attractive, she always has a sneaking concern that her looks are getting things for her — even more so when entering a man's world such as Crime Squad. But if Hansen only suspected that this was the case when she received the letter telling her to move her things to the main police station in Grønland, it was confirmed in no uncertain terms when she arrived,.

Egeland had called her into his room, at the end of the open-plan squad office they called the Pit. The chief was pale and overweight, like a hairy, sallow balloon filled to bursting with lard and squeezed into vaguely human form, with a couple of beady black eyes, a tiny nose, a line mouth, a crown of hair and a nylon suit thrown on.

Sitting there, sweating like cheese in a sauna, he told her outright: the only reason he'd advertised in the newsletter was because, after the bastard she was replacing, he wanted someone fresh, who could be taught, formed. Someone malleable, if she knew what he meant. And then it came, looking right at her: the fact that she was the best-looking of the applicants didn't damage her cause either. So how about it? The militaristic cadet uniform did it for him — the jackboots and cap. They could draw the blinds, get right down to it.

When she just stood there, staring at him, trying not to let the disgust show on her face, he laughed off the rejection and told her that her success or otherwise in the Crime Squad was in her own hands. If she wanted to be seen as any more than a piece of tail, she would have to prove she wasn't.

From Egeland, the chauvinism dripped down the ranks of his cronies like scum from a badly poured beer, taking different forms as it made its way. Inspector Solberg — slick, slim, fit, well-dressed and handsome, in a reptilian sort of way — seemed to think he could simply ooze his way into her panties with aggressive charm. That he thought he actually had a chance was the worst of it. Inspector Halvorsen, the man to whom she had been assigned, was mentally and physically dense, a copper of the old school who had only got to where he was because Egeland was his uncle. He seemed to know he was a lapdog, but not to care, and simply came out with a stream of innuendo-ridden jokes and comments. But he talked about his brassy wife as much as anything, and had never actually come on to her, which was some kind of blessing. The rest of the faces in the Pit, Dahl, Brunstad, Forgaard, were more of the same — leering looks, bawdy comments — but she hadn't had much to do with them yet. She was only four weeks into the job.

Egeland's personal secretary, Vera, and the Pit secretary, Agnes, showed no solidarity, either. They resented her, and Hansen could understand why. No one likes a person who gets a job off the back of their looks, especially women in a men's world.

The first few days, Hansen had gone home to her top-floor studio in Grünerløkka stunned.

Just in stepping over the threshold into the Pit, she seemed to have slipped through a wormhole and landed back in the seventies. Making the short journey in, seeing all the hallmarks of modern Scandinavian equality — fathers pushing prams, women CEOs being bussed around by drivers — looking out of election posters appealing for votes for the parties they were leading, she couldn't quite believe the previous day's experiences had actually occurred.

But as soon as she passed through the time portal again and showed up in the Pit the next day, she knew it had been real, and she started telling herself she was going to quit. Everywhere else in the country it *was* the twenty-first century, for God's sake. There were other departments, other regions, if necessary. But she didn't quit, and by the second week she had grown indignant. She dropped the uniform for civvies, and was looking into making formal charges of harassment, taking her grievances all the way to the top, if necessary. But again, she didn't, because towards the end of that week, she realized that, even if she did get Egeland and his cronies out — which she doubted — she'd never get another position, in any region. No one would want a snitch. And anyway, by then she knew she'd been fooling herself.

This was just part of a process she was working through — the process of acceptance — and by the end of the third week, Hansen was telling herself she'd be damned if she was going to quit such an opportunity just because she'd been born lucky, with good looks. Although her encounter with Egeland had left her shell shocked, in due course she managed to unearth a positive from the experience: he had presented her with a challenge.

It seemed likely that Egeland's words about getting anywhere in Crime Squad were knee-jerk, a reflex threat: if elsewhere in the department she gave out what she wouldn't give him she'd be gone — but that didn't matter. It showed the psychology of the beast. If she proved she was professionally capable, she would earn his respect, and that would drip down to his underlings just like the sleaze. Not that she wanted his respect, particularly, or that of Solberg or Halvorsen — these men disgusted her, after all — but coupling their desire with admiration would allow her to turn the tables on them. It would make her the Alpha. Queen bee. They'd be putty in her hand.

She'd have to play it carefully, of course, particularly with Egeland — the frustrated, belittled Alpha male is a dangerous creature, especially when he's being replaced in the affections of his men — but if she could overcome this, she was pretty sure she'd be able to handle any situation she came up against in what she intended to be a long and fruitful career. She was going to take the bull by the horns. It's what Pepper Anderson would have done in *Police Woman*.

The phone on her desk started to ring. She grabbed the receiver.

'Crime Squad. Hansen speaking.'

'It's the desk. I've got a caller worried about someone.'

'A missing person? You need — '

'No. Says she's heard something. Thinks someone's in danger. You want to take it?'

'Put her through.'

* * *

Following a series of *yeses*, *reallys*, and *are you certains*, all the while jotting notes, Hansen thanked the caller and hung up.

'So, Sugar-tits. What was that?'

Halvorsen had arrived moments earlier and was standing at her desk, holding a McDonald's bag, his daily twin Egg McMuffins inside releasing their grease over the paper.

'Morning, Mel,' she said, looking him up and down. Halvorsen looked like he had spent the first half of his life fighting, the second drinking. Pretty much like Gibson. 'The years haven't been kind to you, have they? *Lethal Weapon* was a long time ago, huh?'

'I'm in rehab,' he said, dropping his breakfast on his desk, right behind Hansen's, and putting his jacket over his chair. 'I'm no longer an alcoholic. Not even a racist, praise be. But I did pick up a new sex addiction. You want me to show you how that works? All us celebrities have it these days, you know?'

'Just as well you've got all that money.'

'Keeps me in clam.' He pulled out an Egg McMuffin, unwrapped it and took a bite, perching on the edge of her desk now. It creaked. 'So?' he said between chews.

'An anonymous caller.'

'Ooh.' Egg fell from Halvorsen's mouth and

116

landed on Hansen's desk.

'Says Henrik Bonde's in some kind of danger,' she said, flicking the pieces of food back at Halvorsen.

'The politician?'

'Yeah. She said she overheard people talking about having Bonde 'taken out'.'

'Those the words she used?'

'The very ones.'

'In what context?'

' 'Within political circles', she said.'

'Shit, Hansen. They're probably talking about a celebratory dinner.'

'She didn't seem to think so.'

'Then 'out' of the running. So he loses his seat. Big deal. What's that? Political misconduct, maybe? Not for Crime Squad.'

'The caller sounded alarmed. You know what I'm saying here, Halvorsen.'

'Do you know how many anonymous calls we get about people like Bonde? Every immigrant in the country's alarmed by the Advance Party. And some days it seems like every one of them with a phone calls us about it. Some to make threats.'

'How many threats do they *report*? And from within political circles? Besides, the caller sounded Norwegian.'

'So why stay anonymous?' He stood, pulling a hair from his mouth and inspecting it. 'It's a crank, Hansen. Whoever put it through should know better.' He dropped the hair and wiped his fingers on his tie.

'Maybe,' Hansen said.

'What do you want to do? Stand guard? Tell

117

Bonde not to show his face? Because an anonymous guardian angel said he shouldn't? The day before elections? Come on.'

'We could advise vigilance, maybe.'

'That's good.' He looked impressed.

'So I'll call his people?'

His face dropped.

'No, you don't call his people. To make that call, we have to believe there's a credible threat. If we believe there's a credible threat, we have to be prepared to throw manpower its way, launch an investigation. That's you and me, sweetheart, and as senior inspector, I don't see any reason to think there's a credible threat here. But I'll tell you what.'

'What?'

'We'll send everyone else out, bring the lights down, and you can give me a little lap dance.'

★   ★   ★

After Hansen turned back to her desk, Halvorsen saw Solberg arriving and wandered away. On the Internet, it took Hansen all of twenty seconds to find the number for the Advance Party's HQ on Youngstorget. She picked up her phone and punched in the number.

'The Advance Party,' the voice said at the other end. 'Renewing Norway for the People. How can I help you today?'

Hansen didn't want Halvorsen to overhear this call.

'Henrik Bonde, please,' she said as quietly as she could.

'May I ask who is calling?'

'Oslo Police.'

'One moment, please.'

Hansen waited a few seconds, glancing over the partition. Halvorsen was laughing with Solberg, jabbing his head her way. She sat back down when the receptionist came back.

'Mr Bonde's out of his office at the moment, I'm afraid,' she said. 'May I take a message?'

'Can you tell me where he is? Or give me his cellphone number?'

'May I ask who in the Oslo Police is calling, please? What seems to be the problem, officer?'

Hansen hesitated. She hadn't wanted to leave a trail.

'I'm Sergeant Ingrid Hansen.'

'One moment, please.'

Hansen got the hold tone, then another voice came on, female again, older, colder.

'May I ask which department you are with, Sergeant Hansen?'

'Who's this?'

'My name is Eli Moe, Mr Bonde's secretary.'

'Do you know where he is, Ms Moe?'

'Mrs. And yes, of course I do. I'm his secretary.'

'Do you mind telling me where that is? I need to get in touch with him.'

'I understand that to be your request, Sergeant, but I'm sure *you* understand that Mr Bonde is a very busy man. I ask you which department you are from in order to discern the urgency of your call. Is it a general enquiry that can wait until he returns, or — '

'I'm Crime Squad, Ms Moe,' Hansen said.

'Call my Super if you need to, but make it quick. I need to know where Bonde is and I need his mobile number.'

'Mr Bonde is currently on a Colorline ferry.' Her tone was ice now. 'It's coming into Oslo harbour this morning. His telephone number is — '

Hansen jotted it down, wondering if she should tell the secretary to keep the call under her hat, but deciding that would just rouse her curiosity even more. 'Thank you, Ms Moe,' was all she said in the end.

'Is everything all right, Sergeant?'

'Everything's fine, Ms Moe,' Hansen said. 'This is just precautionary.'

Hansen heard a sharp intake of breath at the other end of the line and banged the receiver down, angry with herself. Precautionary? Only doctors and police use that word. And it was hardly reassuring coming from either. Composing herself, Hansen took up the phone again and called Bonde's number. After six rings it went to voicemail. By the time the automated message had run its course she had decided not to leave a message. The next number she tried was to the police box at the harbour. It was answered after a couple of rings.

'Harbour, Dragvoll speaking.'

'This is Hansen, Crime Squad. There's a Colorline coming in this morning. I'm looking for a passenger on it. What time's it due?'

'About ten minutes ago. Sorry.'

'Disembarked?'

'Last ones coming off now.'

'Shit.'

'Anything else?'

'No.'

Hansen hung up.

She was still in her trial period in Crime Squad and she had just reached the edge of her official investigative powers. Anything more would constitute stepping off into active pursuit. She didn't have clearance for that yet, but if she was going to move further on this, that's what was needed, because Bonde could be more or less anywhere by now.

She straightened in her chair to look over the partition again. Halvorsen was at the coffee dispenser, beyond Dahl and Brunstad's desks. Solberg was nowhere to be seen, nor his sergeant, Forgaard. At the end of the Pit she could see Egeland in his office through the slats of his Venetian, leaning back in his chair gazing at the lawn outside, already half-covered in bronzing, bikinied bodies.

Hansen picked up her phone and hit 0. It was answered immediately.

'Desk?'

'This is Sergeant Hansen, Crime Squad.'

'Morning, Sergeant. It's Madsen. Those degenerates treating you all right up there?'

'I'll live. How are you doing?'

'At your disposal. What can I do for you this beautiful morning?'

'We need you to put a call out.'

'All units?'

'All units. We need someone found. Shouldn't be too difficult.'

121

'What's the name?'

'Henrik Bonde, the politician.'

There was a brief silence, each waiting for the other to pass comment. When neither did, Madsen said:

'All right, Sergeant. Who's authorizing it?'

'Inspector Halvorsen.'

'Priority?'

'Priority.'

'Your wish is my command, Sergeant. We'll be in touch.'

★ ★ ★

The old man knew exactly where the mark would be. Hobbling at a pace, he'd led Curt from the bridge through town, past the station, zigzagging southwest through the gridded streets behind the Bourse where the hookers plied, and finally through a gate into the grounds of the old fort — Akershus Festning — a public park now. They'd moved straight past the old buildings and outhouses — barracks and museums these days — and had come out on the far side, overlooking the water seventy feet below.

A ferry had been coming in right in front of them. Beyond it, a kilometre away on the other side of the water, lay Aker Brygge, the redeveloped dockland area, the old red-brick buildings cramped in next to the glass and steel, all fancy restaurants and bars now, with pleasure cruisers and seaplane taxis buzzing on the water. To the right, after the chain of tourist tall ships and steamboats, were the twin towers of the red-brick

Fascist-chic town hall, and beyond that the centre of town.

When the ferry opened up, the old man had pointed out the mark — this Bonde guy. He was middle-aged, with silver hair and a blue suit. When he'd stopped to talk to a bunch of journalists, Curt had watched him take possession of an envelope from a man in *Top Gun* sunglasses. Bonde placed the envelope in his briefcase. The envelope was what the old man wanted. When Curt asked, the old man refused to tell him what it contained. There was no time to insist. Curt shifted down an old cobbled drive that led from the grounds of the fort to the waterside. By the time he hit the newly asphalted road people were streaming off the ferry, and the journalists were packing up.

The mark was gone, swallowed in the flow.

Beckoned by a movement, Curt's eyes moved upwards. There on the fort's ancient battlements, like some lunatic imagining he was commanding an army from his castle, the old man was waving his arms northwards, towards the town hall.

Somewhere between running and walking, Curt moved in that direction, dodging and darting between the shuffling people, checking every face, every suit. He passed the customs houses and the old steamers, and was drawing alongside the docked tall ships berthed before the town hall when he spotted him, thirty feet ahead. Such a public space was not the place for a mugging. Too many people to stop him running off.

Bonde pulled up beyond the boats, before the town hall, at the edge of the road. Curt stopped by one of the tourist boats and pretended to read the history board next to it, not knowing what to do. Bonde was trying to flag down a cab. But none stopped, they were all taken and after the third one passed him by he gave up and moved on again, to the pedestrian zone in front of the town hall.

The landscape there was all marble fountains, statues and benches. The place was busy in the sun with tourists, police, kids, clowns, sailors, fishermen and beggars moving in all directions, and skate boarders buzzing around on the steps like flies.

Maintaining distance, Curt let Bonde move up past the town hall's red-brick towers. Having looked a little pissed off at his failure to hail a cab, Bonde appeared to lighten up now. His stride stretched out and he was holding his head high, like he owned the city. Curt followed him round the side of the town hall, back into the trafficked zone. The shade in the crescent street came as a relief: it was cooler, but still with plenty of people spilling out of the cafés, strolling between the waterside and the centre of town, or looking for parking slots.

On the far side, Curt followed Bonde up Roald Amundsens Gate, moving out into the city's main strip, with the palace up the hill to the left and the station way down to the right, and shops and hotels in between.

Here was no better for the grab. There were places to run — metro stations, buses, any

124

number of streets — but also cops.

Bonde crossed the main street and took another turning up by the university, towards the national gallery. It was a little quieter there, and Curt had closed the gap to ten metres by the time Bonde hung a right.

Curt wasn't expecting the quietness that greeted him on Kristian Augusts Gate. There wasn't another person around, not even any trams.

Curt looked up.

Every window was shut — the wonder of air con.

Up ahead, a little beyond Bonde, the street curved, cutting off further view.

They were alone. All he had to do was grab the bag, push Bonde to the floor and sprint away.

Curt extended his stride. The distance between them was fifteen feet when Bonde hit the start of the bend. Curt's walk became a trot. He looked behind. Still no one. And no one ahead.

Ten feet.

Curt brought his hand out of his pocket, ready to take the briefcase handle. He was just about to do so when the bend straightened.

From nowhere the road opened out onto an intersection, six streets converging on one spot. Bonde walked straight out, but Curt stopped dead. To his right, people were seated at tables and chairs outside a café. Beyond it was a hotel. It was busy with new arrivals and departures. More people were waiting at a tram stop outside.

Right over the way was a shining modern white building with a rack of granite pillars holding it up. Above the door, the sign said *Oslo Tinghus*. A bunch of people were outside the building, coming and going, smoking and chatting, tussling with locks at the bike rank. Curt saw a uniformed police constable amongst them, keeping watch.

He had a feeling he'd just missed the best chance he was going to get.

★   ★   ★

Hansen stared at her phone for the next two minutes, willing Madsen to ring. He didn't, so she tried Bonde's mobile again. Her call went straight to voicemail this time. Again she left no message, trying party HQ again instead, anonymously this time. He was still out of office. After that, with Halvorsen in Egeland's office now, she fetched herself a cup of coffee and was halfway through it when Solberg's head appeared over the partition.

'Ingrid,' he said through a lipless smile.

'Inspector Solberg.'

'Call me Trond, please.'

'What can I do for you, Solberg?'

He raised his barely discernible eyebrows. 'Ah, the endless possibilities.'

Hansen looked at her monitor and started clicking at the mouse.

'Halvorsen says you hooked a crank this morning,' Solberg tried again.

Hansen didn't answer or look up, and kept clicking.

126

'Bonde,' Solberg continued. 'And you wanted to advise vigilance.'

She could hear his wry amusement at her rookie enthusiasm, and couldn't help shooting a glare over the partition. His smile widened, pleased that he'd got any reaction at all.

As they were exchanging looks, the phone on Hansen's desk started to ring. Hansen glanced around at other phones on other desks. None of them was lighting up. The call wasn't coming through the general Pit line. It was coming to her phone and her phone only.

'You've got a lot to learn, Hansen,' Solberg said.

'Oh yeah?' Hansen said, suddenly unable to think of a comeback, all her powers of concentration focused on not looking at the phone; on not showing her desperation to answer it.

'Of course. Everyone does when they come in. But don't you worry.'

'Do I look like I'm worrying?' she said, certain that was exactly how she looked.

'I'm here to teach you. Are you going to answer that?' he said, nodding at the phone. 'Go ahead. I want to hear how you are over the wire. Call it lesson one.'

'When you've fucked off,' Hansen said, as light-hearted as she could manage, 'I might just do that.'

But Solberg didn't fuck off. He stayed. And the phone rang on, jangling in Hansen's eardrums, and then Solberg's arm appeared over the partition board, reaching for the phone.

Hansen whipped the receiver off its cradle before Solberg's hand could get there.

'Hansen,' she said, her voice higher than normal; tighter. 'Crime Squad.' Too deep now.

'Hansen, it's Madsen. We've got him.'

'Hang on, sweetheart,' she said.

Madsen was yelping something at the other end when she held the mouthpiece against her shoulder. 'Sorry, Solberg,' she said. 'This is private. D'you mind?'

'Boyfriend?' Solberg said, looking mock-hurt.

She didn't answer, raising her eyebrows instead.

'Mother, right?' he said, smiling, nodding. 'I knew you only had eyes for me,' he added, backing away, giving her the double gun fingers as he moved.

When he was gone, Hansen put the phone back to her ear.

'Madsen? Sorry about that. One of the degenerates, you know? Put me through will you? Who's got him?'

'Constable Kobberrød.'

'*Kobberrød?* What sort of a name is tha — '

'I'm from the south,' a different voice said. 'Get over it.'

'Where are you now?' Hansen said.

'At the courthouse.'

'And Bonde?'

'Just went past, heading eastwards.'

'Towards Youngstorget? The party building?'

'I can catch him up and ask, if you want.'

Hansen grabbed her car keys and wriggled into her jacket. When the phone was back at her ear, she said, 'No. I want you to follow him.'

'I can't just leave the courthouse.'

'Yes, you can,' Hansen said, then cupped her hand around the mouthpiece and said, 'There may be a threat, okay?'

'Then I should approach him,' Kobberrød said.

'No. It's unspecified and uncorroborated. See him to the party building. I'm on my way.'

Hansen slammed down the phone and grabbed Halvorsen's jacket off the back of his seat. Spotting the man himself coming out of Egeland's office, she strode towards him and threw the jacket his way.

'What?' he said, catching it.

'Come on.'

'Where?'

'Youngstorget. They found him.'

His face rippled with confusion.

'Found who?'

'Bonde.'

His nostrils flared a little.

'You put out a call? On whose authority?'

'Yours,' she said. 'I'm driving.'

★　★　★

Bonde had continued right over the intersection, and Curt, recovering himself, had moved across too. He held at fifteen metres, moving due east, flipping left past a grey tower block, then right down a passage that came out at the corner of a cobbled market square.

The square was built on a hill, dug out flat,

leaving a drop at the topside of about thirty feet. These days the market itself was no more than a couple of stalls flogging Patagonian trinkets, but built into the vertical was a raised open-air colonnade, vaulted like a cellar, where you could sit at tables outside cafés looking over the square through a long row of arches. Access to the colonnade and its cafés was by steps going up from the market floor at either end or by steps going down through the mini castle turrets that sat at the topside corners of the square.

Curt had arrived at the northern corner, up high, and drew to a halt. He spotted Bonde just as he was entering the north-corner turret twenty-five metres away.

Curt resisted following him down. Instead he headed down the road ahead of him that sloped down to the low side of the square. At the bottom, Curt scanned the arches of the colonnade. It was busy all the way along: people sitting eating breakfast; some drinking coffee standing up, some smoking.

Curt caught sight of his man just as he was taking the last free table, halfway along. A waitress came out and took his order. Bonde gestured at a building on the south-east side of the square and tapped his watch, and after the waitress left he started patting the table with both hands, drumming out a high-tempo beat as he waited — impatient, maybe excited, definitely keen to get on. And into that building?

Despite the crowd, this looked like it was as good as it was going to get. At least the briefcase would be loose. He would walk along, lift, try to walk on unnoticed. If he was spotted, he'd just have to barge his way through.

Curt moved towards the steps leading up to the colonnade. By the time he got to the top of them, Bonde was restlessly leafing through the pages of a paper.

Curt started to move along the colonnade. As he did, he became aware of the glances coming his way. The pristine suits and bronze complexions looked like they had all just discovered they'd been served up an espresso cup of shit instead of coffee. In turn, their experiences of delight made Curt aware of just how out-of-place he was there, in his beat-up shirt, torn cargos, worn-out All Stars and black skin. But it was too late now. He just had to keep moving forward.

* * *

Hansen stopped the Volvo outside the Advance Party headquarters and was out before Halvorsen had even unbuckled his seat belt. All the way there he'd been demanding to know what the hell she thought she was doing. And he'd made his stance perfectly clear — if this went tits-up, she was taking the hit. So Hansen wasn't about to wait for him and let that happen. She saw Kobberrød standing at the east corner and went straight to him. 'Where is he?'

Kobberrød pointed at the colonnade.

'Getting a coffee,' he said.

Hansen saw Bonde straight away, and scanned the rest of the colonnade. The usual clientele, suits, lawyers, politicians, and a black guy, dripping with sweat, his shirt open all the way down.

'There,' she said, turning to the Volvo. 'You see?' Halvorsen was heaving himself out. She shook her head. 'Come on, Kobberrød. I might need you. Take the west steps.'

They both started to run.

★ ★ ★

The attention Curt was drawing made him feel claustrophobic. The claustrophobia made it hard for him to breathe. A rasping sound was coming from his wind-pipe every time he drew in air. He could feel the eyes as he made his way along the colonnade, as plain as the smell of the coffee and the French cakes and the smoke. Hundreds of them, table after table, person after person, just watching him, wondering what the hell he was doing there — *knowing* what the hell he was doing there. A man in a panama looked at him like he could hear his heart, which wouldn't have surprised Curt a bit. It was all *he* could hear, playing a rag on his ribs like a sugared-up kid with a xylophone.

Curt spotted the briefcase. It was on the floor next to Bonde's chair. Curt would have to crouch to reach it.

Sprinting up the steps, Hansen started pushing her way through the people, along the colonnade, ignoring the objections, the sarcastic 'Now *there's* a girl who wants her coffee' comments. Up ahead she made out the man. He

132

was already practically at Bonde's table, and he was taking his hand out of his pocket and stooping.

'Out of the way!' she yelled. '*Move!*'

★ ★ ★

A split second after he heard the woman scream in Norwegian, just as his fingers met the briefcase, Curt felt a blow to his back. Winded, instantly gasping for breath, his cheek slammed onto the table and his arms were twisted up behind his back.

The same woman said something in Norwegian behind him and Curt felt his wrists being fixed into handcuffs.

'Hey!' he shouted back over his shoulder. 'What the fuck is this?'

But no one was listening. Not the suits, horizontal from his viewpoint, nor the hefty guy making his way through them, nor Bonde. He just stood there, looking more disgusted than anyone.

★ ★ ★

Had Curt been looking the other way, he'd have seen one coffee drinker who was not fleeing the commotion. Surrounded by hysteria, the man wearing the panama was holding his espresso cup in one hand, its saucer in the other, while watching as the young policewoman and the uniform pushed the black vagrant into an ugly green Volvo 240 estate. The girl drove, the uniform went in back with the prisoner.

This activity was of only mild interest to the man, however. Of more interest, and greater disappointment, was the conversation that was taking place between the stout senior police officer and Henrik Bonde just a couple of metres from his table. The cop was inviting Henrik Bonde to accompany him to the Grønland station, an invitation Bonde was accepting.

The man in the panama watched the pair leave the premises. He then finished his coffee and wiped his lips. He dropped a two-kroner tip on the table, then ascended the west stairs and made his way to a midnight-blue 1992 Lancia Thema 8.32. He removed, rolled and pocketed his hat, then opened the driver's door and got into the car.

Starting the Lancia up, he paused to listen.

Her purr never ceased to please him.

8

Britt Petersen did not shed a single tear for her mother. She arrived in Oslo with Ivar four days after Sigrid died. They both knew the city. They had grown up there and only moved to Drøbak, their mother's hometown, following their father's death. Britt had left her school in Oslo and went to work in Bergstrom's boatyard as soon as they arrived in Drøbak. The twin loss of her father and all social connections contributed to her promiscuous behaviour. But on seeing Ivar with the destroyed body of their mother in his arms, waving their father's knife at the gathering crowd, something in Britt's mind shifted so vehemently that she felt it physically. It tied her gut in knots and bristled across her skin. From then on only one thought filled her mind: we are orphans now, and Ivar is my responsibility. My *only* responsibility. I am no longer merely his sister. I am his mother, his father, his teacher, and his protector.

With this in mind, she pulled Ivar into her arms and away from the crowd — leaving their mother's body on the roadside for the gawpers to pick over like crows at carrion. She carried him to their home, removed the kitty from its hiding place, packed one bag with clothes and one with food and money. Then they said goodbye to

Drøbak, and walked and hitched north to Oslo.

They arrived just in time to see the first German troops marching up Karl Johans Gate, the city's main street. The little money Britt had found beneath the loose floorboard in the kitchen didn't last long, but by taking them in, the Jensens — family friends from when their father was still alive — helped Britt to stretch it out. Mr Jensen still worked in the mill while Mrs Jensen looked after their four children, aged between two and nine.

When Mr Jensen found Britt a job as a clerk at the local post office, she took Ivar to a two-room basement apartment that a friend of the Jensens had offered her for low rent. That didn't last long either. The son of the Jensens' friend thought reduced rent meant increased privileges with Britt, and when that happened, Britt put some of her mother's lipstick on, dressed herself and Ivar in their best clothes and headed west, into Frogner, the smarter end of town, where she signed up for a luxury apartment in one of the mansion blocks there. With smiles and laughter, she talked the landlord — male, mid-forties, nagging wife — into letting them forgo the required deposit until their parents arrived, and that gave them a month to find somewhere realistic. By the time they got booted out, Britt had managed to find another place, which is where they were now.

It consisted of two peeling rooms: one containing a double bed, a small cupboard and nothing else; the other containing a table, two chairs, a water stand, a stove cooker, a fireplace

136

and a paraffin lamp.

It was ten months since their mother had died. The evening dark came early in February and by the light of the table lamp Britt was sewing a patch onto the knee of Ivar's spare pair of trousers while the boy himself was on the floor, wearing the rest of his clothes, practising the tying of a fishing fly, their father's coronation knife at his side. They both needed to be wearing all the clothes they could because, while the fire was laid with newspaper and wood, neither it nor the stove was lit. Their breath was coming out of their mouths in plumes of white mist.

But when a knock at the door came, they both involuntarily took a gulp of air and held it. Their eyes met. Ivar looked like feral prey down there on the floorboards, the whites of his eyes shining bright in the gloomy lamplight, ready to run just as soon as he needed to, just as soon as Britt told him to. Britt flicked a nod towards the bedroom door and he stood immediately, slipping silently into the bedroom, leaving the door ajar and watching through the remaining crack. Britt cut the thread of her sewing with her scissors, tied it off and placed the bundle on the table and got to her feet.

The latrines and bathrooms were a floor below. The two of them were quiet tenants. They kept themselves to themselves. Ivar didn't react well to noise these days, it was true, and occasionally he released his anger and sorrow and confusion in an almighty tantrum, but that hadn't happened for a while now. He was doing well. Which meant no neighbour had any reason to be calling.

The rap came again: firm, rapid, confident. One, two, three.

Britt pulled her thick jersey down over her trousered hips, then approached the door, but didn't open it, instead standing to one side and saying 'Hello?' in an uncertain voice.

'Hello?' a male voice came back.

'Who is it?'

'Sofie sent me.'

'Sofie?'

'Our mutual friend.'

Britt unlocked the door and opened it a little, then said, 'Oh my God!' and pulled it wide.

The man standing in the doorway wore his hair combed back across his head. His skin was healthy. Britt let him pull her up into a hug and, threading her arms around him beneath his snow-flecked coat, she felt his shoulders and back, broad and muscular beneath the wool. She looked up at him. Even his teeth, which he was showing in a wide grin now, looked right. Ten months had turned the gawky adolescent into a man. He was actually handsome. Heroic-looking, even. And boy did it feel good to be held by a pair of strong arms.

'That's some transformation, Håvard,' she said, closing her eyes. 'You look so — *well*.'

'Well, you're as beautiful as you ever were,' he said, holding her out and looking down at her.

'I'm a mess,' she said, breaking from his embrace. She pushed him further into the room and stuck her head into the darkness of the corridor. It was deserted. She held still for a few seconds, listening for the tiniest sound. Hearing none, she closed the door and locked it. Then she said: 'I thought you were still in Drøbak.'

'I was, and then I wasn't. It's been ten months. A lot's happened.' He took hold of her hands in his. 'But I never stopped looking for you, Britt.'

'I didn't know you were — you know — *involved*,' she said.

'Involved?' Håvard answered.

'You know — with Sofie.'

'Oh,' he said, pulling her into another hug, closing his eyes as he burrowed his nose into her hair. He took a deep inhalation, drinking in her smell.

He'd been telling the truth when he said he'd never stopped looking for Britt. He left Drøbak a fortnight after her. Found her a fortnight after that. But he had not approached her. He had watched her from afar. He didn't want things to go back to the way they had been in Drøbak.

When she left so suddenly, he'd felt abandoned, of course, but he loved Britt unconditionally, and knew she could not be held responsible for her extreme reaction. So many bad things had befallen her over the years. He knew what she needed was rescuing. All she needed to realize was that *he* was the man to rescue her. To do that, he believed, she would have to see him as the kind of man she had taken up with and told him about in Drøbak. A soldier was such a man.

On the street, the Germans were polite to Norwegians. Officially, in the papers they were circulating, they were pronouncing to their friends.

Norway, they said, was like a little brother to Germany. They were all part of the superior Germanic peoples. In this together. German soldiers helped old ladies across the street, were respectful to the women, treated the men like equals, offered their kids sweets.

When Håvard heard about the division the Germans were setting up for Norwegian volunteers, the 5th SS Panzer Division, 'Wiking', he decided to enlist immediately. They put him into training and transformed his weedy body just as he hoped they would.

Meanwhile, as he watched Britt go about her daily business, it did not take him long to realize from her own secretive behaviour that she was involved in the resistance. To Håvard this was one more danger she needed to be rescued from. The Germans were reasonable people, he'd found, but when it came to resistance to their presence in Norway — well, quite understandably, they could not tolerate it. He had heard some rumour about a Hauptsturmführer called Fehmer. Fehmer was the Gestapo man in charge of discouraging any resistance. The stories weren't pretty. They involved torture. Someone even told him Fehmer had been known to use his German Shepherd to extract information.

Håvard didn't want that happening to Britt. And there was an alternative. An alternative he could use to show Britt just what a man he had become.

He had heard about another SS man too, an Oberführer senior to Fehmer, who was open to approach by concerned citizens. If you were worried about friends or family dabbling in resistance, you could go to him, and avoid them falling into Fehmer's hands. This Oberführer would make sure the people whose names he received were treated fairly, and persuade them, using only words — no dogs — to avoid such pitfalls of occupation. When he approached the man a week ago, Håvard had been about to be deployed to Poland. The Oberführer promised to see to it that Håvard could remain in Oslo and save Britt from the trials of war, from the resistance, from Fehmer; a rescue for which she would prove so grateful she'd fall into his muscular arms and they would live happily ever after.

All this was why, with his lungs filled with her smell, Håvard withdrew from Britt's hair and said:

'Everything's going to be all right now, Britt.'

'What do you mean?' Britt said from his chest.

'You've been through a lot, Britt. First it was your father, then your mother, then this occupation, looking after Ivar. But now I'm here. Here to take care of you.'

Britt looked up at him, smiling.

'When have you ever taken care of anyone, Håvard?'

She was teasing him, just as she always had. But his reaction — only there for a moment before he stifled it — was not one Britt had seen before. His body stiffened in her arms. His nostrils flared slightly. The muscle in his cheek trembled for a second or two. It was anger, frustration, but then it was gone and he smiled back at her.

'Things change, Britt,' he said, locking her gaze.

Britt stared right back at him, forcing her body to remain relaxed, keeping the smile plastered across her face — her eyes narrowed, her ruby lips stretched tight over her teeth, hoping she was better at smothering her instinctive reactions than Håvard was. She was pretty sure the only change in her expression that might have hinted at the deep feeling of unease that descended into the pit of her stomach was a fast double blink — one, two. But she couldn't be sure.

'Too much,' she said.

Håvard was no longer the boy she'd known. That was plain to see. He'd changed. But whatever appearances said, her gut was telling her the change was not for the better.

Håvard glanced round the room.

'Where is Ivar anyway?' he said.

Britt slipped out of his arms.

'Sit down,' she said, making her way across the room, shifting the sewing further up the table. 'I'll fix us something to drink,' she added, stuffing her hand into her pocket.

She did not answer Håvard's question. She didn't look over at the bedroom door or call Ivar out.

Behind the door, Ivar knew better than to announce his presence without invitation. But he didn't know what was going on. Why had Britt not told Håvard that he was just in the other room? Why had she suddenly grown breezy? And why had she placed her sewing scissors into her pocket with such apparent secrecy?

Håvard did not sit down, but went to the fireplace instead.

'It's cold in here, you know. Why don't we light that fire?'

'Fuel costs,' she said, lighting the stove instead. 'Like everything does now. This'll do us fine.'

'I'll bring you some more,' he said, getting to his feet. 'Let me light the fire. It's too — '

'No,' she said sharply, before he could start moving towards the hearth. 'Leave it. I'll make you some tea.'

'Fine,' he said, raising both hands and finally sitting down. He looked at his watch.

Britt filled a pot with water from the bowl in the stand. When the pot was filled and she had placed it on the stove, she turned back to face Håvard again.

'He's all right,' she said. 'Ivar, I mean. He's getting better. It takes time, though. I just need to keep things quiet. Routine. That's what he needs. So, do you know Sofie well, then?' Britt moved to the window.

Håvard smiled. But he did not look relaxed.

'Pretty well,' Håvard said, watching her. It was a lie. He had no idea who Sofie was. The SS-Oberführer had told him to gain entry by using her name, so he had. That was the length and breadth of his knowledge about Sofie.

Out the window, the snow was falling, but by the cloud-diffused moonlight Britt could see a dozen men double-marching up the road.

Suddenly Håvard was by her side at the window and, seeing the soldiers drawing to a standstill below them, he started rubbing the back of his neck. Britt stepped away from him.

Her eyes shifted to the bedroom door, then back to Håvard.

'What have you done, Håvard?' she said.

'It's not what you think, Britt,' he said, edging towards her. 'He can help you. We'll be able to — '

'How could you do it, Håvard? To us?'

'You don't have to worry,' he said, putting his hand out. 'I can take you away from all this. From everything. I can take care of you. All he wants is information.'

She backed up to the window, disgusted, but not scared.

'Sit down, Håvard,' she said, but he did not stop moving towards her. She glanced back out the window. Beneath, a limousine was pulling up, stopping right outside the building, next to the waiting soldiers.

'Come on, Britt,' Håvard said. He was confused. This wasn't going as he'd imagined it would. Britt was meant to be falling into his arms with gratitude. 'It's me. You *know* me. I wouldn't let anything happen to you.'

'What about the others, Håvard? What about all the people fighting to make this country free?'

'They just need to be shown that the Germans — they mean us no harm. They're our friends. We can live *with* them.'

'Our *friends*?' Britt spat. 'They walked in here, Håvard. They took over. What sort of a *friend* comes into your house, declares it theirs, then tells you they're going to be nice enough to let you stay?'

'They have the power, Britt,' Håvard said,

taking her hand in his, beseeching her now. 'That's just the way it is.'

In the street, the Nazi soldier driving the limousine had already got out.

'My God, Håvard,' she said, pity filling her voice now. 'What have they done to you?'

Pity was not what Håvard was looking for. He stiffened again.

'They turned me into a man for you, Britt.'

Outside, the driver was approaching the car's rear passenger door.

Håvard swallowed, taking control of himself. He put his hand to her cheek.

'Come with me. You'll be safe. Let me take care of you.'

'And if I don't?' Britt said. 'What then, Håvard?'

'If not . . . well, you're resisting, Britt.'

'So I've got no choice?'

'You want Ivar to be safe, don't you?'

'And in exchange you expect me to become your whore? To be grateful? That's what you're looking for?'

'Why not?' he snapped, the anger returning, unstifled, superseding affection. 'You've been everyone else's. Now be mine.' He paused, trying to force the tenderness back into his voice. 'I'll be kind to you, Britt. I was always kind to you, wasn't I?'

She glanced out of the window. The driver was opening the back door. She turned back to Håvard.

'I never fucked a Nazi stooge, Håvard.'

He lowered his hand.

145

'I was the only one who loved you, Britt. Me. But I got nothing. Now I'm the only one who'd take you. Look at yourself. You live like a tramp. Which is fitting — because that's what you are.'

She made to slap him across the cheek but he caught her by the wrist.

'And you finally want your piece of me,' she said.

He grabbed her other wrist and forced her hands down by her hips. He tried to kiss her, but she turned her face away, towards the window. The driver was saluting now, as a pair of knee-high black leather boots appeared from the rear seat of the car. Håvard released her right hand and forcibly turned her face towards him. Then he planted his lips on hers.

Britt slackened in his grip and kissed him back. Feeling this, Håvard released her second hand. He moved to hold her head in both his hands and, in the rapture of the realization of his dream, he closed his eyes. Britt's eyes were open, however, and filling with tears. As their tongues continued to dance, she placed her right hand to his cheek and slipped her left into the pocket of her trousers. As her right moved round and gripped his hair, her left came up and drew the blade of the scissors across his throat.

His eyes, opened now, widened in shock as comprehension dawned. Britt pushed him away. The blood took a second, but then it began to flow. Håvard grabbed her hands. Britt let the scissors fall to the floor. His grip was firm at first and he tried to speak, but as more and more blood ran from his neck, his hold on her

146

weakened and the words were just gurgles. He released her and dropped to the floor, and Britt sprang over to the bedroom door, open now, Ivar standing there, staring.

'Y-you killed him,' he stammered. 'You killed Håvard.' He sounded more amazed than scared or sorry.

Britt took him up in her arms.

'It's okay,' she said. 'Ivar, listen to me: it'll be okay,' placing him down again. 'I promise you. Just stay there.'

She moved to the fireplace, crouching and pulling the grate out a few centimetres, but then came a sharp knock at the door. She stopped and looked at Ivar. His eyes were wide with terror. Turning back to the fireplace, she pushed the grate back into place and grabbed him, holding his head so he could only look back at her face, not at Håvard or the door.

'Listen to me, Ivar,' Britt said. 'You know what you have to do. Get to the Jensens, tell them to send word to Sofie. Only Sofie. No one else. Do you understand me? Don't trust anyone else, Ivar. Only Sofie. Say it.'

'And you.'

'No. I'm staying. If I come, they'll find us both. There's no time.' She reached for the coronation knife and pushed it into his pocket. The knocking came again, harder, more insistent.

'What about you?' he said, trying to tug the knife out. 'You'll need it.'

'No,' she said calmly, pulling him into a hug, tears rolling now. 'I won't. Now remember. Only Sofie. Say it.'

'Only Sofie,' Ivar whispered into the wool of her jersey.

'I'm sorry, little brother. Now you go, and be safe.'

She kissed him on the forehead, then pushed him towards the fireplace, unhooking a rope that was hanging down inside the chimney, giving it a tug. She then handed it to Ivar and he took a hold.

The knocking was thunderous now, and accompanied by shouting voices. Ivar was shaking, terrified at the prospect of leaving his sister there.

'Twenty seconds,' Britt said, ignoring the surging instinct to grab him, to go with him and protect him herself. 'Now go. *Now*.'

Ivar obeyed her and hauled himself up into the chimney, through the sixty-centimetre gap above the laid fire. He disappeared into the black of the flue, hand over hand, scrabbling for footholds in the sooted brick, sending fragments scattering back down to the room.

Britt stood and began to count. She moved to the stove, lit a match and waited.

The door's lock and hinges were starting to buckle, the men outside banging on it with their boots now. But still she waited, until finally she reached twenty and put the match to the fire with a trembling hand.

★ ★ ★

When the door finally splintered and gave, three soldiers entered, each levelling a Mauser. They

148

spotted Britt first, then Håvard, but seeing no imminent danger, they moved aside, allowing the portly, greatcoated figure of an SS-Oberführer to come into the apartment. The Oberführer's eyes landed on Håvard, lying with his limbs all a tangle, the pool of blood still growing around him, and removed his cap. The Oberführer was Gerhard von Westarp.

He focused on the figure at the far side of the room. Britt was crouching by the fire, facing away from him. Von Westarp scanned the rest of the room but saw no sign of the blade that he adjudged to have opened Håvard's neck.

Britt did not look round. She wanted this to go as slowly as possible. The longer it took, the further Ivar could run. He needed five, six minutes to be sure. They had practised the route together, over and over: up the rope, out of the widened stack at the top of the chimney. That took the twenty seconds she had given him. Now he would be moving east over the top of the pitched slate roofs, slowly, arms out for balance like a circus performer, from one stack to the next, ten metres between each. It was tricky, especially in the dark, during the winter, with the snow falling. But he was skinny and light and all that skiing — both day and night — had given him a good sense of balance. After four chimneys, he would reach the end of the block. At the end of the block, with the help of another rope they had tied in place, he would shin down a drainpipe. After climbing down two storeys, he would enter the building through a third-floor window that opened into a stairwell. They went

149

into this building every morning to check that the window remained open and the rope attached. This morning everything had been in place. From the stairs he would get onto the street, and from there he would be able to disappear into the night, to the Jensens, to Sofie, to safety.

Having waved the rifles down, von Westarp was now standing over Håvard's body. He tutted. Britt clenched her fist around the scissors, ready to move.

'*Und so weiter, und so weiter,*' von Westarp said, sounding as relaxed as Britt was tensed. '*Das Überleben des Angepasstesten.*'

'What did you do to him?' Britt said from the fire.

Von Westarp raised his eyes to her. Still she was not facing him. 'I, Fräulein Petersen?'

'He was just a boy.'

'No, not just a boy, Fräulein Petersen, but a boy *in love*. And therefore better than any blood-hound.' He turned his head a fraction and flicked his hand. '*Lassen Sie uns,*' he said, and his men filed out, pulling the broken door shut behind them. Alone with von Westarp now, Britt stood and faced him, defiant, her right hand obscured by the folds of her jersey.

Recognition skewed von Westarp's face.

'*You,*' he said.

'You,' Britt said.

Von Westarp removed his *Totenkopf* ring and started picking his gloves off a finger at a time. Britt watched him, letting the seconds tick by. By the time his left glove was off, von Westarp had composed himself.

150

'What a pleasant coincidence this is, Fräulein Petersen,' he said. 'Britt, yes?'

Britt didn't say a word. The Nazi knew she was resistance. Nothing she could say could save her. But she could help Ivar. Fear rendered her silent, but even through the fear she could see that silence was the best move here. It would stretch things out.

'My name, Britt, is Gerhard von Westarp,' he said, pulling his right glove from his hand. 'May I please sit down, Fräulein Petersen?'

Again Britt did not answer.

Von Westarp pulled a chair from the table and lowered himself into it and took from his pocket a piece of material. He placed the material on the table and proceeded to unfold it, revealing a large, white sausage. He pointed at it. 'Please, I judge from the inauspiciousness of our surroundings that you are probably hungry. Come sit with me and sample my *Weisswurst*.'

Ivar would still be doing his balancing act across the roofs, praying the soldiers in the street didn't look up through the naked trees and see him against the moonlit clouds. He needed more time. And if Britt was going to have any chance at all of getting out of this, what she needed was an opportunity to put the scissors to use again. If she could take von Westarp out with a single clean blow, like she had done with Håvard, and get him to drop without a sound, with the soldiers gone she could then douse the fire and use the escape route herself. If he had the chance to call out, they'd come in shooting. She therefore required two things: to be close to von

151

Westarp, and for von Westarp to be off his guard. That way she could slam the scissors into his throat and cover his mouth and he'd be dead in a matter of seconds.

Without saying a word, she moved towards von Westarp. He watched her come, visibly pleased by her apparent capitulation, his fleshy lips splitting his pale face in two with a wide grin.

He slid the second chair out for her and she sat to his right. He gestured at the sausage lying on the napkin in front of her. Britt looked at it, then at von Westarp.

'Fräulein Petersen,' he said, offended. 'Why would I go to the lengths of poisoning you? If I want you dead, I need only call a single word to my men. Come. I am not a man of violence, you will find. I want only to converse with you. So please. Eat.'

Britt picked up the sausage with her left hand and bit into it, meeting his gaze. She chewed and swallowed, slipping the scissors between her right thigh and the seat of the chair. She was ravenous and this was the first meat she had consumed in weeks.

'So?' he said.

She nodded. 'Good,' she said, and took another bite.

He leaned forward, raising his eyebrows, expectant.

'And?' he said. 'What do we say?'

She smiled sarcastically. 'Thank you,' she said.

He smiled too, leaning back in his chair again, satisfied with his victory.

'Gambling is not in my nature, either, Fräulein Petersen. And yet I find myself on one side of what could only be termed a wager. The second party, with whom I have made this wager, is one Hauptsturmführer Siegfried Wolfgang Fehmer. I assume you have heard of him?'

'Everyone's heard of him,' Britt said, taking another bite.

'Of course,' von Westarp said. 'He is a most charming and handsome man, I must say, a poster boy for the Reich. Unfortunately for you and your comrades, he has made it his personal mission to eradicate the resistance movement. This endeavour has brought to his attention a name. Sofie. So simple, just a name, and yet, Fehmer believes, the key to eliminating the resistance.'

'Never heard of her,' Britt said.

Von Westarp smiled approvingly.

'I told Håvard here to use her name to gain entry.'

'I recognized his voice.'

He tutted in disappointment.

'No, no, Fräulein. Do not insist on feigning ignorance. Such lowly dishonesty does not befit you.'

He leaned forward, into range. Britt stuffed the last of the sausage into her mouth, slipped her left hand under the table and passed the scissors into it. She was about to swing the blade out, when von Westarp pushed his chair back and stood.

Britt swallowed the last of the sausage and breathed. She could not jump the gun. Patience was essential. He was standing at the window now, looking out, but if she rushed him from across the room, she was dead, even if he was, too. If she stood and approached without his asking her to do so, it was sure to arouse his suspicion. She had to wait until he beckoned her to him or returned to the table.

'We know that the person to whom the name Sofie is assigned is one of your network's senior members. As you may suppose, Fehmer is very, very keen to find her, and when the Gestapo wants something, very little gets in its way, as I am sure you have heard. And when Fehmer finds Sofie — ' he looked back at Britt. 'Well, let us say hers will not be an enviable position.'

'You won't get anything out of me,' she said, remaining at the table.

'No, no, Fräulein Petersen. You misunderstand me. I am not here on behalf of Fehmer. Rather, I, too, for reasons wholly my own, would like to find Sofie, and before Fehmer. Thus was our wager born. I am not particularly opposed to Fehmer's techniques, you understand — they have their place, certainly — but what he fails to understand is that that place is not Norway. He has not studied the Norwegian as I have, so it is not clear to him, as it is to me, that the best of you will not succumb to his blunt and brutal methods. I knew that, to find Sofie, more subtle means would be required. And so here we are. Now, Fräulein Petersen, tell me where Sofie is, and I assure you, she will be fairly treated, as will you. You will find I am a reasonable man.'

'Go to Hell,' Britt said.

He chuckled.

154

'Didn't you hear me?' she said. 'Torture me, do whatever you want, you won't get a word out of me. I promise you that.'

He was nodding now, admiringly.

'*What?*' she demanded.

'I should have known. It was there in you at Drøbak.'

'What was there?'

'The very characteristics that make Sofie appeal to me.'

'Characteristics?'

'I seek strength, courage, intelligence and honour, Fräulein Petersen. Unlike our friend Hauptsturmführer Fehmer, I do not seek to destroy the resistance. To me, it is the very essence of the Norwegian. You fight valiantly against a foe of superior force for the good of your kind. To me, the Norwegians are to be deified, not fed to dogs.'

'*Deified?*'

He gazed at for a moment, as though considering divulging a great secret. Then he turned to the window again.

'I am a theozoologist, Fräulein Petersen. A student of the animal kingdom, of which I consider we humans very much a part.'

'The zoo's down the road,' she said.

Amused, von Westarp pointed out to one of the leafless maples that lined the snow-strewn street.

'If we listen to Darwin, all life is a rootless tree,' he said, tracing the tree's growth with a finger as he spoke. 'At the base of the trunk we have the most basic of protozoan life, floating in the primordial soup, and from there up springs all existence, branching off into the flora and fauna that populate our world, dividing and sub-dividing. We ourselves are part of the class *mammalia*, which possesses the greatest brain capacity, does it not?'

Britt didn't know what he was talking about and really didn't care. She just wanted him to come back within striking distance.

'I suppose so,' she said. 'Whatever you say.'

'Do not suppose,' von Westarp said, still holding his finger to the glass. 'Which other creatures exhibit the ability to learn and teach and remember across generations? Which other has conquered life in all nature's environments? On land, at sea, in the air — mammals are everywhere. And within the mammal family, those with the greatest brain capacity belong to the order of the primates. Within the order of primates comes the division of simian and prosimian. Prosimians include lemurs, bushba-bies and suchlike, while within the group simian, one finds the monkeys, and the apes. And so the divisions continue, within each group. Of the two simian groups, the apes have the greater brain capacity. And within the apes you find the lesser — gibbons and siamangs — and the great — being chimps, orang-utans, gorillas, bonobos and, of course, us. The humans. Just as in other areas, the brain capacities of these animals are also different, with man the clear winner. And the divisions do not end there, either, so in the gorilla family you find eastern and western gorillas, and within those, the eastern and western lowland gorillas, the cross-river gorillas and the mountain gorillas, and even within the society of each single type there are endless subdivisions. As it is with the gorillas, so it is with the other great apes, including humans.'

He turned to her, and she saw the image of a tree drawn in the condensation of his breath on the window.

'Evolution, Britt. The *theory* of evolution. It is an idea. Theozoology proposes an alternative one. It is very similar to Darwin's, but simply turns his tree upside down.'

'Devolution?'

'Precisely. You see, as I said — intelligence. A rare facet in one so beautiful.' He said it as though he was considering a scientific specimen. 'Where the Darwinist believes life started with the most basic and grew in complexity, the theozoologist believes that the whole process of life started from the top and travelled down. Therefore, in the beginning, there must have existed the purest of all beings, the Theozoa, unknown, un*earthly* beings of supreme power and purity with whom all life started. From them came the purest of *earthly* beings, a master race. Then certain of this breed altered, minutely — through environment, experience, climactic shifts — and, once that alteration occurred, so started the process of devolution, of *dilution*, the permutations continuing through the millennia, creating all those subdivisions through the orders, until the master race was eradicated, and here we are.'

He moved from the window to the fire and

stretched out his hands to warm them.

'You look doubtful, Britt,' he said. 'I am pleased to see that you question things. But consider this: the theory broadly accepted today proposes that Ape became Man. If that is seen as reasonable, can you really say that it is *unreasonable* to suggest that Man can become Ape? Once you have accepted this as a possibility the rest becomes obvious. We humans possess by far the greatest brain capacity of any creature on this earth. We must therefore be the most closely related to this master race. Within the human race, if the Africans are the closest to the apes, then the Aryans are the furthest from them, so it stands to reason that it is they who remain most closely related to the master race. This is borne out by the fact that it is the Aryan that possesses those characteristics which I have already told you are only found in the best of humans: strength, courage, intelligence and honour. The combination of all these is found in no other human subgroup. The African is strong, certainly, but unintelligent. The Jew is clever, but cowardly and conniving. The Oriental is brave and honourable, but small and weak. And in truth even the Aryans of our earth are nothing compared to this long lost master race, who themselves are pale shadows of the Theozoa.'

'If this super-human was so wonderful,' Britt said, 'then why did he get eradicated?'

'A fine question,' he said, turning from the fire to warm his rump. 'But easily answered. The Norwegians are a wonder to behold, undoubtedly, and one to be harnessed, certainly, but your relative purity dictates that you are entirely free of deviousness, that you be a noble and honourable people, and though this is to be celebrated, it also means that you are more than ordinarily susceptible to the connivances of lesser beings.'

Britt's patience was paying off. He was becoming completely preoccupied by his religion or whatever on earth it was. He wasn't concentrating on her. Which gave her more of a chance to make her move.

He gravitated back to the table, and sat in the chair next to her again.

Under the table she moved the scissors to her lap and gripped them with both hands.

'But the Norwegian need not fear,' he said. 'You can see for yourself, I think, that I am not of such pure blood as you. But my impurities, my understanding of the connivances of the impure, mean that I am the ideal candidate to serve as your custodian. It is my belief that it is only by breeding the finest *with* the finest — that is, the strongest, the bravest, the most intelligent and the most honourable — that the master race can be reborn. And from the master race, we can recall the Theozoic titans.'

Von Westarp was leaning back in his chair. If she lunged, he would see it coming and block her. She had to wait for him to lean in towards her.

'And then order will be restored. Balance. And for this the Norwegians are the key, because in all the world they are of the purest stock. This is the land of the Vikings and the Varangians

159

— Thule itself — and I have come here to instigate a breeding programme that will return to us the perfect being. By refusing to inform me of Sofie's whereabouts, by defying me when we first encountered one another in Drøbak, you exhibit just the characteristics I require.'

He wasn't moving forward, so Britt leaned forward herself, gripping the scissors in her hands like a dagger, looking at his neck, the soft fatty flesh just behind the bone of his jaw — the scissor blade would slice straight through it.

'You expect me to spit out little Nazi babies for you? Go fuck *yourself*, why don't you? I won't do any of it.'

She was about to thrust the scissors around from beneath the table, but something about the grin that slapped itself across his face made her hesitate. It was so confident, so knowing, so *certain*.

'What are you smiling at? Didn't you hear me? Nothing.'

'I heard you, Fräulein Petersen. I thought this would be your reaction — and I would hope for nothing less.'

At that point von Westarp finally leaned forward, so close to Britt that she could smell the German tobacco on his breath as he spoke. 'But before you say, or do, more, let me first pull at your heart strings.'

Still she hesitated.

'What do you mean?'

'Håvard did not just bring me to *your* door, Britt. He was good enough to inform me of the movements he observed you making also. But since *I* am here, I sent Fehmer to a family whose house you frequent. The Jensens, I believe.'

All strength drained from Britt's body. The hand holding the scissors slumped back into her lap. 'Oh my God . . . ' she whispered. 'Ivar.'

Von Westarp nodded apoligetically. 'Yes. If you do not comply with my wishes, I'm afraid your brother will remain in Fehmer's hands.'

Her eyes widened. 'He's only a boy,' she said.

'But if *you* come with *me*, I will see to it that *he* comes with *us* to the mountains.'

'I'll do whatever you want,' Britt said.

Von Westarp looked at her for a moment, satisfied.

'Your superior nature demands it,' he said, then over his shoulder called out, '*Wächter.*'

His soldiers immediately reappeared; but his next words were for Britt. 'Please start by placing the scissors you hold in your hands upon the table.' And to the soldiers, '*Wecken die Nachbarn.*'

'*Ja, Herr Oberführer.*'

One of the soldiers left.

'*Und nehmen Sie auf die Strasse,*' von Westarp said to the remaining two.

They moved in. Slack in her seat, Britt allowed them to lift her and shake the scissors from her hand, then they carried her towards the door and led her down the staircase to the street. Von Westarp followed behind. At the front door, she was greeted by hundreds of eyes. All the neighbours had been woken and ordered to the street. He was trying to break her, to render her utterly subservient. He was making sure that after this there would be nothing to go back to. But it didn't matter. As long as Ivar was safe, it didn't matter what anyone thought of her.

She didn't bow her head in shame. She just made her way down the steps to the street, across the snow to the Mercedes, where the driver saluted and opened the rear passenger door for her.

Before getting in, she turned to look at the faces. She saw shock, disgust and confusion. Then something caught her eye. Through the bare trees, up on the roof, a plume of breath was lighting up silver in the moonlight. Someone was sitting on the roof. A boy. Craning to see what was happening, Ivar moved his face into the light.

As long as Ivar was safe, it didn't matter what anyone thought of her. He *was* safe, or at least he wasn't running into Fehmer's hands. And what he thought — that mattered — and he was seeing his sister collude. He was seeing her give in.

Von Westarp was coming out of the building now, down the steps, across the snow. He arrived at Britt's side and tried to usher her into the car. She didn't move.

'I thought I had made myself clear, Fräulein Petersen. We should arrive at the Jensens before Ivar. Please.'

Britt looked around again, at all the faces. She arrived back at von Westarp in front of her. He looked at her, the smugness of victory written all over his face. Then she spoke, staring into his eyes, loud enough to be heard on the roof, and

162

gradually his expression changed, to confusion, then panic, and finally, as he realized what she was doing, rage:

'My name is Britt Petersen. I love my country. Today you look upon me as a traitor. I am not a traitor. I will always fight. Never give in. Never let them win — '

Von Westarp plunged the scissors deep into her belly.

Britt gulped as she felt the rush of pain, then the warmth of her own blood on her belly. He shoved, harder, and upwards, digging the blades in to meet her heart. She slumped against him and he pushed her backwards, letting her fall onto her back in the snow.

As her consciousness began to swim, she saw von Westarp looking down at her.

He considered her prostrate figure for a moment, then turned and lowered himself into the back of the Benz. He spoke a couple of words to his driver before the door was closed. Before he got in, the driver announced:

'The body shall not be removed. Any who touch it shall be arrested and delivered to Victoria Terrasse. By the edict of Oberführer von Westarp.'

As the limousine departed, and the infantry marched off down the street, people gathered around Britt. A man pulled the scissors from her gut and threw them aside. Unblocked now, blood flowed from Britt's wound onto the snow. She felt a hundred pairs of hands grasping her body and raising it into the air to meet the snow that had begun to fall.

Her vision moved from them as she weakened. It drifted up to the trees, through the descending snow, to the roof of the building beyond, the chimney stack, where a boy sat weeping, watching his sister die, swearing vengeance upon a man whose face he had not seen, but whose name was seared into his mind.

Britt Petersen died before the people got her inside.

164

9

The interview room was more like something from an asylum than a police station. The walls and ceiling and floor glared white under the neon strip lights. Inspector Halvorsen should have been taking Bonde's statement, but had left him with a junior officer. He didn't want to miss this. It was Hansen's first interrogation.

Halvorsen sat the suspect down in the chair on the far side of the table, cuffed his hands behind his back and took a seat in the guard's chair by the door, ready to observe.

Hansen took a seat in the chair opposite the suspect and placed a large manila envelope on the table between them.

'Your file,' she said.

'Good for you.' Even in English, Halvorsen could tell this wasn't the first time the suspect had been in this situation. Snide, yet non-committal, and avoiding eye-contact. He had experience of this.

'Ex-soldiers are easy to trace, Corporal Curtis, especially if they keep their tags around their necks.' Hansen's tone was like that of a teacher. Weary. She pulled a folder out of the envelope, opened it, and took her time to read, murmuring a couple of interested *hms*. Usually rookies dived right in, but she was letting him brew. Halvorsen

165

had to admit it was a promising start.

'Corporal Jeffrey Winston Curtis,' she said at last. 'Discharged from Her Majesty's Engineers in January, for — '

'Actually,' Curtis interrupted, looking at Halvorsen, 'I go by Curt here. It helps me fit in. Not too many Yefs around, you know? So are you going to tell me why I'm here or are you just going to sit there and hope I panic?'

Halvorsen shrugged and pointed at Hansen.

'You're here because of a woman,' Hansen said. 'That's what it says here, anyway. But she's in Bergen. And you're here.' Hansen closed the file. 'So I guess that didn't work out then?'

Jabbing straight in with the personal. Another clever move. The reference to the woman appeared to travel through Curtis like a wave of nausea. Hansen had hit a nerve.

'You want my whole life story?' Curtis said, composing himself after the initial blow, donning the familiar armour of sarcasm. 'Tell me why I'm here and I'll tell you the whole woeful tale, from a neglected childhood on the estates of North London, to gang life, to life inside for auto theft, to probation as a mechanic, two years and four tours in the Engineers, all the way to the door of a squat in Sjursøya. I might even tell you about little Jenny Thiamou and what we got up to behind the bike sheds. But before we get cosy, how about that explanation? Or is it illegal to beg in this country?'

'You weren't begging, Mr Curtis.'

'Then what was I doing?'

'If you were begging you would have

approached every person along that colonnade. You stopped at the table of only one person. A specific individual.'

'He looked generous.'

'You are claiming that you did not know the identity of that person?'

'Which person?'

'Henrik Bonde.'

'There are only two kinds of people when you're asking them for money. Those that give, and those that don't. And none of them have faces, let alone names.'

She had started strongly, but it was fizzling out. Her line was getting soft, obvious. Any hood would be able to swat these questions down. Halvorsen decided to give her a couple more minutes.

'Henrik Bonde is a well-known and divisive politician, Mr Curtis. This morning we received a phone call informing us that he's in danger. Then, of all the people you could have approached at that café, you chose him. Are you telling me this is a coincidence?'

Halvorsen winced, internally at least. That was it. She'd given him all the information they possessed. After that she had nowhere to go, she had nothing left to throw at him, which wouldn't matter anyway, because worse, she'd just handed him the ball. Halvorsen would let her have the sting of what was coming — it was the only way she'd learn, and seeing as this was an empty case anyway, it was a better one to learn from than most — but then he'd close it down.

'Are you telling me they don't exist?' Curtis

167

said, smiling. 'Listen, darling, it's nice you care about the citizens of your city and all, and want to keep us safe, but correct me if I'm wrong, that guy I was asking money from, Bender you call him?'

'Bonde,' she said. 'Henrik Bonde.'

'Right. Well, last time I saw him, he was alive and well, so what are the charges here?'

Curtis stared at Hansen over the table. Halvorsen couldn't see Hansen's face, but her speechlessness and the satisfaction written all over Curtis's face told him she now understood what she had done. It happened to everyone, of course, but fresh out of school you adhered to the rules. You didn't necessarily know that a threat or a display of unpredictable aggression could win back the ball. She would have to be shown how that worked.

Halvorsen got to his feet, the scrape of his chair breaking the silence. He slowly removed his jacket, the pair of them watching him from the table.

'Curtis,' he said, rolling up his shirtsleeves, but before he could go on, the door behind him opened and the face of a young uniformed officer appeared in the gap.

'Inspector Halvorsen?' he said. 'You're wanted in Superintendant Egeland's office, sir.'

Halvorsen nodded and let the officer close the door again before turning back to the room.

'You better start talking to Sergeant Hansen here, Curtis,' he said. 'If you haven't given her anything by the time I get back, I'm going to take over, and I'm not as nice as she is. You understand me?'

* * *

Hansen had got one thing right about Inspector Halvorsen. He was a fighter. Or had been, anyway. The trophies and medals on his mantel at home told the story of a pretty decent middleweight, and he'd continued to box after he'd joined the force. But Egeland, Halvorsen's mother's sister's husband, had jigged his nephew's Sergeant's paper, which had seen him onto Crime Squad. A heavy with the built-in loyalty of family was a good thing for Egeland, but boxers weren't known for their brains. He didn't want to give the internal affairs division a reason to look into his nephew's exam results, so when he'd said the boxing had to stop, Halvorsen had stopped.

He still regularly hit the heavy bag at the gym, though. This was mainly in an attempt to maintain the shape that had originally attracted his wife, Else, a former ring-girl ten years his junior. Even though she'd given up the job for motherhood — Ronald was six, Linda three — Else was still only in her early thirties, a natural blonde with a rack to die for and legs up to here. At forty-three, with a growing fondness for the numbing effects of alcohol, and middle-aged spread beginning to hit, Halvorsen was more aware than ever of the attention his grade-A, turbocharged super-vixen wife received wherever she went, especially in this heat.

Else made Ingrid Hansen look like a clueless schoolgirl — pretty, sure, but an object of sex? Come off it. He only made the sexist comments because if he didn't he knew he'd end up paying for it with the other guys in the squad room somehow. Hell, if he was actually *nice* to her, she'd probably think he actually did want to get with her, and they'd both end up paying the cost. But that would have been like chasing his niece or something. Just plain wrong. He guessed his mind had been adjusted by Else. Praise be.

He would work double-hard at the gym tonight, try and get rid of some of this gut he was tucking his shirt around as he came into the Pit. He noticed the privacy blinds were down on the glass walls of Egeland's office straight away. Something was up. When he knocked and entered, though, Egeland was sitting behind his desk, looking out the window at the bodies baking in the sun, just as he had been earlier that morning.

'Lukas,' he said, as though surprised to see his nephew there.

'You asked for me, boss?'

'I did.' Egeland spun in his chair and pointed across his office, to Halvorsen's left. 'You know Mr Bonde, of course.'

Bonde was sitting in a leather armchair by the wall, his briefcase at his feet, a half-drunk glass of water on the coffee table at his side. It was depositing a pool of condensation on the cheap veneer. Halvorsen stepped towards the politician.

'We met in the car from the scene. How are you feeling, Mr Bonde?' he said, holding out his hand. Halvorsen knew Egeland was an Advance supporter. Most of the force were. They promised an increased police budget, greater

170

police freedom. None of the other serious parties did. He figured they were working away to cook the suspect as publicly as possible.

'I'm fine, Inspector,' Bonde said, getting to his feet as he took Halvorsen's hand. He was sweating; who wasn't in this heat? He also looked a little shaken by the whole affair, like it had left him wired. 'Your uncle's been telling me all about you.'

There was the hint of amusement in his tone, a millisecond's glance at Egeland. Uncle Lars had been telling him all right. Not too clever, but eager, enthusiastic, does his job. He's a good boy. He'll do what he's told.

Halvorsen felt his body temperature jump a couple of degrees.

'How can I help?' Halvorsen said to them both.

'Superintendent Egeland?' Bonde said, looking towards Egeland.

'Mr Bonde has asked me to release the — ah, are you calling him a suspect, Lukas?' Egeland's tone was patronizing. It was this treatment that had pushed Halvorsen to the bar. Being treated like a special child at work, while thinking himself over-the-hill at home. It felt like his head was being whisked.

'Jeffrey Curtis, a former British soldier living on the streets here. We're — '

Egeland leaned back in his chair.

'Frankly, Lukas, it's a case we could all do without. Mr Bonde doesn't want any untoward attention so close to polling; we don't need the grief — and from what Mr Bonde says, the kid

171

didn't actually *do* anything. That about the size of it, Henrik?'

'Thank you, Superintendent,' Bonde said, approaching the desk. 'I'm most grateful to you. And I'll make my exit now, if that's okay. Busy times, and you have this in order.'

Egeland stood and took Bonde's proffered hand.

'Go ahead, Mr Bonde. They'll have a couple of forms for you to sign out there, but bear with them and they'll get you out of here as soon as humanly possible. Again, congratulations, and good luck. You know you can always count on us. Right, Lukas?'

Bonde had crossed to the door and opened it.

'Yes, sir,' Halvorsen said, his own obedience disgusting him. 'I guess 80 per cent of the force votes Advance.'

'And the Advance Party won't forget it, Superintendent Egeland, Inspector Halvorsen. As you know, an effective and well-funded police force is fundamental to our vision for the future of our country. Gentlemen.'

The door closed, Halvorsen turned back to Egeland, and saw instantly that his pleasantness had evaporated.

'What the *fuck*, Lukas?' he said, leaning across his desk, his weight on his knuckles, as though he might actually launch himself at Halvorsen, like some kind of obese, bald, albino gorilla. 'Starting an investigation based on an unsubstantiated threat from an anonymous caller? What are you, twelve?'

'Youthful exuberance, Uncle Lars.'

'Don't Uncle Lars me, you fucking retard,'

Egeland said with real violence, spit showering over his desk, his face changing colour, a vein appearing and dissecting his forehead as it pulsated. 'You're meant to be controlling her, teaching her the fucking ropes. If you can't even do that, what good are you to me?'

Halvorsen shrugged, a beaten schoolboy.

'I thought the experience would do her good.'

'You signed the call off, *Inspector*, so you get to do the paperwork. Personally.'

That would take Halvorsen most of the day, and Egeland knew it. It was his punishment, like a child made to write out lines for talking in class.

'Now get him the fuck out of here,' Egeland spat, picking up a piece of paper from his desk. 'I've signed it myself this time, so there can be no oversights, no fucking exuberance, youthful or otherwise. Understand?' Egeland flicked the form at Halvorsen. It fluttered to the floor. Halvorsen had to bend to pick it up off the carpet, sending even more blood to his head.

★ ★ ★

Despite what he'd said to the pretty little policewoman, Curt didn't believe in coincidences. In the five minutes since the big guy with the pug face had left, he'd sat there, listening to the police woman reiterate the same question over and over, as though he was going to open up and admit something. At the same time, he'd cultivated a desire to learn the answers to a couple of questions of his own: Who made the

173

phone call she was talking about? What were the police doing there at all? Who the fuck did that old man think he was messing with?

He wouldn't be asking anyone in here, of course. They were questions to save for when his silence landed him back on the street and he met up with the old man again. Then he'd ask. Loud and clear. And he'd get himself some answers.

Just then the door flew open. The big guy stamped back in, heaving like a cartoon bull. He slammed the door shut behind him.

'*Ga han deg noe?*' he puffed.

When the police woman just shrugged, the bull hit the recorder on the wall, stopping it, and moved behind Curt. Curt craned to see him, but couldn't. Instead he just heard his heavy breathing, then felt a hand on his shoulder, and the whole world shifted. Curt slammed backwards onto the floor. His cuffed arms were sandwiched between the aluminium of the chair back and the lino. His whole body weight came down on top. The hard metal of the chair drove through the soft tissue of the muscles on his forearms. Curt screamed. He opened his eyes to see the bull lowering himself down on top of him. He placed his knees on Curt's shoulders and let them dig in. Curt's forearms were bearing the entire load across the aluminium bars. The pain was excruciating. He squealed, and the cop grabbed his face, squeezing his cheeks with powerful, thick fingers.

'What do you have?' he said.

'I don't know what you're talking about,' Curt said, wincing.

The cop leaned forward, adding more weight. At some point Curt's arms would simply snap.

'What do you have?' he repeated, and this time hit Curt across the face.

Curt managed to look at the girl, still on the other side of the table. Through the blur of his rattling eyes, he could see that she had her hands covering her mouth. She was frozen.

The pain increased as the cop leaned even more heavily on him. Curt didn't know what would come first: the sound of splintering bones, or blackout from the pain. But then it stopped. The cop was off him, hoisting Curt upright again. Then, heaving a breath like he himself had just been relieved of some great weight, and straightening his jacket, the cop pointed at the door.

'*Ut, Hansen,*' he said. But she didn't move and he had to take her by the shoulders and lead her out. He shut the door behind them and Curt was alone, heaving for his own breath.

* * *

Outside, Halvorsen was also recovering, leaning on a wall with one hand.

'I guess he didn't know anything, then,' he said, suddenly over-excited, his blood up. 'If he did, he'd have spilled.'

Hansen had never really been close to violence like that before. She knew it would come with this job, she might even have been disappointed if it hadn't, but she hadn't expected it to occur right here at the office, at the heart of the city's law enforcement, *from* the heart of the city's law enforcement.

'Who do you think you are, Halvorsen?' she said. 'Mike fucking Hammer?'

He actually looked surprised at her reaction, but a little pleased with the comparison.

'Come on,' he said, grinning into her face, sweat dripping from one sideburn. 'You can help me write it up.'

'And say what? That you physically abused a restrained man?'

'It was a little roughing up.' Now he was patronizing the little girl. 'It's the way things are done around here sometimes. The way they have to be done.'

'And what if he makes a formal complaint?'

'He won't.'

'You can be sure of that?'

'Who's going to believe a vagrant? *The suspect arrives bruised, sees a chance, makes a false complaint pertaining to police brutality,*' he said, like he was reading the report out loud. 'But it won't come to that. We're trouble he doesn't need. Come on.'

Hansen didn't move.

'That's not the point.'

'Yes it is.'

She stared at him a moment. This was an argument she could never win.

'Then what about the threat?'

'Sweetheart, if Bonde doesn't care about the threat, we don't care about the threat, okay?'

'And he doesn't?'

'He told my uncle we should forget the whole

176

thing, release the kid. Doesn't want negative press or something.'

'That'll be the day.'

'Got the release form right here,' he said, pulling it out of his jacket pocket.

'You're kidding, right?' Hansen said, taking it from him. 'Let me have a look at that.'

'My uncle signed it himself,' Halvorsen said, starting to make his way up the corridor back towards the Pit, leaving Hansen standing there, inspecting the form.

'Halvorsen,' she said, her tone authoritative all of a sudden. He stopped, waiting for her to catch up.

'What is it now?'

'I don't understand. Why would this be anything but good press for Bonde? The Advance Party is all about law and order, not to mention anti-immigration. Surely he should be milking it for all it's worth, calling in the networks as we speak. It's a gold-plated stunt ticket for him, whether Curtis was a threat or not. Why's he throwing it away?'

Halvorsen was shaking his head, but she could see in his eyes that he'd thought the same thing.

'You think too much,' he said. 'I admire your commitment, but this is finished now.'

'There's something going on, Halvorsen. Can't you see? We've got to — '

They re-entered the Pit and she was cut off by cheers. Every person there was standing by their desks, Dahl, Brunstad, Forgaard, Vera, Agnes, and others — even Solberg was back from wherever he'd been for the occasion — every one

177

of them clapping and grinning, the sarcasm as thick as the applause was loud.

Halvorsen's high was gone. 'Get him out of here, Hansen,' he said.

★ ★ ★

Hansen picked her way through the mock 'congratulations', but it was Solberg who had the most deflating words for her. 'Don't worry, Hansen,' he said, taking her hand in both his, cold, clammy. 'We were all in your position once. You'll learn how things are done around here soon enough.' If someone else had said those words, in another situation, they might have been reassuring. But somehow he made them sound like an attempted seduction — the tone, the tenderness — and that was bad enough. But what really hit Hansen was the idea that he might be right; maybe she *would* learn. That was why, after slumping in her seat and sitting motionless for thirty seconds, she sat up again and picked up her phone and hit 0.

There was something odd about Bonde's reluctance to press charges, that was for sure, and she knew Halvorsen had seen it. He might be able to let it go, but she couldn't — and she didn't want to. That would be the first step to becoming like them. She'd already screwed this up anyway, so what would it matter if she took it a little further?

'Madsen?' she said when someone picked up.

'Yeah.'

'Hansen again.'

'What can I do for you?'

'There are two civilian men in this building. One's a suspect about to be processed for release, a Jeffrey Curtis. The other's Henrik Bonde, the politician.'

'And?'

'I want a tail on each of them. Use Kobberrød again if you can, okay?'

'Under Halvorsen again?' He sounded reluctant.

'That's right,' Hansen said, brassing it out.

'You sure about that, Sergeant?'

'I am.'

'Are you being careful, Hansen?'

'I guess not.'

'You should be. Your chief's bite is worse than his bark, you know?'

'I'll keep it in mind. Just give me the tails, will you?'

'All right, Hansen. It's your head.'

'I know. And Madsen?'

'Yeah?'

'The guy I replaced.'

'Skarnes?'

'Yeah. Let me have his number, will you?'

10

1941

The sign above the café on Ruseløkkveien used to read *Svendsens*. These days it simply read *Bakeriet* — the Bakery. As well as baked goods, the menu included traditional Norwegian fare. Ruseløkkveien lay in the shadow of Victoria Terrasse, and while the location was good for business (each lunchtime saw it flooded by the staff of the Gestapo headquarters), its proprietor feared the effect this would have on his reputation amongst his fellow Norwegians; so he had changed the name of the establishment. But Tord Svendsen was no sympathizer, and Jonas Grevle knew this.

Grevle had been an ordinary, middle-aged, middle-of-the-road clerk for the Oslo police force, working out of the building on Victoria Terrasse. He'd eaten at Svendsen's nearly every day and the two men had grown friendly over the years — they both had two daughters, their wives were both from the west country — so when, just before Christmas 1940, Grevle came in and started railing against the new regime that had seen him out of a job, Svendsen had silenced him with a shot of aquavit. Knowing that the place was growing in popularity amongst the *Sicherheitspolizei* workers, he said, 'Drink this and shut up,' leaning in to add, 'and wait.'

Until that day, Svendsen had taken a daily walk across Karl Johan's Gate to the National Gallery. However, with the rest of the previous day's post, he had received a letter informing him that the Germans had placed a member of Quisling's Nazi-sympathizing *Nasjonal Samling* party as Director of the gallery. This increased the risk of using it as a drop-off point, as he had been; but security at the gallery remained lax, and it was still a place a man could frequent without suspicion. The method of passing information was not to alter. Instead, to increase security, another link was to be added to the chain.

Once the Germans had vacated the café premises that afternoon, Grevle had joined the movement. That was why he kept up his routine of coming here every day, even though he no longer worked nearby. Over lunch or just a cup of coffee, he would talk to his old friend about the world, their wives, their daughters, the weather. But to this routine Grevle had now added a new habit. With time on his hands, he had developed a hitherto undiscovered passion for the art of the National Gallery. Or at least for one picture in particular. Wiping his mouth with a napkin, which he then idly slipped into his pocket, he left the café and headed for the gallery and, from the foot of the main stairs, contemplated the enormous painting called Åsgårdsreien — the Wild Hunt — that hung above the half-landing.

After a minute, he took the stairs up to the landing, where there was a donations box attached to the wall beneath the picture. Instead of money, he dropped a stamped, unaddressed envelope through the slot, which had been widened for the purpose. The envelope had been folded into Svendsen's napkin.

In dropping this envelope into the donations box at the National Gallery, Grevle was passing coded information pertaining to the movements of the residents of Victoria Terrasse to senior resistance members via agents among the gallery staff. Grevle did not know the key to the cipher. He did not know the names of the operatives within the gallery, nor the identity of those they passed the information on to. Svendsen to Grevle, Grevle to the National Gallery. It was as simple as that.

New orders; changes of plan; any information at all to which senior members wanted to alert the men — it all came through the post, in letters signed only with Haakon's monogram, H7. In case of emergencies, Svendsen's handlers had him memorize a telephone number, which he, in turn, made Grevle remember by heart, but neither man had ever used the number. The whole thing was set up so that they would have as little as possible to give up under torture.

When Grevle came into Bakeriet on 21 November 1941, it was lunchtime, and the premises were busy with the usual clientele. Grevle did not order any food, though, or even a cup of coffee. He was looking preoccupied and did not stop at the counter or utter a word to Svendsen. He simply ducked straight under the hatch, grabbed the telephone, and pushed his way through the swing door into the kitchen. Svendsen had customized the cord to a length at which calls could be made in privacy.

This atypical behaviour had Svendsen concerned straight away, but he knew his role under such circumstances. Despite the uneasy feeling in his gut, outwardly he maintained the good-natured light-heartedness for which he was known. He tutted, and raised his eyebrows. At the same time he stuck out his foot. This stopped the two-way door from swinging, sealing the kitchen from the main café and preventing Grevle from being overheard by idle Nazi ears. To make sure, at the sound of the tut, Svendsen's nephew Stefan upped the tempo and volume of the tune he was playing on the chipped upright in the corner.

Svendsen turned to face the restaurant. The place was filled with Germans, uniformed and in civvies. At the counter a man in the uniform of an Untersturmführer was lighting a cigarette. He was looking at Svendsen, mildly curious. Svendsen did not recognize him. He was not a regular.

'Looks like he's in a hurry,' said the Untersturmführer, whose name was Bitzler.

'His wife is nearly ten months pregnant. He comes in here every day to call her,' Svendsen said, moving between the Untersturmführer and the door. 'She looks like a Zeppelin!'

The German almost laughed.

'More coffee, Sturmführer?'

'Why not?' the Untersturmführer said.

Svendsen reached for the coffee pot and

183

refilled the officer's cup.

'Something to eat, perhaps, Sturmführer?' Svendsen tried. 'I have a delicious range of sweet buns.'

But Bitzler ignored him, craning his neck to watch the man in the kitchen. The Norwegian father-to-be was holding the telephone receiver to his ear, his brow sweating, despite the cold, his eyes jerking from the telephone and out through the window in the door. He didn't know *where* to look.

Then the man's eyes settled. Bitzler was surprised to find the Norwegian looking through the round window directly at him. As a German soldier, no one looked at you in this snow-laden hell-hole. Even when you addressed them and they answered, usually they didn't meet your eyes. It was like the uniform was a light, too bright to look at. But this guy was looking right back at him —

No. Bitzler realized he was wrong. The man wasn't looking at him. Or he wasn't seeing him, anyway, and their eyes were not meeting. The Norwegian's eyes were directed further afield. Beyond him. Through him.

Before Bitzler could discern what the man was looking at, his gaze dropped to the phone again. Number dialled, he raised his other hand to take hold of the receiver with both and he began to talk, fast. Bitzler couldn't hear what he was saying through the door and over the piano, but the man looked concerned — naturally — then he nodded and spoke some more, and concern seemed to turn to sorrow — bad news?

The man wasn't talking any more. He was listening, nodding almost imperceptibly. He raised his eyes again and once more stared through the round window, beyond Svendsen, beyond Bitzler, beyond the soldier's compatriots enjoying the music. His gaze went beyond the café itself, into the snow-covered street, up to the front of the main entrance to Victoria Terrasse, to a child, ragged and dirty, standing there motionless but for his uncontrollable shivers. The kid was staring up at the entrance of the Gestapo headquarters. Uniformed soldiers were moving past him, not one of them paying the slightest bit of attention to him or to the metal glinting in his right hand.

The man wasn't making a call about an unborn child. For whatever reason, he was discussing the kid out there. Bitzler knew it and, ignoring the wittering proprietor, he threw some coins next to his coffee cup and made his way to the exit, watching the child all the way.

* * *

Due to lack of nutrition, Ivar had grown less than an inch since February. His felt hat was pulled down over his forehead, shadowing a hollowed face smudged with dirt. His clothes — torn and inadequate in the chill of winter — hung from a 12-year-old body whose muscles had reduced to stringy sinews. His shoes were worn through and let in the snow. But he was not cold.

Nine months; 274 days: the period it takes a child to grow in its mother's womb. Seeing Britt

185

die, Ivar knew Håvard had compromised the Jensens as well as the girl he loved. Ivar had never met Sofie, but likely the Jensens had given her up to save their children, and even if they hadn't, the Jensens were his only contact. He was entirely alone, and over the past nine months he had lived wherever he could find shelter, begging food from the back doors of restaurants and houses. When people saw him standing at their door, half-starved, dirty, freezing through the winter months, they tried to coax him in, to distract him from his task, but he had resisted. He had never faltered. He took the food they gave him, or a hat, a jumper, and walked away, always moving, counting each day, obsessively racking them up in his brain, searching the city for one man.

Ivar did not see the face of Britt's killer from the roof that day, but he had a name.

Oberführer von Westarp. In the spring after Britt's death, when the snow was nearly melted, he had put a photographic face to the name. On a stained scrap from a newspaper, he'd seen the name printed beneath a torn picture. The picture showed a man standing in that same black Nazi greatcoat, proud, cruel, cold. Laughing.

Now, finally, all those months of traipsing had paid off.

Ivar had spotted the man in the picture three days ago, striding from the great white building on Victoria Terrasse, in his smart outfit, nothing to indicate that he had stabbed a girl in the belly and left her to die. Not one drop of regret or penance.

Ivar had been watching the building from a doorway for the three days and nights since, observing the man's coming and going. Now, though, his impatience for vengeance had got the better of him. It was time. The man always appeared at lunchtime and Ivar had been standing on the same spot for more than an hour, waiting for him to appear, grasping the coronation knife in one freezing fist, the picture from the newspaper in his other. He would call out his name, see the fear in von Westarp's eyes, and then plunge the knife into his belly. Whatever happened to Ivar afterwards would not matter. Britt's killer would be dead, killed right outside the most feared building in the country. The Germans would see the consequences of their actions, just as the people outside their block had been shown what happened to those who resisted.

At long last, Britt's killer came out of the building into the crisp winter sunlight, wearing his black greatcoat and cap — dressed just as he had been on the day he murdered her. Every footstep he placed in the snow crunched in Ivar's ears. Every breath he took was audible to the boy. Ivar could hear nothing else, in fact, and as tears cleaned lines down his dirty, concave cheeks, he could see only his sister's murderer, and Britt lying there, bleeding into the snow.

A man holding a leashed dog stopped Britt's killer three metres away from Ivar.

'Von Westarp,' Ivar said, but his voice came out as a croak, fear constricting his throat. He swallowed.

'*You*,' he said, louder this time, but still the German did not respond. Ivar took another step forward. '*YOU!*'

Finally the German responded. Frowning, he turned from the man he was talking to and faced Ivar.

He was not Gerhard von Westarp, but Ivar did not know this. He did not know that the picture he had found was a fragment of a whole, a whole which had shown *two* men laughing together. He did not pause to consider that the single name printed below had referred to the other man, whose image he did not possess. Why would he? In his desperation to find Britt's killer, he had grasped hold of hope, of opportunity, of destiny. He had no idea that Fate had, in fact, laid him in the path of a man even crueller and more sadistic than his sister's murderer, a monster, to whom the panting hound held leashed by his compatriot at his side was no mere pet, but a favoured method of torture.

Hauptsturmführer Siegfried Wolfgang Fehmer looked into Ivar's eyes, then moved his gaze down to the steel shining from the boy's right hand.

'It seems I have done something to upset you, young man?' Fehmer said in German, amused at the sight.

Ivar stared back at him. He did not understand a word of German, in which language Fehmer continued to speak, saying something to his companion holding the dog's leash now. But Ivar understood the laughter that followed.

188

'Come, my boy,' Fehmer continued in German. 'Whatever I have done, I am certain we can come to some understanding.'

Ivar raised his hand, and pointed the knife at Fehmer.

The scene was starting to gather attention. Passers-by saw a child holding a knife, challenging an officer, challenging *Fehmer*, of all people, who even the Germans feared, and were stopping to watch with unmasked fascination. The guards either side of the entrance to Victoria Terrasse noticed the audience forming and approached, levelling their guns when they saw Ivar.

'No, no,' Fehmer said, raising his hand so that the guards too joined the audience. The German then crouched to stroke his dog. 'This boy shows spirit. More than the rest of his people combined. While others creep in secrecy against me, he comes here to meet face to face. A child.' Fehmer was staring at Ivar, nodding slowly, impressed. Then he said: 'Tell me, boy: what is it I have done to be the subject of such courage?'

Ivar said nothing.

'Clearly it is a matter of the heart. Your tears tell me this much. We stand here to settle a score of the blood, do we not? A *vendetta?*'

That word Ivar understood.

'You killed — my sister,' he said.

Fehmer turned to his companion, who translated.

'Ahh,' he said. 'And blood must beget blood, is this not so?'

Fehmer rose to his feet and started unbuttoning his coat.

'I cannot apologize for her death, boy. I am certain I would not even remember her name. I do my duty, just as you have come here to do yours. Where all others cower at my name, you come here with honour to face me. For this I will grant you — ' He removed his coat and his cap, and threw them at one of the guards — 'a single chance to achieve that which you have come for.'

Fehmer stepped forwards, into the empty space between them, unhooking his Luger holster from his Sam Browne.

'I will stand here.'

He threw the holster onto the snow a few feet away.

'Unarmed.'

Next he removed his Sam Browne from around his waist and over his shoulder. It joined the Luger on the ground. Fehmer tutted, then wagged a finger at Ivar, smiling.

'Yes, of course. You are right. Many of our soldiers carry an additional weapon in the waistband of their trousers.'

He unbuttoned his jacket.

'And the wool of my uniform is thick. Your mean blade would not penetrate. But my shirt is of the finest Egyptian cotton, against which it will not struggle.' Jacket off, Fehmer threw it aside and slowly rotated 360 degrees, holding his arms out as though crucified. 'And now you see — I do not carry a secreted weapon. I am like you, boy, and conduct my affairs with the honour of a true soldier.'

Fehmer stopped turning, and faced Ivar.

'I will not move. I will not defend myself. And

190

you have my word that there will be no consequences if I fall. All these people have heard me speak. No one shall prevent you or arrest you. Kill me, and you will walk away free, your duty done.' He turned to the crowd. 'Is that clear?' he said. 'This boy wants blood, and for his courage he shall have his chance.' Then he looked again at Ivar. 'You have shown heart, boy, so I show you mine,' he pointed to his chest. 'And here my liver. Here my jugular. Choose your spot.'

Ivar did not understand the man's words, but he could not mistake his gestures. He was being invited to take a chance. In all his months of hunting, he had never imagined the day of reckoning to be like this. He thought he had planned for every possible situation: an ambush in a dark alley; running up to him in the street and sliding the blade into his gut; cutting his throat in a cinema as he laughed at the screen. Calling out his name, looking in his eyes, and plunging the knife into his belly.

But not this — this public display, this performance, this *theatre*. The man was making sport of him.

Ivar stood there, staring at Fehmer. He stared and wept, the tears blurring his vision, the people around them vanishing in the snow-white swirl. All but for him, Britt's murderer.

Whatever the circumstances, this *was* the day of reckoning. He had chosen the stage. He had not waited for his victim to enter an alley or a cinema. He had approached him and called out to him. He *wanted* to see his eyes as he drove

Britt's knife into his belly. He *wanted* him to know what was happening to him and why.

Ivar wiped his eyes, and glared into those blue crystals staring back at him. All trace of amusement had vanished from Fehmer's face.

'Come,' Fehmer said, and the crowd fell silent. 'I order you. Avenge her death.'

Ivar ground the toes of his shoes into the snow, dropped the scrap of newspaper at his feet and pushed off. He was so weak his run was more a tragic stagger than a sprint, his feet dragging in the snow, but he willed his spent body to move as it was built to, gripping the hilt of the knife with all his strength.

Fehmer watched him come, the boy staring straight back into his eyes, pitiful, broken, the tears streaming down his face.

Halfway, Ivar screamed out unintelligibly, raising the knife up above his head.

With a metre between them, Fehmer closed his eyes, and lifted his arms into the air either side of himself, inhaling through his nostrils, welcoming the attack.

Ivar willed his legs into a final leap, and brought the knife down onto Fehmer's chest. He felt it penetrate the flesh, and pushed harder, with all his weight, surely into the man's heart.

Fehmer opened his eyes the moment the knife hit, and wailed out — half in pain, half in euphoria.

Ivar let go of the hilt and fell to the ground, face down.

Above him, Fehmer grunted, and Ivar heard a thud in the snow next to him. He turned his head. The sound was not Fehmer falling dead next to him, but the bloodied knife, dropping to the ground beside the foot of a black leather boot. Ivar looked up. Fehmer was covering a growing bloodstain with his hand, located not over his heart, but between his shoulder and chest, his bright blue eyes, alight with ecstasy, looking down at him.

Ivar had injured him, caused pain, even, but the man was alive. Very alive. And he appeared to enjoy the agony.

'You had your chance, boy,' he said. 'And you have done all that could be expected of you. More. But you have failed.'

Fehmer stepped to one side and picked his holster up off the snow.

The sport was over.

Suddenly animated, Ivar rolled onto his back, and started shuffling and slipped backwards through the snow, kicking it up as he tried to scrabble away, the crowd parting for him as he moved. But Fehmer followed him, his paces slow, as though trying to give Ivar a chance to escape as he pulled his Luger from its case.

'You are a courageous child,' he said. 'Now you must die, but die knowing that your bravery will stand as your epitaph.'

Fehmer raised the gun. Ivar scrambled into the road, and stopped as Fehmer took aim.

'Now sleep, boy. Close your eyes and sleep.'

Ivar did not close his eyes, but everything went black.

The black was not the black of death, though, or even of unconsciousness. It was Dodge black, a sedan delivery car skidding to a halt on the impacted snow between him and Fehmer.

The goods door on the side of the vehicle was already open and hands reached for Ivar, pulling him inside, pushing his face down onto the back seat. Confusion suddenly wiped across the German's face. The German soldiers around him suddenly found their voices and started screaming orders. But the vehicle's engine roared, the tyres squealed for grip, and it was moving. Over the noise of the motor and the shouting voices within the vehicle, for Ivar one voice was clear, calm, warm, the words soothing and kind and female: 'You're safe now, Ivar. Safe.'

Outside Victoria Terrasse, Fehmer crouched to pick up the scrap of paper the boy had been holding. It was one half of a newspaper photograph showing his own handsome face. The caption beneath it read: 'Oberführer von Westarp laughs with Hauptst — '

★ ★ ★

The vehicle shuddered to a standstill and Ivar's hat was pulled down over his face. He felt hands hook beneath his armpits and he was lifted out onto snow-covered ground, his feet between two other pairs — one male, one female — whose owners led him along the side of a building then up a flight of ice-shined steps.

Inside, he could tell the building was not a home or an apartment block. They were moving across a large, cold foyer, the woman's heels

194

clip-clopping on the tile floor. Ivar managed to twist his head, and saw a window through which a middle-aged woman was watching them, nodding solemnly. Then they went through a door into darkness and he heard distant music. His hat was pulled off. In front of him was a man, tall and broad, like a labourer. He smelled like one, too: sweaty, unwashed. Like an animal.

Ivar heard the woman's voice from the darkness behind him.

'Ivar, this is Leif,' she said. 'Okay, Leif. Take care of him.'

Half-excited, half-impatient, the man took Ivar's hand in his enormous fist.

'I will,' he said. 'Come on, kid. It's not been going long.'

The man opened another door and the volume of the music increased. They moved up an ascending passage and emerged into a huge room with row after row of seats, a third of them occupied. A great screen showed a monochrome moving image of two young women in their beds, alarmed by something, pulling the covers up. Then one got out and went to the bedroom door.

'Front-row seats,' the man called Leif said, shoving a paper bag into Ivar's hands, and adding, as he led the boy down the aisle to the front of the cinema, 'Nothing but the best today. All this shit got to you, kid. You just enjoy this. And don't worry, you'll be taken care of, okay?'

Ivar said nothing, but sat and opened up the bag. A chunk of bread and one of cheese. He took a bite from each and began to watch the film and the man sitting next to him in equal measures. The hairy giant stared up at the screen, loving every moment.

Not a word had been spoken by anyone in the car after the woman had whispered those words in Ivar's ear. Nothing had been explained. And now he had just been dumped here, expected to watch a movie with a child-man as though nothing had happened, as though he hadn't just been snatched from the jaws of death.

You're safe now, Ivar. Safe.

The woman knew his name. Was that a good sign? And this giant, his guard, he had said he would be taken care of. What did that mean?

Maybe they could help him. Why not? They were his own kind, after all, fellow Norwegians, and they weren't working with the Germans, that much was plain. But what did they want with him? For them to take the risk of picking him up like that, it had to be something important. These people were secretive. Like spies. And how did they even know that he would be there, or what he was doing?

But whoever they were, von Westarp was still out there, with no more than a flesh wound, which meant Ivar didn't *want* to be safe and warm. These people might help him. But more probably they would pack him off as far from von Westarp as possible. *For your own good,* they'd say. Ivar could not risk that. He had a job to do.

He glanced at Leif, a big, strong, lumbering man. Slow. Ivar was sure he could get away from him, but there was no reason to reject the food.

196

He could fill his belly first. He would eat, wait until the place was at its darkest, then make a dash for the exit. He'd left the coronation knife at the scene so he'd have to find a weapon somewhere. That would be an obstacle, but not an insurmountable one. They hadn't driven long enough to be in a different town. They were still in Oslo, which he knew as well as anyone now.

★ ★ ★

'Don't you see? This is a perfect opportunity. You're not thinking about this logically.'

'Logically? This is a child we're talking about, Arne.'

'More like an animal now.'

There were four of them in the room, a basement store about five metres by four. A wooden table sat in the middle of the concrete floor. The two longer walls, opposite one another, were taken up by shelves stacked with celluloid cans. The third had a door, the fourth a window facing onto the street at ground-level, blacked-out with thick material but for a centimetre-square peephole. Geir Larsgård had his eye to it, his back to the room, a Suomi KP machine gun slung over his shoulder. The man by the door, holding a Soviet-issue Nagant revolver, was Reidar Thomassen.

The two had met in the volunteer corps fighting with the Finns against the encroaching Soviets. They'd returned to Oslo together, with their weapons, just in time to see the Nazis invading. Sixteen days after coming back from

197

Finland, the pair had encountered Arne Stornes, the man standing by the table there in the cinema storeroom, with whom Geir had served his national service. After their time in comms, Stornes had started studying for a degree in engineering at the University of Oslo, which was where he had met the beautiful, dark-haired woman now sitting at the table. She had been studying physics, and became his wife in 1939. Neither of the couple's degrees had been achieved. In August of 1940 they had both been approached and recruited by the resistance for its fledgling intelligence branch, what came to be called the XU. Arne had added Thomassen and Larsgård to the team soon afterwards.

'Reidar's right,' Arne said to his wife. 'The boy's gone feral. By rights he should be dead after living rough for that long, but he's alive, and what do you think it was that kept him going? It damn well wasn't food — there's hardly a gram of flesh on him. It was hate. His desire for revenge. He screwed up today, by going after Fehmer. For us that was lucky. But with our help he'll do it right next time round.'

'So you're not talking about just a straight assassination?' she said.

'Von Westarp's too valuable to kill — you know that. He's got contacts all the way up thanks to the Thule, even if he is currently holed up in the middle of nowhere.'

His wife shook her head, disgusted.

'What's the Thule?' Reidar said, breaking the silence.

'A secret society,' Arne said, still looking at

her. But then he broke away and faced Reidar. 'Politically hardline right wing, with all kinds of mystic rubbish thrown in on top of the Jew- and Communist-hating. Started by a crazy ex-monk by the name of Liebenfels in the late 1910s.'

'Von Westarp would have been a kid back then,' Geir said, turning from the peephole.

'He was,' Arne said. 'The Thule was made up of moneyed Münchners. The von Westarps are mid-level Bavarian aristocracy. London says Gerhard fell for his cousin, the Countess Hella, when he was, what? Eleven?'

'Yeah,' the woman said reluctantly. 'But she was twenty-six.'

'Ambitious,' Reider said.

'Bavaria was declared a free state for a bit back then and ruled by the Communists,' Arne continued. 'In reaction, a whole raft of right-wing societies sprang up. The Thule was one of many. The situation didn't last long, but before the Communists got the boot, they thought the Thule was planning a coup, and their forces raided the society's premises and arrested seven members. They executed them by firing squad in the basement of a Munich secondary school. Countess Hella von Westarp was one of the seven.'

'He's fifteen,' Arne's wife broke in. 'Three years *older* than Ivar, all cut up. No one understands what he's going through. Soon enough he ends up on the doorstep of Hella's Thule Society, He meets the requirements of membership — '

'Three generations of pure Germanic heritage.'

'And an academic by the name of Dr Walther Ziegler takes this highly impressionable kid under his wing. Teaches him what's what.'

'Ziegler's almost as bad as Liebenfels. But more reasonable,' Arne said.

'More science, less God,' his wife said, and then fell to thinking.

'And growing up an aristo, von Westarp already knows there're certain divisions within society. Ziegler shows him that's true not only of society, but of humanity, too, and that's why von Westarp's here. The name Thule, it was a place described by an explorer in ancient Greece, thought to be the most northerly place in the world, full of mountains and blonds. Sound familiar? To the society it represents the birthplace of the Aryan, a mythic land of the pure.'

'So he's a nut,' Reidar said. 'Why does all this make him a target? I mean like a Nazi who we *don't* want to kill? Do we want to get to this Ziegler through him or something?'

'Not Ziegler. It's bigger than that. In 1919, two Thule members called Anton Drexler and Karl Harrer established the *Deutsche Arbeiterpartei*. It was renamed the following year. It became the *Nationalsozialistische Deutsche Arbeiterpartei*. That got shortened to NSDAP, or the even catchier Nazi Party. See what I'm saying now?'

'Who're we looking at?'

'Various prominent Nazis filtered through the Thule at one point or another. Drexler was Hitler's mentor in his early years; Hitler dedicated *Mein Kampf* to Dietrich Eckhart, another member . . . Hans Frank, Alfred Rosenberg, Rudolf Hess, Hermann Göring — the list is long.'

'Holy shit.'

'Yeah,' said Arne. 'But only one man matched Ziegler in his passion for theory, and the doctor saw that his new apprentice Gerhard became firm friends with this guy. Thought he'd be a positive influence on the new recruit.'

'Who was it?' Reidar said.

'Heinrich Himmler.'

'Wow,' Geir said.

'Von Westarp's friendship with Himmler is how he came to be so powerful, so untouchable, playing God in his Aryan bird's nest in the mountains,' Arne continued. 'He's high up in the *SS Rasse- und Seidlungshauptamt*, the Nazi department in charge of safeguarding racial purity, and he can do whatever he wants, wherever he wants, with total impunity. No one's going to stop him, here or in Germany, precisely because of that friendship. So if Himmler plans to come here again, which is likely considering his views on the Norwegians, wherever he is, von Westarp's going to be the first to know. And if we get a man close to von Westarp, we'll know it too. And there'll be no pulling out this time. Because finally our leaders have realized that if they actually want the movement to succeed, then we can't afford to be held back by the threat of repercussions.'

Geir whistled, impressed.

'Shit — I see why you two are leading this troop.'

'London keeps us informed, we keep you informed. That's our job here. Maybe sometime it'll stop being purely about information, and we'll get in on the action. It's about time — '

'What did you mean no pulling out *this time?*'
Reidar said.

'Himmler was here in January, overseeing the Norwegians who were signing up to be members of the *Waffen SS*. We knew his procession route in advance; we had a chance, had it planned, but word came to snuff it before we got you involved. They feared the reprisals.'

'God knows how many they would have killed,' his wife said, looking up. 'They were right to be concerned.'

'The action should have been taken irrespective of ramifications,' Arne said. 'That's how they're thinking these days. It's the only way we'll get anywhere.'

'They're even willing to put the lives of children on the line,' she said.

'He'll be fine,' Arne said, facing her. 'All he'll have to do is keep his ears open for news of Himmler coming, feed it back and leave the rest to us.'

'But now Fehmer knows who Ivar is.'

'He saw him, but he doesn't know *who* he is.'
She looked round at the others.

'There's no way we can entertain this idea. I'm sorry. He's a child. Burning with hate. Who knows what going up there will do to him. You're crazy to even think of it, Arne.'

Her husband looked at her.

'I didn't think of it,' he said. 'You did.'

'What?' Disbelief was audible through the anger in her voice. A frown creased her porcelain forehead.

'You planted the seed, anyway,' Arne went on.

202

'When Britt died and Ivar didn't turn up at the Jensens, you said von Westarp better find that boy or he'll have someone after him for the rest of his life. You remember that?'

'And that got you thinking, did it?'

'Listen,' Arne said, trying again to reason with her. 'With all the theatre of today, maybe von Westarp will hear of it — maybe. But he'll just think the Gestapo killed the boy's sister. God knows they've killed plenty of others. What reason is there for him to think the kid has anything to do with him?'

'Von Westarp isn't a man who forgets, Arne.'

'And that's why we fiddled the records, remember? Ivar Petersen died of hypothermia three weeks after Britt was killed. He's perfect.'

'That was to keep him safe while we looked for him, not so that we could send him behind enemy lines when we did.'

Arne had been bending down, leaning on the table. Frustration made him straighten up and run his hands through his hair, but he held short of letting anger take over. His wife was the leader of the unit. If only for the sake of their relationship, he needed her to approve this operation, and he knew that she was more sensitive than most when it came to the subject of putting children in jeopardy.

He took a deep breath and composed himself. Then said: 'You're not thinking clearly about this. Emotion is clouding your judgment — '

The screech of her chair silenced him. She got to her feet, looking at him sideways, barely even able to do that.

'I'm thinking perfectly clearly,' she said. And then more quietly: 'He's twelve years old, Arne.'

Arne moved around the table. He took hold of her upper arms and turned her towards him.

'But you know I'm right,' Arne said. 'Ignore your personal feelings and think as the leader of this unit. What if it was a grown man we were discussing? Geir, here, or Reidar or Leif. Me, even. You'd say this is an opportunity that won't come again; hard though it would be, you'd send any one of us in. But this will only work with a child. Only a kid will be able to infiltrate. To pick up the information we need unnoticed. And this child is the only one we've got. He's tough. He's committed to our cause, and his hate will make sure he stays that way. But he'll take convincing to do this *our* way.'

'You'll be gambling with his life, Arne. You do realize that?'

'Yes, but we're gambling it against the lives of so many others . . . '

He was slowly succeeding. He recognized the way his wife was looking at him, her body language. He'd seen it before when trying to persuade her to do something she didn't want to do — go to his parents in the country for the summer, skip lectures, make love by the lake in the forest — but there was something new as well. Usually, when the issue at stake was more minor, he was left feeling only slightly guilty — the fruits far outweighing the efforts. But not this time. This time the process was making him feel nauseous. He had never broken her heart before, but that's exactly what he was doing now, and he could see it in her eyes: the sadness, the disappointment.

He lowered his voice and, with a hand on her shoulder, lowered her back into her chair, before pulling the other one up for himself and facing her.

'It'd be for the very highest stakes,' he said.

'He can't be exposed,' she said flatly. It was done. 'Only we can know. We four. London's like a sieve. You can't tell them anything about this. If word got out . . . Only we can know, okay?'

Arne reached across and took her right hand in both of his.

'We'll train him ourselves. You and I. And no one beyond this room will know what's going on. He's already come this far. He's survived everything — remember that.'

'That's what makes him fragile.'

'No, it's what makes him strong. All that hate for this one man, it burns inside him like a furnace in the cold. The problem will come in persuading him to not kill von Westarp when the opportunity arises.'

'But you think it can be done?'

'I know it can. We just have to convince him that the greatest punishment for von Westarp will come in failing his masters.'

'Revenge by betrayal.'

'Exactly. London says they'll — '

'You've spoken to London about this already?' she interrupted, pulling her hand from his, dismay turning back to anger in an instant. 'And after what you just said?'

He nodded, mentally cursing himself. That

little slip could lose her. The face looking at him now was stone.

'You went over my head,' she said.

'I did. I apologize. I'm sorry. But don't let that distract you. They agree that it's more than likely Himmler will come here again, and they approve a plan to utilize that fact. But they don't know about Ivar. It will just be us that know. I won't pretend it's not risky, but surely it's a risk worth taking?'

She shook her head again, composed now.

'Nothing is worth the life of a child, Arne.'

He paused for a moment, but then said, 'Joining the resistance was.'

She had been pregnant when they were approached. He'd asked her not to get involved, but she had proved as determined to fight as he was. One night, after a particularly gruelling operation, he was woken up by a warm wetness seeping across the mattress. It was blood. He had had to wake her up. Since then she had let herself be consumed by the work. Always the work, never allowing herself time to grieve, and for fear of breaking her he had never probed. There would be time for mourning when the work was done, when peace returned.

'You bastard,' she said.

He hated doing it, hated how it made him feel, how it made her feel, but it was the only way he could see. He stared back at her and she looked away from him, the iciness melting into the tears that began to fill her eyes.

'I need a smoke,' was all she could say.

'This is war,' Arne said, taking both her hands

in his, her letting him. 'We didn't ask for it, but we've got it, so we must fight it. So take your time, have your cigarette, take a shot of aquavit if you need one, but then go and talk to him. Convince him. Please.' Arne paused again, hoping she would forgive his next words. 'Try to make the death of our baby mean something.'

★   ★   ★

Following the frame that said 'The End' at the movie's conclusion there was a moment of complete darkness between the screen fading to black and the house lights coming up, and that was when Ivar lurched from his seat. He was running at full pace before Leif even noticed he was gone; halfway up the aisle before the giant got to his feet.

Ivar dashed past the shadowed faces as they creaked from their seats. At the top he slammed into the doors, threw one open and sprinted down the passage into the foyer. He burst out onto the steps outside and flung himself down them, slipping on the ice as he went, falling to his knees and climbing back to his feet again.

Rising, he glanced back at the cinema, at the curved corner steps, the three-storey pillars and the words *Soria Moria* at the top. He knew this place. He was on Vogts Gate. He was in Torshov. They'd taken him north. He could be back at Victoria Terrasse and waiting for von Westarp in half an hour. But he'd have to find a weapon first. Something bigger, nastier than the coronation knife. A gun, or a longer blade.

Just then the deep wail of a foghorn came over the air, all the way up from the water, and he knew just what he needed and where to get it: a docker's hook. He'd be able to slip quayside, onto a ship, and then he would get it right; this time he would jam it deep in that bastard's neck. He'd bleed out in a second.

Ivar heard frantic voices coming from the cinema foyer and broke into a sprint again. He did so without looking where he was going, and slammed into something. It let off a shriek. It was someone. They both went down, and Ivar's head hit the ice on the street.

He sat up, rubbing his head, and looked at the person who had got in his way. It was a dark-haired woman with pale skin, wearing a thick, man's overcoat, her cigarette still smoking on the ice next to her.

'Ivar?' Her voice was familiar. 'Ivar, don't go. Please.' He had heard it in the car. *You're safe now*, she had said. *Safe*. But she didn't say that now. Now her voice was colder, more formal, less comforting.

'I want to talk to you,' she said. 'The man you attacked today — he wasn't who you thought he was. He wasn't von Westarp.'

'*What?*'

'His name is Fehmer. Hauptsturmführer Fehmer.'

'But I — I — '

'I know you must be scared, Ivar — '

He stiffened. 'I'm not scared,' he said.

At that moment, Leif appeared at the cinema's entrance at the top of the steps, flanked by three more men. They were about to carry on towards the pair sitting on the ice, but then the people leaving the movie appeared, flowing out of the exit and crowding down the steps in front of them, and they stayed right where they were, at the top of the steps, watching.

'And I don't want to talk about von Westarp,' Ivar said to the woman. 'I want another weapon. And I want to kill him.'

'We'll arm you, Ivar,' she said, keeping her voice low. 'And we'll make sure you get to avenge your sister's death. But you must do it our way, for the good of the cause. For your country, as well as for Britt.'

'I don't care about my country or any cause,' Ivar said and got to his feet, but he did not move away. He was looking down at the woman, his resolve starting to seep out of him as he spoke. 'Why should I listen to you anyway?'

The woman smiled.

'No reason at all,' she said from the ground. 'But at least let me feed you. Get you back to health.'

'Why should I?'

'Because I told Britt I'd look out for you.'

'What do you mean you told Britt? Who are you?'

'My name is Sofie.'

11

The girl, fourteen, was lying under the snow-laden spruce trees on the ice-caked road in the suburban hills of west Oslo, the falling snow settling with gentle thumps on her twisted legs, on her opened coat and on the immaculate striped dress beneath. The speed of their descent did not increase, but the beat of the snowflakes landing on her hair and angelic face was increasing in volume — *whump-whump-whump* into her open eyes.

Blink, Ida. Blink.

But she did not blink. Her eyes just gazed out, in slightly different directions. Unmoving.

The rest of the scene was just as still, all but for the snowflakes, which drifted down like feathers.

Please, Ida. Blink.

He could see, but he was not in this freezing place. He was floating, impotent, somewhere else, somewhere hot and close and oppressive.

Just once, Ida. Please.

The siren came closer in the black winter afternoon, louder and louder, until it drowned out the pummelling snow.

Please, Ida. Just close your eyes and open them again. Once.

Still nothing but the snow moved.

Come on, Ida. Just give me a sign.

The blizzard got thicker, denser, until he could hardly see through the bright blanket of white, and panic hit, mangling him.

Ida. Give me a clue. Please. Please!

But finally the siren blew him out of there, before it arrived, before anything could be done.

He was in bed. He was sweating — from the dream, from the sun beating through the break in the curtains. He reached out, picked up the phone by his bedside, killing the siren, but not the images that went with it. They were still alive and well in his brain.

'Skarnes,' he said, his dry voice croaking so violently it didn't sound human.

At the other end, a female voice said, 'Wow. You even sound like a dinosaur. You know I really didn't think people like you existed any more.'

'The last of a dying breed, I guess,' Skarnes said, not knowing who on earth this person was or what she was talking about, and not caring. 'Do you mind telling me who the hell I'm wasting my time talking to as I edge towards extinction?'

'Who in this day and age doesn't have a mobile telephone?'

'Someone who doesn't want to be contacted, probably.'

Skarnes tried to sit up, but a weight in his head pushed him back down.

'Who the hell is this?' he said.

'My name is Ingrid Hansen.'

'And who's Ingrid Hansen?'

'A sergeant with Crime Squad.'

Skarnes felt his pulse quicken a fraction. It made his head pound.

'The whole place has already collapsed without me, has it?' he said, without a trace of humour, or conviction, rubbing his temples between his thumb and forefinger, trying to massage his head back into shape. He smacked his lips. His mouth felt like he'd been drinking sand all night.

'No.' She was bemused.

'Then what are you calling me for, Ingrid-Hansen-a-sergeant-with-Crime-Squad?'

'I — '

'Hansen,' he interrupted, licking the fur that he had discovered coating his teeth, and considering the name. 'You're new.'

'That's right.'

'Who did you replace?'

'You.'

He started to nod his head, but stopped. It made his shrunken brain rattle.

'Me.' he said. 'They swapped me for a junior. That's charming. What do you want, Hansen?'

He heard her take in a breath.

'Your help,' she said.

A breath of laughter made it from his lungs, deflecting off the mouthpiece into his nostrils — stale smoke and cheap blended whisky, a smell acrid enough to get him to sit up.

'Hansen,' he said, using the bed sheet to wipe the sweat from his face and chest, scanning the room. 'You took my job.' Amongst the mess, the piles of papers, the clothes, the empties, he spotted what he was looking for — the brown glass of a bottle.

He rose, slowly, and grabbed it. Beer. He held it up to the shaft of direct sunlight coming through the curtains. And half-full. He put the bottle to his lips and pulled at the warm flat liquid. It felt good travelling down his shrivelled pipes. 'And you work with the people I despise most in the world. What makes you think I might help you? Even if I could? Because haven't you heard? I'm a washout. So if you don't mind, I'm going to get back to cultivating the first-class hangover you're interrupting.'

'You *should* help me, you know,' she said, her voice suddenly grasping and desperate.

'Don't you listen?'

'Not really.'

'Well that's one thing you've got going for you, I suppose. Good luck to — '

'I don't listen,' she cut him off, 'and I don't want to be like them, these people you despise most in the world, I mean. They brought me in so they could shape me; to teach me to *fit*. But I don't want to fit. I'm calling you because they've already shut me down for trying too hard. I'm twenty-four years old, Skarnes, a psychology major just out of college. I don't know how this works. You do. And I've got something here no one wants to know about. And that's why you should help me. Because if you do, you'll be sending them a nice big gift-wrapped 'fuck you'. Come on, what else have you got planned?'

Skarnes felt the sun on his face, stronger than he'd ever known it at this time of the morning, at this time of the year. And it was only going to get stronger, each hour hotter than the last. He closed his eyes, trying to bask, but his heartbeat, punching at his skull with its diamond knuckles, came through stronger than ever.

'I'll buy you breakfast,' she said.

He opened his eyes again and caught his reflection in the mirror on the wardrobe. He was backlit, and could only make out his outline, a silhouette, a shadow.

'I'll even come and pick you up.'

'You'll have to,' he said.

★ ★ ★

Having had his arms nearly snapped in two, Curt had discovered that maybe he wanted to live after all, or at least that he wanted to be the master of his own demise. But a couple of splintered radia didn't get you anywhere, in life or in death. Just jelly hands and a lot of pain.

He came out onto the green in front of the police station rubbing his bruised forearms, and, without pausing, started to pick his way through the bodies basking in the heat. Halfway down to the road, he spotted the old man on a bench, lounging with the rest of them. He must have sensed Curt coming, because just then he opened his eyes, and seeing Curt, beamed like he was a father welcoming his son out of Pentonville. Curt sent him back down — to the ground — with an open fist.

'What were they doing there, old man?' he said.

The sudden violence, the aggressive voice, and the old man's yelp as he fell, caused the sunbathers to look their way en masse.

Up on an elbow, the old man wiped his beard and looked at his hand like he thought he might be bleeding.

'You have just been released by the police,' he said. 'You are standing outside a police station. And now you hit a helpless old man to the ground?' He held his hand up to Curt.

'I saw an opportunity to give you what you deserve,' Curt said, looking down at him and taking the hand.

'I don't know why the police were there, Curt,' the old man said, using the hand to clamber back onto the bench.

'But you're here.'

'I got to Youngstorget just in time to see you getting bundled into the police car.'

'Of course you did.' Curt shook his head. 'But I don't care. Because it's over. Just hand over what you owe me.'

The old man reached out his hand and opened his fist. Lying on his palm was the single little nugget of gold. Curt didn't take it.

'You said you had more.'

'No. I said that there *was* more. And there is. I don't have it, but I know where it is.'

'Where?'

'In a wreck at the bottom of the fjord down by Drøbak.'

'What sort of wreck?'

'A Nazi warship. And this is one of tens of thousands.'

Curt shook his head and snorted.

'I'm supposed to believe this?'

'I believe it. I *know* it.'

'Oh yeah? How so?'

'Because the man who was bringing it over during the war gave me this one and told me about the rest.'

'And why'd he do that?'

'He was bargaining for his life.'

★ ★ ★

Less than a hundred metres away, a man wearing a panama hat was sitting on another bench outside Grønland police station, watching the pair with casual interest.

Following a brief stint in the 18th Recon Regiment in Bialystok, Piotr Wojciech moved into the world of security. He started off as a guard in a bank, but soon shifted to the more lucrative, less stringent role of bouncer, at a Warsaw go-go club named *Klub Angelika*. It was owned by *Organizacja* — the Organization. Wojciech worked his way up, proving his worth both tactically and physically, and was head of security by the time he moved again. A septuagenarian near the top of the tree named Wilkowski came to hear of him and put him under the command of one of his lieutenants, a middle-aged man called Wonsowski.

The Organization had operations going in the States, Britain, Germany, France, Italy. Wonsowski was getting sent out to establish a branch in Norway. Wojciech was going with him. This was back in 1994 when he was twenty-five years old.

Not many places are unsullied by organized crime, but Norway during the nineties and the early years of the twenty-first century was as close as you got to virgin territory. When the Organization arrived, the Norwegian people and state had been innocent to the devious minds of organized criminals. Security had been minimal. What's more, oil had made the country rich: for the ex-Yugoslav gangs, the Albanians, Bulgarians, Iranians and, of course, the Poles, it was easy pickings in an unguarded candy shop.

Then, not long after the turn of the century, stories began to circulate — a young Chinese immigrant couple who couldn't pay off their travel-masters turned up in an Oslo apartment, strangled to death with barbed wire; three Kosovans floated up on a kids' beach in the fjord, their ears and noses cut off. Prostitution was hitting a record high, visible on the streets in the form of skinny Eastern Europeans and pneumatic West Africans; drug addiction amongst kids had skyrocketed, as had homelessness and beggary. As the country came of age, the Norwegians fast caught up on the game. The biggest bank heist in the country's history, in which 56 million kroner was bagged, had been a native hit, so too the Munch heist in which three priceless masterpieces were stolen from the National Gallery.

The territory had lost its innocence. Which is how Wojciech came to meet Advance Party Leader Akse in the late nineties.

The Polish old-country powerbase owed their Slovak counterparts for breaking some senior guys out of a Bratislava prison. The Slovak outfit had heard about Norway, how it was the new promised land of organized crime, and knew the Organization already had a footing there. To pay off the debt, in part at least, Bratislava decided Warsaw would help their newly assembled Nordic crew to get started.

This task came down the chain of command to Wonsowski. To start them off, Wonsowski handed the new arrivals some compromising photos of Akse. A married man with a couple of whores at one of Wonsowski's own houses. The Slovaks made the approach themselves. Akse didn't know who they were. He thought they were a bunch of hoods off the ferry trying their luck. He resisted their demands. As a sign of further goodwill to Bratislava, Wonsowski offered to push the politician to pay the Oslo Slovaks the blackmail money they were requesting. Wojciech got the job.

When approached by Wojciech — who, with his monotone bass voice and ice-cold manner, had never been considered a hood, even when he was one — Akse asked outright what would happen if he continued to resist paying. Wojciech didn't need to explain to Akse the chain that had brought the two of them together. He just told him that if he didn't pay up it would reflect badly on everyone involved, which no one wanted, least of all Akse himself.

Akse handed over the cash later the same day, but also persuaded Wojciech to give him his number. Soon afterwards Akse called Wojciech up and asked him to do a little digging. Wojciech

218

passed it by Wonsowski. Wonsowski passed it by Wilkowski back in Warsaw, and Wilkowski okayed the move, passing Wonsowski information pertaining to a shipment of dope. Wonsowski passed it to Wojciech. Wojciech passed it to Akse, and the Slovaks were imprisoned for the cocaine racket they were setting up before it even got going. Akse's picture featured in all the papers, so he got to look strong, and suddenly his party was on the up. The set-up was good for Wonsowski because he got rid of the new rivals he'd been forced to help establish, without a bit of dirt falling his way. And for Wojciech it was the beginning of a lucrative relationship — Akse paid him more for the lowdown on the Slovaks than Wonsowski paid him in a month.

Wojciech liked working with Akse. He had money, of course, and he paid well. He was also a little afraid of Wojciech, and didn't expect violence as a matter of course. If at all possible, he wanted to avoid it, in fact. Akse merely needed his problems solved, to be neutralized. If his problem was a person and that person suddenly disappeared, that led to questions. The sort of questions politicians didn't like. So he paid more to avoid them.

This was a situation that suited Wojciech. The older he grew — and at his next birthday he'd hit the big 4-0 — the more he became a man of figures, of probabilities, and it was plain to him that the fewer people you killed the less likely you were to go to jail for murder. Twenty-one years was the maximum sentence in Norway, with no capital punishment, but his pa had died

219

at fifty-eight and Wojciech didn't fancy dying inside. But of course, fulfilling his contract had to take precedence. If he failed to do so, he would stop being called on, and the link to the political classes was one Wonsowski, and Warsaw, valued highly. If no other method was available, therefore, Wojciech was still quite willing to kill.

Today all this presented him with something of a dilemma. Akse's successor wanted Henrik Bonde dealt with. Normally this would not have been a problem. Wojciech was very effective at persuading people to reconsider their positions. But this case wasn't so straightforward.

Wonsowski had an ambitious son, called Cezary. Wojciech had heard through the grapevine that Cezary was working a deal off his own back, trying to impress his father, and the whole camp back home, show them all he was fit to take over the Norway operation when the time came for old man Wonsowski to step aside. Cezary'd met Bonde through one of his contacts in the police force. Bonde was looking to take power. He had the support to take it within his own party, but needed to make such a takeover stick. That meant he needed to prove a success in the general election. He wanted enough votes to see him into parliament as prime minister. Cezary told Bonde he could supply them. Fifty million kroner. It was pocket money for what it was buying, but that was sort of the point. This was about having the leader of the country over a barrel, and keeping the amount low would make it easier for Bonde to make himself their man. Bonde would know they couldn't just kill him if they wanted to retain influence, though, so they needed something over him. Something concrete. They had to be able to threaten something more powerful than death, and that something was ruin. He'd paid his 5 per cent deposit by drop-off. The rest would be made in person and the meet, set for an abandoned brewery next to the river north of town, would be photographed from four angles. That way, if Bonde got tricky in future, they could start the squeeze. He would be their guy until the end of time. A good position for the Organization to be in. One that, Wojciech admitted, it would be worth ditching Nygard for.

Wojciech had heard Cezary had spent months, and a lot of Organization money, collecting the votes. Students, addicts, the disaffected — they were all willing to sell; and union leaders were happy to exchange wads of cash for wads of member ballot papers, it turned out. Altogether it was looking like a smart move that *would* impress Warsaw — but only if Bonde came through with the money. And despite the amount, that was increasingly looking like a big 'if'. Bonde'd already missed several meets. And now the elections were tomorrow. He had until midnight. Today was his last chance. And it was Cezary's last chance, too. If Bonde failed to pay, Cezary couldn't just *give* him the votes. Wonsowski's kid would be lumbered with a stack of out-of-date ballot papers and a lot of explaining to do. He'd kill Bonde certainly, but that would only be temporary relief from the shit that would fall his way. And his dad's.

But that was midnight. A long way away.

Bonde still had time, and Wojciech did not want to screw it up for Cezary by dealing with Bonde for Nygard. He'd find out, and whatever Wonsowski thought of either of them, only Cezary was his son. If Wojciech messed up the kid's big move, Cezary would make sure he ended up out in the cold. And Wojciech didn't fancy being left out in the cold. But nor would Wonsowski be too happy if Wojciech lost them their only current political contact. Nygard was useful. And Wojciech had the relationship. He'd cop the blame if Nygard cut loose due to failure to deliver.

It was a tough call, and sitting on the bench outside the police station, Wojciech still didn't know which way to go.

The young black guy who had been taken in by the cops for approaching Bonde on Youngstorget and the old white guy he'd met up with afterwards were still talking when Wojciech clocked the pair of uniforms chatting at the entrance to the station, trying to look like they weren't talking about the sideshow. They both practically stuck their heads in the ground when Bonde suddenly strode out of the building's exit right next to them and started across the green. One of the uniforms moved zigzag from tree to tree after Bonde. The other uniform remained in place at the station entrance. Bonde didn't notice either of them. He'd looked wired as he passed Wojciech's bench; worn out.

Wojciech stood, strolled down to the road, got in the Thema and followed both Bonde and the uniform back to Youngstorget. It looked like the cop was tailing the politician, because when Bonde

222

entered the party building, the cop started walking a beat around the square, round and round.

Wojciech sat in the driver's seat of the Thema and waited.

★ ★ ★

The uniformed police officer who remained at the station entrance after Bonde took off was Constable Kai Kobberrød. Kobberrød was twenty-nine years old. He'd been on the force for seven years and was still a constable, but he wasn't bitter. He wasn't too bright, but he had other things going for him. Looks, for one. And physique. He kept himself fit; he'd appeared in the force's charity calendar for each of his seven years, and had even done a little professional modelling — shirt-off, catalogue stuff mainly. But he liked the police, he liked the army-style uniform, and so did Karin, his girl.

Kobberrød knew exactly who Sergeant Hansen was. He didn't like the way she had got her job any more than anyone else did, but he understood how things worked, and the few times he had dealt with her she had been civil. And while Karin was a babe, Jesus, Hansen was something to see, and *that* he really could appreciate. Frankly, he could look at those almond eyes, those high, sharp cheekbones, and those perfect lips all day long. Even the mole high on one of her cheeks was perfect, the speck of imperfection that gives a face character.

Not that Hansen was short of that — character. News of her bringing Bonde in unnecessarily,

223

and making the arrest, had already filtered throughout the force, and Kobberrød liked her style. He
could picture them in a spread together: 'The
Face of Oslo Police' — guns, uniforms, pecs,
stockings. Sweet.

The courthouse was a good gig. Flirting with
the woman lawyers in their suits was fun; but
even better was getting them *out* of those suits
and down to their black lingerie — always black
with lawyers. But lawyers spent most of their
time in court, and standing around all day was
boring as hell when no cameras were flashing,
which was why he'd agreed to leave his post and
help Hansen.

Besides, what could possibly go so wrong that
the others assigned to the court today couldn't
handle it? If doing this for Hansen led to him
dealing with her more, following this couple of
dudes awhile was worth the risk of a dress-down.

Pulling out his phone, he snapped a picture
of the old man and the black guy and started
keying in the line 'let me know if you need
more'. That was pretty smart, the double meaning. He wondered if she would get it.

Kobberrød hung back near the station, and
kept watching. When they moved, he would
move. For Hansen. He hit send on his iPhone,
and the photo took off into the ether.

★   ★   ★

'Well I think it's great, Atle,' the caller was
saying. *'It's high time something was done about
immigration in this country. Stoltenberg just lets*

224

them stroll in. I'd vote for Nygard, and I'd vote for Bonde.'

'What do you say to that, Bernt?'

'I'd just like to say that I don't like any of them, Atle — Nygard or Bonde or the Advance Party. But you can't help but feel sorry for Nygard on this. He's done a lot for Advance, and now this could end it for him, for the whole party . . . '

'Bernt, Kalle, we'll have to stop it there. Thank you both for calling in. So, listeners: Henrik Bonde, can he do it? Can he take the Advance Party into parliament? Or is he ruining the whole game for them? Your views, on Oslochat FM, after this from — '

Skarnes lived up in the Ryen district, in the northeast of the city. Hansen was sitting in her car outside his apartment block. She switched off the radio when the door to the block opened.

What she knew about Skarnes's daughter, Ida, was common knowledge. Just fourteen years old, she had turned up dead on the side of a respectable residential street in the west of town, knocked down and killed by a car while coming home from school one evening two winters ago. The driver had hit and run. No witnesses. The culprit was never found. Oslo Police wasn't so big that a story like that didn't get passed round. It was pretty much the only piece of Skarnes's story Hansen could consider concrete. Apparently he was meant to have picked his daughter up that day, but didn't because he was working a case. His wife left him soon afterwards; that too was true, but some versions had the split coming because she blamed him, others because he had turned to prescription drugs and alcohol to numb the guilt, others still because he had started getting unpredictable, violent even.

Who knew which was true? If any. Apparently it was the violence and unpredictability that had got him the boot from the force as well. One interpretation said he had lost control in the Pit, while another said it was all cooked up, that they were looking for a way to get him out. Hansen thought most likely it was a combination — they were looking for a reason and he served one up.

Skarnes pulled open the door of Hansen's 240 Volvo and slumped into the front passenger seat. The rush of air that came in when he slammed the door shut carried the smell of booze to Hansen's nostrils in a sudden rush, and it was all she could do not to slap a hand over her nose.

'Inspector Skarnes,' she said, holding out a hand. 'I'm Sergeant Hansen.'

Under a crumpled grey-black herringbone jacket, he was wearing a blue shirt, unbuttoned to his breastplate. Returning his gaze, she saw eyes that managed to look bloodshot and jaundiced at the same time; sleepy, melancholic. His cheeks were crisscrossed with thin veins and his lips were cracked. He was slim but out of shape, his jawline sagging into jowls.

He took her hand. His was clammy and cool.

'*Ole* Skarnes,' he said, then pushed sweat-wet strands of hair back over his scalp. 'The squad car budget's all spent, is it?'

Even Skarne's breathing was heavy and nasal. He was shaking, quivering all over, almost imperceptibly. The constant tremor of burnt-out neurons never given the chance to re-grow. Such an injured creature, Hansen understood, had to be handled carefully.

'She's mine. I've already signed out two tails for this under Halvorsen's name. A car, and he might start wondering.' She patted the wheel. 'She'll do the job. So, Ole,' she said, smiling and putting the Volvo into gear, like the prettiest, most amenable taxi driver in the city. 'Where are we going?'

'Bislett,' he said, leaning back on the headrest and closing his eyes. 'Sofies Gate. You can tell me what you've got on the way.'

12

After what Ivar had done to Fehmer, the city was no longer safe for him, and that very night, Sofie and Arne Stornes took him from the Soria Moria cinema to a single-roomed cabin in the forested hills north of Oslo. As Ivar slept under a blanket in the back seat, the couple established their plan of action. They made one small alteration to what they had agreed in the cinema storeroom. As well as Geir and Reidar, they would have to let two other people in on the scheme: Svendsen and his wife.

The following morning, with the moonlight still filtering through the trees and the small square window into the musty timber room, and Sofie still asleep, Arne woke Ivar. The man's hand remained on the boy's shoulder, preventing him from getting out of bed.

'I know you want to avenge Britt,' Arne whispered to him. 'And I understand that. I want to avenge her myself; she was like Sofie's surrogate child, but I need to explain something to you, so listen carefully. This resistance we're running here has finally got organized. It's called *Milorg*, and we're all over the country; we're in touch with the government-in-exile in London and the King and the British SOE and SIS. Some of us commit acts of violent sabotage and

228

assassination; but we also have people who are trafficking men and women out of the country and moving arms, and plenty more fighting through civil disobedience — printing and distributing illegal material, like Britt was doing. But what all these people need, what the Allies need to win this war, is *information*. Intelligence is the fuel of the anti-Nazi war effort, and that's what the XU does here in Norway. We gather intelligence. That's how we'll win the war, and that's how we'll get von Westarp, because he isn't like you or me, Ivar. If you just kill him, he'll think he's dying because he failed. He believes only inferior beings fail, and that inferior beings do not deserve to live, so if somehow you ever find yourself pointing a gun at his temple, don't expect him to beg for his life, to cry out apologies for his sins. He'll demand you pull the trigger. But if you kill him, you'll be doing him a favour. So ask yourself this: where is the vengeance in killing a man *asking* you to take his life? Ivar stared at him through sleep-filled eyes.

'But there is a way to take vengeance on a man like that,' Arne continued. 'If you really want him to pay for what he did to Britt, then you have to make him betray his masters. Use him and use him. And when he can be used no more, show him what you've been doing. Then, when you see the look in his eyes, you'll know you've succeeded and he'll probably *beg* you to kill him. But you won't, because you'll know that survival will hurt him more than death.'

Ivar rubbed his eyes in response.

The boy looked weak and helpless lying there,

his eyes jerking around like a feral cub.

'You'll be safe here, Ivar,' he said. 'They won't find us — no one but us even knows we're here, and no matter who they are, no Nazi can ever understand or survive in these forests and mountains like we can. They're in our blood. Our bones, down to the marrow. But this isn't going to be easy, on any of us. This is a small cabin. It's going to be cosy, and it's going to be tough, I give you my word. And it's going to take time, time that'll take us out of the loop and prevent us from fighting. All I want from you today is a promise — your word that you'll see this training through. That's all. If you can't give me that, we can leave right now, and we've wasted no time.'

Ivar's eyes had stopped moving and settled on Sofie, stirring in the bunk the couple shared. Then he looked Arne in the eye and nodded.

'I'm in, Arne.'

'Then let's eat.'

★ ★ ★

As the three of them sat at the table between the bunks, eating a simple breakfast of bread and cheese, Arne began to lay out what the immediate future held for Ivar.

'We'll start with German language. It's the most important element of your training. You don't have to pass as a native, or even be fluent. You just need to be able to comprehend what you hear. If you can't understand what he's saying, what others are saying to him, can't read

230

his letters, there's no point you being there. Sofie's fluent and knows all the Bavarian dialect inflections, accents and phrases that the target's likely to use. When you're not learning the language, I'll be taking you skiing while the snow's still on the ground, then running when it melts. We need to build up your strength, so it'll just be a little each day to start with, but as you get stronger we'll increase the distances and the pack-loads. We want you fit and strong by the time you go up. That way you'll be more likely to appeal to von Westarp. It will make it easier to get in, but also it'll help keep your mind your own. Von Westarp's working on his own out there, so Terboven, Rediess — the hierarchy in Norway — have nothing to do with him. We're looking for personal communication with Germany, that's all — information pertaining to friends coming here, the top echelons of the Nazi Party. I'll teach you how to communicate this information to us.'

'Until any information comes your way, you'll be entirely safe,' Sofie interjected.

'That's right. You won't be sending out anything that might compromise you. Just innocent letters, in order to keep the lines of communication open.'

'Only we two, Geir and Reidar will know about you, Ivar,' Sofie said. 'Plus one other couple. Tord Svendsen and his wife, Marit. We tried to work it so they wouldn't know, but there's no way. Letters are the only way to do this safely, and Svendsen's the only one who ticks all the boxes. He's got the real history to

231

make things stand up. Svendsen's sister and her husband were killed in a boating accident five years ago. They had one son, Snorre, about your age. He was born in May 1927 — eighteen months earlier than you — but that'll be fine. The food shortage is taking its toll. Kids' growth is slowing down everywhere. When his parents died, Snorre went to live with Tord and Marit, but when the Nazis arrived, the couple shipped the boy out to his father's family in America. We've changed the records. For all intents and purposes, Ivar Petersen no longer exists. If they ever happen to look, the Germans will see that he died of hypothermia soon after Britt was killed. And Snorre Nilsen didn't go to America. He's still living with his Uncle Tord and Auntie Marit, and you're him. Only with their daughters and his business, pretty soon Tord's going to find he hasn't got the space or the time or the money for you. So you'll get sent to Marit's sister Heidi and her husband Johann Gulbrandsen out in Voss. Their niece on Johan's side, Tone, already works at von Westarp's Dove's Nest. Tord will suggest she finds you a position there. Heidi and Johann can't afford to keep you any more than Tord can. They're only taking you in because Tord's telling them wartime Oslo's no place for a boy your age. They won't know you're not Nilsen. Only Tord and Marit will.'

Sofie looked at Ivar. Already he was looking exhausted, and it wasn't yet 11 a.m.

'We've got pencils, paper and not a distraction for miles around,' she said.

'I'll go and find us some more wood while you

232

two start on the German,' Arne said. 'We'll ski this afternoon.'

★   ★   ★

The big, ornate grey stone building at 8 Prinz Albrecht Strasse in Berlin was the headquarters of the *Reichssicherheitshauptamt*, or RSHA, the Reich's Main Security Office, of which the Gestapo was a part. The man reading a letter at his seat behind the Chippendale desk in the best of the wood-panelled offices carried a deep scar across his face. He told people it was the result of a duel he had won as a student. The truth was more mundane — a schnapps-induced car accident — but no one was about to question him: he stood at six feet seven, but more than that he was SS-Obergruppenführer Kaltenbrunner, *Chef der Sicherheitspolizei und des SD* — top dog in the whole building. Himmler was his direct superior. Himmler's boss, the Führer himself, was looking down at Kaltenbrunner from a gilt-framed canvas above his head.

The letter Kaltenbrunner was reading was from a nobody Untersturmführer stationed in Oslo called Bitzler. The letter was hand written and addressed personally to the Obergruppenführer. This was in contravention of protocol. There was a structure to be followed. Bitzler should have written to his direct superior, and the information contained in his letter would move up the tree, each boss deciding if it was important enough to go one higher. Untersturmführers didn't go about writing to Obergruppenführers as though

233

they were penpals. Even if he thought an Ober-gruppenführer might give a damn about what he had to say. By writing the letter straight to Kalt-enbrunner, this Bitzler was risking everything, and he'd have known it, too. If Kaltenbrunner disapproved, he was out, finished, one more dead German private on the eastern front. But if Kalt-enbrunner approved, then his rise could prove fast.

Kaltenbrunner admired Bitzler's balls. He liked the gamble he was taking. All or nothing. It was the sort of brawny manoeuvre the Reich was being built on. But more than that, Kaltenbrun-ner admired the Untersturmführer's insight.

The structure of the enemy's intelligence outfit in Norway, the XU, was narrow. So far as they could tell, very, very few knew the identity of the people calling the shots. For obvious reasons it was a closely guarded secret. It was also, for similarly obvious reasons, a secret Berlin wanted to get their hands on. In their hunt for those senior members, they had only one clue, one name, probably a codename at that. *Sofie*. And they weren't getting anywhere with it.

Kaltenbrunner had heard the stories going round the building about what had happened with the kid in Oslo. Bitzler said in his letter that he had watched the whole scene. Whilst doing so, he thought he had also observed something else. Something much more interesting. But he was worried.

The Gestapo's top man in Oslo, the star of that piece of theatre, was effective, there could be no question of that. Hauptsturmführer Fehmer's sadistic reputation had made him a figure of genuine fear throughout the country, infamous for his viciousness and cruelty. Kaltenbrunner thought the stories were probably exaggerated, folklore always was, but even so, he had to admit that building up a culture of fear like that was no mean feat. But while Bitzler was admiring of Fehmer in his letter, he made it clear that he believed that his superior officer's techniques were to the detriment of his intelligence gathering. A man like Fehmer is rarely a man to gain access to the innermost sanctums of the enemy, the letter implied, and that was precisely what Bitzler hoped he was in a position to offer. Thus he was asking Kaltenbrunner to send someone in from the outside. Bitzler had chosen his words carefully — there was nothing that could be construed as insubordinate — but in effect he was saying that on this occasion he thought somebody steadier was required at the helm.

Kaltenbrunner put down the letter and picked up the telephone. The possibility of locating 'Sofie', and what she might lead to, justified the affront to Fehmer, he had decided, and he knew just the man for the job.

'Get me the Teacher,' he said into the receiver.

★ ★ ★

In the month that followed Ivar's arrival in the forest, the basic Phase-1 training regime was adhered to. In the morning, Arne woke Ivar and together they went through the reasons for what

235

they were doing. After a couple of mornings, Arne got Ivar to put it into words himself, and as the weeks progressed, Arne allowed the boy to whittle and hone the information into his own mantra. Soon Ivar was opening his eyes and immediately speaking the words:

'The Nazi does not fear death. The Nazi fears only his master. Only by making him fail his master, will I bring the Nazi to disaster.'

Arne liked it for two reasons. First the vague and childish rhyme made it easy to remember. Second, Ivar of his own accord had decided to call von Westarp simply 'the Nazi', dehumanizing him, making him just an object to be used, not a man with a name to be hated.

Breakfast followed the recital, study with Sofie followed breakfast. After lunch Ivar trained with Arne. When that was complete, he went through his back-story, and they both blasted him with questions. After supper, exhausted by his day, Ivar retired, Arne prompting him to recite the mantra a final time before putting his head down. Once he had gone to bed, Arne and Sofie went to sit under blankets outside, Sofie smoking her cigarettes. Ivar could hear the murmers of their voices from inside, but not the meaning.

About a month into his training, Arne and Ivar were skiing through the forest. Sliding down a valley side to a frozen, snow-covered stream, Ivar slipped and fell sideways into the snow. Already up the other side, Arne watched the boy struggle to get to his feet. Ivar swung his skis round so they lay parallel, gathered up his poles and pushed them into the snow, and when they

236

gained purchase against the ice of the stream beneath, he began to hoist himself up. Halfway, one pole, fast followed by the other, shot deeper through the snow. They had pierced the ice.

Ivar looked to Arne for help, but the older man remained watching from the top of the bank. Now it had been broken, the ice beneath the snow — beneath Ivar — began to creak. The boy retracted his poles and jabbed them into the snow again. But as soon as he laid any weight on them, they sank once more. Anger and panic began to rise in Ivar, and he began to stab the snow with the poles at random, hardly waiting to see if he could raise himself. Still Arne observed him and soon Ivar was flailing. With the added movement, the ice gave way beneath the snow even more and Ivar began to sink. Seeing this, Arne removed the length of rope from over his shoulder and was tying it round the trunk of a tree, when from behind him he heard Ivar's voice whispering to himself.

'*The Nazi does not fear death. The Nazi fears only his master.*'

Arne turned. Ivar had stopped thrashing and had flipped himself onto his belly. He was shivering, but managed to thread his hands out of the loops of the pole handles and was moving his fingers down the pole shafts. He took hold again at the base of each, then he reached out and dug the sharp metal point of one through the snow of the bank into the frozen earth, and pulled. He repeated the action with the second pole, then again with the first, hand over hand, until he had dragged himself all the way up the bank to Arne, each jab and pull emphasizing his words: 'Only by making him fail his master will I bring the Nazi to disaster. The Nazi does not fear death. The Nazi fears only his master.'

At the top of the bank, he pulled himself to his feet, using a narrow spruce trunk for support. Breathing heavily, he glared at Arne in triumph. Then skied off further into the forest.

That night the murmurs coming in to the hut from outside sounded different to Ivar. Where days before Sofie had been content, as happy as Ivar had ever seen her, that night he heard alarm in her tone.

The conversation, whose specific meaning Ivar could not hear, started with Arne saying, 'He's getting much stronger, you know.'

'He's doing well,' Sofie replied, 'but he's still weak. It takes time to get back nine months of living on the streets. And he's growing so fast, like he really is playing catch-up. What we're able to give him isn't enough to sustain that sort of growth. He needs meat.'

'I know, but there's nothing around. He gets his protein from the cheese and beans. And oats. They keep him going. He's fine.'

'He's as skinny as a rake, Arne.'

'Boys that age are meant to be skinny.'

They were quiet for a time, both of them gazing up at the moonlight filtering through the snow-laden pine trees.

'You know,' Arne said at last. 'We were skiing today, and he fell, got stuck in the snow. He couldn't get up and was beginning to panic. But do you know what he did?'

'What?'

'He controlled it.'

'Good for him.'

'I know, and do you know how he did it?'

She looked at him.

'The mantra. His funny little song. And by the end of it he was up and skiing again.' Arne paused, then said: 'He's ready, Sofie.'

'No. He's not ready. He's too weak. He needs more time.'

'Maybe ready's the wrong word. He'll never be ready. But he's as ready as he'll ever be. And time is not a luxury we have.'

'No, Arne. You can't. It's too early. We'll lose him.'

'No we won't.'

'It'll undo all the progress we've made.'

'You won't let it, Sofie. This needs to be done.'

★ ★ ★

The next morning, Ivar was awoken earlier than was usual — not by Arne speaking his name, but by the shock and force with which he was pulled from his bed by his feet, through the cabin and out into the snow. Ivar was tossed face-down in the cold before he knew what was going on, and spun round to see the black leather boots, and the black plus-fours and uniform jacket of an SS officer. Beneath the cap he saw the face of Arne.

Ivar burst out laughing.

'What the hell are you doing, Arne?' he said. 'You — '

But he did not have time to complete his

sentence before Arne grabbed him by his hair and lifted him to his knees.

'Ow! That hurts, Arne. Let go.'

'She begged for her life, you know?' Arne said in German.

'What do you mean?' Ivar said, the amusement vanishing from his face.

'Your whore sister.'

'Arne, what are you doing?' The look on Ivar's face was confusion now, but already Arne saw that it was slipping into anger.

'Before she died, she begged like a dog to be spared.'

And there it was, uncontrolled rage, looking him right in the face.

'It made watching her die all the more enjoyable.'

Ivar suddenly came to life, and lunged at Arne, but Arne just slapped his face and sent him to the ground again.

'And do you know why she had to die?'

Ivar was lying on the ground, Arne's blow, the confusion, the rage, all combining into a surge of power that made him jump to his feet and launch himself at Arne in one movement, like a cat. But Arne simply stepped aside, tripping Ivar as he went, and Ivar landed back in the snow.

'Because she was worthless. And so are you.'

Ivar lay there steaming for a moment, and then flipped onto his back. Arne, the Nazi, whoever the hell he was meant to be, was gone.

Ivar clambered to his feet and found his way into the cabin. Sofie was waiting for him with open arms. Arne was nowhere to be seen.

240

The exercise was repeated irregularly over the next month or more. Ivar never knew when it was going to be. Arne no longer lived in the cabin. He was only the Nazi, sporadically appearing. The taunts came. The goading worsened. But eventually Ivar became capable of just standing there, allowing the jibes to pass him by unheard, repeating in his head: *The Nazi does not fear death. The Nazi fears only his master. Only by making him fail his master, will I bring the Nazi to disaster.*

And from the window of the cabin, Sofie watched as a wild, angry boy in need of care and affection became a numbed, gangly adolescent; and as she watched, the knowledge and regret that she herself had sanctioned the transformation grew inside her like a cancer.

★ ★ ★

One morning, when the snow was receding and the first green of spring was sprouting from the suffocated earth, Ivar came out of the cabin to see Arne sitting in the driver's seat of a Dodge sedan, picking at his teeth. He wasn't in uniform.

'Get in,' he called.

Ivar did not move.

'The Nazi's gone,' Arne said. 'We're moving on to the next stage, okay? Come on.'

Ivar walked to the car, opened the passenger door and sat next to Arne.

Arne looked at his own hand. In it he was holding a strip of black material.

241

'When a Viking boy came of age,' he said, 'his father would blindfold him and lead him into the forest as the sun was rising. The pair would walk for as long as the sun was visible above the mountains. When it disappeared over the ridge, they stopped walking and the father turned his son to face due east, kissed his forehead and returned home, leaving his boy standing there in the forest. The land was wild with bears and wolves back then, but the boy didn't move, he didn't even take off his blindfold until he felt the warmth of the sun on his face the next morning. He did this because he knew that if he could resist the desire to see, he would learn to control fear, the sort of fear that, as a man and warrior, he was certain to experience in battle.

'When finally he did take it off the next day, he could easily have found his way back to his village — even a boy your age would have been able to read the stars back then — but that wasn't the challenge his father was setting for him by leaving him out there. The challenge was survival, pure and simple. The boy knew his father would return to the very same spot after three moon cycles. If his son was there, alive, he would be able to call himself a man and fight for his people.'

Arne raised the material, but Ivar flinched away from him.

'The Viking's son became a man at the age of twelve, Ivar. You were thirteen this year. You've got a year on him. Now, I won't leave you out here for three months — we haven't got that long. But I'm not going to tell you when I'll be back, either. You've got to learn to survive, on your own, surrounded by danger.'

Ivar allowed the material to cover his eyes. He felt Arne tie it off. Then he heard the engine start. They drove for nearly twenty minutes, Ivar guessed. Then the engine cut out. His door was opened. He was raised from the vehicle and his blindfold was removed. Ivar waited for his eyes to adjust. The pine trunks of the forest came into focus. It was dusk. His vision fully cleared and he realized that the lie of the land was completely foreign to him. The rock formations. The trees. He couldn't recognize any of it. This was the forest, certainly, but not part of it he knew. He turned. Arne's car was not on a road, or even a track, and he saw that Arne was already back in the driver's seat, leaning from the open window.

'Good luck, Ivar,' he said, then backed up, turned the car around and drove away.

Ivar was utterly alone, without food, without water, without shelter.

The first night, Ivar sat beneath a pine, shivering in the darkness and listening to the forest come alive. The day that followed he looked for food but found none. By the third he was consuming leaves and insects, his starving mind giving fearsome images to even the most innocuous of night sounds. On the fifth night, this reached its apotheosis.

Just as on the previous nights, he was leaning against a tree trunk with his knees drawn up to his chest. Every rustle from the woods, every flutter and every shriek unnerved him. He had eaten some ants, a moth, some algae, some moss, some black berries he hoped were elder, but his stomach remained empty and bloated as a balloon, and rumbled like a storm was brewing inside it, as it had so often during his months living on the Oslo streets. Nonetheless, his head eventually began to loll, his eyelids to sag. He was just about to drop off at last, when a scuffing sound in the darkness shocked him into wakefulness.

It had been close by.

It still was.

He could hear the breathing of a creature, and now the shuffle of steps, then out of the darkness came the misted breath and at last the lumbering, dense form of a brown bear.

Ivar remained completely still. He did not move. He just watched the animal carry its enormous, powerful frame towards him. A bear like that could take his head off with a single blow. He knew fear was the natural reaction. But his pulse wasn't racing. His breath wasn't shallow. He was perfectly relaxed. Rather than terror, a sort of euphoria of calm had overcome him. As it put its enormous head before his and snuffled its great, rough wet nose up his neck and across his face and hair, it was as though the creature was drawing panic and fear right out of him.

For a few seconds, the bear stopped smelling him, stopped moving, and looked at Ivar, its slow, warm, acrid breath condensing on his cheeks.

Ivar looked back, into its dumb, indifferent eyes.

Then the bear turned and wandered back into the darkness. Ivar watched it go, then wiped his hand across his face. Next thing he knew, he was waking to the morning sun.

Ivar could recall the look of total, indisputable and unassailable power in the animal's eyes, yet he was not certain the encounter had actually taken place in the physical world at all. But real or hallucinatory, the memory of the experience, and its effects, would last longer than any other part of his training. It was a moment that Ivar would recall and draw on frequently for the rest of his life, but he never mentioned it to a soul — not to Sofie, and certainly not to Arne when he returned in the Dodge after ten days, to find a boy grubby, cold, torn, and yet somehow alive and well.

Ivar was sitting precisely where Arne had left him, his blue eyes staring out from behind the dirt entirely without expression. He stood and approached the car.

He was only a little shorter than Arne now, 170cm maybe. He was lean, fit and strong for a kid his age. Not powerful, but resilient. He had been linguistically prepared, debriefed, desensitized, and was in control of his emotions and instincts. He was ready to be put into play, in a role that might turn the tide of the war in Norway.

* * *

Arne did not want to run the risk of travelling into Oslo with Ivar: if any of them were

245

recognized, it would put the others in danger, so they said their farewells there in the forest, as the sun of early summer was beginning to warm them.

In the cabin, Arne hugged him. Ivar did not hug him back.

'You've done well, Ivar,' Arne said. 'But now you're going to do better. Just you remember — '

'The Nazi does not fear death.' Ivar's voice had broken into a deep monotone. 'The Nazi fears only his master . . . '

'Only by making the Nazi fail his master will I bring the Nazi to disaster. We all have to make sacrifices, Ivar. Whether we know it or not.' Arne smiled and let him go. 'Good luck. Just keep your head down, let them come to you, and you'll be fine.'

Sofie was waiting for Ivar outside. Geir was sitting in the Dodge a little way into the woods. He was to drive Ivar to the outskirts of Oslo, from where Ivar would go on foot to the train station.

Sofie took him by the hand and began to lead him over.

She did not say anything at first, but then she stopped in her tracks and turned Ivar to face her.

'Be careful,' she said, holding his face in her dirty and cracked hands.

Ivar placed his hands on her shoulders. She had been the single sympathetic female face and voice he had known since Britt had been killed. The only one he now knew.

'I will be,' he said, trying to form a smile. 'It'll be okay. *I'll* be okay.'

'Just remember,' she said, drawing him close to kiss his cheeks. 'Write to me, at least once a week. You'll have to fill the letters to Tord with something, and the words you write, they'll be coming to me. And the letters you get back, they'll be *from* me. And if you have any suspicions — the first sign of danger — you get out of there. Into the mountains. These idiots couldn't ski if their lives depended on it.' They both smiled. Then hers faded. 'If nothing comes to the museum for more than a week, I'll know to come and get you.'

She kissed him again, and shoved a small bundle of oiled rags into his hand. It was heavy.

'It's a .38 Colt snub-nose. A Detective Special, like from the movies, you know? They call it a belly gun. If you have to, don't hesitate for a second, you understand?'

Even though they were out of earshot of both the cabin and the car, she had dropped her voice to a whisper. She stuck a finger into Ivar's stomach, mimicking the employment of the weapon.

'Just go like this and pull the trigger.'

Ivar nodded and slipped the weighted oil rags into his pocket.

Sofie let him go and watched Ivar walk to the Dodge. He got into the passenger seat and Geir dropped the clutch. She watched the car until it was out of sight.

13

Late-braking, swinging the corners, high-rev gear changes — she could drive, but none of it was doing Skarnes's head any favours.

'That's pretty thin,' he said, once Hansen had laid out how the morning had gone down — the anonymous call, the official reaction, the take-down, the interview, the humiliation and lastly her call for help.

'So can you explain why Bonde let him go?' she retorted, without taking her eyes off the road.

'I don't need to explain it to believe there's nothing strange going on. There could be any number of explanations, from Bonde needing the bathroom, to having a meeting, to wanting — '

'Or there's something going on.'

'It's one of about four hundred on the list of possible explanations, and right at the bottom.'

'So you want me to turn around?' she said, glancing at him as she took a right.

'I didn't say that.'

'So you're going to help me on this? Despite its 'thinness'.'

'A gift-wrapped 'fuck you', isn't that what you called it?' he said, grabbing the handle above his head as she swung into a particularly acute turn. 'Involving me might not end up doing you any favours. You understand that, don't you?'

She pulled up at some lights.

'I understand that. But if there's nothing to it, it won't be a fuck you. It'll — '

'Just prove that neither of us is meant to work the rest of our lives under Egeland.'

She shrugged, eyes on the red lights.

'It'll do,' she said, then the lights changed and she moved the car off.

He recognized the brazen disregard for authority, the young, eager eyes always looking forwards, never backwards, and he could feel the smile creeping onto his face, creasing the skin in a novel way, just as some outer-space beep emanated from somewhere in the transmission tunnel. Not loud, but just the right pitch to tear through his head. The smile fizzled as soon as it had appeared.

'What time did you get to the Pit this morning, Ingrid?'

'What?' She frowned, but still kept her eyes on the road.

'What time? This morning.'

The beep came again. It echoed in Skarnes's head. He knew old cars made odd noises — clunks, rattles — but this wasn't mechanical. It was futuristic. In a mid-nineties Volvo?

'A little after seven. Why?'

'And you live where?'

'Up in Grünerløkka. A studio. It's not much but it keeps me and Mister — '

'So you were up this morning at what? Five-thirty?'

'Five. I went for a run.'

'And did you shower afterwards? You know — to wash the sweat off?'

'Of course.' The frown was turning into mystification.

Beep.

'A lot of soap, then?' Skarnes said, trying to ignore the noise, sounding like the very thought of Hansen in the shower had aroused him. 'Steam? You're naked? Rubbing yourself all over?'

She sighed. 'Not you as well. If we're going to work together — '

He shook his head, eyes closed, partly because there it was again, shrilling through his mind: *Beeyeep*; partly because she wasn't getting it; partly because he knew he couldn't carry it off.

'That's how they talk to you,' he said, changing his tack.

'What?'

'Hansen,' he said. 'You're ambitious. You want to make it in Crime Squad. That's why you've called me in, isn't it? So you could show them you're more than they think? That you should be measured on your police work instead of your cup size?'

'I guess.'

Skarnes shook his head again.

'No. Again. More decisive this time.'

'Yes. That is what I want,' she said, enunciating every word.

'Then take it from me: do not under any circumstances arrive early again.'

'Why not?'

He gritted his teeth through another pulse. The sound was making him short-tempered.

'I just tried to show you how the minds of Squad men work. And it makes you look naive, which you are, and it's charming — too charming. How long have you been in the job now?'

'Nearly a month.'

'Long enough to know that in Crime Squad you don't want to be charming or naive. Arrive late, Sergeant. On time if you're really pushing a case. You want to prove yourself, stay late.' He looked at her. 'You're a beautiful girl. Anyone can see that. On the street, the catwalk, it might do you some good. But in the Pit, it's a handicap.'

'You're lost on police work, Skarnes,' she said, raising an eyebrow his way. 'You should get into self-help writing.'

'I'm just saying,' Skarnes said, eyes front, irritated, the sound there again, feeling the sting of her remark's implication — why would anyone take life advice from him? 'You need to wipe the slate clean and realize that if you do anything that could be construed as actually caring about your appearance you won't be a policewoman. You'll just be a woman, and fair game.'

'Why don't we stick with the police work to start with, all right?' she said, prickling.

'Fine,' he said. 'The first principle of detection is *work the evidence*. And work it and work it, until something gives. If there *is* any evidence, of course, and not just a hunch, which is what you have. So for now we follow, and see where it gets us. I'll take Curtis, you can take Bonde — And what *the fuck* is that Goddamned noise drilling in my head?'

'It's my phone.'

'Persistent. Why don't you answer it?'

'I like to see a man in pain.' She pulled up at another set of lights and reached into the console and looked at the screen on her phone. 'It's a message. From Kobberrød, the man on Curtis. A photo.'

She tossed the phone into Skarnes's lap and moved off the lights.

Rubbing his forehead with one hand, he picked up the phone with the other. The screen showed a green lawn covered in sunbathers — he recognized it as the one outside the police station. Amongst the sun worshippers were a couple of bedraggled men, one young and black, the other old and white, conducting an apparently animated conversation. Skarnes stopped rubbing his head.

'That's Curtis on the left,' Hansen said. 'I don't know who the other one is.'

'I do,' Skarnes said.

★   ★   ★

'Even if I believed you, old man — which I don't — there's no way I could get down there, if that's what you're proposing here. I'm a half-decent diver, but there's no way. So I guess it's just the one piece.'

Curt reached for the nugget, but the old man wrapped his fingers round it again and leaned back on the bench.

'If you *want* the rest, you won't need to dive for it.'

'What's that supposed to mean?'

'The man you tried to rob for me — Henrik Bonde — he knows of the gold's location, too. That's what I had you trying to steal from him. I couldn't try to take the envelope myself. He knows me. And this is a small city. For a man with that many friends in the police, I'd be easy to find. If someone completely unrelated stole it, he'd have no reason to seek me out. If you'd got the envelope, he wouldn't have been able to get the gold up; but as it is — '

'He could have made a copy.'

'No way Bonde was going to let anyone else make a copy.'

Curt shook his head in disbelief.

'And how do you know all this, old man?'

The old man smiled.

'I gave the envelope to his delivery boy this morning.'

Curt smiled, too, now. It was amusing, but a little pitiful.

'Why tell him where this gold is if then you're going to steal the information back off him? You're a little mixed up, I'm afraid. Nice try, though.'

'I wanted to die free.'

'What's that supposed to mean?'

'He got me out of prison. The deal was that when he did that, I would give him the location of the gold. Had I the chance, I would have vanished, but they were there right out of the gate.'

'Prison, huh?'

'Yes.'

'So why go to him in the first place? Plenty of

people would be interested in gold. Influential people. Why not ask them for help?'

The old man stared out beyond Curt for a moment, drinking in the sun. At length, he said:

'Because only someone like Bonde would be willing to deal with someone like me.'

'You're talking in riddles again. What do you mean, *someone like you*?'

'My so-called crimes are not of a sort most who can influence a parole board would want to risk association with. Bonde's an old-fashioned, far-right politician, Curt, sympathetic to the cause I was supposedly fighting for. That's why he was willing to help me, and that's why he can't win this.'

'What were you in for?'

'Treason.'

'*Treason?*'

'They said I betrayed my country to the Nazis.'

★ ★ ★

'This country is sick.'

The cameraman slowly pulled focus from Aker Brygge, the rejuvenated dock area, bustling with boats and people basking in the morning sun, and the politician in the foreground grew sharp. The camera was angled slightly from below. Bonde's chin was set — strong, stern, determined — but his eyes were pained. The impression created could not have been bettered. This was a statesman for the modern era, the images said, a man of conviction and power, saddened by the current state of his country's affairs, but resolute

254

in his desire to see them changed for the better.

'It needs to be healed,' he went on. 'Labour and their coalition have proved weak, slipshod and indecisive. They have had their chance. It is clear that only one party has the policies that constitute the medicine required and the will to implement them — the Advance Party. Unfortunately, as I have toured the country over this last fortnight, people have been coming to me, people from all walks of life, people of all colours, people of all political persuasions. And what have these people said to me? They have been saying, *Henrik, please help us.* No one can deny that Karl has done a fine job, but sometimes, in order for the correct medicine to be administered, one must change doctors. We need more decisive and wilful leadership. *Henrik Bonde*, they say, *your country needs you*, and that is a call I could not ignore. I have been asked to challenge Nygard for leadership of the Advance Party, and today, though it pains me to lay down a gauntlet to a man I respect so much, I see that I must think first of my country and its people.'

He looked directly into the camera now.

'If you give us your mandate, I will lead the Advance Party into government, and the country to peace and prosperity. I will . . . '

Schloop. With one brisk nasal intake, the first of the two lines he had cut out on the mirror went up the rolled hundred-kroner note. The powder combined with spit and mucus and, sitting up, he could feel it trickling down his throat, the familiar bitterness, the immediate raid

255

on his bloodstream, the instantaneous confidence, the knowledge that he knew best.

Henrik Bonde was in his office at party HQ. He was sixty-four years old. He and cocaine had been introduced to one another by one of the roadshow secretaries in the mid-eighties, at his fortieth birthday party, and they had proved close friends ever since. Only in the last year had they become business partners. Bonde's political career had been in the doldrums. But as plans for his domination of the Advance Party and Norwegian political life strode forward, so his intake grew.

The police station hadn't been the place for a top up, of course, and the lines he'd taken in his cabin on the ferry were long gone, but he had still been riding a high all morning. This was the biggest day of his life, after all. Adrenalin was pushing him on. After treading water for so long, after all the work that had gone into setting this up, the whistle had just been blown and today was the day it all came in: at the same time as staging a political coup that, if successful, would see him leading the Advance Party into government, he was organizing a crew of international mercenaries to haul a load of gold out of the sea in order to pay off gangsters who would make sure the coup was successful.

But he knew endorphins alone wouldn't be enough to see him through. Moving the note to his other nostril, he bent again and, *schloop*, line two was gone and it was time to get on with the job at hand.

He put his hand in his left jacket pocket. It

was empty. He checked the right. Also empty. Inside, both sides. He pulled out his wallet, a screwed-up Kleenex, but no phone. He checked his trousers, too, then grabbed his briefcase and opened it. More papers fell out, including the envelope, but no phone. He rifled the inside pockets. Nothing. His phone was gone.

He massaged his temples and tried to remember when he had last used it — the police station? The café? He hadn't used it in either place, as far as he could recall. The ferry. He must have left it on the ferry. He grabbed the landline off his desk.

It took his secretary a moment to pick up in the next room.

'Eli,' he said.

'Mr Bonde?' Eli said. 'I have Prinsdal from VG on one, *Aftenposten* on two, Margaret Gulstad at TV2 on three, a whole raft of your fellow politicians vying for your attention, and Mr Nygard's tried three more times.'

'Who's keen?'

'Well, you knew Strandberg would be with you from the start, Bøhler too, I think.'

'He hates Nygard.'

'That's good enough.'

'You're right. Who else?'

'Gunnar Saxegaard sounds interested, but he'll play it safe until he knows which way this is going to go. And it sounds like Nivestad is potentially open to persuasion, but she was playing it close with me. Have you started thinking about a cabinet?'

'Come on, Eli.'

257

'Of course you have, but you need to make the calls. And soon. They need to feel like they're first on your list. The faster you do it, the greater the number of people who will feel that way. Time is of the essence.'

'All right, Eli,' he said. 'Just give me a couple more minutes then we'll start fielding. In the meantime, find me a phone, will you?'

'What?'

'A cell. I left mine on the ferry. Call them up. It'll be in my cabin.'

'This is going to be the busiest day of your life, Henrik. You're going to need your phone.'

'You don't know the half of it, Eli. So find me one, okay? I need to be mobile. Redirect the calls from my number to the new number. Got that?'

'Okay.'

'As fast as possible, Eli.'

He hung up with his finger and punched a number into the keypad. After four rings, a recorded voice told him he'd got to the voicemail for Matthias Eggen — the political editor for the TV News at NRK, the national broadcasters.

'Matthias, this is Henrik Bonde,' Bonde said. 'I want to offer you an exclusive interview for tonight's news. To get it you'll have to sign off on at least five minutes. Call me back if you're interested.' He jerked his left fist into the air, sliding his shirtsleeve back over his watch-strap. 'You've got half an hour. Then I'm calling Gulstad at TV2.'

He replaced the receiver, then picked up the envelope, unfastened it and pulled out a single piece of A4 paper. He lifted the lid of the fax next to his iMac, placed the paper face-down on the glass, dialled a number then hit send. As the machine whirred and scanned, he took up the phone receiver again and dialled another number. It was answered before the second ring.

'Are we ready?' a voice said at the other end, in English, but tinted with a Provençal accent.

'I'm sending it through now,' Bonde said to Broussard, just as his second line started flashing. 'Get moving as soon as it arrives.'

★ ★ ★

Georges Broussard, the owner of that Provençal accent, had worked for Total and Elf as a diver; then, when a serious case of the bends permanently surfaced him, as a dive-team leader. The contracts for that dried up after he lost a man — the corporate ones anyway. Salvage and excavation had become his game next, as a freelance private-dive coordinator, bidding for jobs then putting teams together. This world was far less regulated than oil, and there was a wealth of former rig divers looking for a quick bit of danger money. Broussard had positioned himself as the go-to man for both divers and clients. Even though he'd moved off the rigs, he confined himself to working with ex-rig divers. He and his business partner, Pierre Fallon (who was permanently surfaced after diving too frequently at Exxon), had never gone military before.

A recommendation by Himberg (for which Himberg would receive a 2.5 per cent commission) had bagged Broussard and Fallon the Oslo contract. It was a good gig. Two hundred and fifty thousand dollars for one wreck dive in the fjord, if they surfaced with a haul of gold. A quarter of a million for half a day's work.

Broussard had put the job out to tender through the usual channels. Two or three groups he was familiar with had submitted for the same amount — 125K — 50 per cent — but one offered a pedigree the rest could not match. Lieutenant Colonel Henry Henderson was ex-SBS, and would bring with him five more from the same stable. One of whom, Archie Jones, was his nephew. He also had two Dutch ex-MARSOF men, de Veer and Klandermans, a former South African Commando called Palmer, and a Bulgarian with time in the Black Sea Sharks by the name of Bukhalov. This was a ninety-metre dive that required men willing to work without permits or insurance. For a group such as Henderson's, these conditions were the norm. Military precision, Broussard and Fallon agreed, could prove no bad thing under such circumstances.

Broussard met Henderson once before the job, in London, in a fancy restaurant on Piccadilly — the Wolseley — to discuss the intricacies of the operation. Georges, with his sailor's visage, build and manner, felt like an impostor amongst the bankers and Bond Street shoppers in the cut-glass eatery. Henderson, on the other hand, with his Sandhurst voice and tidily parted blond hair, was fitted to the surroundings as well as his tailored suit was to his lean and wiry frame. He had an easy charm about him, too, but behind the smiles the waiting staff received, Georges noticed that the man's blue eyes were entirely expressionless, dead, yet all-seeing, and when you knew he had been SBS, you knew too that they were the eyes of a cold and calculating killer of men, and not at long range with a rifle, but close, with a knife, his bare hands even; eyes that had seen, and had grown accustomed to seeing, life drain from another human.

This chilled Broussard somewhat, but also convinced him that Henderson was the man for the job, and he had not mentioned his impressions of the dive leader to Fallon on his return to Caen.

The next time Georges had seen Henderson was in Drøbak, one week ago. Henderson had arrived in a forty-five-foot blue-hulled dive boat called the *Penguin II*, along with his men, equipment and enough weaponry to fight a small war — to cover any eventuality, foreseen or unforeseen, Henderson had said. Georges and Pierre had exchanged raised eyebrows over the arsenal, but had not discussed it. Both knew these were not the kind of men one fired from a job, and anyway, there was no time to rearrange. The dive was imminent. Or at least they'd thought it was.

For the last week all twelve men had been living on the *Penguin II*, mooching around the fjord on the *Chick*, a twin-engined Revenger, which the *Penguin II* had hauled behind it, as though they were on a fishing expedition. The *Penguin II* was a tight fit for that many men, and the longer the wait went on, the less convincing they became as a group of friends gathered for a jolly.

The call from Bonde came as a welcome relief and Georges, Pierre and Henderson were on the bridge waiting for an image to materialize out of the fax machine.

As they waited, Georges had begun to fret about the clouds beginning to show in the sky.

'If it's a storm, Henry, in this humidity it could get rough. I'm not sure we can risk it. And I don't like doing it in daylight, either. The currents down there are strong enough without having to worry about the atmospheric pressure and traffic up here.'

'Georges,' the Englishman said, leaning on the console. 'I quite understand your reservations, but jobs like this are always laden with risk — it is the nature of our business, you know that. One of my roles is to weigh one risk against another. Think of it like this: we are not being paid by the hour here, and three of the men on this boat are wanted by authorities in three different European countries. Every moment we remain here constitutes an increase in risk, far outweighing that of the weather, or indeed a few motorboats, and as such, I determine that the sooner we complete, the better it will be for everyone involved. We — '

That moment the fax started whining and the three men watched an intricately drawn diagram of a battleship edge out. It showed a side view and a plan. A thick cross marked the centre of both. Georges shook his head.

'That is too deep into the wreck. The risk is too great.'

'It is the divers who will take that risk,

Georges. I lead those divers, and I say we dive
— immediately.'

Henderson reached across Georges and tore
the sheet off the roll then plucked the tannoy
receiver from the console.

'Get ready, gentlemen,' he said, his voice
amplifying into every cabin on the boat. 'It's
time.'

★   ★   ★

Bonde switched lines with a couple of taps.

'Eli?'

'I have Eggen.'

'Put him through.' Bonde waited a second,
heard the click, and the change of background
noise. It sounded like he had NRK buzzing. 'So,
do you want it, Matthias?'

'What are you doing, Henrik?'

'You'll just have to wait and see, Matthias. Do
you want it?'

'Of course we want it.'

'The full five minutes?'

'I can offer you four. That includes our run
time.'

'Leading?'

'After the floods.'

'This is less important than some water on a
different continent?'

'Tragedy sells, Henrik. You go second. Unless
you can pull something else out of the bag before
eight p.m.'

'I'll see what I can do.'

'Where do you want to do it?'

'Ullevaal Stadium. And I can't go out live. We'll have to lag it. I'll be there at seven fifteen. Get there early, too.'

'Why?'

'I'm a busy man, Matthias. I've got somewhere to be at eight.'

Bonde hung up, and waited for Eli to come back on the line.

He didn't have anywhere to be. There was a match at Ullevaal tonight. Kick-off was at 7.45. By eight the area around the stadium would be deserted. At 7.15 it would be throbbing with fans. If Bonde chose his backdrop carefully, dropped a few thousand kroner in the right hands, the crowds would make it look like he was on the campaign trail, that he had the sort of rabid support that in reality only sport could muster.

'Mr Bonde?' Eli said. 'Nivestad's on three.'

Bonde pressed a button that was blinking its LED.

'Aase?'

Aase Nivestad was one of the new breed, a female version of Nygard. They were the golden couple of the party. But there were rumours of bitterness on her side. A couple of years older than Nygard, she had wanted leadership for herself, but had had to step aside for Akse's golden boy and settle for Deputy Leader, a nothing position. To the public, watching on television, she just appeared to stand in Nygard's shadow looking pretty, like the First Lady of the Advance Party, when in fact she was one of *the* driving forces of the new look, and the party members knew it. It would be a coup if Bonde could get her on side. She killed two demographic birds with one stone. With her aboard, Bonde would show he had won over both the female contingent and the modern. Nygard would vanish, melt into his Jaeger suit.

'You've got some balls, Henrik Bonde.' She wasn't entertained, or impressed. She was stating facts.

'Why, thank you.'

'I'm not going to piss around, Henrik. Who have you got?'

'Bøhler, Saxegaard, Fuglestveit — '

'I mean who that matters.'

'Okay,' Bonde said. 'Kaland, Iversen, Strandberg. I just got off the phone to Wik — '

'Did you say Iversen?'

'I'm a thorough man, Aase. You know that.'

'That conniving little fucker.' Now she sounded impressed.

'No — just sensible,' Bonde said. 'He knows I have the backing of our members.'

'What are you offering?'

'You're in?'

'That depends what you've got to offer.'

'What do you want?'

'Foreign Office.'

'Aase, it's yours.'

She was silent for a second. Then she said 'I'm in' and hung up.

Bonde hung up with his finger, kept it down for a second, enjoying the moment, then released it again and got Eli.

'Eli, find me Magnus Iversen's cell number.'

After a couple of seconds she recited a number. Bonde hung up and hit the digits on the keypad.

'Yes?' Iversen's voice came.

'Iversen?' Bonde said.

'That's right,' came the reply. 'What can I do for you?'

He didn't sound right.

'Is he in the room with you?'

'That's right. Very busy.'

'How is he?'

'But we're quietly very confident.'

'Good.'

'Really?' His voice didn't relay an ounce of concern — he was making out that the caller had imparted some information of mild interest. Probably he was raising his eyebrows at Nygard and whoever else was in the room.

'Relax, Iversen. If he thinks he's untouchable up there on the fifth floor, we'll just let this play out. That arrogant bastard doesn't know what's about to hit him. Just make sure he keeps his confidence. Everything's going according to plan here. Sit tight. If I need more from you, I'll call. If he plays any more, call me. Otherwise, I'll see you in parliament.'

He hung up and got Eli again.

'I'll take Nygard now,' he said.

He waited.

'Henrik?'

'How are you, Karl?' he said, kicking back in his chair, but leaning forward again almost immediately.

'What are you doing, Henrik?'

'I'm saving the country, Karl, and our party along with it.'

'You're killing both of them.'

'I'm doing what you will never do,' Bonde retorted, suddenly sharp. 'I'm going to lead us into government.'

'Don't be a fool, Henrik,' Nygard said with an annoying calm. 'It's not too late. The situation can still be rescued. You still have time to back down. We can sell all this as a simple misunderstanding.'

'This country is an orphan child, Karl,' Bonde said, as though addressing a crowd rather than an individual on the other end of a telephone line. 'Wandering into the dark. I want to adopt it; and lead it into the light.'

'You may have the media panting like dogs, but don't bother me with your cheap parlour tricks, okay? Just understand that it would be in all our best interests for you *not* to run as leader, will you?' He paused, then added, 'And that includes yours.'

That was more like it, Bonde thought. Nygard was resorting to empty threats. Bonde turned to look out across the square, the people walking across it. Tomorrow their world would start to change.

'Leadership's over for you, Karl,' he said. 'Take it with grace and I'll find you a cabinet position.'

'Fuck you, Henrik.'

'Fuck me?'

'Fuck you. And don't say I didn't warn you.'

Bonde was still laughing to himself a full ten

seconds after Nygard hung up. To hear Nygard panicking felt good. That's when you see the real mettle of a man — when he hits the ropes. And Nygard was unravelling; Bonde had heard it in his tone.

★ ★ ★

'But you didn't betray your country to the Nazis?'

'No,' the old man sighed. 'I didn't. I was working *against* them. That's why I've got to stop Bonde getting this gold. He's no better than they were.'

Curt shook his head. 'Old man, why would I believe anything you say?' Curt placed a foot on the bench now, leaning down towards the old man. 'The last time I did what you suggested, I ended up arrested, you remember?'

'I did not know the police would be there, Curt. I give you my word.'

'Then why did he have me released? If he's this hard-right immigrant-hating figure I've been hearing about, me robbing him's a golden opportunity.'

The man shrugged, delighted.

'Because he doesn't want the attention, of course. Because of what he's about to do. He's been waiting for this for a year. I don't doubt everything has been ready and arranged since the day my release date was confirmed. Plus the news is saying he's challenging for leadership. The day before elections. That's highly irregular. I wouldn't be surprised if the gold had something to do with it, would you? He's bringing it up today. He doesn't want to change his plans because of you.'

'I don't know,' Curt said, trying to fight temptation. 'How do I know I'm not a patsy for some plan you two have going?'

'I suppose you don't,' the old man said. He opened his hand again and raised the nugget to Curt. Curt took it, heavy in his palm like a little weight ball. Even if everything this old man was saying was rubbish, which it sounded like, could it hurt to check? What did he have to lose? And thousands of nuggets the same as this one? That was something to gain.

The old man could see in Curt's eyes that he couldn't resist, and smiled.

'Gold does funny things to a man, doesn't it?' he said. 'Millions of pounds, Curt. Think about it.'

Curt closed his fist.

'Drøbak, huh?'

'That's right.'

'All right. Show me.'

★ ★ ★

Asking a man broken by the death of a daughter for assistance and then mocking him? Hansen regretted her joke about Skarnes writing a self-help manual almost as soon as she'd made it. But thankfully the picture Kobberrød had sent had made Skarnes forget about it. He was too busy to think about the misguided humour of a person he'd just met — busy staring through

269

the windscreen, trying to extract all the information he could from a head swimming with self-administered poison.

'You don't recognize him?' he said.

'No. Should I?'

'That's Snorre Nilsen.'

'The Nazi guy?'

'They must have released him under a false identity or it would have been all over the news.'

'What exactly did he do?'

'Doesn't your generation know anything?'

'He's history.'

'He was turned. Became a sympathizer during the war. A colluder who gave up his own people to the Nazis. Imprisoned for treason as a war criminal, they say he never repented. Certainly he didn't like it when his old comrades did, when they started cooperating to reduce their sentences. He saw it as weakness and killed them off, one by one — shoelace, belt, length of wire, anything he could get hold of, his bare hands if necessary. He was a maniac.' Skarnes looked at the photo some more, then said, more quietly, 'I can't believe they let him out at all.'

'What?' Hansen said.

'I said he makes your hunch a bit more interesting,' Skarnes answered. 'Suddenly we have something that looks a little like evidence. Circumstantial, but still evidence. So work it. Question: Why has Nilsen linked up with Curtis?'

'Why are they trying to attack Bonde? And why won't he press charges?'

'Does this picture look right to you?'

'What do you mean?'

'Is Curtis not the last person you'd expect a man like Nilsen to be associated with?'

'Maybe.'

'So what are they up to?'

'You mean Curtis could be a fall guy, and it's Nilsen and Bonde who are really working together?'

'Why not?'

'Cooking up some election-day excitement for the Advance Party, you mean?' She shook her head. 'It doesn't run. He didn't press charges. Anyway, Bonde's all over the news today. That would be a small distraction at best, compared to his challenge for leadership on the eve of the election. If he's working with Nilsen, for Bonde it has to be worth gambling everything on. He's going to be on every front page in the country tomorrow morning. Yet he risks associating himself — and his party — with a war criminal, a traitor, a Nazi, for God's sake.'

Skarnes was nodding, and went on with his line of thought.

'If it leaks, it'd finish him, the party too if he wins leadership. His votes would drop like rain. But this picture was taken right outside the station. Nilsen was waiting for Curtis to get out. He knew he was coming. He knew Bonde wouldn't press.'

'Which adds to the likelihood that they're somehow working together,' Hansen said.

'So what are they up to? Why *would* Bonde risk it? What's in it for him?' Skarnes pointed at a road running to their left. 'Up here.'

271

'You interested now?' she said, taking the turn. Skarnes was smiling again.

'We'll let it play.' He pointed at a car. 'That's me.'

'The Merc?'

'Yeah.'

Hansen pulled up behind it. Beige, formerly high-range, now used, the paintjob cracked, the exhaust sagging — the 1982 230CE looked a lot like Skarnes in sedan form.

'Call in, will you?' he said, climbing out. 'I need to know where to find Curtis.'

14

The western seaboard of Norway is so island-rich that it looks like it has shattered, as if the country suffered some kind of colossal impact in its formative years. The point of that impact could have been the Sognefjord. This waterway cuts into the country like a jagged axewound for more than two hundred kilometres. Further inlets run off it like runaway ice fractures. One of these is the Nærøyfjord. Here, mountains thousands of feet high shoot vertically out of inlets only a couple of hundred metres wide. Johann and Heidi Gulbrandsen's home was in a small village called Gudvangen at the very end of this fjord, sitting by the water at the foot of a mountain. At the very pinnacle of that mountain, above the village, commanding views up the waterway in one direction, and across the peaks and valleys of more mountains in the other, was Dueredet — the Dove's Nest.

The three-storey main building was constructed in the traditional Norwegian fashion. Stripped, interlocked pine trunks formed the outer walls. They were dark brown, almost black, treated against the weather with some kind of creosote stain. The window frames were white and small and regularly spaced. The roof was steeply pitched and covered in shiny black tiles.

The place had been a convalescent hotel until the Germans took over, built on the top of the mountain for the air, and named for the birds that roosted there. What made its appearance different from most other buildings in the region, other than its size and the drama of its views, were the elaborately carved flourishes sprouting forth from the top angle of the pitched roof, like dragon's tails curling up from under the eaves. This throwback to Viking ship figureheads, coupled with the location, gave the place a sense of wonder, of unreality, as though a big boat had somehow been stranded high up a mountain after a monumental flood.

Johann Gulbrandsen and Ivar were coming up the footpath from the village on foot. It was May 1942, six months before Ivar's fourteenth birthday. A good layer of snow remained on the ground, but the bright high sun was melting it fast. Nearly at the top, Johann, a beefy fisherman to whom everything seemed to be an irritant, struck away from the path and led Ivar across country, until they hit an icy gravel drive that ran away from the former hotel down the other side of the mountain. Ivar could see the road snaking away into the distance. Closer in, only a little way down, was a second building, a single storey, with a number of doors divided in two on the horizontal. Stables. Above it was the dovecote. But he didn't see any birds, or any horses. Just two offroad Kübelwagens parked outside, a six-wheeled Mercedes G-4 next to them, itself parked in the shadow of an Opel Blitz personnel carrier.

The other way, the way they were walking, the drive led up to a flight of twelve steps, which in turn led to a heavy wooden door, which led into the main building.

Other than the vehicles, the two German soldiers stationed either side of the door were all that suggested the place was no longer a convalescent hotel. Stopping at the foot of the steps, Johann told the soldiers why they were there. The soldiers looked sleepy, indifferent, and one of them raised a hand. Johann stopped explaining. The other soldier pulled a rope behind him and Ivar heard a bell ring somewhere inside.

A few seconds later the door was pulled open by a solid, middle-aged and grave-looking woman dressed in a long-sleeved, long-skirted, all-white nurse's uniform. She didn't say a word, just looked Ivar over for a moment then nodded and held out her hand. Ivar looked at Johann. Johann nodded, too. Ivar went up the stairs and into the building.

Through the door was a hall. To the right were two more doors, both shut. Straight ahead was a broad stairway doubled back on itself to the floors above. There were additional closed doors either side of the main stairway, one to the left and one to the right, with a soldier standing outside the one to the left. Between that door and another one immediately to the left of the front door was a large fireplace that warmed the whole building like a heart pumping blood around a body. Apart from the grey stone of the hearth the whole place was painted a dazzling white.

'My name is Frau Gärtner,' the woman said in German, standing in front of Ivar now. 'Tone is this way.' She led Ivar through the door to the left of the front door, and along an equally white corridor. 'Tone will explain your duties here. You will do them. You will stick to them. You will work hard. You will not roam, in or out of the facility. Sundays will be your own. Leisure activities — sport, games, hiking, will be overseen. Since you will not require money while working here, your earnings will be sent home to your family.'

At the end of the corridor she opened another door. The kitchen was beyond, another white room. Four women were bustling around a large central table and a large stove. A door led outside and was manned on the exterior by another pair of soldiers.

Frau Gärtner stopped inside. Ivar did too. The four women turned to look their way. Two were middle-aged, two young. One of the young ones — slim, blond and pretty in a stern sort of way — came forward.

'Snorre?' she said.

'Tone,' Ivar said.

* * *

Once Frau Gärtner had gone, Tone removed her white apron and said 'Follow me'. She took Ivar back along the corridor to the hall and up the stairs. The wood was painted white all the way up. They bypassed the second floor — a white landing with white corridors running right and left — and carried straight on up to the third, which was built into the slant of the roof. Its layout was the same as the one below. Tone led Ivar along the corridor to the right, also white, to a room at the end — his bedroom, evidently, white and slant-ceilinged on three sides. Ivar dropped his bag on the white floorboards and only then, with the white door closed, did Tone start to talk.

'I'm sorry about your parents, Snorre. My mother died, too. My father, Johann's brother, is all I've had for a long time, and because of that, I want to get one thing clear here, okay? He's old, my father, frail. The money I earn here at Dueredet is the only thing keeping food in his belly. Do you understand? You may be family, but I don't know you. My father raised me. If you mess this up, they'll get rid of us both. And I won't let that happen. So don't go around asking questions and poking your nose into what doesn't concern you, all right? Just do your chores and keep out of sight.'

Ivar sat on the bed. There was a white chair in the room and a chest of drawers with a small mirror on the top of it and a small window looking out over the mountains.

Tone smiled.

'I'm sure we'll be friends. I just felt we needed to get that clear. Okay?'

'Okay.'

'So to your duties,' Tone continued, her tone light now. 'Dueredet is a maternity home now. A happy place.'

'Then why the soldiers?' Ivar asked.

'As you can imagine, not everyone thinks Norwegian women should be communing with Germans. The guards are precautionary. Women come here in the early stages of pregnancy, but only very few stay for the duration. We only have ten bedrooms, each with two beds, so there's not much room, but there are plenty of other homes. Staff sleep up here — that's you, me, the three ladies you met downstairs, and Frau Gärtner has the room at the far end of the corridor. There's a washroom and WC next door to my room. The soldiers are in the stables, and the mothers' rooms are down on the second floor, along with one birthing room, two bathing rooms, two WCs and one nursery. On the bottom floor we have the kitchen, a laundry, separate leisure rooms for staff and mothers and a dining room for mothers only. Staff eat in the kitchen. The guards do everything over in their own quarters. We deliver their food. The mothers' sheets are changed twice a week, staff and guards' once, and the babies' every day. You will strip the beds, remake them, then take the soiled sheets to the laundry where you will wash them, then you will hang them on the lines at the back of the building. And then there are the nappies.'

'Nappies?'

'Maternity homes contain babies. So far we have seen three pregnancies to birth. Their mothers nurse them to six months, but once weaned, the women depart.'

'They are taken from their children?'

'The women leave them here. And happily. We do not have facilities to let the mothers stay once their babies have been weaned, but our nursery is sizeable, and life for the babies will be better here than any the mothers could hope to provide on the outside. There is no war at Dueredet, Snorre. It's maybe the only peaceful and happy place in the whole of Europe. The babies will be safe here. And the mothers know that. We will care for them as long and as well as we can. But like all babies, the Dueredet babies soil themselves. You will wash and soak the nappies once they are soiled.'

'Overall it sounds like I'll be kept busy,' Ivar said.

'If boys get bored, boys get curious, and while this a happy place, Frau Gärtner runs a tight, and strict, ship. We adhere to the rules here, so for the good of us both I'm going to make sure you don't get bored.'

'What about correspondence?'

'Letters, you mean?'

'Yes.'

'You're free to write letters if you have anyone to send them to. Frau Gärtner can supply stamps.'

'I brought a supply just in case.'

'Then you won't need hers. But your letters will still be checked before they go out. The soldiers post them in Voss. So just make sure you keep things happy and vague. Like I said, we don't want any trouble. Understood?'

'Understood.'

'Then let's get to work.'

★ ★ ★

Half Ivar's duties were to take place on the second floor. Coming down from the third floor, the white corridor to the left was the longer of the two, and ended in a window which lit twin lines of doors, five on each side. Behind each door was a bedroom. Each bedroom was as white as the rest of the place and contained two beds. Each bed contained one pregnant Norwegian woman. A couple looked set to burst, a couple were hardly showing, while the rest were somewhere in between. All were in their late teens or early twenties. Most were blond, some just fair, and a couple were a little darker. All were pretty and healthy. Tone told Ivar he was to strip the bed sheets and remake the beds when the women were eating or taking the air or washing or being medically checked. Each time Tone opened a door, she wished the women a good morning, and again when she closed it, but she did not introduce Ivar to the women.

She then led Ivar into the opposite corridor. This one was shorter than the other, and ended in a door instead of a window.

'Your duties on this side involve the three rooms on the left only. None of the others. Come.'

Arriving at the last door on the left, Tone raised a finger to her lips before opening it.

The curtains were drawn. The room was a dim grey. In the gloom, Ivar could see three cots lined up against the far wall. Numbers were stencilled on the headboards in black paint — 1, 2 and 3. Ivar moved forward and saw three babies asleep, each a different size. 3 was small,

280

still gulping in its sleep like a just-hatched bird. 2 was a little larger, 3 a little larger still.

'There's room for plenty more,' Tone whispered. 'And that's where their nappies go.' She pointed to a pot next to a changing station. 'Empty it three times a day.'

The next two rooms were washrooms. They contained tubs, sinks, a shelf full of towels and a basket. Each towel was used once before being placed in the basket. Ivar was to empty it once a day.

Tone showed Ivar the WCs, which he was to clean daily, and then took him back downstairs. The guard who had been standing by the door between the fireplace and the stairs had gone. Tone showed Ivar the rooms to the right of the front door. The first was the dining room for the women. A large, white, heavy dining table took up much of the space and the windows looked down on the fjord far below. The second room was a leisure room, with similar views, containing three card tables and shelves of games and books. The door to the right of the stairs was a cupboard for coats. The doors along the corridor to the kitchen led to the laundry and the staff's leisure room. It was in the latter that Ivar asked Tone about the door between the fireplace and the stairs, where the guard had been standing. All she said in reply was, 'We don't know, and have been told to neither enquire nor investigate.'

And so Ivar settled to his duties, keeping his head down and waiting for them to come to him, just as Arne had told him to.

SS-Sturmbannführer Alfred Neumann was a small, wiry man, with thin lips, inquisitive eyes and a halting, somewhat apologetic manner. He had been a teacher of primary-school children before hostilities began and claimed it was this work that prepared him for his wartime role in the SS. He was patient and methodical, and his experience of making school children succumb to his will had enabled him to develop a theory of what he termed psychological pressure points. Since joining the SS, he had determined which of these pressure points continued to exist in adulthood. His lack of scruples in selecting the level of pressure to apply had seen him rise fast to his particular niche within the organization, and these days he travelled throughout the Reich, to wherever his talents were required. He taught people to see things his way, to see things the way of the Reich, and the Teacher had never yet failed. He was much in demand.

When Kaltenbrunner first called, Neumann had been tied up in France, where he had been sent by the SS-Reichsführer himself. The Nordic mission was not a task to be taken lightly. Kaltenbrunner wanted the best. And had been willing to wait. And now the Teacher had finally arrived in Norway.

In Oslo, only Reichskommissar Terboven knew he was coming, but by the time Neumann got there, the Gestapo's Oslo man, Hauptsturm-führer Fehmer, had also learned of his arrival. Terboven had told him. The Reichskommissar wanted the pair to work together. This displeased Neumann. He worked alone.

Neumann waited in Fehmer's own office for fifteen minutes before the Gestapo man arrived, saluted and sat behind his desk.

'So, Sturmbannführer,' Fehmer said. 'I understand you come armed with information for me.'

'Information for *us*, Hauptsturmführer,' Neumann said. 'I come to act on classified intelligence that Berlin hopes will lead to the arrest and interrogation of senior XU members, and ultimately to the dismantling of the entire Allied intelligence network in Norway. The operation will commence through observation alone. Only once I possess all the information I deem pertinent shall we act. Is that clear?'

Fehmer, Neumann knew, was not a man likely to endorse the idea of a surveillance operation. He had been actively working to dismantle the resistance himself since coming to Norway — bone by bone, according to some — and doubtless he considered Neumann's arrival on his turf something of an insult. By immediately establishing his intentions, Neumann was stamping his authority on the operation, and also on the Hauptsturmführer. Fehmer might be sadistic and bloodthirsty, but Neumann knew he was not a stupid man, and was not surprised that he resisted voicing the opinions that his eyes could not hide. A Sturmbannführer was a Hauptsturmführer's superior. Neumann had been sent by Kaltenbrunner personally. Kaltenbrunner was friendly with Himmler, who in turn, of course, had the Führer's ear. That was a short chain.

'I am afraid such tactics are not in my nature, Sturmbannführer,' was all Fehmer said in response, leaning back in his chair and placing his boots up on the desk — an act of insubordinate bravado he hoped would cover his anger.

Neumann considered the soles of Fehmer's boots for a moment.

'So I understand,' he said in his quiet, unassuming voice. 'But in order to proceed without stumbling, we must first light our way.'

★ ★ ★

The nurses at Dueredet talked about '*der Vater*' and promised Ivar he would meet him at some point. Ivar knew to whom they were referring, but he did not search von Westarp out, and he did not enquire after him, and for the first weeks at Dueredet, he did not encounter him once. He had been told by Arne, by Sofie, by Frau Gärtner and by Tone to keep his head down, to do nothing more than his Dueredet chores. And sure enough, by doing nothing more than that, the situation at Dueredet started to develop of its own accord.

It was lunchtime and the women were eating in the dining room downstairs. Ivar was upstairs making up beds, but was unable to complete his task before the door of the room opened and a mother-to-be, gowned and fresh from bathing, was ushered in by one of Gärtner's older nurses. Keeping his head bowed, Ivar apologized, saying he thought all the ladies were eating downstairs, and made to leave.

'No, don't leave on my account,' the woman said.

Ivar glanced at the nurse, who, though plainly incensed by his presence, nodded; so Ivar returned to the bed and went on smoothing the sheet out over the mattress as the nurse helped the woman into the bed he had already made. After that, the nurse departed, leaving the door open, and Ivar was alone in the room with the woman, who lay still in her bed. Ivar paid her no heed until he heard her speak. He turned and saw that she was caressing her stomach. Ivar watched transfixed as she stroked and cooed over the naked dome, but when she looked up at him, he felt the warmth of his cheeks reddening and averted his eyes, and busied himself with the sheets once more.

'It's okay,' he heard.

Ivar looked back at the woman, her head lying on the propped pillow, her blond hair splaying over it like liquid gold flowing from her scalp. She was smiling at him, her eyelids heavy as though half asleep.

'I'm sorry,' Ivar said. 'It's just that I've never seen it before.'

'Never?'

'Not — you know. Naked.'

'You've no younger siblings?'

'No.'

'Cousins? You never saw your mother or aunt pregnant?'

'No. My mother and father died.'

The woman tried to smile in sympathy, but in her state — emotional, physical and hormonal

— the tragedy of orphanhood brought tears to her eyes.

'Perhaps one day you'll have a wife and a child of your own,' she said.

'Like you?'

She wiped her eyes.

'Yes, like me.'

Ivar smiled and started to tuck the edges of the sheet beneath the mattress.

'I hope so,' he said.

The woman watched him work for a time, then said: 'Boy. Come over here.'

She was reaching out a hand. Ivar moved to her and she took his wrist and placed his hand on her belly. He felt something flick his palm through her skin and flinched. She laughed.

'You feel it?'

'Doesn't it hurt?'

'Not usually.'

'That's . . . ' But he petered out as he felt the child kick again.

'There's a whole new life in there,' she said. 'Isn't that wonderful?'

Ivar didn't answer, but let the woman move his hand over her stomach searching for the next kick.

'He's sleeping now,' she said, stopping. Ivar kept his hand on her, though, and watching him stare at her belly, the woman said, 'Do they treat you well here?'

Still looking down, Ivar said: 'They feed me, and send money to my family. And I have my own room.'

'So they are good people, you think?'

Ivar looked up from her belly to her face. He wanted to tell her the truth, who these people really were, what the Nazis did to Britt, a girl not much younger than her, that they would take her baby away from her almost as soon as it was born, but he held back. That wasn't why he was there, and to speak up would be to compromise himself. Sacrifice, knowing or unknowing, that's what Arne had said, and it was what Ivar was saying in his head when, out loud, he told her, 'Yes, I think so.'

The woman looked down at her belly, and stroked it again.

'You see, Hans?' the woman said to the unborn child. 'I told you. They're just jealous.'

'Who are?' Ivar said.

'Oh,' she said, almost as though she had forgotten he was by her side. 'Just my parents' neighbours. They said some horrible things to my mother when they heard I'd agreed to come here. Made her weep. But they were just jealous.' She smiled. 'What's your name?'

'Snorre Nilsen,' said Ivar.

'Well, Snorre — this is Hans in here. And I'm Grethe. Ingessen.' She stuck out her hand and Ivar took it. 'We're pleased to meet you, Snorre Nilsen.'

'I'm pleased to meet you. And don't worry. It'll be okay.'

Ivar was not smiling as he spoke those final words. He walked out of the room, and turned right towards the staircase, but then he stopped in his tracks.

'Boy,' he heard from behind him. The voice was male. Ivar had not set eyes on another male upstairs in the hotel. The guards were not allowed beyond the hall. The fathers of the newborns and yet-to-be-borns were never seen — Ivar presumed visiting was discouraged. This was a world of women, of fair voices and feminine smells — soap, flowers, scent — and yet what he heard was a deep voice, and he could smell the aroma of foreign tobacco. But it was the accent that made his scalp prickle. Bavarian.

Ivar spun around. A man was leaning against the wall between two doors, his shirt sleeves rolled up and his hair a ruffled mess. He was inspecting the bowl of his pipe.

'Snorre, isn't it?' he said.

Ivar knew immediately who he was, so different from the Nazi he had attacked in Oslo — squat and round and repulsive, where Fehmer was tall, slim and strong. Ivar had been desperate to believe Fehmer was von Westarp, but now, unquestionably, here was the real culprit, the man who had driven the scissors into Britt's belly and taken from him the last of his blood kin. He recognized the shape of the man he had seen from the roof; his manner. And he was smiling at Ivar. *Smiling*.

Ivar's head started pulsating, the blood rhythmically swelling everything in his field of vision. His skin started to prickle. But it was not born of fear. Just as when the bear had sniffed at his hair in the woods, he was not afraid. The prickling sensation was born of anger, and he felt his own fingernails digging into his palms. Somehow he managed to bow his head in deference.

'How old are you, Snorre?' von Westarp said.

'Thirteen, sir.'

'It is very interesting.'

'Excuse me, sir?'

'Women who come here can be somewhat apprehensive, Snorre.'

'Yes, sir?'

'I was watching you in there, with Grethe.'

'Yes sir?' Ivar replied, keeping his head down.

'And she spoke to you.'

'Yes, sir.'

'This is what interests me, Snorre. Do you know why?'

'No, sir.'

'When she met you she saw two things. First of all a fellow countryman, a kindred spirit. But also an orphan child. An innocent lost, and like that,' he clicked his fingers, 'her heart was unlocked. Suddenly she was completely at ease, and this caused her to open herself up to you. The ability to make someone open their heart is a very powerful tool, Snorre.' Von Westarp nodded to himself, as though lost in thought, then he said, 'This evening, once your chores are done, come to my study.'

Then he turned and walked off down the corridor, leaving Ivar drinking in the tobacco-tinged air and waiting for his vision to return to normal.

★ ★ ★

After that first encounter with von Westarp, Ivar's nappy- and sheet-washing duties reverted to the housekeeping staff, but he continued to

289

make up the beds in all the rooms. In fact, whether sheets required changing or not, Ivar's primary duty was to make sure that wherever a woman could be found alone she was persuaded to take this orphan into her confidence. He would report these conversations every evening when he performed his final duty before retiring — delivering supper to von Westarp in his study at the end of the corridor next to the nursery.

The first thing Ivar noticed about von Westarp's study was that, while everywhere else was characterless, this room, although painted white like the rest of the building, was cosy. There was a carpet, a desk, an armchair, books, shelves, pictures on the walls, and it had its own fire, the only room to have a direct source of warmth other than the hall and the kitchen.

On his first few visits, Ivar held a grip on his hate and merely gave the German a one-word report on the mental or physical state of each woman — Grethe, excited; Linnea, anxious; Nora, fatigued — and departed before his desire for retribution boiled over.

One evening, before listening to Ivar's report, von Westarp asked the boy to polish his boots. Ivar complied, and sat across the carpet from Britt's killer, buffing the boot leather with the brush — *shhht-shhht shhht-shhht* — chanting that familiar mantra in his head. Yet with each sweep of his hand, he glanced at the rotund Oberführer, sitting there in his armchair pushing food past those hideous fleshy lips, and in Ivar's mind each one of these glances carried with it a vision of him slitting von Westarp's throat as he ate, or holding the man's own Luger to his forehead and pulling the trigger, of him grabbing the stoker from the fire and lunging it through his ribcage and into his heart and watching his Nazi blood bubble on the hot metal.

After that evening, Ivar was always expected to shine von Westarp's boots before delivering his daily report. Food eaten, von Westarp would push the tray aside, light his pipe and start to ask Ivar questions about his conversations with the women. These questions were apparently casual, but Ivar knew this was not really the case. Von Westarp was fishing for any criticisms of his *Lebensborn* home that the women might pass on to Ivar — like the words of Grethe Ingessen's neighbours.

Whilst battling to control his hate, Ivar also had to make von Westarp believe that he was successfully mining the boy's brain for intelligence, while actually denying von Westarp any information that might incriminate others. If he was unsuccessful in this subterfuge, he knew that von Westarp would simply ask him outright, and then he would have no choice but to reveal what the women had told him. Thus each of these evening sessions was like a dance, but one in which von Westarp could not know that Ivar was watching him move for move.

This practice continued for some while. Ivar was embedded in Dueredet throughout the summer, without remarkable incident, seeing to his duties, writing letters to his uncle Tord every week, listening out for information, reading whatever he could get his hands on, reporting on events in the house to von Westarp, seeing children born, women coming and going, and hating every moment of it — but always, always reciting his mantra. Until one cold, blizzard-strewn October evening in 1942.

On entering von Westarp's study, Ivar went through the familiar routine. Von Westarp sat in his armchair and ate his supper, while he himself sat on the stool and applied polish to his boots. But the German ate with noticeably reduced verve that evening, and afterwards, rather than wiping his lips and shooting questions at Ivar, he domed his fingertips before his lips and gazed deep into the fire's flames, his cognac untouched on the table at his side. He was in a thoughtful frame of mind, it seemed, and when finally he spoke, his words reflected his outward appearance.

'Fire, Snorre,' he said. 'What is it?'

'Herr Oberführer?' Ivar said, looking up from the boots.

'I asked you what fire is.'

'I'm not sure I understand the question, Herr Oberführer.'

Von Westarp parted his fingers and gestured at the fire.

'Burn a log of wood and when the burning is done, what are you left with?'

The boy said nothing, and von Westarp looked at him.

'Ash, Snorre. Ash.'

'Yes, Herr Oberführer.'

'And what is ash?'

Again Ivar did not reply.

'Carbon,' Von Westarp confirmed. 'And carbon?

The most basic of elements, the simplest and purest of nature's building blocks. All the impurities lying in the piece of wood vanish into the air as smoke. So fire? Burning? It is the process by which nature attains purity. But look at it — fire is hypnotic, is it not? The licking flames are uniquely capable of holding one's attention. They are pure in themselves. Are they not?'

'Indeed they are, Herr Oberführer.'

Von Westarp passed his tongue over his lips. The spittle made them glisten.

'So we agree that the process of purification is in itself pure,' he said. 'This pleases me.'

Von Westarp held Ivar's gaze for a moment. Ivar was the first to avert his eyes, returning to his polishing duties. After that both were silent, until Ivar placed the brush in its box and made to rise.

'Herr Oberführer?' he said. 'Forgive me, Herr Oberführer, but if that is all for this evening, I will — '

'No, Snorre,' von Westarp said. 'Never ask for forgiveness.'

Ivar had thought that there was no music to dance to that night, but he was wrong. The music had changed, that was all, to a tune he did not recognize.

★ ★ ★

Two weeks earlier, coming back from his afternoon constitutional, von Westarp had entered the hall to see Frau Gärtner descending the main stairs to meet him.

293

'Herr Oberführer,' she said. 'Your guest has arrived, sir.'

'My guest?' von Westarp said, removing his coat and giving it to the woman. 'Since when have you known me to entertain guests, Frau Gärtner?'

'The guards let him in,' she answered, brushing snow from the coat. 'So I assumed — '

'*Never* assume, Frau Gärtner. Who is he?'

'A Hauptsturmführer,' she said, bristling at von Westarp's tone. 'A most *handsome* man.'

Von Westarp knew immediately who was waiting for him upstairs, and nodded.

'See to it that we are not disturbed,' he said.

'Very well, Herr Oberführer,' she said. 'Your hat?'

'No. For him, it stays on.'

* * *

The snowfall was light, not yet the blizzard it would become by evening, and the sun was shining through the clouds, the snow glaring off the white mountainside so brightly that the man in von Westarp's study had to narrow his eyes as he gazed out of the window at the fjord far below.

The man turned when he heard the door opening behind him.

'Hauptsturmführer Fehmer,' von Westarp said. 'To what do we owe the pleasure of your company?'

'*Heil* Hitler,' Fehmer said, saluting.

Von Westarp waved his own hand.

'*Heil* Hitler,' he said. 'I asked you a question, Hauptsturmführer.'

294

'You did, Oberführer,' Fehmer said.

Von Westarp waited.

Fehmer waited.

Then he said, 'You know of Sturmbannführer Neumann, I presume?'

'The Teacher?' von Westarp replied, sitting down in his armchair and taking his pipe up from the table next to it. 'By reputation only.'

'Then perhaps you do not know that he is currently in Oslo, working with me in dismantling the XU.'

'What happened to your *canine* German Shepherd, Hauptsturmführer?'

'Very droll, Oberführer. Very droll,' Fehmer said. 'But this is no laughing matter.'

'His methods do not match your own?' von Westarp said, lighting a match and placing it to his pipe.

'We are different men, with different styles,' Fehmer said. 'He is thoughtful, I am dynamic. But we complement one another. So much so, in fact, that we have unearthed a cell that we believe could lead all the way to the top of the XU.'

Satisfied that his pipe was lit, von Westarp leaned back and said, 'I am most pleased to hear that you are defeating the enemies of the Fatherland, Hauptsturmführer, but I fail to see why you have travelled all this way just to inform me of your success. Surely a postcard would have sufficed? Unless, of course, you have something more to tell me.'

'You are as perceptive as ever, Oberführer.' Fehmer bowed almost imperceptibly.

'And so?' von Westarp said.

'Surveillance shows that this cell has infiltrated our ranks.'

'Our ranks?'

'*Your* ranks, to be precise. I am sorry to have to report it, but it seems you have a rotten egg in this nest of yours.'

'Really?' von Westarp said, amused himself now. 'And why would the resistance seek to penetrate a place that is of no strategic significance whatsoever?'

'We could not explain it either. Not for a long time, anyway. Dueredet is, as you say, an establishment purely *ideological* in nature.'

'So your surveillance was mistaken,' von Westarp said, sucking noisily at his pipe again.

'Unfortunately not, Oberführer. The Teacher does not make mistakes. Our surveillance had been thorough, and is accurate. And yet, though a spy there most certainly is, this place is, as you say, of no strategic interest, so no information of significance has been passed. So we watched. And we watched. And still nothing. And then it became clear. The resistance has imbedded an agent here in waiting.'

'In waiting for what?'

'For the moment of your betrayal.'

'Betrayal?' Von Westarp whipped his pipe from his mouth. 'How dare you, Hauptsturmführer! Need I remind you of who — '

Von Westarp broke off. Fehmer nodded.

'The ideology that brought you here, Oberführer, stems from your association with one man, just as you were about to point out. That man is second only to the Führer himself in all the

Reich. The spy awaits your unknowing betrayal of Himmler himself. It is the only conceivable reason for their being here. An idle comment, a casual mention of a Thule reunion here at the Dove's Nest, in Oslo, wherever. Only then will information be passed.'

'And you are here to propose what precisely?'

'I have come to ask you to drip-feed this agent just such information — but false, of course. It will pertain to a visitation, the details of which shall grow progressively clear and specific. It is our belief that by making this spy appear to be successful, we will draw more woodworm from the woodwork. The longer we extend the process the more will come out. And then, as they are all crawling from their holes, we will strike.'

Von Westarp had composed himself and, as Fehmer spoke, had been thinking.

He said, 'I am always happy to assist the Fatherland, Hauptsturmführer, but you are yet to offer me proof even of the *existence* of this so-called agent.'

'Of course, Oberführer,' Fehmer said, delving into his jacket. 'I have it here — evidence too that will finally settle our wager. In my favour.' His words, spoken casually, nevertheless informed von Westarp of the real reason Fehmer had come. The man was there to brag.

Von Westarp's association with Fehmer had begun when they first arrived in the country, in Oslo, where they had competed to capture one resistance fighter in particular, for different reasons and using different methods. The longer Sofie evaded capture, the more von Westarp wanted to meet her. The more he wanted to use her. And both men had failed in their attempts — until now.

'You've found her?' von Westarp said, irritated and excited in equal measures.

'Oh, it is better than that, Oberführer,' Fehmer replied, finally taking some items from his pocket.

Von Westarp placed his pipe back on the table. 'Talk,' he said.

'Very well, Oberführer,' Fehmer said. 'The spy is called Snorre Nilsen. We do not know if this is his true identity, but we do know that he pursues a vendetta against you.'

'*What?*'

Fehmer's eyes showed amusement at von Westarp's outburst, and seeing it, von Westarp immediately reined himself in.

'And how do we know this?' he said, through pursed lips.

Fehmer crossed the room and placed the first of the items on the table next to von Westarp's pipe. It was a knife, some kind of coronation souvenir. Haakon the Seventh.

'By the simple fact that he came to kill you, Oberführer, with this knife, on the street, in broad daylight, in front of the most feared building in the country. Only he thought I was you, because of this.'

Fehmer placed the second item on the table next to the knife. It was a dirty, torn newspaper picture. The picture showed the handsome Hauptsturmführer Fehmer laughing at something or someone featured on the second, missing half of the picture. The name in what remained of the caption below was von Westarp's.

'And these things led us to this.'

Fehmer placed two envelopes next to the knife and newspaper scrap. One was addressed to Mr Tord Svendsen. The second to Master Snorre Nilsen.

Von Westarp knew instantly that there was only one act he had committed since coming to Norway that could have earned him such hatred in a Norwegian. When Ivar Petersen did not fall into the Gestapo's hands, von Westarp had passed an order demanding that any intelligence that arrived relating to the boy be forwarded to him. Three weeks after he had killed Britt, reports came through that the boy had died of hypothermia not long after his sister.

'Fortunately, on the day he came for me, the boy was rescued before I could terminate him,' Fehmer said.

'By Sofie,' von Westarp said.

'Svendsen is part of the Stornes resistance unit. They must somehow have persuaded the boy that revenge was best served through betrayal. And so your actions, which caused the boy to swear blood vengeance against you, will finally deliver Sofie — to me.'

Fehmer's tone was respectful, but he spoke slowly, milking the moment.

Von Westarp was already thinking of the future and smiled at the thought.

'Congratulations, Hauptsturmführer.'

'You are most gracious, Oberführer,' Fehmer

said. 'May I ask — do you recall the circumstances that drive the boy Nilsen?'

'Oh, yes.'

'And?'

'And they do not concern you, Hauptsturm-führer,' von Westarp said, 'but I will feed Nilsen the information as you desire, with only one condition attached.'

'You want her.'

Von Westarp nodded.

'If you agree that the wager is done with,' Fehmer said.

'I do,' von Westarp said.

Fehmer smiled. 'Then it is settled,' he said, and bowed again, almost imperceptibly, closing his eyes at the same time. 'Come the day, she will be yours to do with as you please, Oberführer. I will deliver her to you myself. And now, if you would be so kind as to have one of your lovely nurses provide me with house stationery, I will be on my way. The Teacher has a letter of his own to write.'

* * *

Fehmer left soon afterwards, and von Westarp sat alone in his study, thinking.

The boy's death certificate had been a resistance lie. He had lived to become a spy for the XU. Von Westarp knew then that he should never have believed the story. After all, what was the likelihood that a wandering orphan's death from exposure would be so efficiently recorded? And he should have recognized those blue, blue

Petersen eyes, too. But Dueredet was so far removed from that night in Drøbak when he had first met Britt, or the evening in Oslo when he had encountered her for a second and final time, that the similarities between the two had never struck him.

It mattered little now, though. Fehmer had made it quite clear that Ivar was a boy who not only shared his sister's eyes, but also the qualities von Westarp had most admired in Britt Petersen.

Before his evening meal arrived, von Westarp wound the radio-telephone on his desk — the only one in the building — then picked up the receiver. After a moment of silence the connecting operator in Voss came on.

'How can I connect you, Dueredet?' the girl said.

'I need a number in Drøbak,' von Westarp said.

'What's the name, please?'

'Langeland,' von Westarp said. 'Mrs Berit Langeland.'

★   ★   ★

'Do you know why I tell you never to ask for forgiveness, Snorre?' von Westarp said at last. 'Because the need to do so exhibits weakness. You must *mean* what you say and do, and stand by it. That is the secret to being a man. And you are on your way to being a man, are you not?'

'Yes, sir,' Ivar said.

'I enjoy our evenings together, Snorre,' von Westarp said. 'I feel we are becoming firm friends, you and I.'

301

Ivar bowed his head. 'You honour me with your words, sir. And if you are finished with me — '

'Sit, Snorre. Sit and talk with me a moment. There is something I wish to discuss.'

'Very well, Herr Oberführer,' Ivar said. 'What is it you would like to speak to me of, Herr Oberführer?'

'Don't worry, Snorre. You have nothing to fear. You have not angered me. Pass me my boots, will you?'

'As you please, Herr Oberführer,' Ivar said, doing so.

'In fact, Snorre,' von Westarp said, pulling on a boot, his mood brightening, 'I need your help.'

'My help, Herr Oberführer?'

Von Westarp straightened, both boots on now.

'I mean — of course, Herr Oberführer. It would be my pleasure. Anything you ask. I do not mean to question you. You merely arouse my curiosity.'

Von Westarp smiled and raised his glass.

'Then let us first toast the future of humanity,' von Westarp said. '*Skål*, Snorre,' and he poured his brandy down his throat, slamming the glass back onto the table. 'And then let us set to work immediately.'

'Immediately, Herr Oberführer?'

'Immediately.'

Von Westarp placed a hand on Ivar's shoulder and led him to the door, resting his other hand on the knob.

'You know, Snorre, if you are to help me, you must understand why it is that I am here with you in these icy Norwegian mountains, holed up in a place called the Dove's Nest,' von Westarp said, and he opened the door and ushered Ivar into the corridor before taking the lead towards the stair.

'This home, as you know, houses women who carry the children of superior men, just as in any other *Lebensborn* home, yet here at Dueredet we do not only breed children to fill the ranks of the German army.'

He paused at the top of the stairs.

'This home, Ivar — *my* home, is special.'

As he continued to speak, von Westarp began to lead Ivar down first one then the second flight.

'We are here because I seek *Lebensborn*, Snorre — in the truest sense of the word. The fount of life. Quite literally. The beginning. Bit by bit, baby by baby, it is my aim to reveal purity in mankind. So I go somewhere that is pure, and to that place I bring the pure, and set to work.'

At the bottom of the stairs, von Westarp turned right to face the door between the staircase and the fire, where a soldier stood sentry. Von Westarp nodded at him, and as the soldier unlocked the door with a key from his pocket, von Westarp continued to speak to Ivar.

'And the work we are doing at the Dove's Nest, the work with which I want your help, will change the world, Snorre. For the better. The women who give birth here will be the saviours of mankind, for through them the Theozoa will be reborn — the Supreme Being. I am not a man of war, but a man of peace. I want the best for the world. And is a purer world not a better world?'

The guard swung open the door. It was dark beyond, until the guard flipped a switch and a chain of electric lights lit the interior. There was a staircase, leading downwards, a 45-degree tunnel cut out of the mountain.

Von Westarp stepped through the doorway. Ivar looked at the guard, who nodded. Ivar followed von Westarp. The guard followed Ivar, pausing to close and lock the door. As the trio descended, over the smell of damp rock, Ivar could smell disinfectant in the air.

'Strength, courage, intelligence and honour — these are the ingredients that I look for in my subjects, Snorre. These are the quintessential Aryan traits that I believe will lead us to the rediscovery of the perfect original beings who inhabited this earth.'

Fifty metres ahead of von Westarp, Ivar saw an ancient, riveted iron door that would have been more at home in a medieval castle. As they neared it he made out a small sliding hatch. The peephole was protected by a thick wire gauze. Like the dungeon of a medieval prison.

'Subjects?' Ivar said.

Von Westarp stopped outside the door and pulled a key from his pocket and placed it in the door's lock. He twisted the key and Ivar heard the lock give, but before von Westarp opened the door he turned to the boy.

'Strong, courageous, intelligent, honourable,' von Westarp said, nodding solemnly. 'These are words that describe you, Snorre.'

He placed his hand on Ivar's shoulder. And then he opened the door.

The space beyond was more a cavern than a room, but painted completely white, every inch of it. It was windowless and almost circular, about ten metres in diameter. The rough ceiling stood two and a half metres high at its highest point, and then sloped down to meet the more or less flat floor, giving one the impression of being within a shallow white dome, or rather, it seemed to Ivar, like being trapped in a giant buried lightbulb. In the centre of the room, beneath a real lightbulb, was a white hospital bed, a twisted pile of white sheets adorning it.

The Oberführer followed Ivar into the room. The guard did not. Instead he closed the door, and Ivar heard him lock it again.

'And they are also words that describe *her*.'

The sheets on the bed moved. A girl rose from them, swinging her legs over the side, the sheet slipping from her body. She was completely naked, her face freckled, her electric-red curls tumbling over her pale shoulders down to breasts just beginning to swell into womanhood. She could not have been more than fourteen years old.

★ ★ ★

It had been more than three years since Ivar had set eyes on Eva Langeland. Though her eyes still held their deep blue innocence, she had changed. Her face was less childish, more angular, there was less fat on it, so too on her body. The pair

305

had attended the same school, but had never been friends, and when Ivar faced von Westarp the German knew immediately that Ivar did not recognize Håvard's sister, and smiled. And then he watched.

15

The old man produced a map from inside his jacket and unfolded it. Curt sat down on the bench next to him. The map showed the Oslofjord. The old man pointed to the water south of the city, to Drøbak. Then he drew his finger up a fraction. Just north of Drøbak the water widened out, but there was a large island placed right in the middle, creating narrow channels either side of it. The man's finger was pointing at the water in the east of these channels.

'Here is where the wreck lies,' he said.

'What are those?' Curt said, pointing at four tiny dots in the middle of the east channel.

'The Askholmen islands.'

'They're too small for houses. Where does the wreck sit in relation to the traffic channel down there?'

'Directly beneath it,' the old man said. Curt was nodding. 'Why?'

'In this heat, the traffic channel will be busy with everything from dinghies to cruise ships,' Curt said. 'They won't be able to just park over the wreck and dive down. That sort of dive'll take time. They'll go beneath the traffic. The first man will take a guideline down one side, swim along the seabed to the wreck, enter, find the gold — if it's there — navigate on through, then come up. The rest of the divers will follow the guideline, looking for the gold, each one bringing up what he can carry. Maybe they'll loop the guideline back to the boat, but it'd be easier to run it straight and come up somewhere convenient on the other side of the channel. Somewhere there won't be anyone to trouble them.'

'Askholmen.'

'It's what I'd do.'

'So . . . ?'

'Bonde's only one man, and guys doing a dive like this won't be the sort of people you want to piss off. Ideally we'd take it after the handover's been made, but we don't know where that's going to happen. The wreck-site's the only concrete location we have. Once it's gone from there, it could be heading anywhere.'

'You're going to try to steal it from the *divers?*'

'The way I see it, it's our only option. In a wreck at ninety metres, it'll be entirely dark, though, and a ship that's been submerged 60 years will be fragile. They won't want a crowd down there. Which means they'll probably go down at intervals. What's certain is that on that sort of dive they'll be sitting out hefty deco stops.'

Curt gazed out over the glistening, bronzing bodies rotating on the lawn like hotdogs.

'Deco?'

'Decompression. To prevent their blood turning to Coke, they'll have to pause at depth, several times probably. But they won't be able to just sit in the water clutching gold. It'll pull them straight back down. A shallow diver will go back and forth taking it off them and bringing it up to the surface. They'll have to put the gold somewhere.'

Curt got to his feet.

'Come on. We're going to need a boat.'

★　★　★

The phone's spiral cord was stretched to breaking point. The cocaine was hitting its peak now, and Bonde was pacing the laminate flooring of his office, dynamic, forceful — the Man. He had dialled a further number and was waiting for his call to be answered.

Finally the ringing stopped. He could hear breathing, but whoever was there didn't say anything.

After a couple of seconds, Bonde said, 'Do you know who this is?'

'Of course we know who this is. We have seen you on the television today. Before full payment has been made we feel your announcement to be somewhat premature.'

'You got the deposit,' Bonde said, halting. 'You know I'm good for it.'

'Five per cent buys you time, and that time runs out at midnight tonight.'

'Just make sure I get what I'm paying for and I'll make sure you get paid.' He was on the verge of leading his country to glory. How dare they question his character? 'Failure to deliver can go both ways.'

The man did not respond.

Bonde could only hear the breathing at the

other end. Regular, unbothered. Pretty much the opposite of his own, and that irritated him.

'Do you hear me?' he said.

'The arrangements have been made. Make sure the payment is, too. There can be no turning back.'

'Is that a threat?'

'You know who we are, Mr Bonde. If you entertain any doubts as to our abilities to carry out *anything* we have promised, perhaps you should ask Rafik Hariri.'

'Don't use my name!' Bonde hissed.

'Or Bernardo Vieira, perhaps, Mr Bonde.'

'What are you talking about? Who are these people?'

'Yitzhak Rabin?'

'The dead Israeli?'

'Benazir Bhutto, Mr Bonde?' He was enjoying himself.

'*Stop using my name,*' Bonde spat. 'I get it. They're all dead politicians. Assassinated.'

'So you *do* know who we are, after all, Mr Bonde.'

'You're threatening my life.'

'We seek only to clarify the situation for you, Mr Bonde. To make you sure of your responsibilities. Are we quite clear?'

'I'm *going* to pay you. That's why I'm ringing you, for God's sake!'

'Midnight, Mr Bonde, or we will be forced to start proceedings against you.' He said it as though he were a lawyer, with an authoritative finality.

The next thing Bonde knew, he was standing there listening to the dialling tone, his head

310

pulsating. A minute or more had passed. He whacked the receiver against the base, once, twice, three times, then took a deep breath, composing himself, and put the receiver back to his ear.

'Who's next, Mr Bonde?' Eli said.

'Kim Larsen,' he said.

'Kim *Larsen*?'

'Get me his number, Eli.'

'Why do you need to talk to Kim *Larsen*? Today? Now? Mr Bonde, I don't mean to be . . . but he's not — '

'Eli, get him on the line. Now.'

★ ★ ★

Skarnes left the Volvo, walked past the Mercedes and approached the door of an establishment on Sofies Gate that had fraying red-and-white awnings over its windows. The peeling hoarding called it *Sofie's Mat og Vinhus*. He buzzed the intercom and waited.

Hansen was still in the car. She scrolled from the photo to the number it had been sent from and hit *call*.

The constable's voice came on after a couple of rings.

'Kobberrød,' he said.

'Thanks for the picture, Kobberrød,' Hansen said. 'Where are you now?'

'Heading into Aker Brygge,' he said.

'Have they made you?'

'I don't think so. It's busy down here, and I'm hanging way back.'

'I'm sending someone to take over.'

The door to *Sofie's Mat og Vinhus* opened and a man in a vest and boxer shorts appeared. Skarnes exchanged a few words with him. Then the man handed something over. Skarnes patted the man on the shoulder, then turned and started moving back towards the Volvo, holding his hand up, a car key dangling from his finger. The barman must have taken his keys the night before.

'He'll find you on the boardwalk,' she told Kobberrød.

'What if Curtis moves on?'

'Go with him. My guy will find you.'

'Do I know your guy? What's his name?'

Skarnes opened the door and leaned in.

'Inspector Skarnes,' she said.

'Jesus, Hansen!' Kobberrød said.

'You'll have nothing to do with him. He'll meet you and take over; you go back to the courthouse. You don't have to *do* anything. Just watch. Come on, Kobberrød — he's already on his way. And if this takes us anywhere — '

'All right, Hansen. I'll watch.'

'I owe you, Kobberrød.' She hung up, and said, 'Sorry about that,' to Skarnes.

He smiled slightly. 'I'm just glad my good name still manages to elicit a reaction. Nothing worse than being forgotten. So it's Aker Brygge for me. Where's Bonde?'

She started up the Volvo.

'I'll find out on the move.' Then she held up her phone. 'With this magical piece of equipment I picked up from the future.'

312

He closed the door, and watched her drive off with a smile spreading on his face.

Skarnes opened up the Merc and sank into the worn upholstery and let it hold him for a moment, wondering what his daughter would have been like if life had let her get to Hansen's age. Hansen had a fairer complexion, but the easy relationship, the sheer good-natured honesty of her words, they were familiar. And then, just like that, he felt tears welling. With no bottle to hit, he caught himself and slammed shut the door of the car. He wiped his eyes, then slid the key into the ignition and twisted it. The starter turned over. And over. And over. But it didn't take.

He tried again.

Over, and over, and over . . . and at last she took.

He shifted her into Drive, and pulled out.

★   ★   ★

Along the boardwalk from Kobberrød, Curt and the old man hung a left onto the jetties of Aker Brygge marina. The network of floating walkways were flanked either side by boats. The boats got bigger the further out you went. Curt wasn't interested in the cruisers and yachts. He was looking for something small and fast.

Curt glanced at every boat they walked past. Every one of them was chained and padlocked to a steel loop. The loops were welded into the structure of the jetties. And nine out of ten of the outboards were brand new or as good as:

313

immobilized, secured with trip switches so no one like him could come along and hotwire or pull start them under the cowl, so taking the time and risk of picking a padlock was pointless.

Curt stopped walking. Sensing his frustration, the old man offered him a cigarette. Curt took it and let the old man light it. He took a long drag and was about to move further, but didn't. He heard voices behind him, one male, one female, loud, laughing, carrying over the water and the bubbling of a slowed engine. Curt looked over his shoulder. Fifteen feet of black-and-red inflated rubber bumped into the jetty twenty feet away, and a pair of long tanned legs in a black sleeveless mini-dress sprang up onto the slatted wood, then stumbled. The woman fell on her behind, a beer bottle spinning across the jetty and rolling to a standstill. She flicked her honey hair back off a heavily made-up face. Twenty-two, maybe. She looked at the man, twenty-five, who was still in the boat. They both burst out laughing — loud, uninhibited, drunk. Laughter reducing to a dazed smile, she tried to climb to her feet, but collapsed back down and out came a new burst.

Curt scanned the marina for life. The jetties weren't busy, but the boardwalk was. Certainly too busy to risk getting physical.

Curt moved over to the female and put out his hand. She looked surprised for a second, but then grabbed it and Curt pulled her up. They came face to face and she smiled at him.

'*Tusen takk, helten min,*' she said. It sounded sarcastic, but she gazed into Curt's eyes, and

314

Curt stared into hers — blue, young and excited.

Then she turned, walked over to her beer bottle, and bent from the waist, straight legged, to pick it up. The short black dress rode up over the back of her narrow thighs and Curt saw black sheer underwear shading the curves of her rump.

'*Jeg er en heldig mann,*' the man said to Curt. *A lucky man.* Curt nodded. She looked over her shoulder and deliberately lifted the skirt, flashing the underwear at both of them again.

'*Ser dette fortsatt greit ut for deg?*' she said. Curt didn't know who she was talking to. But she was asking how it looked, so he turned to the man. The man pulled the key from the ignition and pocketed it, then lifted a three-quarter-inch rope, and threw it towards Curt.

'*Her,*' the man said. '*Fortøy oss.*'

He was asking Curt to tie them off. Curt stepped forward and picked up the rope. The woman weaved back towards the water's edge, draining her bottle, the man stretching a hand out towards her.

'*Bare en øl,*' the man said, shaking his head. *Only one beer.* He looked and sounded excited, too.

Curt took the rope and knelt at the loop.

'*Bare vent til jeg har fått to innaberds!*' the woman said — *you should see me after two* — and she threw the beer bottle into the boat.

Curt bowed his head. So far they had been jovial, but things could turn on less than that and the man looked handy enough. Curt finished his knot like he'd not even noticed the female. She

315

pulled the man out of the boat, both of them laughing at Curt's apparent awkwardness. But then another sound replaced that one, a metallic pitter-patter like it had started to rain. Half of the handful of coins they dropped for Curt fell through the slats into the water below, some landed on the wood, some in the boat. Curt looked up — they were already walking away towards the restaurants for that second beer.

Curt watched them to the end of the jetty, then started gathering the coins. He got into the boat, picking the coins there up too, then stood and took hold of the steering wheel ready to lift himself out. But when he applied a little weight, it turned. And the engine at the back of the boat moved with it. It wasn't locked, or immobilized. And the whole boat was only secured by a rope he himself had tied. And the couple had melted into the boardwalk crowd.

Curt moved to the rear of the boat. The engine was large — a Johnson V-6 that promised to spit out a hundred horsepower. On the back of a boat this light, that meant real speed. There was even a spare jerry of fuel fastened to the plastic decking, which a kick told him was near-full.

He looked up at the old man standing on the jetty. His eyes were wide.

'Help me aboard.'

'I don't know what I'm going to find down there,' he said. 'But if even half of what you've been telling me turns out to be true, one thing's for sure — I'm going to need to be mobile. And you're not exactly fleet of foot, remember?'

The old man looked forlorn.

316

'Look, I'll go down there alone. If there's no activity, I'll wait. If they are there . . . well, I'll see how it looks. In the meantime, you stay here and wait for me. If they're there, if they find anything, if I get my hands on it, we can't be walking around town with sacks of gold and no plan. I'll find a place to stash most of it, and bring just a portion back here. We pawn it, get ourselves cleaned up and buy some tickets. Then we pick the rest up and get the fuck out of here. Okay?'

The old man still looked a little dejected.

'That's a lot of ifs. Here's another. If this is all just some figment of your imagination, I'm going to want to come back and dunk you in this water. So you just make sure you wait for me, okay?'

Curt was smiling.

The old man smiled too.

'Okay,' he said.

★ ★ ★

'Larsen?' Bonde said.

'Who wants to know?' The voice at the other end sounded like its owner might have his mouth full of food.

Bonde was reluctant to answer the question, but he had no choice.

'This is Henrik Bonde.'

'And?'

'We have friends in common, Mr Larsen.'

'And?'

'Are you still — how do I put it?'

317

'I don't know.'

'Do you still — you know?'

'What?'

'Deal.'

'Maybe. Maybe not.'

'I need something if you do.'

'What sort of something?'

'Do you want me to say it on the phone?'

'You offering cash?'

'I'm not about to write you a cheque, am I?'

'Cut the jokes and I'll see what I can do.'

'Fine. Where can you meet me?'

'You want what I've got, Mr Bonde, you come and get it.'

Bonde hung up and Eli came on again.

'I've got Gulstad at TV2 for you, Mr Bonde,' she said.

'I haven't got time now. Tell her to come to Ullevaal with a crew tonight at around six forty-five, all right?'

'All right. Ullman at *Aftenposten* wants to do a piece, too. You want to talk to him?'

'Later.'

'And Bredesen at VG is asking for a phone interview. What times should I give them?'

'Eight thirty and nine. That'll see us into the morning editions. Have them call you, then you patch them through. They don't need to be getting my number. And how's that phone coming? I'm heading out in a minute. I'll need a car, too.'

'I got you one. Pick it up on your way out with the key. Are you meeting Larsen? I really don't see — '

Bonde hung up on her.

Curt watched the old man turn back up the jetty, then at the rear of the boat he flipped the four jubilee clips protruding from the engine cowl, removed the plastic casing and slipped his hand into the guts of the engine. He felt around until he found the fuel primer. He threw the valve around 180 degrees to open it up and squeezed the pump a few times until he could hear the petrol squirting. Then he flipped the valve back. On the top of the engine was the flywheel. With one hand he spun it until he felt resistance, at the same time searching around the housing with the fingers of the other, all the crevices and gaps. He found nothing but warm metal and oil until finally he located what he was looking for. A quarter-inch nylon cord wrapped around a small T handle. He unravelled it and tied a knot in the end of the cord, then slotted the knot into a notch on the flywheel and wrapped the cord halfway around.

Bracing himself to pull, he froze when he heard a voice behind him, close.

'Trøbbel?' it asked — trouble.

★ ★ ★

Hansen had set Kobberrød onto the black guy, not the old guy, but she hadn't said anything about what to do should the pair split up, which they were now doing.

Kobberrød didn't know what course of action to take. Hansen was off the leash with this, he

319

knew that, and now she'd let on that she'd brought the former Inspector Skarnes in on it. Kobberrød didn't know too much about Skarnes other than he went batshit after his daughter died, but one thing was for sure: the man was bad news. Meanwhile, here he was, Kobberrød, tracking a man who had been pointedly declared of no interest to the police by none other than Superintendent Egeland. Now it looked like that man was stealing a boat in broad daylight.

So what was he meant to do? If he intervened, it would be a legitimate arrest, of course — the guy looked like he was hotwiring the boat — and if Hansen approved then it'd earn Kobberrød points with her. She'd said his primary task was to stick to him, so probably she'd be grateful, and who knew where that could take him. But then again she might not want the guy arrested yet. Presumably she wasn't going behind Egeland's back just to get Boat Theft stamped on this guy's record.

Then there was Egeland himself to consider. This was an arrest that he definitely wouldn't want — if word of it got out, it would be humiliating. This was a man his department had just released. Plus, with Hansen operating off-piste, it would show the Super didn't have control over his stable. A humiliated Super was not something you wanted to be responsible for. He'd be looking for someone to blame. With Kobberrød off his beat, Egeland could arrange for a whole shitpile to fall out of the sky over him. Kobberrød just hoped Skarnes arrived in time to make the decision for him. And where the hell was he anyway? Bislett to Aker Brygge shouldn't take this long. And now the old man was coming up the gangway.

'Hey,' Kobberrød said, approaching the old man.

'What?' the old man said, playing innocent. 'Me?'

'I need to talk to you.'

'You need to talk to me?' the old man said, sticking his face in Kobberrød's. 'What do you want with an old man like me when there's a crime in progress down there?'

Kobberrød followed his pointing finger. The old man was pointing at his associate down in the Zodiac.

He was giving up his own man now?

'What is this?' Kobberrød said. But he got no answer, because when he looked back to where the old man had been, the space was empty. The old man was gone, swallowed up by the stream of people on the boardwalk.

★ ★ ★

Skarnes stopped at the barrier that kept cars off the pedestrianized zone, hauled himself out of the Merc and started moving past the marble fountains towards Aker Brygge. He spotted the uniform cop two hundred metres up the boardwalk. His dumb pretty face was looking troubled, confused. Skarnes broke into a run.

The promenaders seemed to him like they were moving through honey; they were shocked speechless by the sweating, grunting man barging through them. Skarnes swore them out of his way, but the running was hard going on his

321

punished body. His feet pounding the paving jarred through his body. After thirty metres, his legs were lead-heavy, his lungs wet sacks of mucus, his gut kicking, calves shrieking. Halfway there he was down to somewhere between a fast, painful walk and a stagger.

* * *

Curt turned, and blew out his relief. The voice didn't belong to the cops. It was a couple, but not the drunken owners of the Zodiac. These two were middle-aged. Returning from a long lunch, tipsy, moneyed, friendly. A polo-shirt and his woman.

'*Nei*,' Curt stuttered. '*Takk*.'

The man's eyes lit up.

'English,' he said more to his wife than to Curt.

Curt clenched his teeth.

'Yeah. English. The, ah — the solenoid's gone. You don't have a hammer on your craft, do you?'

'A hammer?'

Curt mimed hammering.

'You know, for the solenoid? It might help.'

'Ah, yes. A hammer.'

The man did the mime himself, nodding and laughing.

'Pål will be able to help you. We will come,' he said, leading the woman towards the larger boats. 'One minute.'

Curt waited for the nautical couple to move a little way, then pulled on the handle with all he had. The engine spat but didn't take. He reached over beside the steering wheel and moved the throttle lever up a fraction, then he rewound the cord around the flywheel, and pulled again. The engine coughed a bit, but nothing more, so he reached in to flip the fuel pump valve again and squeezed a little more fuel through. He heard the man's voice again, further off now, calling for his man Pål. Curt closed the valve, turned the flywheel, wound the cord and pulled.

The flywheel spun into life, the engine howling, the whole boat jerking forward and throwing Curt onto his face. But his mooring knot held and the boat strained like a dog at a leash, the engine roaring to heaven, water spewing up onto the jetty. Curt scrambled for the thrust lever and pulled it to neutral. The boat settled instantly, but people along the jetty were twisting to see what the commotion was about, crews craning for a view over and between boats.

Stooping, Curt pulled the mooring rope free from the jetty. At the wheel again, he fought the desire to gun the boat right out of there, away from the watching eyes. That would just bring more suspicion, because only someone with something to hide shoots right out of a marina. Crawling out is the accepted etiquette. So he spun the wheel and crawled.

'Hey!' a voice came from the jetty. The man was holding a hammer in the air. 'I have hammer. And Pål.'

Next to him stood a squat and tanned polo shirt. Then a third man drew up on the jetty next to them, not so smart — balding, pink, sweat-drenched and heaving for breath, about as out-of-place there as Curt himself.

Curt waved as he crawled away from the marina, and smiled. Accepted etiquette.

*   *   *

When Bonde came out into Eli's office, his secretary held out a Nokia and a car key without speaking a word or looking up. She was obviously offended by the hang-up.

Taking the items, Bonde leaned over the desk and kissed her forehead.

'I know what I'm doing, Eli,' he said. 'But I can't do it without you. Today you're the woman behind the man, sweetheart. Tomorrow you'll be the woman behind the Prime Minister.'

Her chilly façade cracked with just a hint of a smile.

'The ferry says there's no sign of your phone.' The tone was mock-offended now.

Bonde smiled.

'There wouldn't be. I was using it when I was waiting to get off. I must have lost it after that.'

His smile vanished.

Those last words had come out of his mouth without him actually thinking about what he was saying. His subconscious had released information he had been unable to consciously call on. But now it was unlocked, he knew: that was the last moment he had seen his phone, at the top of the gangway. After that, only the café and the police station were left as possible locations for its loss. But he was pretty certain he didn't use it in either place. He was absolutely certain it hadn't rung. In fact, now he thought of it, it hadn't rung at all since he'd announced the challenge, and that was odd. That was more than odd. It was impossible. He should have been fielding calls even as he was talking to the journalists. But that didn't happen, which meant he must have lost the phone somewhere between the top of the gangway and the huddle of reporters.

'That fucking leech,' he said, and then he turned and marched out of Eli's office, leaving her frowning at her desk. Before Bonde could think it over, he was violently punching a number into the Nokia, and shoving it to his ear as he got into the BMW.

★ ★ ★

'I've taken steps, Magnus,' Nygard was saying. 'And Henrik Bonde will not get through this day without some kind of mishap befalling him.'

Iversen was still in Nygard's office on the fifth floor. It was just the two of them now. People had been coming and going all morning, seeking assurances and receiving them in no uncertain terms. Now that they were alone for the first time since Iversen's arrival, Iversen had just asked Nygard what made *him* so confident. He had to know if Nygard was playing some kind of game, too.

'You mean a political mishap?'

'I should think so.'

'But you're not certain? It might be more than that?'

Nygard just looked at him. His expression was a strange combination of connivance and righteousness. He didn't say anything. And it was then that Iversen's phone started to ring.

He pressed the answer button and placed the phone to his ear.

'You little fucking rat,' Bonde spat at the other end.

'I'm sorry?' Iversen said, trying his damnedest to keep his tone light. But he couldn't help turning his gaze away from Nygard's. 'What's wrong?'

'I'm going to take a great deal of pleasure in crucifying you, motherfucker,' Bonde shouted.

'I'm afraid I don't know what you're talking about.' Iversen looked at Nygard again, frowning, as though he was speaking to a random raving lunatic.

'You people are all the fucking same — sneaking around playing the odds. Well I'm going to rip your yellow fucking heart out, Iversen, and piss on your guts. No one's going to want you by the time I'm finished with you, you little cunt. Not even Nygard. I — '

Iversen hung up, shaking his head.

On the other side of the desk, Nygard raised his eyebrows in question.

'My number must have leaked on the tour. I'm getting calls from raging liberals all over.'

'Have your number changed.'

'I will. In the meantime, sir, if you've taken, er, precautionary steps, then perhaps it would be prudent to prepare for the aftermath.'

'What do you suggest?'

Iversen thought for a moment, then said, 'Might I be right in thinking that Rune Kolbu is Bonde's doctor?'

* ★ ★ ★

Hansen's phone was ringing, too. It was the third time Halvorsen had tried her. She threw the phone back on the seat next to her, letting it pass to voicemail again, and looked up out of the windscreen.

Only a couple of minutes after Hansen had pulled up on Youngstorget, she had watched Bonde leaving the party building looking angry. When he marched around to the back of the building, Hansen moved her car to the corner to see him get into a black 5-series BMW sedan. In the minutes since then he had been making his way pretty much due north.

He was driving like he had somewhere he needed to be, weaving in and out on the dual carriageways, and kicking the BMW down to second and overtaking on the singles. She followed him all the way to the suburban outskirts and the two-storey rows of residential wooden houses. But he didn't stop there. He continued right on towards the university and now they were arriving at its north point, marked by woods, and a lake called Sognsvann. Instead of pulling into the car park next to the lake, Bonde took a left onto a dirt track that led between the Sports Science building and the woods lining the southern lake bank.

Slowing to a crawl, Hansen hung right back. Beyond the Sports Science building, the track became tree-lined on both sides. Beyond the trees to the left, in front of the Sports Science building, was a sports field, accessed by vehicles

327

through a gap in the tree line. A few other cars were parked around the touchline, but no one was on the pitch. Hansen passed it by and beyond the sports field was an agricultural field. At the end of that field, through the trees, she made out an isolated red timber house at the end of the track, outside which Bonde was pulling up. The place looked like a farm, and maybe it still was. But other than Bonde not a person was to be seen.

Hansen stopped the Volvo behind a stand of trees and watched Bonde get out of his car and make his way through the gate and up to the front door. He knocked and waited. Then the door was opened and he entered.

Hansen opened her door, got out and stalked towards the house. Getting closer, but still in the shade of the trees, she could hear voices inside, but only muffled remnants, nothing of what was actually being said. At the end of the trees, twenty metres from the house, she stopped to scan the scene. The ground-floor windows had blinds drawn, and from this low angle Hansen could only make out whitewashed ceilings through the upper windows.

Outside, the house was in disrepair, paint peeling, some visible rot around the windows and the garden fence. The American-style postbox bolted to the fence by the gate had an enamel finish that had formerly matched the dark red of the house, but it was just orange rust now. The white characters roughly painted onto it remained legible, however. They spelt out the name Larsen. That was something. A door number or street address and she could run it through the police databases. But she was side-on to the door. If it had a number, she'd have to move to see it.

She stepped out from behind the tree, but as soon as the sunlight hit her face, her phone, still in the Volvo, started to ring again. She backed into the shade and jogged back to the car and reached through the window.

She was about to shut the phone off, but the number on the screen wasn't a station line. It was Kobberrød's.

'Kobberrød?' she said, eyes back on the house.

'It's Skarnes, Hansen.' He was breathing heavily, heaving for breath, but the irritation and disappointment in his voice were audible.

'What is it?' she said.

'I lost him.'

'*What?*'

'Your man here let him steal a boat and take off.'

'You mean he *watched* him commit a crime?'

'Would seem so.'

'Did they both go?'

'Just Curtis.'

'So what about Nilsen?'

'He lost him too.'

'On a jetty? An 80-year-old man? How on earth — ?'

'Don't ask. He's gone. Where are you?'

'Bonde's stopped to visit someone. I'm waiting for him to come out.'

'Who?'

'The postbox says Larsen.'

329

'Any ideas?'

'Who knows?'

'Well, you let me know where you end up, all right?'

'*Ha!*' she whisper-laughed. 'And how exactly am I meant to do that when you have no cell of your own?'

'I — ' he tried, but she wasn't about to let him.

'I'm a big girl, Skarnes. You want to do something useful?'

'Sure,' he said. 'What?'

'Halvorsen's looking for me. I'm already ignoring his calls. If I call in, he'll close us down. You, on the other hand, have already been closed down. Do you still have any contacts?'

'On the force?'

'No — in the Natural History Museum . . . Yes, on the force.'

'Some — maybe. I suppose we'll find out. What do you need?'

'Run the name.'

'Larsen?'

'Yeah.'

'Is that all you've got?'

'Hang on. Maybe I can get you the street name.' Hansen looked at her phone, and punched away at the touchscreen.

Waiting for the GPS to find her, she heard voices.

Bonde had appeared at the door of the house, looking like a spooked doe, a plastic bag in his hand. Unsmiling he turned to shake the hand of another man — blond, one-eighty high, one-twenty heavy, well-built in a wife-beater and jeans — not a politician's man. Hansen got back in her car, but didn't turn the ignition over. She watched Bonde back to the 5-series. Watched him get in, close the door, then cock his arm as he keyed the ignition.

Hansen turned the key in the Volvo a split second afterwards. The diesel started up and she flicked the gear stick into reverse and pinned down the accelerator. Bumping up the track, she steered violently through the gap in the trees and into the sports field. She carried on careering backwards over the grass for a few seconds then, switching pedals, slid the car to a halt, slipped it into first and waited, the engine growling.

Twenty seconds later, Bonde in his BMW passed by on the track on the other side of the trees. Hansen drove back to the field entrance, waited until the BMW was up by the Sports Science building, then pulled out.

If she'd looked in her rearview mirror, she'd have seen a Lancia Thema pulling out of the very same sports field just before she turned onto the metal road, but she didn't. She only had eyes for the BMW, and moving back into town the Lancia became just one more executive saloon on the road.

Coming down the road, she glanced back down at her phone. The GPS had found her, a blue dot edging across the map. She put the phone to her ear.

'You still there, Skarnes?'

'What are you doing?'

'The car may be a piece of crap, but the phone is state of the art. GPS.'

'So?'
'I'm in Sognsveien.'

* * *

Skarnes hung up. Sensing the unease in Kobberrød at his side, he didn't look at him and just dialled a new number into the constable's phone.

Skarnes had come up with Tobias Edinsen in Crime Squad. They'd been drinking buddies until they had children, then the bars had turned into weekend BBQs and cabin trips and teaching the kids to ski, right up until Edinsen moved over to Kripos to work organized crime on the national level. That had been what? Six years ago now? Edinsen was a busy man these days, but the voice answering his office landline was his own.

'Tobias?'

'Who's that?'

'Ole Skarnes.'

'Ole. Jesus. The prodigal son returns.'

'Not exactly.'

'How're you holding up?'

'Yeah — all right. And you? How're you, bigshot?'

'You know, crime pays the bills. How are you paying yours?'

'I'm getting by, more or less. All the pay-offs I kept under the floorboards, you know? But I do need to ask a favour.'

'Anything.'

'I want you to run a name.'

'Oh, that sort of favour.'

'Can you do it?'

'Have you gone private now?'

'It's a Larsen, at an address on Sognsveien.'

Tobias laughed. 'Sognsveien runs all the way from below Kirkeveien up to the university. How many Larsens do you think I'm going to get? Give me a clue for Herdis, will you?'

'Herdis?'

'My secretary.'

'Your *personal* secretary?'

'I'm far too much of a bigshot to run my own searches these days.'

'Wow.'

'I know. So?'

'Rightwing,' Skarnes said. 'Far.'

'All right. I'll see what we can do, okay? Is it urgent?'

'Depends what you find. I mean what Herdis finds.'

'All right. And Ole?'

'What?'

'Why don't you do that? Go private. Get yourself a licence — and keep me out of trouble in future?'

'Thanks, Tobias.'

'Don't mention it. And how about a meal soon? Yeah, come on over, see Unni and the boys. It'll do you good.'

'I'll be in touch.'

'Make sure of it. Have you got a number I can get you on?'

Skarnes turned to Kobberrød. 'What's the number on this thing?'

'Uh-uh,' Kobberrød said, looking panicked. 'I've got to go. I'm off my beat. No way I'm waiting around here for the shit storm coming this way.'

Skarnes glared at him for a moment then turned. The boardwalk was lined with restaurants. The nearest one was a Big Horn. Its number was printed on the red awning. Skarnes read it off for Tobias.

'Just ask for me, okay?' Skarnes said. 'I'll be waiting.'

Skarnes hung up, and tossed the phone at Kobberrød. Skarnes considered him with disdain as he fumbled to catch it.

When Kobberrød saw Skarnes watching him, he said, 'It's an iPhone. You know how much these things cost?'

Skarnes left him on the boardwalk and made his way into the steak house, past the waiters and diners at their tables, the smell of seared flesh and deep frying turning his stomach. He went straight up to the bar and took a seat.

'What can I get you, sir?' the barman said.

★　★　★

Doctor Rune Kolbu was fifty-three years old. He'd heard about the day's developments on the radio. He'd been a member of the Advance Party for a few years now. A lot of the senior members lived close to his practice in Frogner. That's how he had got interested, and then eventually involved. Henrik Bonde was one of quite a few he was on good personal terms with, but even so, he had to admit that, in party terms, he thought Bonde's recent move was unwise.

He was in his office between patients when his mobile rang.

Dr Kolbu?'

'What can I do for you?'

'This is Magnus Iversen, Mr Nygard's advisor at the Advance Party.'

'I know who you are, Mr Iversen. How can I help?'

'I want to talk to you about Henrik Bonde.'

'Indeed. I suppose he must have Mr Nygard running scared if you're ringing individual members. But you needn't worry about me.'

'I'm glad to hear that, Dr Kolbu. Very glad. But I'm not calling individual members. I'm calling *one* individual member. You.'

'And why is that, may I ask?'

'Because you're Mr Bonde's doctor.'

'So?'

'So I want to discuss his condition.'

'And which condition would that be?'

'His mental condition, Dr Kolbu.'

3

16

The building was damp and cold, like a corpse dumped in a winter field. At least the end of the cold was in sight. It was the beginning of March, 1943. Another month and the dead brown grass would be showing through patches in the snow, then it would turn green and the sun would be up in the sky nearly all day and food would grow again.

The resistance met in all kinds of places, and this certainly wasn't the worst of them. Geir had used the flat a number of times. Number 11, the end apartment on the ground floor, had access both through the building and from the yard, as well as a basement and enough cubbies to keep a raid searching for weeks. The person he was there to meet wasn't actually resistance, though — at least not yet. This was a recruitment meeting. Desperate times bring disparate people together, and the chain of events that had led to him picking his way through the dingy corridor was a convoluted one: Geir's sister's husband had a cousin who had been taken on as a maid at Terboven's residence — the Crown Prince's former home out in Skaugum, southwest of Oslo. That meant she would be cleaning his bedroom, his office, his dining room, handling all manner of items both personal and professional.

As such, there was a good chance she might come across information useful to the cause.

Word of her appointment had trickled back to Geir and, seeing the chance, he had engineered the meet. It was perfect. Terboven's people would have made extensive checks into the girl's family and friends, her life before the war and during, and she must have come up clean as a whistle. That was why she got the job. She was the perfect mole, and her willingness to agree to meet Geir suggested she was sympathetic. But no doubt she'd be nervous. His job today was to convince her that the risk was worthwhile, and to assure her that he would be her one and only link to the clandestine world. She wouldn't even see him again after today, because his second job was to arrange the means of secret communication.

Geir glanced up and down the corridor. It was empty. There were sounds — there were always sounds — a cat somewhere, a crying baby, the strained, hushed tones of its parents trying to calm the child, and beyond that the constant drawl of military industry from the water — but nothing suspicious.

Geir slipped the key into the lock and opened the door. The girl of course didn't have a key. He was supposed to be the first there. But just a second after he'd opened the door he knew he wasn't. But it was already too late. He was over the threshold and the door closed behind him. There were soldiers standing either side of it. Either side of him.

He turned and looked through the doorway to

his left into the living room.

The man sitting in the chair by the stove was uniformed, German, handsome, smiling. Fehmer. His German Shepherd was lying at his feet, panting and alert. Hungry.

'Good afternoon, Herr Larsgård,' he said.

'You're in the wrong uniform,' Geir said. 'I'm here to meet a maid.'

'I am sorry to disappoint you.'

Geir spat on the floorboards, then said, 'You won't get anything from me.'

'There is nothing you could tell me that I do not already know,' Fehmer said, dropping his hand to stroke the dog between its ears. 'So let me tell you a story. When I was a boy, my mother's Linzertorte was the toast of Munich, you know? Once, after taking it out of the oven, she neglected to place it in the pantry to cool, and left it unguarded in the kitchen. Its scent beckoned me. The room was deserted, and temptation proved too much to bear. I cut myself a modest slice, and placed it in a teatowel and stole to my bedroom to consume it. But before a mouthful passed my lips, the door was thrown open. My father. The Linzertorte was for my parents and their guests, he said. Not for impudent children. It was a childish misdemeanour that could have occurred in any house in Munich. And yet the punishment dispensed for the transgression remains with me to this day.

'Before my parents' guests arrived,' he went on, 'my father sat me in his seat at the head of the dining table, and placed before me the slice of torte I had stolen. Furthermore, he told me

341

that I was free to eat it, and that if I did so, no further punishment would be visited upon me. I sat there, eight years old, unable to believe my luck, wondering how this man could construe such treatment as punishment. But punishment it was. You see, my father also told me that I was to sit in his seat for sixty minutes. He then placed the rest of the torte on the table, and said that if I could resist the single piece for the full hour, when it was over, I could take the entire cake. Then he left, and I sat there, staring at the torte — the sweet, crumbly pastry, my mother's beautiful latticework only half hiding a treasure trove of sweet nuts inside. Fifteen minutes passed, and I did not move. Thirty. Forty-five. Fifty-five. And finally all sixty. When my father returned, I cried, 'Look, Father. I have done it!' And do you know what my father did next? He threw me to the ground and struck me with his belt.'

'I like the sound of him.'

Fehmer smiled.

'The whole thing had been a test, you see, all the way down to the placing of the torte in the kitchen instead of the pantry. I had failed it. Resisting the torte showed admirable self-discipline, yes, but not eating it showed fear, weakness. I should have waited for him to return and then consumed the whole thing while staring him in the eye.'

Fehmer sat back, pleased with his story.

'That's a shitty story,' Geir said.

'But a fitting one.'

'Really?' Geir said it without a gram of interest.

'Certainly. Because I have waited, Herr

342

Larsgård. But now the sixty minutes are up. And you are my first slice.'

Fehmer nodded briefly, up-down, and Geir felt each of the soldiers behind him grab hold of one of his arms, twisting them back. He struggled, and felt the joints at his elbows and shoulders strain against the pressure. Then he heard a pop, and a crack, almost simultaneously, and a sharp driving pain ran through his body, like his blood had been turned into electricity.

★ ★ ★

There was no manual for fighting the clandestine battle, no list of rules you had to read and adhere to in order to take part, but operating procedure was quite clear nonetheless, especially when it came to breaches of security: if there was even a hint that one had occurred, if someone's behaviour inexplicably shifted, however subtly, you locked down. If someone seemed to be looking slightly better-fed, for instance, or cleaner, operations were suspended until further notice. The whole enterprise dissolved, and everyone linked to it melted back into civilian life. But if one of your unit vanished into thin air, then what?

Sofie's view on the matter was entirely clear, especially in this case. You get your operative out. And then you run. The same day Geir went to meet his brother-in-law's cousin and didn't come back, while Arne tried to find out what had happened, Sofie sat down at the small wooden table in the cold apartment she and Arne were staying in, laid out a sheet of paper and wrote a letter.

The contents of the letter were mundane and brief — she spoke about the weather and passed on family news, mentioning girls called Wenche and Nina, and then signed off as Uncle Tord. She post-dated the letter with the following day's date, placed the letter in an envelope, addressed the envelope to Snorre Nilsen at the Dueredet address, and then pulled the stamp she had purchased that day from her pocket. She laid the stamp face down on the table and wrote three characters, scratching them through the gum: U, T and 3. She then licked the stamp, checked her spit had not made the marks smear, and stuck the stamp to the top right-hand corner of the envelope, above the address. She flattened the stamp down with the ball of her palm, then held the whole thing up to the window. The light streaming through the window penetrated the cheaply manufactured envelope. She could see the paper inside, and the words on the paper, and in the top right-hand corner the stamp created a dark square.

Satisfied that her message was invisible, Sofie left the apartment through the back door and hit the city streets. Had she been heading for the post office, to send the letter to Ivar as she usually did — by regular post — she would not have bothered making sure she was not being followed. But regular post was slow. Too slow. So she doubled back on herself four times in quick succession before making her way out into the more rural surroundings of the hills to the west, where large wooden houses sat in unfenced gardens looking down on the fjord. She came to a large, white church in an area called Ris and entered the graveyard.

The graveyard was not yet filled to capacity, but the graves that were occupied were arranged in sectors. Each sector was organized into rows of headstones, each row sightly curved, fanning out from the church itself. Sofie worked the sectors methodically. Along a row, all the way, then on to the next row, then the one after that, checking the name on every grave, looking for one in particular. One sector done, she moved on to the second, and worked it in the same way. She found the name she was looking for in the second row of the third sector, amongst a handful of graves hidden by the low, arcing branches of a row of spruce.

The gravestone featured a small arch in which you could prop flowers. On the floor beneath the arch was a stone plaque, about 25cm by 25cm, engraved with Sinne Marklund's epitaph: *To The Lord I Go*. The pinnacle of the arch was about three feet high, face-height if you were kneeling, which Sofie did, as if to pray.

In front of her on the left and right of the arch, on the inner sides of the uprights, protected from the weather, were twin alcoves. Each alcove held a tin cup. Each tin cup held a candle. Only the candle in the cup to the left was lit. Sofie used that candle to light the second candle and returned the cup holding the newly lit candle to its slot. Allowing the wind to blow out the candle in the cup she still held, she returned the cup to

345

its alcove on the left of the arch. Setting it in place, Sofie allowed her buttocks to rest on her heels, as though falling to contemplation. Her right hand slipped from her thigh to the stone plaque with the epitaph. Her fingers found the edge of the stone, and she used her fingernails to raise it. The plaque was a tile, no more than a centimeter thick. Beneath it was a space about thirty centimetres deep, a void into which an urn containing Sinne Marklund's ashes had been placed. The urn was still there.

Sofie tugged her letter from her pocket and dropped it next to the urn and lowered the tile back into place. She then crossed herself, got to her feet and left.

* * *

Within the hour, Sinne Marklund's grave received another visitor, a second amongst the select few to be given her name. That person saw the change in the candles and knew what it meant, and collected Sofie's letter and started it off on its onward journey to the western mountains, where it would arrive the following day.

* * *

There was a lot more snow at Dueredet than there was in Oslo. Even so, less than twenty-four hours after Sofie had visited Ris church, a resident of Gudvangen arrived on skis at the doorstep of Dueredet claiming to have a letter from Johann and Heidi Gulbrandsen for Snorre Nilsen. The letter was taken from the villager by the soldiers, opened, checked, then given to its addressee. Ivar kept the letter in his trouser pocket all day, waiting until he was back in his room to read it.

Once in his bedroom he opened the envelope, read the letter once, dropped it on his bed and turned his attention to the envelope. The stamp was in place, firmly gummed to the paper. It didn't look like it had been lifted by the guards. Very carefully, Ivar peeled the stamp from the envelope. It brought some of the fibres of the envelope up with it, but not so much that the message printed on the underside of the stamp was illegible. He could read it fine. It consisted of two letters and a number. The letters — U and T — spelt a word. *Ut.* Out. And the number — 3 — meant three days.

★　★　★

Sitting in his office in the Gestapo building at Victoria Terrasse the same day Geir was taken, Alfred Neumann picked up his telephone and said, 'Get me Fehmer.'

The disappearance of Geir Larsgård changed the playing field. That had been the point of Fehmer's move. Neumann had not authorized it. But Neumann was not angry with the Hauptsturmführer's impatience. In the past months he had taken all he could from surveillance, and the information von Westarp had been feeding the mole at Dueredet had had

347

the desired effect. Numerous XU heads were now sticking out over the parapet. Perhaps more could be drawn out, but it had also become apparent to Neumann that Fehmer's character had affected him in ways he had not previously noticed. The Teacher, despite his usual disposition for patience, found he was in no mind to wait longer. He wanted action.

'Sturmbannführer?' Fehmer's voice said at the other end of the line.

'It is time,' was all Neumann said.

'At long last,' was all Fehmer said back.

Neumann sat at his desk in silent stasis for a moment, then he opened his desk drawer, pulled out the Dueredet stationary Fehmer had brought him and started to write.

★ ★ ★

Neumann's letter was addressed to Uncle Tord, as those coming from Dueredet always were, and was written in what the Teacher thought to be a very decent approximation of the handwriting featured in those letters. He had been practising for many weeks now, and was satisfied. The contents of his letter were as unassuming as Sofie's and concerned people previous letters had referred to — people called Heidi and Johann and Tone. He signed off, 'Your nephew, Snorre', then placed the letter in the envelope Fehmer had brought from Dueredet. He sealed the envelope, wrote Bakeriet's address on it, and then took from his desk a stamp he had prepared even before he had given Fehmer the order, which he stuck onto the envelope.

Bakeriet was just across the road from Neumann's office, but instead of making a personal delivery, he took the letter to the civilian post office two blocks away. He told the fearful clerk behind the counter to make sure that the rubber stamp he used to start its processing did not include the location where it was posted. The clerk was only too happy to comply.

★ ★ ★

On the third day, in the evening, with all but one of his duties seen to and his evening meal consumed, Ivar retreated to his room before undertaking the last of his chores: going to von Westarp's study to start the dance afresh. And, of course, polish his boots.

He was sitting on the edge of his bed before heading down, staring at the floorboards, recalling that evening four years ago when he had sat with Britt in their room in Drøbak, him tying a fly, her rolling cigarettes, the pair of them conspiring to formulate a plan that would see him sneaking down to the water to join his sister and her friend Håvard in fishing. And their mother, downstairs, oblivious. All of them oblivious of what was to come.

Feeling the heat of sentiment rise, Ivar pushed his thoughts away from that evening, from the past entirely. *This* evening was not one to cloud with emotion. *Ut 3.* He was going to follow that briefest of instructions to a tee. He was going to get *out* after *three* days, and the three days were up. He was to meet Sofie at the shepherd's hut tonight and get away from Dueredet forever. Away from von Westarp forever. That was why he had added a couple of complicating factors to the plan. There was a job to be done, and though that job was born purely of emotion, to succeed and survive, he had to forget the reasons for doing it.

Tonight he had only to *act*, not *feel*. He could *feel* when he was out of there, in the mountains, with Sofie, with Eva, with the baby, away and safe.

The morning of that same day Neumann's letter finally arrived at Bakeriet.

★　★　★

The breakfast rush was long over when Grevle came in, but still two tables were occupied by German uniforms. Four junior officers were sitting by the window, their jovial tones drifting over the counter towards Tord Svendsen. Nearby an older man, a plump mid-level Gestapo Hauptscharführer, who Svendsen didn't recognize, sat alone at another table.

Svendsen laid a napkin down on the counter in front of Grevle and placed a cup of coffee on top of it.

'Give me an aquavit, too, eh?' Grevle said.

Svendsen reached for a glass and the bottle and poured out a measure and set it next to the coffee.

'So,' Svendsen said. 'How're those girls of yours doing?'

Grevle sipped his coffee, set it down again.

'You know girls,' he said without humour.

'Yeah, I know girls,' Svendsen said.

'Yeah,' Grevle said, draining his coffee, lifting the napkin to his lips, wiping them, folding the napkin, placing it in his coat pocket, and picking up the aquavit. 'Remind me — how old are they now?'

Svendsen smiled.

'Thirteen and fifteen.'

'That sounds like trouble.'

'You can say that again.'

'Growing up fast.'

'Wenche — the 13-year-old — she's got the whole world figured out. Even now, with it like it is. And Nina, she's just like her mother — got the boys running round her like dogs. But she's a good girl. How about yours?'

'Yeah.' Grevle drank the aquavit down. 'They're younger. They're all right really.'

'Different ages, different problems — but always problems, am I right?'

Grevle put down the glass and turned up the collar on his coat.

'You got it all coming with your girls, Jonas,' Svendsen said.

'Tell me about it,' Grevle said.

'Be seeing you.'

'Yeah,' Grevle said a final time and left.

Svendsen watched his friend pull his hat on, tuck his hands in his pockets and leave. The sun was out, dazzling off the slick of the melting snow, but still it was cold out there and Grevle hunched his shoulders against it.

351

Svendsen let out a breath of relief. He picked the phone off the counter, took it through the door into the kitchen and dialled a number from memory.

★   ★   ★

Ivar had only been with the girl once. On that single occasion, von Westarp had overseen every awkward movement of the coupling. As Ivar and von Westarp left the basement cavern following the enforced intercourse, and the two older nurses streamed in to attend to the girl, von Westarp had made it abundantly clear that Ivar was not to spend any time with the girl at all, even though she was to remain at Dueredet. 'Sentiment only muddies the purity,' he'd said in explanation. 'Not to mention the mind.' Von Westarp did not want any bond developing since Ivar would be called on to perform again in future, and emotional attachment to any female could prove detrimental to his performance. As it happened, Ivar had not, in fact, been 'introduced' to any further females as yet, but in case doing so jeopardized his revenge, he had not sought the girl out. Instead he watched her belly swell with his child from afar, stealing glances as he passed her room or as she walked the grounds.

Ivar had never had a woman, or girl, before that day; he had never had to contemplate fatherhood. Neither had he ever, to such a degree, required love before, so the self-imposed distance served only to intensify his feelings for the girl. An intensification which had at last, the night after he received Sofie's letter, driven him to approach her once again.

Considering that he awoke her at midnight, and by covering her mouth with his hand, he should not have been surprised to see fear animating her eyes: pure, unadulterated horror. But even after he had calmed her down and assured her that he meant no harm, he was dismayed to see that the fear remained — an unavoidable legacy of their first meeting. This cut into his heart, because this perfect, beautiful and innocent face had become his beacon of hope and assurance in that place of uncertainty.

'Please,' he whispered, retracting from her immediately, appalled that he could engender such a reaction. 'Don't scream. I don't — please — I'm — '

She didn't scream. Her face had changed already. In the moonlight she must have seen the gentle pleading in his eyes, and hers softened.

'Why are you here?' she whispered, sitting up.

'I've — ' Ivar stuttered.

'Look what you did to me,' she said, pointing to her pregnant belly, as though it was a schoolboy prank and she was seeing the funny side. 'I'm going to have a baby, Ivar. *A baby.*'

'I — ' Ivar tried again.

'I think it'll be exciting. Don't you?' the girl continued. 'The ladies here all say it will be. They're — '

Ivar was looking at her stomach, wondering how she could be so chipper, so childish, and yet a mother nevertheless, when her words finally penetrated. He looked up at her, terrified.

'You know my name,' he said.

'Of course I do.' Her face was still as light as could be. 'It seems like I'm the only one who does. Why does everyone go about calling you Snorre?'

'It's a — a game. A nickname.'

'I thought that must be it.'

'You haven't told them my real name — have you?'

'Of course I haven't. You know me — I'm not going to spoil a game.'

'*I* know *you*? What do you mean? What's going on?'

She laughed.

'Oh, you are silly, Ivar.'

'Please tell me how you know my name?'

He took hold of her arms and pulled her towards him, insistent. Suddenly she looked crestfallen.

'Don't you know who I am, Ivar?'

'I — ' He looked at her, not knowing what to say, not wanting her to weep, but needing to know the answer. He let her go.

'Oh, stop winding me up, Ivar,' she said, slapping his arm, a broad smile transforming her face again. 'Of course you do. How could you mistake all this hair? Just like Håvard's.'

'Eva?'

'*Eva!*' she mocked. 'Of course Eva,' she said, tutting, suddenly serious. 'Now what are you doing here at this time of the night, Ivar?'

'Why are you even here, Eva?'

'Håvard's friend, Mr von Westarp. You know

354

him as *derVater*, of course. He says Håvard's been doing wonderfully in Oslo. Mamma says I'm terribly privileged to be here.'

He didn't want to recall the answer to the next question, but he heard himself asking it anyway, maybe just to get away from the subject of Håvard.

'H-How old are you now, Eva?'

'I'll be fifteen in May. And you're fifteen in November, aren't you?'

Ivar took hold of her arms again, more gently this time.

'Eva, listen to me. I'm taking you away from here. Do you understand? Away.'

'From here?' she said, looking concerned. 'Why would you do that? Everyone's so nice. Mamma says I should be grateful — '

Ivar reconsidered his words.

'No, Eva. We're not *really* going away,' he said. 'It's just another game.'

'Oh!' Eva made to clap her hands, but Ivar caught them before they could make a sound.

'Do you remember at school?' he said, forcing a smile. 'When the teacher would ring the bell all of a sudden and you had to run outside as though there was a fire?'

'A drill?'

'Exactly. A drill. This will be like that, only it's a wartime drill, and during war they're special. More exciting. We're to be tested. We have to pretend everyone wants us to stay, but we have to get away. They want to make sure everyone can get away if they need to, you see?'

'In case the English come?'

'Precisely. And if we can't they might *make* us leave.'

'Leave?'

'Yes. You don't want to leave Dueredet, do you?'

'Certainly not.'

'So it's very important that we make absolutely certain that no one sees us. Do you understand?'

'I think so.'

'Good.'

'It sounds awfully strange, though.'

'I know, but these Germans have some funny ideas, don't they?'

Melancholy flickered across her eyes as she lowered them and said, 'I suppose so, yes.'

'Eva, I need to know,' Ivar said, raising her chin with his hand. 'Do you think you can ski in your state?'

The sadness was gone in an instant, pushed once more to the back of her brain.

'Of course I can,' she said sitting up straight for the challenge. 'I was regional champion. Didn't you know that?'

Ivar almost laughed.

'That's wonderful, Eva.'

'Shall we get going then?' she said, sweeping her sheet aside.

'No, no, no,' Ivar said, holding her in place. 'It's not tonight. I just wanted to get you ready. It's — ' He was about to tell her, but thought again. 'They spring it on us. It's a surprise, to keep us prepared. But it'll be at night time. I'll come for you. Just you be ready for me.'

'I will be.'

'And remember — '

'Don't worry, Ivar,' she said, watching him melt into the darkness again. 'I won't tell a soul.'

★ ★ ★

Arne and Sofie were in their apartment. They had their coats on. Their rucksacks were packed and on the bed. They were ready to leave. And someone was knocking at the door.

'Who is it?' Arne said.

'Who do you think?' a voice said. 'Open up.'

Arne shook his head wearily and opened the door.

The giant frame of Leif was standing in the space.

'Don't you know the code word?' Arne said, watching Leif lumber over the threshold.

'Any word?' the huge man said, watching Sofie sling her rucksack over her shoulder. Loaded, she went to the bed and lifted the corner of the mattress off the floor. Beneath it lay Reidar's old Nagant pistol. She pushed it into her coat pocket.

'No,' Arne said.

'What are you thinking? It's been days now.'

Arne shrugged. There were only two options — either he'd been taken, or he went. Arne was clearly thinking the worst.

'Come on,' Leif said. 'There's no way Geir would do that.'

'But why would they just take someone? Just like that, with no further action. One person.

357

And not a very important one, either, in the grand scheme. Geir doesn't know anything.'

'But if they've turned him, then why pull him and spook us without moving?' Leif said.

'I don't know,' Arne said. 'But whether he's gone over or was taken, if we don't know where he is there's nothing we can do for him. The brass'll find out, and if anything can be done, they'll act. *Our* orders are clear. And sensible. We have to leave.' He turned to Sofie. 'All of us. So let's go.'

Arne had moved to the bed and was picking up his own backpack. Leif and Sofie moved to the door. Arne threaded his arms through the straps and began to make for the door when the phone by the bed started to ring. Arne frowned at Sofie for a moment.

She returned his look, thinking for a moment, and then nodded. He picked up the receiver.

'Yes?' he said.

'So my nephew wrote.'

Arne recognized Tord Svendsen's voice immediately.

'What?' he said.

'Yeah,' Svendsen continued. 'I've sent it on. Thought you might be interested — it's carrying a fascinating stamp. You'll pick it up?'

Arne had still been looking at Sofie, but he turned away now.

'Yes,' he said, and hung up, but left his hand on the receiver in its cradle, his head lowered, thinking.

'What is it?' Sofie said.

Arne turned to face her.

'He's sent a new letter.' His face was grave, his tone apologetic. 'I need to get it, Sofie.'

'Don't be ridiculous,' she said. 'We'll see him tonight. If there's anything in it he can tell us then. He knows we're coming.'

'That's exactly why I have to go. Why would he send a letter if he didn't want us to read it before we left? You know what that means, don't you?'

Leif looked to Sofie, his face an amiable blank.

'We've got to go,' Sofie said. 'It's too dangerous for us. Sensible orders, remember?'

'This is it, Sofie,' Arne said. 'With all the whispers we've been hearing, that everyone's been hearing, and Ivar writing now, it has to be.'

'Maybe Ivar sent it before he got my letter. Maybe it's just another whisper. Or just a letter.'

'Or maybe not. Maybe Himmler's coming, Sofie, maybe the operation won't be worth nothing after all. And this time we'll be ready and there won't be any stepping back.'

'Not us, Arne,' she said. 'We have to go.'

'I know not us,' Arne said. 'I hate it, believe me, but I know. We can't let the others miss this chance, though. It's too big an opportunity.'

She stared back at him. Their time with Ivar in the forest had started it off, but since the boy had gone, things had got worse. Her focus, and thus her involvement in the struggle, had been in decline ever since, and the longer this war went on, it seemed, the further apart they grew, physically, mentally, emotionally. Since taking over the unit, Arne had been preoccupied with the fight. Most days Sofie did not even see him.

He spent every waking hour organizing sabotage missions, thinking about safehouses, weapons, communication. He had put all that time to good use — boats had been limpet mined, barracks firebombed, offices burned — and they were still alive.

'We still get him, Arne.'

'Absolutely.'

She nodded. 'Okay,' she said. 'How?'

'You take Leif, go to the station, buy the tickets. The letter's on the move already. I'll get it, transcribe on the hoof, safe-drop the transcription and meet you there before the train leaves.'

Sofie looked doubtful. 'It leaves in forty-five minutes,' she said. 'We have to be on it, Arne.'

'Sweetheart,' Arne said, pulling tight the straps of his pack. 'I'll be there.'

★ ★ ★

Ivar's chest of drawers, never stuffed full, was now almost entirely empty. His clothes were in two rucksacks, themselves stashed in a cupboard in the kitchen in which the ironing boards were kept. In with them was food he had saved over the three days, and next to them two sets of skis and poles. These last had been the most challenging element of his preparations. Not the locating of the skis — that was easy at this time of year. Everyone had a pair. During winter the snow was deep and you skied instead of walked. The challenge came in stowing the skis without being noticed. Ivar could simply have left them outside, but then he had no guarantee that they

360

would still be there when he absolutely needed them to be. Frau Gärtner was always complaining that they were left there — by the guards, the women, staff — and maybe they would be cleared away. Maybe not — probably not — but he couldn't risk it.

But it was not as simple as just carrying a couple of pairs inside. The kitchen door was guarded at all times, just like the front door. So how to get the skis in safely without that guard asking him what he was doing? He could pretend to be clearing them up for Gärtner, but odds-on the guard would tell him to ignore the old crone. If he refused, it might arouse suspicion. Again, not worth the risk.

The problem occupied Ivar's thoughts from the moment he came back from waking Eva and telling her the plan. He watched the kitchen guards as he worked the problem through his mind. And then they presented him with a solution.

Usually, in most places, when a guard changed, the replacement came and relieved the previous man. However, so little happened at Dueredet — especially at the kitchen door at 3 a.m. — that the guards had grown lazy. Eager for the night's sleep that was coming to him, the incumbent guard left his post and headed to the sleeping quarters in the stables. There he presumably awoke his replacement, because another man appeared back at the post by the kitchen some ten minutes later, bleary-eyed and cold, grumbling to himself.

Ivar decided that the time to bring the skis in and stow them in the kitchen cupboard would be during this break in the guard.

This course of action presented its own problems, however. During the day Ivar could walk the corridors of Dueredet without any nurse batting an eyelid. But traipsing around at 3 a.m. might arouse suspicion, and the staff had to tend the women at all hours, of course.

Therefore, when he made his move the second night after the letter arrived, stealth was the name of the game: stopping, listening, timing, skipping across doorways, he kept his footfalls as light and quiet as possible and succeeded without mishap.

All the equipment was in place, ready to be grabbed when it was needed.

Ivar knew the mountains around Dueredet now, the slopes and runs, and he damn well knew he could ski better than anyone else in there. And at night? It would be easy. Or would have been, if he hadn't had Eva to worry about.

He couldn't be certain she would be up to it in her state. She said she could ski, but she was nearly six months pregnant. But he wasn't about to leave her or his unborn child behind. He just had to hope that, once they were clipped in, Eva would prove to be as good as her word. A true Norwegian. Because they would have to make a dash for it, barge past the guards, and disappear into the night before a bead could be drawn on them. They would be pursued on their way out of there, no question about it, because right before they left, Ivar was going to kill von Westarp.

* * *

362

After Svendsen hung up, he went back through the door into the café, leaving the phone in the kitchen.

'Herr Svendsen?'

Tord turned to see that the older of the soldiers, the solo Gestapo Hauptscharführer, had risen from his table and was approaching the far end of the counter.

'Yes, sir?' Svendsen said, moving along to him.

'Herr *Tord* Svendsen?'

Suddenly Svendsen felt a chill. Those words sounded innocent enough — it was just his name, for God's sake — but they dropped a weight in his gut and he knew without any doubt what they meant. That letter was a fake. This was a set up.

He glanced beyond the officer. The soldiers at the table stopped talking and turned, as though synchronized, towards the counter.

Svendsen held the panic. He could never make it to the door to warn Grevle. He was already out of sight. Svendsen knew there was no chance for his old friend, just like he knew there was none for him.

He picked up the coffee pot.

The best he could do was make it back to the kitchen, to the phone, wedge the door before they made it round, redial, hope to hell Arne was still there. It wasn't much, but the most he could hope to achieve. And it would give some of them a chance.

'That's right,' Svendsen said. 'At your service. More coffee?'

Before the German could respond, Svendsen

swung the glass jug. It smashed over the soldier's head, glass and hot coffee showering over him. Svendsen dived for the kitchen door before he could see the results, but he heard the cry and the scrape and banging of chairs as the soldiers flew out of them. Svendsen grabbed the chef's knife off the food-prep board, slid it between the door and the floor with one hand, pulling on the door with the other, until the handle wedged in and stuck it fast. Scrambling out of the line of fire, he grabbed the phone and started to dial the number, each rewind taking an age. It was then that he realized that the door wasn't splintering with gunfire, or even receiving a bootpounding. Nothing. No one.

Svendsen picked put the receiver to his ear and dared to rise up on his knees, centimetre by centimetre, as he waited for the call to go through. The moment he saw the older soldier through the circular window, wiping coffee from his face, his skin burnt red and blood seeping from a gash above his ear, Svendsen realized he was listening to nothing. No voice, no ringing, not even a dialling tone.

★   ★   ★

To be absolutely certain of achieving his aims at Dueredet, and then absolutely sure of escape, Ivar had quickly known what was required. The snub-nosed Colt.

Taking a gun to Dueredet when he first arrived would have been suicide, so he had hidden it at the bottom of the Gulbrandsens'

364

wood store when he first got to Gudvangen. The second night after Sofie's letter arrived, Ivar did not return to his room after placing the skis and rucksacks in the kitchen cupboard. He stole away from Dueredet and in the moonlight traipsed down the mountain to the village and on to the Gulbrandsens' woodshed.

After nearly a year, the oilskin was still there, covered in cobwebs and bark, between two logs right at the bottom, all the way back, hidden from view. And the Colt was still wrapped in the oilskin. He unwrapped it, opened the gun, emptied the rounds, and fired the barrel right the way round. *Click, click, click, click, click, click.* The mechanism was fine. This wasn't precision shooting he would be doing. The Americans did not call these weapons belly guns for nothing. The revolver worked — that was all that mattered. He reloaded, flipped the safety on, stuffed the gun in his trouser pocket and left.

By the time he got back to Dueredet, the sky was growing lighter. It was early morning. The guards at the front door just thought he had left through the kitchen door for some chore or other, and Ivar walked straight in and up the stairs to the second floor.

He crept along the corridor to von Westarp's study and put his ear to the door. He heard nothing. He moved to the door next to it — von Westarp's bedroom — and made out the regular nasal breathing of the sleeping Oberführer. He moved back to the study door. He checked behind him. No women, no staff. He eased open the door to the study, slipped in and closed it

365

behind him. Less than a minute later he left again, having secreted the weapon in the shoe-shine box, ready for the evening.

That had been this morning. Now it was evening. The time had come.

Ivar stood up from his bed.

To start with, this evening had to go like any other. He would go down to von Westarp's study. The German would be sitting in his armchair, already in his socks, the boots waiting for Ivar by the fireside. Ivar would go to von Westarp's desk behind the armchair. He would take from the bottom drawer the shoe-shine box, and that is when routine would be broken. This day he would not carry the box to the fireside. He would open it, take out the Colt and hold it to the back of von Westarp's head. He would circle him and then, when they were staring into one another's eyes, he would tell the German who he was, he would make him remember Britt — and then he would blow his Nazi brains out of the back of his skull.

★ ★ ★

The senior German officer in Bakeriet — Hauptscharführer Wolf — had purposely spoken to Svendsen only when Grevle was out of sight of the establishment. Grevle therefore did not see any of the activity that occurred in the café, instead making his way across Karl Johans Gate at his leisure, past the university, and to the National Gallery. Walking through the main entrance on Universitetsgata, he came into the dark foyer and made his way through to the great hall. As ever, these days, only a few people were around, the shining marble floor lit from the glass roof high above, a flight of stone stairs sweeping up to a landing in front of him, which split off to the left and right, leading visitors on to different wings.

Grevle never ventured further than the hall, however, and today, like any other day, he stopped at the foot of the first flight and looked up at *Åsgårdsreien*. A massive canvas, two and a half metres wide, one and a half tall, hanging on the huge wall above the first landing, the painting depicted the Norse gods, a sea of them — Thor waving his hammer, towering above the Valkyries leading the charge; the warriors of Valhalla were plucking naked women up from earth by their hair; swords, spears, bows and arrows were all going off in different directions, their owners stampeding through the air, the sun rising beneath the hooves of their rearing, bolting horses. Behind them and above them was the place from which they were racing, from where the horde continued to pour — Åsgård, the land of the Gods. Its light was brighter, more brilliant, more violent than even the sun.

Supposedly this was the so-called Wild Hunt of myth, and wild it was — the whole enterprise looked utterly out of control, a mess, a mad dash, a battle-charge rather than a hunt. Grevle had been coming there three years and still he couldn't figure it. A hunt requires prey, and in the picture there was none.

Grevle mounted the stairs, feeling in his pocket, moving the envelope from the folds of the napkin. At the top, he slipped it into the donations box as usual, thinking. Who had any to spare these days?

He descended the steps once again, but just before leaving the hall for the foyer, he did something he'd never done before. With the paper dropped, he was usually keen to get out of there as soon as possible, but today he turned back to look at the picture once again, and was staring up at it when a voice spoke close to his ear.

'You know why we allow this picture to remain, Herr Grevle?' it said. 'In so prominent a position?'

Grevle looked to his side. The man standing next to him was also gazing up at the picture with his hands clasped behind his back. He was suited, bespectacled, frail. Contrary to the sinister threat associated with the full-length black leather Gestapo coat cloaking his body, Neumann's voice was calm and friendly. Beyond him, manning the exit, Grevle saw two more wearing the same outfit.

'It shows the world as it is today,' Neumann continued, still looking at the picture. 'The earth's sun is not rising, you see. It is descending. And not merely for the night, but forever. This is not something to bemoan, however. You can see that the world in the painting is ruined — nothing more than black rock and remnants of dead trees. This signifies the descent of the world, of Europe, into a mire of weakness and mediocrity.'

Neumann paused to smile slightly.

'But all is not lost, Jonas,' he continued. 'Thor

368

is arriving from the fires of Åsgård with his minions. He comes to protect mankind with all his great strength and destruction. Just as in the picture, in reality the fresh dawn of the new sun has arrived, and with it have come the gods amongst men to save the world. You know, they say that if a man should see the wild hunt, and is unworthy of becoming a god himself, he shall perish in its path.' Neumann finally looked at Grevle. 'Because *he* is the prey. And so it is with the new world of the Führer.'

Grevle made no attempt to run. He just stared into his eyes, because, after so many visits, and so many hours of deliberation, in the mere seconds it took this strange little fellow to speak his words, suddenly the meaning of the picture became clear to Grevle, and he understood why there was no prey.

'No,' said Grevle, almost laughing. 'You're wrong. It's not about before. It's not even about now. This picture shows the future. And in the future the so-called Gods are a mess, drunk with power. They are not hunting any more. They're running. *They* are the prey. You're right — it is a new dawn, but the sun is rising on the darkness, chasing the rapist gods from the earth they have scorched, away even from their origins, into the wilderness. To die like dogs.'

'But they are gods, Herr Grevle, not dogs. And it is I who am out hunting today, is it not?'

Grevle did not care that the man's smile had turned into one of pity, of mockery, and nodded.

'Today,' he said, then turned from the picture and walked with the man towards the exit.

369

*   *   *

Before heading to von Westarp's study, Ivar
moved along the corridor where the women's
bedrooms were located. His intention was to
pass by Eva's door, catch her eye, give her a wink
or a nod, somehow let her know that tonight was
the night, and tell her to be ready. But when he
got to her room, she was not in her bed. She
should have been. He stuck his head through the
doorway. She was not in the room at all. Only
one of the older nurses.

'Where's Eva?' Ivar said.

'Who?'

'The redhead. The girl.'

'Oh, she was moved this morning. I believe
Frau — '

Ivar was running before she had finished, back
along the corridor, past the stairs, to the door of
von Westarp's study, pounding on the door.

'Yes,' he heard von Westarp say. 'Come in.'

Ivar swung the door open.

'What have you done with her?'

Von Westarp was not sitting in his armchair, or
nursing a brandy. He was standing, leaning on
the mantel, and now, quite calm, he moved to
the door and closed it.

'And by 'her' you mean . . . ?'

'Eva.'

'Yes, of course.' The German shook his head. 'I
told you not to allow any emotional ties to form,
Snorre. That it would only lead to heartache.
More importantly, it will sully the purity of the
child she carries. Emotional distress will affect

his developing mind. Keep in mind what we are creating here. Besides, as I told you, there are other girls I shall be introducing you to.'

'They're not carrying my child.'

'*Your* child?' he laughed. 'No, no, Snorre. That baby is the property of the Reich. If it belongs to any one man, it is the Führer. The same is true of myself. And of you.'

'What have you done with her?'

'What I needed to. She is quite safe. You need not concern yourself with her, or the child. And may I remind you to whom you are speaking.'

Ivar and von Westarp stared at each other. It was Ivar who finally gave in. Eva was gone. But if he didn't kill von Westarp now, the German would see to it that he would never track her down. She was still under his power. There was only one way he was going to see her again. And that was to follow the rest of the plan.

'Forgive me, Herr Oberführer,' Ivar said, bowing his head. 'I should have listened to you. I apologize. I am your servant. I still have much to learn. Allow me to show my gratitude for your mercy and penance for my behaviour by having the privilege of polishing your boots for you.'

Ivar started to move towards the desk, but before he could reach it, von Westarp took hold of his wrist.

'That is not necessary, Snorre,' he said, his tone conciliatory.

He had overdone the subservience. It was out of character.

'I insist, Herr Oberführer,' Ivar tried.

'No, no. Absolutely not, Snorre. You are a man now. You cannot continue as a mere polish-boy. It is time you were promoted.'

'But I don't mind, Herr Oberführer. Really. Please — '

'No, *I* insist, Snorre,' von Westarp said, pulling Ivar towards him, away from the desk.

Ivar looked down. Von Westarp's boots were still on his feet. And his Luger holster was on his belt.

'I need your help once again,' he was saying. 'Come now.'

Ivar had no choice. To insist again would be suspicious. There would be another chance. There had to be.

'Very well, Herr Oberführer,' he said.

★ ★ ★

Per Bjerke rose from his seat at his desk in an out-of-the-way office in Oslo's National Gallery, put on his sheepskin coat and his hat, opened the door, locked it behind him, and then started up the red marble corridor.

Directorship of the gallery had moved from Jens Thiis's aged hands to NS member Søren Onsager in 1941. Onsager's main achievement since then had been to arrange the *Kunst og Ukunst* exhibition of 1942, in which 'genuine' art was placed next to 'degenerate' art. Only *he* did not arrange the exhibition, nor the removal from the premises of all the 'degenerate' art once the exhibition had closed. Onsager was an artist and part-time teacher and possessed no practical experience in managing galleries. His appointment had been made purely by virtue of his political affiliation. Onsager was a puppet, fed demands and directives by his German masters; a miniature version of his leader, Quisling.

The staff of Thiis's tenure had been retained to ensure administration continued smoothly. Bjerke, fifty-five years old, had arranged the 'degenerate' show, and all subsequent exhibitions. He had received no praise for his efforts, but he did not expect it. He'd worked at the National Gallery for fifteen years, and all things being right — before the war arrived and placed Onsager at the top — he had been a shoe-in as Thiis's successor. But he didn't mind this either. And nor did he mind that, in all his years of service, he had never seen the place in such a state of disrepair. Plaster was coming off the walls all over the building, pipes were dripping, the cold was freezing the water and creating cracks everywhere. The building was dying. But despite all of this, and despite attendance being down to a record low, the war years had thus far been those in his life of which he was most proud.

He had retained the pictures he was now walking past for the nation. *The Scream*, Lunds, fjord landscapes by Askevold, Adelsteen and Tidemand and Gude — they only remained in the country because he'd told the SS that leaving them in place would boost public morale; it would show the Nowegian people that the Nazis were not there merely to rape their country, that there was meaning to their occupation beyond

373

just domination. Then he told Onsager of his fears that the works might be lost entirely, as had happened in France. Removing those that did not adhere to Nazi ideals from the gallery walls was one thing, but to steal the images of Norway's historical and cultural identity was something else. If the Germans did that, then surely they could expect to see a rise in resistance to the Nazi presence.

The sycophancy he'd had to show in order to retain all these works left him feeling disgusted with himself. This revulsion at his own behaviour was salved in part by the result of the toadying — an unsavoury means to a worthy end — but also in another, more clandestine way.

At the far end of the west gallery Bjerke turned onto a flight of stone steps. Making his way down, he pulled from his pocket a small key attached to a string that was tied to a belt loop on his trousers. He checked that there was not a soul to be seen, then guided the key into the lock on the wooden donation box on the landing beneath Arbo's *Åsgårdsreien*. He removed the single envelope from within, placed it in the inside pocket of his coat, relocked the box, and left the building.

Outside, he waited for a tram in the melting snow. They had reached that glorious time of the year when it was both warm and cold, and dazzlingly bright. He raised his face to the sky and closed his eyes, basking, until finally a tram arrived, which took him east then north up Akersgata. He alighted at Trinity Church, walked along the front and made his way to a large green neoclassical building, then went up a flight of steps leading between ionic columns and entered the building beneath a sign that read *Deichmanske Bibliotek* — the Deichman Library.

Six minutes later he came out of the library, found another tram and travelled back to the gallery. He went straight to his office, removed his coat and hat, sat behind his desk, and began to leaf through the post that had been deposited on his blotter since he had left for the library. He pulled a letter knife from his desk drawer. He was about to slice an envelope open when a knock sounded at his door. He dropped the letter on the desk as the door swung wide. The letter knife remained in his hand.

Two men walked in. One, fifty years old maybe, was much smaller than the other, who was in his thirties. Both wore civilian suits, but on their lapels Per spotted swastika pins glinting in the sunlight.

'Herr Bjerke?'

The smaller of the men was thin, drawn and wore glasses. He looked and sounded weak, in need of the muscle he brought with him.

Bjerke looked from Neumann to the blade in his hand and back again.

Seeing Per's fist gripped around the hilt of that puny, blunt scrap of metal, the Teacher smiled.

★ ★ ★

Von Westarp led Ivar out of his study towards the staircase.

'They consider me a scientist in Berlin,

375

Snorre', he said. They pool me with the likes of Mengele and — '

'Mengele, Herr Oberführer?'

Von Westarp started down the staircase.

'A butcher operating unhindered under the aegis of science. Stories of a most distressing nature reach me from Poland. But I consider myself an artist. A painter must choose his paints, mix them on his palette, apply them to his canvas and eventually, over time, with talent, practice, hard work and inspiration, he hopes he will create his masterpiece.'

On the ground floor von Westarp turned to the door situated between the stair and the fireplace. The guard saluted. Von Westarp saluted back. Then as the guard opened the door, von Westarp said:

'Our endeavours here are much the same as the painter's, are they not? The only difference I perceive is that, if I am to create my masterpiece — or if I am to rediscover Nature's — I must *separate* rather than *mix*. That is all. Certainly we are not butchers, and the association with the likes of Mengele is one to which I object.'

Von Westarp led Ivar down the stairs towards the cavern in which he had watched Ivar impregnate Eva. The guard followed and closed the door, just as before.

'And just as with an artist, it does not please me when my creative process is interrupted by needless intrusions. However, sometimes it does turn out that these intrusions can inspire you to create a masterpiece.'

At the bottom of the stairs, they stopped and

von Westarp looked for his key, saying, 'And thus what before appeared to be an irritant becomes the vital ingredient.' He placed the key in the door and unlocked it, but did not open it. 'When you came to me here, Snorre, I fast realized that I could put you to use, and useful you have been in helping me keep the purity of Dueredet's environment. You have even aided me with a pregnancy. But that was with a mere girl, for I thought you were a mere boy. But you are not, are you, Snorre? You are more than a boy. You are a prime example of the very best of your people. Through your deception and your loyalty, to your country and your sister, you have shown strength, honour, intelligence and courage of the highest order.'

Realization flooded Ivar, then panic.

'You know,' he said.

'I do. And I am not angry, Snorre. I am pleased. Because now you will serve me again, this time with a woman rather than a girl. A woman who shares all your attributes.'

Von Westarp had his Luger in his hand and it was aimed at Ivar's chest.

'And thus shall my masterpiece be born.'

★　★　★

Just after Per Bjerke left the library, Arne arrived. Arne saw the older man walking away, but Bjerke did not see him. Had their eyes met, they would have made no sign of recognition in any case.

Through the entrance to the library, between the ionic columns, Arne came into a large room four storeys high, the roof a grid of opaque white tiles that sent diffused daylight down onto the seven-foot-high rows of bookshelves. Every shelf held only half its capacity. Just as the National Gallery had been purged of its 'degenerate' art, so the City Library had been purged of its 'degenerate' literature.

Arne mounted the spiral staircase to the balconies with the assurance of a man who knew where he was going. He did not encounter a soul, but the clang of his feet on the metal steps echoed out so loud he was certain it would bring people from miles around, who would see him stopping, crouching and scanning the spines of the books of Knut Hamsun.

Hamsun's most famous novel, *Hunger*, wasn't really in keeping with the Nazi ideal — the story portrayed the inner psychological workings of a descent into madness — but plenty of his other books illustrated man's pastoral life and his close relationship to the landscape, which was more consistent with the Nazis' image of the Germanic people. Even if that were not the case, Hamsun's books weren't about to be burned. The author was still alive, and though getting on for ninety, he was a sympathizer — and a vocal one. He'd sent his Nobel prize to Goebbels.

Vagabonds was the man's longest novel. In these hard times the chances of someone checking out such a brick between the moment Per Bjerke slipped an envelope between pages 443 and 444 and Arne Stornes coming to pick it up were slim. It hadn't been borrowed since 1938.

Arne did not look at the writing Svendsen had covered the envelope with. It was purely diversionary. The numbers and letters were meaningless. If found by the Germans though, they would assume it was a code, and look no further. The real intelligence was elsewhere, Arne knew, hidden from prying eyes. Arne carefully pulled the stamp from the envelope. On the back, in tiny handwriting, was written 'SSR — 22.3'. A chill rippled his skin.

SSR was SS-Reichsführer.

Finally, Himmler was returning. And in three days time. Arne had been right. Ivar had sent the letter because it contained information that needed to be passed on immediately. This was what they'd been waiting for, the culmination of all their work, the chance to change the course of the war, to alter the world for the better.

Arne put the stamp in his mouth and swallowed it, tore up the envelope, then ate each piece. Then he took another envelope from his pocket. This envelope was already stamped and addressed and inside it was a letter. All these were meaningless. Arne wouldn't be posting it in a regular post-box, and it wouldn't be going to President Gate. But he added a name above the address nonetheless: Andreas Vegard Christensen. It was a crude code. Each senior Nazi had a codename. Hitler was Erlend, Terboven was Halstein, Himmler was Andreas. V was the twenty-second letter of the alphabet, C the third. The people who would eventually receive the letter had contacts throughout the city — at the docks, the airport, the train stations. If someone big was coming in, they'd hear the whispers. Now they'd know they were true, when it was going to happen, and what to do.

Arne tucked the envelope into his pocket. Composing himself, he walked along the balcony, descended the steps and left the library.

Outside, the sun was up — of course it was. This was a great day already.

He took out the envelope and dropped it into a waste bin. It would be picked up and delivered to the top echelons of the XU in less than an hour. By which time Arne would be heading west on a train with Sofie and Leif.

To Arne this news meant they could finally complete what senior resistance officers had curtailed in 1941. Himmler. *Himmler!* They wouldn't be a part of it, but the entire XU could concentrate on the piece of information he was passing. The entire XU *would* concentrate on it. They would get everyone in the region involved. But more than that, to Arne, to Sofie, this proved the validity of Ivar's mission. Without that, Arne knew his marriage was dead. If he could show Sofie that sacrificing the boy's innocence for the good of the cause had been worth it, then perhaps there would be a chance to recover and, over time, rebuild the relationship that this war had destroyed.

Arne, preoccupied by these considerations, did not give a second thought to the two suited men — one older, smaller and bespectacled, the other younger, larger, stronger — that he saw getting out of a black Mercedes Benz outside *Deich-manske Bibliotek*. He only recalled having seen them when, some fifteen minutes later, he entered a street a couple of blocks north of the station and spotted a motorcycle and sidecar manned by two German soldiers at the next junction.

Suddenly he was not thinking about Himmler any more. Without breaking stride, he turned to look back up the street and saw the two suited men walking towards him. He picked up his pace and, coming up to the junction, hunched his shoulders, dug his hands into his pockets and avoided eye-contact with the soldiers.

'You!'

He heard the voice, but ignored it.

Instead he looked at his watch. Five minutes until the train departed. He could make it. They didn't know where he was heading. If he could get to the next crossroads he could disappear into the warren around the station, the courtyards, the office and apartment blocks. There they wouldn't have a chance of catching him. He'd grown up only a few blocks away and knew every gap and alley, every hiding place and every route from one yard to the next, and the back ways onto the platforms.

'You!'

This time Arne had to look at them. They were only a couple of metres away.

'*Heil* Hitler,' he said.

'*Heil* Hitler,' both soldiers said.

'You are — '

The soldier on the motorcycle didn't finish, though, because Arne pushed him off the vehicle and was running. The sidecar soldier had his rifle sitting over the bonnet, but he did not raise it. He did not move at all. Instead, the motorcyclist climbed to his feet, and the two simply watched the Norwegian dash headlong down the street, his arms out, working to keep him from skidding on the snow.

Arne covered the distance in less than ten seconds, but at the junction, rather than swerving into one of the streets, he slid to a halt and moved no further. In each of the three roads stood a squad of soldiers, every one of them levelling a rifle at Arne. He raised his hands into the air and turned to see the two plain-clothes men approaching. They wore swastika pins in their lapels.

'He's not coming is he?' Arne said.

'I'm afraid the Reichsführer is a very busy man, Herr Stornes,' the older, smaller one said in the voice of a woman. 'Perhaps if you cooperate you will be fortunate enough to be moved to Berlin and there have the privilege of meeting him.' He stopped in front of Arne. 'First, though, I would very much like to discuss with you a certain envelope.'

* * *

Von Westarp pushed open the iron door to the basement cavern. The room was unchanged but for a wooden stool next to the bed. Von Westarp nudged Ivar in the back with the barrel of his gun and they both entered.

Moving forward, Ivar saw a figure lying belly-down on the bed with a cover spread over it, the face obscured by its longish greasy dark hair. No, not greasy. It was wet, but not with water. It was glistening, with blood, the red seeping into the cotton of the sheets.

'How did you find out?' Ivar said.

Von Westarp looked down, and Ivar followed his gaze. From his pocket, von Westarp pulled a knife with a three-inch blade and a wooden handle. On its hilt was the monogram H7. Not Haakon's, but Håkon's — it was the coronation knife.

Ivar stared at it.

'By leaving this in Fehmer's chest,' von Westarp said, 'you saw to it that he could make a fool of me. It was not an experience I enjoyed. Not at all. But — we are here to shape the future, not malign the past. And so — '

Von Westarp ushered Ivar towards the bed.

'I won't,' he said.

'Oh, you will,' von Westarp said, his flabby lips stretched into a smile. 'Or she will be executed.'

* * *

Sofie entered the station bar and found Leif standing by the exit, looking out to the water.

'It's running on time. We should get going,' she said. 'Any sign?'

'No,' Leif said, picking up his rucksack. 'Wonder what *they're* up to.' He nodded out at the street towards three German personnel transports moving past with two jeeps. Then seeing the concern on Sofie's face, he added, 'Come on. Don't worry. He'll be here. He said he would be and he will be. This is Arne we're talking about.'

'He cares more about the letters than he does about the people who write them,' she said. 'Come on. If he gets here he can meet us on the train. *I'm* not going to miss it.'

She turned and led Leif out of the bar and across the hall towards the platforms. The cavernous hall was busy with people and the echoes of their voices. The gate to Platform 4 was congested by a huddle of people. Reaching them, Sofie and Leif joined the scrum. The smaller Sofie easily elbowed her way to the front. Leif found moving through the people more difficult and he saw Sofie show her ticket and false papers to the soldiers at the gate, who let her pass through without hindrance. On the platform, Sofie stopped to wait for Leif.

'Excuse me, sir.'

Leif instantly heard the German accent on the voice.

He looked down at the man next to him. He was just a man, not a soldier. 'Your papers please, sir.'

'Papers?' Leif said.

'Yes.'

'I don't show them to the soldiers?'

'Not today, sir.'

Leif looked over the heads of the other people. The soldiers at the gate were letting everyone through, barely even glancing at their papers. Behind them, lining the fence that divided the hall from the platform, Leif saw more plain-clothes men. Leif would not have noticed them but for one fact. Each one of them was staring at him.

Sofie saw Leif glance at her. He looked apologetic, and shrugged very slightly, but also shook his head, almost imperceptibly, and she knew straight away that he would not be making it through the barrier. She turned and started walking up the platform, as calmly as possible.

When Leif saw her walk away, he felt a wave of relief, and looked at the German again just as the guard on the platform blew his whistle.

'Papers?' Leif said.

'That's right.'

'Right. Papers. Now I understand. That accent of yours . . . I'm sure I've got something in here somewhere.'

Leif dropped his rucksack on the floor, and as he stooped to rummage within, between people's legs and the railings he saw Sofie breaking into a trot, moving alongside the train, past people waving to loved ones already aboard. Leif willed her to just climb on. *Get in. Let it take you away.*

The guard blew his whistle a second time and waved his baton. A blast of steam came from the head of the engine and the train jolted into motion just as Sofie's eyes fell on a compartment that was almost empty. Only one figure occupied it, suited, hatted, his face obscured. He opened the door for her and reached out a hand.

'Here they are,' Leif said, pulling his hand out of the bag. 'I knew they were in here somewhere.' Instead of standing up, he launched himself at the German's chest, and they both fell into the crowd of people, who shrieked and scattered like pigeons. Leif's great weight came down on top of the man, and his weak body fell limp immediately. Leif leapt to his feet and started to dash across the hall towards the exit, people clearing a path before him. The soldiers standing guard at the ticket office stepped forwards and took their rifles from their shoulders. They both went down on one knee and levelled their weapons towards the lumbering giant. Reaching the main entrance to the station, Leif pulled open the door.

Now running herself, Sofie managed to take hold of the hand stretching from the carriage door, and allowed its owner to haul her in, where she fell onto the seats.

The slamming of the carriage door coincided exactly with the crack of the soldiers' rifles. Both bullets struck Leif in the back, and he fell to his knees. On all fours he crawled out into the sun before collapsing onto the cold wet ground.

'Thank you,' Sofie said breathlessly, finding her seat, trying to compose herself. 'I hope you don't mind — '

She stopped short. Her eyes had fallen upon her Nagant revolver — it had fallen from her pocket in the leap into the compartment and now lay on the floor. She made to reach for the gun, but then stopped.

'Not at all, Fräulein,' she heard. 'I hope you do not object to my canine friend.'

The gun had landed by the panting mouth of a German Shepherd.

She looked up as the man sat and looked

down at her. His aquiline face was handsome. Smiling, Fehmer pulled a pack of cigarettes from his breast pocket.

'Do please take it,' he said, proffering her the packet. Sofie looked up at him. Was he talking about the gun or the cigarette? Was it possible that Fehmer had not seen the weapon? It was under the lip of the seat. But could he really not know who she was? Could this actually be a coincidence?

She took a cigarette. Holding her gaze, Fehmer reached out and lit it, then his own and, leaning back in his seat, released the smoke in a satisfied plume.

'But I am afraid the Nagant is a most unreliable weapon, Frau Stornes. Soviet. And should it misfire, what then shall you do?'

★ ★ ★

Ivar saw his chance and rushed at von Westarp. He moved too quickly for the guard to take aim, and managed to land a blow on von Westarp, sending the coronation knife skidding towards the bed. But his attempt to escape was over as soon as it began. Von Westarp hit the back of his head with the Luger and Ivar fell to his knees.

Von Westarp stepped back.

'Now,' he said. 'Get up. And get to work.'

Ivar glared at him, but clambered to his feet.

'Get on with it,' von Westarp said, raising the Luger.

Ivar turned, and started to approach the bed.

'Who is she?' he said.

Von Westarp tutted and said, 'Complete the sequence of names. Johan and Heidi Gulbrand-sen . . . '

Ivar took the few steps to the bed and placed a hand on the woman's back.

'Tord Svendsen . . . '

Ivar felt for a pulse.

'Jonas Grevle . . . '

She was still alive.

'Per Bjerke . . . '

Ivar raised his hand to her hair.

'Reidar Thomassen . . . '

He peeled back a strand of hair sticking to her disfigured face.

'Geir Larsgård . . . '

And another.

'Leif Tidnes . . . '

The face was bruised, battered and bloody.

'Arne Stornes . . . '

But the eyes looking out at him from behind the gore were unmistakable.

It was as though her soul had been lifted from the beautiful, sorrowful face he had known and shifted into this . . . this inanimate, bloody mess. But the eyes were still the same. They still retained the strength, and were trying to communicate.

'Sofie,' Ivar whispered.

★　★　★

The blow Fehmer had administered had knocked Sofie out. Coming to, pain pounded at her temple. The noise hammering at her head

388

was emanating from the wheels and rails below. She was still on that train. But somewhere different, an empty baggage carriage maybe. A single lightbulb swayed at the end of its cord a metre in front of her. Beyond it sat Arne, his head bowed, unaware that she had awoken. Beyond him was a metal table with some items laid out upon it that she could not identify. Sofie tried to move her hands, but could not. She turned her head in an attempt to assess the nature of her bindings, but another sight distracted her. On the floor lay an unconscious man. His shoes had been removed and his feet were a sticky bloody mess. His trousers were torn, so too his shirt, dried blood staining both. And his face — Sofie turned away in disgust, but soon enough her gaze returned to the poor wretch. His face was swollen like a boxer's, one of his eyes entirely closed up, his cheek below it opened to the bone, the whole visage red with blood and bruising.

'It's Geir.' Arne's voice penetrated the horror. He was looking at the body too. 'Poor bastard.'

She had not seen it to start with — the man on the floor was too mangled to recognize — but now Arne said it, she saw he was right.

'Then who — ?' she tried, looking at her husband.

'Per, Svendsen, Grevle. What does it matter? It's happened. And it's my fault. I should have seen it immediately. The letter. I'm sorry.'

'There's only one person to blame here, Arne,' Sofie said, trying to get him to look away from Geir, at her, his eyes glazed with defeat. 'Fehmer.

389

This is all him. We know what's going to happen here, no matter what gets said. Don't we? Arne? Listen to me.'

'What're you trying to say?' He met her gaze. He was sunk. They all were, the whole unit. And Arne was broken, she could see it in his eyes.

'When that door opens,' she said, 'it will be as good as a bullet into each of our heads. Our lives are over, no matter what happens, no matter what we tell him. But there's no need to let others die today.'

'Ivar?'

She nodded.

'Are you crazy?' Arne said. 'They set up the letter to come from him. They know. The only hope for him is that he's working for them.'

'It's not *only* Ivar. It's everyone. We have to protect the whole organization.'

He smiled despite the tears forming in his eyes.

'What is it?' she said, smiling back.

'Welcome back. I lost the real Sofie for a bit back there, you know?'

'I'm sorry, Arne.'

'Don't be.'

'But we have to protect everyone. You know how this has to go.'

He nodded. 'All right. But no matter what happens, no matter what gets said, it means nothing, okay? I love you. Do you understand that?'

'I do.'

'And, Sofie?' he said. 'Thank you for being my wife.'

Sofie could feel the heat of tears rising in her own eyes.

'I love you, too.'

He leaned back.

'And that's all that matters. What comes next — it's just a bad dream. Okay? A bad dream. We'll wake up from it soon enough and we'll both be there, and we'll hold our baby in our arms, and hold him high.'

His tears were rolling down his face now. He couldn't say a word more, and did not need to because at that moment Fehmer and his dog appeared at the door, accompanied by the two men who had taken Arne.

'Herr und Frau Stornes,' Fehmer said jovially. 'Welcome to this makeshift approximation of Victoria Terrasse. It does not look like much, I know, but let me assure you it is quite sufficient for my needs. Now, I believe you, Herr Stornes, have already met Sturmbannführer Neumann. Allow me to introduce him to you, Frau Stornes.'

Sofie was staring at the Germans, at the panting dog, and had begun to shake uncontrollably.

'Sofie?' Arne said, ignoring the Germans completely.

'Sturmbannführer Neumann only arrived from Berlin relatively recently and therefore does not know, as I do, of the fortitude the Norwegian is capable of exhibiting in times of hardship.'

'Look at me, Sofie,' Arne said, but she didn't. 'Now, Sofie!'

The firmness of Arne's words reached her and

391

Sofie faced her husband. 'Just look at me,' he said. 'And remember.'

'For I, of course,' Fehmer continued, 'have been entertained by your fellow countrymen on a number of occasions. And I am also a gambling man. It is thus that our wager came about. Let me explain. Neumann believes that if we torture your wife before you, Herr Stornes, we will unlock a deluge of information from within you, including the names and whereabouts of all of your contacts, both here and in London, and of course the keys to the codes you employ. He thinks that by telling you that you have the power to spare your wife such treatment, you will accept defeat. I, on the other hand, believe that to have evaded capture for so long, your dedication to the cause must be greater than even the love a husband harbours for his wife. And so,' he clapped his gloved hands and rubbed them together, 'without further ado — let us begin.'

'Neumann?' Arne said to the spectacled German, who nodded acknowledgement of his name with mild interest. 'Are you married?' Neumann nodded again. 'And you love your wife?' It took him longer this time, but eventually Neumann nodded a third time. 'Then you're a lucky man,' Arne told him. 'Me? Not so lucky. Every time I see this beautiful face, do you know what I see? The face of my unborn child. The son she killed for the good of our cause. And Fehmer knows that. You've been tricked, *Sturm-bann-führer*.' He enunciated each syllable with as much mockery as he could muster. 'You

392

know it's not the cause that'll keep my mouth shut. Don't you, Wolfgang? It's hatred. So you may as well hand over your money right now, Neumann, and shoot us both.'

'Clever,' Fehmer said, laughing, 'but I'm afraid, Herr Stornes, a bet is a bet,' and he hit Sofie so hard her chair fell over backwards.

Neumann's man picked Sofie back up. Her head was lolling already. Her eyes looked drunk. Her vision would be blurred and soon enough her body and that woozy head would numb itself to the pain. It had to, because despite his words to her, Arne didn't know how long he could watch his wife, his Sofie, being beaten while pretending he didn't care. And all just for a cause. *The* cause. *Their* cause.

'The information, Stornes,' Fehmer said casually, unconvinced that his demands would be met, already preparing his gloved fist for a second blow. 'Give us the information and all this will stop.'

'No,' Arne said. 'It won't. And I don't want it to. It shouldn't. She killed my boy, and with him any chance of a family.' He could not stop himself from clenching at the rope that held his hands and feet to the chair. 'I despise her.'

Fehmer laughed again, incredulous this time, bending down to occupy Arne's field of vision.

'Do you mean to say that she is incapable of bearing children?'

Arne spat in his face, then said, 'Of course she is.'

'Truly? She is barren?' Fehmer said, wiping the spit off his cheek and looking at it on his

393

fingers. His smile widened into a manic grin. 'Oh, how wonderful,' he said. 'For me. For Sofie, not so good, I'm afraid.'

He spun and hit her again. This time the soldier Neumann had come in with kept her chair in place. Her head whipped back, then slumped forward again. Her battered face was virtually unrecognizable, both eyes swollen shut, her hair lank with blood. She was unconscious.

Fehmer turned to Arne, his eyebrows raised.

'She killed my child!' Arne shouted, looking at her, tears blurring his vision.

'You see, Herr Neumann?' Fehmer said. 'It is as I told you. They are devoted to the cause above all else. In my experience, more creative techniques than patience and crude psychology are required to break the Norwegian.' Then he lifted his finger towards the younger man who had come in with Neumann. 'Take her away. We have no more need for her here.' Fehmer was facing Arne again, with his head tilted slightly, like an artist contemplating his model, stroking the dog.

Arne looked back at him. It was his turn.

'*You* killed my child!' he spat.

* * *

Silence reigned as Ivar crouched by Sofie's side, staring at her beaten face, looking into her eyes, trying to discern the meaning of their expression.

'Get on with it, boy,' von Westarp said impatiently.

'You bastards,' Ivar said, rising back to his feet.

394

Tears were filling his eyes.

The guard wasn't about to be outpaced a second time, and immediately took aim at Ivar.

'What have you done to her?' Ivar said.

'We have Fehmer to thank for that, the fool,' von Westarp said. 'But she will live. And she will breed. Now, *get on with it* — '

Von Westarp was distracted by something behind Ivar. Ivar spun round and saw Sofie climbing to her feet. The coronation knife was in her hand.

'Sofie, I — '

'I have lost one child,' she croaked. 'Not another. I'm sorry, Ivar.'

And she placed the knife to her own throat and dragged the blade across it, blood instantly gushing from the wound. She stood there for a second, staring at Ivar. Then she crumpled, and the boy screamed out as he rushed to her and caught her in his arms.

17

Curt was speeding over the black water of the fjord. The rushing air streaked the sweat back over his face, reducing it to white slashes of salt. He had to turn his face sideways to breathe. The sun was on the dip and the clouds were coming in. This was the least hot he'd felt in months. The fjord was still busy, though — yachts, water skiers, groups boozing on decks in the sun.

Curt gave them all as wide a berth as he could, but even with his meandering course, the boat ate up the knots and in no time he saw an island coming up from the south. Håøya was a great teardrop-shaped line of tree-covered hills sticking out of the water. It nearly blocked up the waterway, and led right up to the narrowest point of the fjord at Drøbak. The wreck site was east of the island, but Curt had already decided to approach it from the south. According to the map, there was a longer line of sight from that direction, which would give him more time to work out how to play the situation without looking like he was prowling. He moved to the right of the land, and bombed down to the southern tip.

Rounding it, he came face to face with a rack of half a dozen six-inch guns pointing right at him. They were situated on a smaller island next to Håøya, that housed an old fort that was now a

396

museum; everywhere he looked people were walking around, holding up cameras. The water was just as busy and Curt pulled the thrust lever down to a crawl in order to scan the traffic for evidence of diving activity. He felt the heat again as soon as he slowed, pounding against his back despite the gathering clouds, sweat instantly soaking into his shirt. He pulled it off. He may not have looked like just another pleasure seeker, but it made him feel less like a black beggar in another man's boat. Even with all the on-water activity, it didn't take him long to find what he was looking for.

Over on the mainland to his right, north of the red, yellow and white timber houses of Drøbak lay a marina, a single jetty with a dozen boats moored to it. A little way out from there, anchored and stationary, sat a blue-hulled motor boat, thirty feet long. Two aerials grew high out of a cabin placed further forward than usual. It made the whole vessel look front-heavy.

This design anomaly was in order to accommodate the large, open-air deck at the back of the boat, currently occupied by a group of men — it was difficult to tell exactly how many there were because each of them wore a black-and-neon wetsuit, and they melded together at this distance. But certainly they were Scuba frogmen. Curt idled at a safe distance and took a better look.

One of them, with a double cylinder on his back and another under each arm, climbed down a ladder into the water, made a hand signal and then sank.

Curt looked directly north. Between the dive

boat and Håøya lay the Askholmen islands. There were four of them, three in a column north to south, with a fourth to the east of the northernmost. They were little more than low humps of grey rock breaking the surface of the water. The northernmost of them was the largest of the group, and had a few trees sprouting, but even that wasn't more than two hundred metres from north to south. He'd been right — if you were running a line to a wreck under the traffic from the blue-hulled boat, those islands would be the place to come up with whatever you found down there.

Curt turned the wheel and headed west, towards Håøya, until the dive boat was eclipsed by the islands. Then he chugged the Zodiac north a way and, when the Askholmen islands were due east of him, the boat directly beyond them, he spun the wheel again, heading straight across, bringing his speed down even further as he drew closer to the largest of the islands, cutting the engine out altogether at twenty metres, allowing momentum to take him forward. As far as he could tell, he was completely out of sight.

The shore of the island was a steep bank, the rocks sinking straight down into dark water, so when the boat made contact Curt lowered himself into the water with the tie-off rope wrapped around his fist. The water was icy compared to the air, and he carried on sinking until he felt rock under his feet just as his nipples hit the cold. Ten feet further out, and he'd be under the surface. The other side would be the same. Fifty out, a hundred, and you had to go down ninety metres to hit a wreck. Curt ducked his head under, wiped off the sweat residue, then edged forwards.

The stone under his battered All Stars was slippery, the current strong, and he lost his footing, floundering for a moment before his left hand found a hold on the bank. He hoisted himself up onto dry land and clambered along the shoreline, pulling the boat through the water next to him until he came to a point where the current tugging at the Zodiac was diverted by a small promontory sticking ten feet out into the open water. He positioned the boat close to the bank, with its nose pointed outward, then dropped a couple of loops from the rope and moved further up onto the island to tie it off at the base of a clawing shrub. He pulled it. Tightened it. Tested it. This was not the time or the place to let a shoddy knot send your Zodiac drifting down to Denmark.

Satisfied, Curt began to move towards the scrubby trees growing at the centre of the island. To start with, the ground consisted of smooth, weathered rock, with a little brush growing from the fissures, but further up it was covered in a loose shale that crunched underfoot. Beneath the cover of the trees, pine needles carpeted the ground and dulled the sound. Dodging between the pillar-straight trunks, he made out a small, gentle hillock of bald stone that rose up ten feet or so, but well below the height of the trees. Curt crawled his way upward, lying flat when he came within arm's reach of the top, edging further to see over.

The trees formed a wreath around the hillock. On the other side, a tree-free path ten metres wide ran all the way down to the water's edge forty metres away. This opened up a view to the fourth island, which was low and treeless, and from his vantage point Curt could see beyond it, across the channel to the dive boat on the other side.

Closer in, he saw as he rose, a thick-set man in dark-blue shorts and a forest-green fleece jacket was walking up the clearing straight towards him. Curt instantly dropped back onto his belly.

'*Eh — Georges. Ici,*' Curt heard, the voice sounding a little further away than he'd expected; it was accompanied by the sound of spitting and the hollow noise of air being released from a regulator.

Curt waited and listened. Hearing nothing, he peeked over the lip of the rock again. The fleece had stopped and was facing the other way now, down to where a second man in a wetsuit and mask was slowly swimming towards the shore. He grabbed hold of the bank and raised himself up onto his elbows. This diver was wearing only one cylinder. A shallow diver.

The fleece made his way down to him. The diver reached up with both hands and passed something to him, which the fleece took with both his hands and lumped down on the rock beside him. It gave out a wet thud.

'*Combien de temps jusqu'à ce que le premier remonte à la surface?*' the fleece said.

The object was muddy and soggy with algae, small enough for two hands to wrap themselves comfortably around it — black or maybe grey in colour, with patches of blue and green.

The diver looked at his watch.

'*Dix-sept minutes. Et puis à cinq minutes d'intervalle si tout va comme prévu.*'

The diver pushed off, swimming back out, but he didn't put his regulator back in his mouth. He lowered his masked eyes beneath the surface, brought them up again, looked at his watch, tutted. But he didn't dive.

Curt waited until the diver drifted to face away from him, then he lifted himself up a few more centimetres. The other man, the fleece, moved out of sight, into the trees to the left. Curt concentrated on trying to listen to the man's movements, but soon he realized he couldn't hear anything but his own shallow breathing.

Here were two divers, and they were bringing something up. Something that looked and sounded heavy.

Curt backed down from his vantage point. His heart was racing. Crouching on level ground, he bowed his head and took in air as slowly and smoothly as he could.

Was it really possible the old man had been speaking the truth? And just like that, Curt's heart was thumping at his chest again. He breathed, concentrated and lowered himself onto all fours before crawling north, watching through the trunks for the guy in the fleece. Sweat rolled down his face and across his bare back, but as he moved, it became apparent that the hillock was only the highest point of a ridge that ran the length of the island like a spine. Amongst the trees again, Curt was almost at the edge of that slope when he heard the voice again — foreign, close, only metres away.

'Nous serons ici toute la journée et toute la nuit.'

As he lay on his belly, Curt caught a glimpse through the trees ahead of the fleece approaching. Just over the ridge from the divers' side of the island, his forehead pressed to the ground, Curt held his breath, staring at the rock and the pine needles in front of his face, praying to God that he wouldn't be seen, that he melted into the rock.

The same voice came again.

'Mais . . . '

The man's footsteps were so close that Curt was sure he could feel vibrations in the rock. Then they stopped, the voice too. Curt was certain he'd been seen, that it was only the sight of him lying on the ground that had stunned the fleece into momentary silence. But there came only a grunt, followed by a dull, metallic thud, and then the footsteps again — receding this time.

'Nous sommes payés pour ça, je suppose . . . '

Curt glanced over the ridge. The man was walking away. Somehow, Curt had melted into the rock. Or at least that was how it seemed. He was in a hollow in the stone, just below the spine, sinking him out of the fleece's eyeline. If Curt stayed down he was completely hidden from view. The only way he'd be seen there was if the fleece stepped over the ridge and landed on top of him.

Up on his elbows, Curt watched the man down to the water, where he nodded at the diver. Curt's heart started up again.

Just over the lip, lying in another hollow, like mutant dragon eggs in a stone nest, was a pile of six sodden lumps, grey, brown and green covering the coarse weave of hessian sacking. Each one measured six inches by ten. And they were completely unguarded.

Curt stretched out his hand and grasped one of the lumps, tried to move it. But he couldn't. *It was too heavy.* He had to use both hands, just as the other men had. Nothing weighing that much was worthless.

Curt started bringing the sack towards his body, but then stopped.

He could take them one by one back to the boat, but there had been at least ten frogmen on the dive boat, and they hadn't started coming up from deco yet. As they rose, eggs would be added to the pile. The more sacks Curt removed from the nest, the more likely they'd notice their disappearance. He needed to substitute.

He pushed the sack back into place, rolled back over the ridge, and moved away.

Back at the Zodiac he didn't have to worry so much about noise, as there was plenty to cover him. Beneath the seat was a storage box. He pushed the cushion off, grabbed a rock from the shore and thwacked the loop, snapping the small padlock. He flipped open the lid and emptied the contents: a couple of life jackets, some spare rope, a ten-litre emergency jerry, a few thick waterproof poly-bags, a first-aid kit. He threw

403

the bags onto land and unzipped the red nylon first-aid kit, tipping it out onto the floor of the boat, rummaging for what he needed: the stitch kit and folding scissors. Unravelling some of the blue nylon thread, he finally succeeded in feeding it through the eye of the needle, tying it off so it couldn't slip back through. Then he wound the thread back up, jammed the needle into the card spool to keep it in place and stuffed the lot, along with the scissors, into his trouser pocket.

Moving to the back of the boat, he lifted the cowl off the engine, primed the fuel, slipped the knotted cord into the flywheel and wound it around, leaving it ready for a fast exit. Then he collected the poly-bags and headed back to the trees again. Before he entered them, he pushed two of the three bags into his other trouser pocket, as far as they would go. Then, dropping to his knees, he opened the third and half-filled it with shale rock chips. Once he had enough, he twisted the slack up and hoisted it over his shoulder. Ducking as low as he could, he moved off into the trees. Coming through the trunks, Curt discerned immediately that the situation by the water had altered.

The guy in the fleece was still down by the water's edge, facing out towards the diver, who remained hanging in the water, but there were also two additional men, up by the stash. One was stripped to his shorts and feeding his diving equipment into a black rubber holdall. The other was removing his buoyancy vest and cylinders. Once they were both in their shorts, they moved to the tree line, away from the stash, and sat looking the other way, watching the water.

Curt needed cover to work in. Next to the stash was a tree and a piece of thick bush. It would have to do. Lying in the hollow would be too awkward. He scampered across and lowered the plastic bag holding the shale onto the needles behind the bush. He then sat against the trunk of the tree and pulled the needle and thread and scissors from his pocket. He opened up the scissors and laid them on the ground next to the bag. Then he unwound a two-foot length of thread and laid that out next to the scissors. Finally he pulled out the two plastic bags he'd stuffed in his pocket and proceeded to untwist one.

The plastic crackled like lightning. Curt stopped and looked over his shoulder towards the water. He could see all the way down. The two divers were smoking at the tree line and the other guy was still down by the water. The shallow diver had gone, though, only bubbles on the water's surface marking his location.

Curt placed the empty bag between his legs and opened it with yet more rustling. Two more eggs had been added to the nest, making eight. He reached over and lifted out the nearest one, dragging it back towards him, a few inches at a time.

Curt placed the sack in the empty plastic bag between his legs, put the blade of the scissors to the top seam of the sacking and carefully scraped away the dirt with a downwards motion, pushing aside the mud and algae until the closing twine was revealed. He did this all the way along the topside, and then cut through each of the stitches. He then lowered the small sack onto its side within the plastic bag, and he heard dull clanks as the contents poured out. He put his hand in the sack and lifted out a handful. Each nugget was different — size, shape, even shade — but that one small handful weighed as much as two litres of water. And there were seven more bags back there waiting, with more being brought up as he worked.

Everything the old man had told him had sounded crazy, but here it was — gold, right in his hands. He'd been telling the truth.

Staring at the handful, Curt could feel his chest and throat tightening again. His heart was playing his ribs like a xylophone. He forced himself to breathe.

If he was going to succeed, he had to keep disciplined, focused. He placed the handful back into the bag and withdrew the empty sack, placing it on the ground to his right. He then filled it with shale from the other bag. When it was full, he sewed it back up with the needle and thread, tied it off and cut the thread. The thread glowed medical blue against the ancient water-damaged sacking, and he smeared it with dirt as best he could. Then he replaced the sack and took another one to work on. Setting it down inside the bag between his legs, he began the process over again, emptying it, refilling it and sewing it closed, just as he had done with the first. It was as he was scooping gravel into the third that he heard the sound of water breaking, and a voice.

'*Eh, Georges,*' it said.

Curt looked round. The diver was back, with company this time. Another masked man.

'*Ils vont remonter régulièrement maintenant. Je vais redescendre.*'

'*Ici,*' the guy in the fleece said to the new man. 'Come here.'

The new diver was already swimming towards him. When he arrived at the bank, his hands broke the surface and he passed the Frenchman, Georges, another small sack. Georges placed it on the ground then reached out again and hoisted the diver out of the water. He wore a double cylinder on his wide back, and one under each arm. Sitting, he removed his mask and flippers, then got to his feet.

'Put the equipment over there,' Georges said in thickly accented English. 'With the rest of these.' He passed the sack to the diver. 'Change, and stay out of sight.'

'How many do we have?' Curt had heard the voice before from a hundred different Sandhurst-trained officers telling him what to do, how and when. This one had taken a different route to Curt, and the disgrace must have taken a different form, but somehow two British Army veterans had ended up in the same place.

'With that one, nine now,' Georges said.

The Englishman started moving towards the trees, sluggish with exhaustion and the weight of his equipment — towards the gold. Towards Curt. He was a hundred feet away.

Curt whipped back behind the tree. He still

had a sack from the nest. It was only three-quarters full of shale, but it would have to do. Curt shoved the needle into the sacking and sewed. Wet with slime, mud and sweat, his fingers slipped along the thin metal of the needle.

He glanced back round. Seventy feet.

Curt cut the thread, tied it, muddied it, lumped the sack back with its brothers and rolled away out of sight behind the bush, lying his dark body over the glaring white plastic bags.

He could make out the Sandhurst diver through the bush. The man stopped a few metres from the stash, placed the sack on the ground, then straightened and began to remove his equipment — cylinders, vest, belt, neoprene gloves, balaclava, and last of all his wetsuit — and placed it all in a black rubber holdall. He looked to be in his forties and was built like a barn, as though he spent all day chopping wood in the mountains. Clipping the bag shut, he picked up a green fleece and headed over to the other two men.

Curt edged off the plastic bags and positioned himself by the tree again. This time he manoeuvred himself into a crouch. With his feet on the floor, and his arms working between his knees, he could be at full sprint in just one push, no delay.

He reached for a fourth sack. When the sack was full, stitched and muddied, he replaced it. He did not take another, however. Four would be more than heavy enough for one trip. He shimmied backwards to the bush, crouched on his feet again and slowly wrapped the slack from the takings bag around his right fist. He felt every muscle in his worn body stretch and tighten. The bag wasn't even half full, but it weighed far more than the shale had. The gold clattered as it was raised from the stone and found its new lie in the bag, and the plastic audibly strained under the mass. Curt put his left hand underneath to support it, and grasped it to his belly like a rugby ball, rising to stand at the same time.

Up on his feet he knew he was exposed, and he glanced again at the men. They hadn't seen him, or heard him, and he crept the twenty feet that took him behind the rise, and once he was out of sight, he shifted up a gear.

At the Zodiac, he placed the bag between the bench and the steering column. By the time he got back to the rise, the situation had changed again, and he edged back out of sight.

A new diver was peeling off his gear up near the stash. Once he had stripped and donned a fleece, he lifted a sack from the ground and placed it with the rest. From where he was standing, Curt could see the plastic bag and the thread just on the other side of the bush from the diver, all bright as torches. But the shrub apparently hid them from the diver, and the man went about his business, unrolling another rubberized holdall and pushing his equipment into it. Then he placed the holdall with the others and headed over to his fellow divers, who were standing now. The Englishman offered the new arrival a cigarette, and they began to talk, too quietly for Curt to hear, gesticulating as though they were sculpting something from the air.

Down by the water, Georges was talking to the shallow diver.

Curt ducked across to the trunk. There he opened the third plastic bag between his legs, plucked a sack and placed it inside the bag. He processed it efficiently, and a second, but had to pause before replacing the next one when two further divers surfaced, almost at the same time.

He waited. Both filled holdalls, but neither added to the stash. Their gold must have come up already. That meant the flow was slowing. One more sack and Curt's bag would be as full as the last one had been.

Once the two divers had retreated to the growing pack, Curt replaced the sack and grasped another.

As he was coming back to position, yet another diver surfaced.

'It's fucking boring down there, man,' he called out, in a voice thick with Afrikaans.

The rest of them cheered, all of them on their feet now, smelling the finish line, full of macho congratulation — back slaps, punches, wrestle holds — raising the testosterone and preventing exhaustion from setting in.

'There's nowhere to spend this, that's for sure,' the South African continued, lumping a sack onto the bank next to him. 'How many have we got now, Georgie Boy?'

'With yours, that's ten,' Georges replied.

Curt got to work, scraping away the mud,

cutting through the thread. He glanced round. The South African was making his way up to the equipment store. Curt emptied the gold into the bag, but stopped when he heard the snap of the diver unravelling a holdall. The clanking of cylinders followed as the man stuffed his equipment in. Then, over the increasing noise from the other men, Curt heard footsteps as the diver came to the store, then that wet, metallic thud again, as another sack joined the nest. Curt waited to hear the footsteps receding, but the sound did not come. Instead Curt heard that distinctive voice counting.

He was counting the sacks.

Curt looked at his feet, At the sack inside the bag.

The South African arrived at the number eight, then started again from one. Eight again. Curt turned his head slightly. Through the bush he could see the face in profile, feet away, counting to eight a third time, confusion written all over it.

'Hey,' the South African said, getting to his feet and lumbering his rugby-player body down towards the other men. 'Georgie Boy.'

Curt broke into action, grabbing shale and dropping it into the sack.

'*Oui?*' Georges's voice said.

'How many sacks did you say there're meant to be?'

Curt put a fifth and sixth handful into the sack, then snatched the needle and stuffed it through the sacking. Over the top, back round, through again.

411

'Ten,' Georges answered.

'Then why are there only eight up there?' the South African said.

'What? That's ridiculous,' Georges answered, unbothered.

'Are you telling me I can't count, my little Frenchie?'

Curt tried to tie off the thread, but his fingers were shaking too much. He pulled it tight, cut it, took a deep breath and held it as he tied a fast, loose half-bow and rubbed his mud-smeared fingers along the thread. The blue still glared out, but he didn't have time to conceal it any further.

'Ridiculous,' Georges repeated. His voice was still a distance away, but coming closer, no doubt about it — as were the footsteps of at least two more men.

'Why don't we just take a look?' the Englishman said.

Curt glanced round the trunk. They were all coming. With both hands he threw the sack towards the others. It landed, rolled over and stopped.

Curt stopped still too. His shoulder was exposed, but if he moved, if he tried to hide himself, he'd be spotted. Total, unerring stillness was his only chance.

Curt couldn't see the men but heard them counting — counting the dummy sacks held together with twenty-first-century blue nylon thread.

The counting stopped.

'Frank is correct, gentlemen,' Georges said.

'But the count is nine. *One* bag is missing.'

The men fell silent.

Curt felt his gut turn to liquid. *One short?* He glanced about himself without moving his head. He saw only plastic bags. One gravel, one gold. No sacks. He hadn't overlooked any, he hadn't been sloppy. *How could they be short one bag?*

'Then what the fuck's happened to it, eh?' the South African said. 'This is fucked, man. Totally fucked. Whichever one of you took it think the rest of us are fucking stupid, do you?'

'We must search the equipment bags,' said an Eastern European voice.

'We'll have to search the whole fucking island,' the South African said.

'No one has been out of sight of the other men since I came up,' the same Eastern European voice said.

'Line them up,' Georges said, his voice agitated now. 'Count again.'

'We counted, Georges. Nine. It should be ten — you said it yourself. And if what this fella says is true, you know what that means. Only you Frenchies been up here alone.'

'Idiot,' Georges said. 'You cannot even count to nine and you dare accuse me — '

Sweat was dripping down Curt's forehead into his eyes. He blinked repeatedly, fighting the temptation to move and wipe away the stinging sensation. If they came for him, he had to be ready. Given their size, and their tiredness after such a dive, he'd be faster — but they'd still be on him before he could get the Zodiac running. Problem was, he'd been holding his breath for so

413

long that he wasn't far away from a sudden uncontrollable intake of air. And that would not be silent. But he had to hold it. Sliding his right hand up, he clamped his nose and mouth shut. Seconds later, his chest started to heave from lack of oxygen. The palpitations were small, but they were growing already.

'Frank,' the Englishman said. 'Do you really think Georges would tell you there were ten when telling you nine would have settled this with immediate effect? He has a right to be offended, don't you think?' Curt's vision began to blur as the Englishman said, 'I put the blasted thing down here when I changed. Forgot to put it with the rest. Nothing more sinister than that.'

The clunk of metal against metal sounded 'And that's ten,' the Englishman said.

The Frenchman said, '*Dix. Pas huit, pas neuf. Dix*,' as Curt's vision clouded. His arm dropped and his hand landed on the ground in the open.

But none of the divers saw it. The hollow, receding footsteps were the last things Curt heard before losing consciousness.

He came to seconds later, his body sucking in air on automatic. As the oxygen rushed through his body he retracted his arm, then heard the Englishman's voice again, further away now, but raised.

'Form a chain,' he called.

Looking round, Curt saw the man organizing the others, Georges at his side. The shallow diver was still in the water, which suggested there were more divers to come, but it looked like they were getting ready to move out nonetheless. Curt would let them do just that. Four sacks' worth of gold lay in the plastic bag. It'd be heavy and he didn't feel good. He'd just sit tight and wait until they were gone.

He heard someone grunt, close by.

It was Georges. Curt saw him through the bush. He was crouching by the nest.

Georges lifted a sack with one hand. But instead of walking away, he passed it to the Eastern European, who was standing at arms' length behind him. The Eastern European passed it to the South African, standing behind him.

'Feel heavier under water, don't they?' the South African said.

It was about then that anxiety started turning Curt's belly inside out.

The South African passed the sack on down the chain. Georges crouched down again, picked up another, passed it on. The Eastern European weighed it in his hand.

'They do. It's strange.'

Curt reached out and started twisting up the slack on the plastic bag, the rustling covered by the continuing conversation.

'Must be the pressure. All that water on top of it.'

The Eastern European passed the sack to the South African and took another from Georges.

The South African passed the sack to the man behind him.

'Or it's the water soaking in,' the Eastern European said.

Curt dragged the bag over, lifted it onto his

thighs and clasped it to his chest, leaning forward and tensing the muscles in his legs.

'Are you serious?' the South African said.

The Eastern European took another sack from Georges.

'But this one isn't light. It's heavier.'

Curt took one deep breath and let it out slowly, feeding oxygen into his bloodstream. And another. He was going to need all the strength he could find.

'Now that *is* weird,' the South African said.

'No, it is not,' Georges said. 'Because this one is full of gold.'

'Then what's in the others? Gravel?' the South African laughed. But then he took the sack from the Eastern European. '*What the fuck?*'

Curt heard tearing, then the sound of shale raining onto stone.

'*What the fuck*, indeed,' Georges said.

Curt drove his foot against the trunk and launched himself. He didn't look back and at first he couldn't tell if the divers had seen him, but then he heard them roar.

He sprinted on, leaping from rock to rock, slipping on loose pine needles, the blood pulsing from his feet as he grasped the bag to his chest. He saw the bank ahead and the Zodiac and threw the bag ahead of him into the boat. Momentum carried him in after it. Leaping to his feet, he pulled the rope free from the boat and grabbed the flywheel cord. Placing his other hand on the body of the motor, he gave the cord all he had.

The engine spat.

But it didn't take.

His hands shaking, he ran the cord through his hand, seeking the knot, looking back for his pursuers. He heard the South African before he saw him coming from the trees, screaming and swearing, leading the charge, the rest coming out after him now.

Curt managed to place the knot in a notch in the flywheel and wind it round. He pulled it off — still nothing. He grabbed the knot in the cord, tried to put it in place again, but it slipped out. He forced himself not to look up at the men coming down at him, to concentrate on what he had to do, and put the knot in, wound it, turned, kicked the throttle up all the way, pushed away from the bank with his foot and then pulled at the cord, and fell face-down into the boat just as the South African made it to the bank. But the diver didn't stop there.

The engine took and the South African flew. The engine roared and the boat shot away from the island.

The South African was in the boat, and was on Curt in a second.

Pain tore through Curt's body as the man pounded at his kidneys with his fists. Then he was flipped round and was looking into pink-skinned fury as the South African whipped his face from side to side. By then Curt was inert with sheer exhaustion, and the South African stopped and looked up, reached out and the engine calmed. Then he faced Curt again, between his knees.

'So you thought you could take our gear, did

you?' he said. 'Well, I've got to say, boy. It was a nice try.'

He looked about them for a second.

'That's quite an engine you got back there.' He was smiling. 'You'd be able to outrun Henry's rusty blue fucker any day, eh?' He laughed and then: 'So really, before you go, I should thank you.'

Curt felt fat muscular fingers wrap themselves around his throat. He could feel his kidneys throbbing, his face swelling, his gut snaking. The fingers began to squeeze, pushing the muscles in his neck in on themselves, constricting his windpipe. Curt tried to struggle, but the man was too strong, and as he wriggled he let air out of his lungs, air that he could not replace. Curt felt his larynx moving as it began to crush under the strain. His body flipped and thrashed, his head shook, anything to get that smiling creature off him, to fill his lungs. But nothing he did had any effect.

'Just go to sleep, my friend.' The South African had lowered his face to Curt's, his voice whispering in his ear. 'This is it for you. Don't make it a struggle. Experience it. Feel it.'

All Curt could see of the man was his neck, thick, strong, veined.

And then the South African screamed, right in Curt's ear, because Curt had succeeded in stretching to one side and had bitten down on that neck with all he had. He had felt the skin under his teeth tighten, then loosen again as it gave way. The man's grasp around Curt's neck loosened, too, and when he lurched away, still screaming, Curt held on like a limpet. His back hit the floor of the boat as the South African finally managed to jerk him away. The anger and pain riddling the South African's face morphed to confusion when he saw Curt lying there, his chin bloodied like a vampire. That became fear when Curt spat a bloody clod out of his mouth onto the deck. With Curt gasping in wet, bloody air, the South African raised his right hand to the great gash in his throat, then lost his balance as his sight failed and life drained from him. He slid over the side, into the black water.

18

As Sofie died, her hand relaxed and the knife fell into Ivar's lap. He grabbed the knife and started swinging it at von Westarp, and the guard as he approached.

'Give him room,' von Westarp said, waving back the guard.

'Open the door,' Ivar said, holding the knife as steadily as he was able, and rising to his feet. Sofie's body slumped to the floor.

'Okay, Ivar,' von Westarp said. 'Okay.'

'Herr Oberführer?' the guard said, holding up his gun.

'Open the door. Let him leave.'

'But Herr Oberführer — '

'Do it, man,' von Westarp spat, and the guard unlocked the door.

'Ivar,' von Westarp said. 'Eva is still here.'

'*What?*'

'She is in my room.'

Ivar ran out.

Watching him go, von Westarp said to the guard, 'Where can he go? He has lost his father, his mother, his sister and now this surrogate mother. His mission here was a secret. The only people who knew of it are in our custody and will very soon be eliminated. We are the only two free men in all the world who know his true identity.'

Von Westarp shot the guard in the heart. The man crumpled to the floor and von Westarp moved to the doorway to watch Ivar as he bounded up the stair.

'And he may still prove of use to me,' he said.

★ ★ ★

The echo of gunfire followed Ivar as he burst out into the hall and sprinted up the stairs, but he paid it no attention. A floor up, he threw open the door of von Westarp's bedroom. Eva was sitting on the bed.

'Is it time?' she said, expectant, but then she saw the blood covering Ivar's chest and stomach, and the knife in his hand, and her expression changed to one of fear.

Ivar nodded and rushed to her bedside. 'Come on.'

'But Ivar, what — '

'There's no time. We've got to move. Take this.' He pushed the knife into her fist, then slipped a hand around her waist and took her by the elbow and hoisted her out of her bed. She was only wearing a nightdress but he had clothes enough in his sack. They just had to get out of there.

He pulled her across the room, along the corridor, down the stairs, but when they descended to the main hall, von Westarp was standing there, flanked by half a dozen guards. Each one of them had his hands held behind his back, their revolvers hidden from the girl lest the sight upset the precious foetus.

421

'Have we passed?' Eva asked her.

They were standing on the landing. Ivar held her to him with both arms. She looked up at him. 'Do we get to stay?'

'Well, Ivar?' von Westarp said. 'What do you think?'

Ivar looked at the girl. Amused suspicion was animating her face.

'He knows your real name. Is he in on the game now? Is he playing too? Or . . . '

'Yes,' Ivar said, releasing her. 'He's playing. It's all right.'

'Oh, what fun,' Eva said, clapping her hands in excitement.

'Well?' von Westarp repeated.

'Yes, Eva,' Ivar said. 'You're staying.'

'That's right,' von Westarp said, stepping forward and taking the girl by the hand as she descended the last flight of steps. 'We are your family now, and we must get you back to bed, my dear. But perhaps first a warming cup of tea in the kitchen.'

Ivar heard Eva say, 'And Ivar?' but he did not catch von Westarp's response as they passed through the door towards the kitchen. The German's voice was swallowed by the sound of the guards' footsteps as they ascended the stairs.

★ ★ ★

Ivar struggled against them, but one of the guards whipped the butt of his gun across the back of his head. Ivar did not pass out, but the blow left him dazed, his vision throbbing and uncertain.

422

They dragged him out of the main building, across the gardens, up the drive to the stables. Throwing open the doors, they dragged him over the floorboards and pulled up a trapdoor in the floor. Under the trapdoor was a short flight of steps. They dragged him down. At the bottom of the flight of stairs was another door, metal and heavy. They unlocked it, pulled it open, and threw him over the threshold. A little light made it down from the stables above and illuminated the room, but Ivar was in no state to take in the new surroundings before the guards slammed the door shut again, and once it was closed, there was no light in there whatsoever.

Lying like a foetus on the cold, hard floor, anger, hate and grief swathed Ivar like a rancid blanket, but after a short time, exhausted, he fell to sleep. As his eyes closed, his tears were still falling. When he awoke, cold through and stiff-limbed, visions of Sofie slicing her own throat flashed bright in the lightless cell. But his tears had stopped, and through the grief he knew escape was his only option. He clawed his mind away from what had happened, determined to concentrate instead on his new domain of darkness, and getting out of it to find Eva and his unborn child.

He crawled on his hands and knees across the uneven stone floor until his head met something. The upright surface was cold and hard like the floor, but flatter, slightly rough, with rows of small dome shapes protruding from it. He moved his face forward until his lips met the surface. He stuck out his tongue and licked it. It tasted like blood. It was metal, an iron wall. He stretched out his arms either side of him and surveyed the entire surface with his hands. It was constructed of sheet metal, belted and riveted together at the seams. Ivar tapped on a panel. At least two centimetres thick. He moved on, and found a framed area two metres high, seventy centimetres wide. The metal inside the frame was slightly sunken. It was a door, presumably the one he had been thrown through. And no inside handle.

His foot knocked into something on the floor at the bottom of the door. He crouched and touched two differently sized metal bowls. The smaller one was full of cold liquid. He raised the bowl to his mouth and sipped it. Water. The larger bowl was empty, to be filled with effluent, he guessed. Ivar moved the bowls aside and returned to the door. At its base, next to where the bowls had lain, there was a panel that shifted slightly when he applied pressure. He tapped it. It rattled slightly. It wasn't riveted in place, and was thinner than the other panels. A hatch, maybe.

Ivar tried to slide the hatch in all directions, but it only moved forwards and backwards a fraction, not left or right, and pushing it upwards he could feel a restraint holding it in place. Locked.

To the right of the door he found a rough woollen blanket. He left it where it was and turned, on all fours again, feeling with his hands as he moved into the space.

So far as he could calculate, the rough, uneven

stone floor covered an irregular oval space of about three metres by four. Up on his feet, holding his hands above his head, he found that the roof was equally irregular, two and a half metres at its highest point, sloping down to the floor, and hewn from rough rock, much like the place where von Westarp had brought him to Eva, and then Sofie. Maybe they had been dug out of the mountainside on von Westarp's orders, or maybe they were naturally occurring caves. Either way they were highly effective jail cells.

Only when he had completed his survey of the cell and was sitting by the door drinking from the water bowl did Ivar consciously acknowledge what instinctively he already knew: he was entirely trapped. If he wanted to get out, he would have to dig through solid rock.

He fell asleep again and when he woke, he found that the bowl of water had been refilled and next to it was a third bowl containing a piece of bread and a piece of cheese. Ivar ate them, and as he was doing so realized he had no idea how long he had slept, nor how long he had been awake before he had slept, which meant he had no clue as to the time of day or even the day of the week. When the bread and cheese was finished he set to work, scraping against the rock where the iron wall met the stone.

After some time — a week? a month? a year? — he was lying on the floor, no longer scraping, when from the darkness stepped a bear. Not any bear, but the very one he had encountered alone in the forest. He knew it was a vision, and not real, and yet he reached out his hand and

425

touched the creature, smelled its musty fur, and looked into its intelligent, indifferent eyes.

'What brings you here?' he asked the bear.

'What brings you here?' the bear answered, and Ivar was not perturbed by its ability to talk. It was perfectly natural. The creature was a vision. A figment of his mind.

'Do you know what time it is?' Ivar asked.

'Bears can't read clocks,' the bear said.

'Then what day is it?'

'If you don't know, I can't know. I'm a product of your imagination. Do you want me to lie to you?'

'Not if I know you are lying.'

'Then a wager?'

'Very well. I bet it is Tuesday,' Ivar said.'

'And I bet it's Wednesday.' And they spoke in this way until Ivar saw the sun filtering through the pine branches around them, glowing shards at first and then a precise, dazzling square, and a human hand appeared above the bear's head, large, reaching, Biblical.

The hand lifted Ivar's bowls out of the cell. When new bowls moved in, Ivar grabbed hold of the hand.

'*Please*,' he said, as politely as his desperation allowed. 'What time is it? What day? Please — we need to know.'

There came no reply. The hand slapped him back, retracted and the hatch was closed.

He had no way to predict when the hand would arrive. He abandoned his digging in favour of the promise of human contact and spent most of his time lying in front of the hatch, talking to the bear, bickering with it, dreaming of the hand's owner looking in — the face turning from Sofie's to Britt's to their mother's to the bear's, staring at him with complete indifference before slamming the hatch shut again.

★ ★ ★

Finally the door opened. First a crack, then wide. The light was gloomy, but still it made Ivar cover his deprived eyes.

'Ivar? Open your eyes, Ivar. Come on.'

A hand took his arm and raised him to his feet, and started to lead him forwards.

'Is — is this real?' Ivar said.

'Look at me, Ivar.'

Ivar let his hands be taken from his eyes and a figure started to come into focus. First the squat outline, then the face. Von Westarp's face. Ivar flinched, tried to break away, stumbling to his knees.

'No, Ivar. Listen to me. Look at me.'

Quivering, Ivar looked at the German. The man's appearance had changed. Though still squat in body, his face was thinner, drawn, older, and those fleshy lips had sagged, making the mouth they framed downturned, like a tragic clown who had washed off his make-up. His eyes were jerking around like he had just been found out. Hunted.

Von Westarp led him up the stairs into the stables and out the door onto the mountainside. If the opening of the cell door had dazzled Ivar, the brightness of the outside world near blinded him. He stopped in his tracks, covering his eyes with his palms again.

He felt von Westarp take hold of his shoulders.

'You're weak, Ivar. Starving. By the looks of things you are suffering from scurvy and malnutrition — at the very least. But I came back for you, If I hadn't come you would have died down there. Understand that, Ivar.' His tone was at once aggressive and conciliatory.

'W-what do you mean?' Ivar spluttered, still rubbing at his eyes.

'There is no one here, Ivar. They have all gone. Look for yourself.'

Von Westarp moved aside, and Ivar lowered his hands. Ahead he saw grass. It glowed electric green in his frazzled eyes, the wild flowers explosions of purple and blue, the mountains over the fjord deep and rich with green moss and trees, the water below a lustrous aquamarine. A flash of blue streaked across Ivar's vision and he followed a jay as it flew to the eaves of Dueredet. Nature was alive, audible, visible everywhere, amplified in his starved ears and eyes. It had reclaimed what man had taken away. There was not a person in sight.

'Wha — ?' Ivar tried. 'I — How long?'

'It is the month of May.'

'What year?'

'1945.'

'I — I — '

Ivar could not speak. He had been in that cell for two years, yet he felt no sadness, no anger. Nothing. But tears started running down his face nonetheless.

'You have not received food for days, Ivar. Here.' Von Westarp pulled some bread and a canteen from the rucksack he carried and gave them to Ivar. 'Do not try to speak.' Ivar took the food and drink and pushed bread into his mouth. As he did so he became aware that von Westarp was not in his military uniform. His clothes were the clothes of a Norwegian: well-worn brown leather boots, hide breeches, a thick woollen shirt and a cloth cap. He was holding an ash hiking stick. 'You will need all your little strength. Just eat, drink and listen.' Von Westarp twisted Ivar to look south across the mountains. In the distance he could make out dust rising on the road winding through the peaks. 'The roads are no good. They're coming. We must head for Sognefjord. Our ships are still moving out. We haven't a moment to lose. We must get moving.'

So the Nazis were leaving Norway. And judging by von Westarp's outfit and behaviour, it was because they had lost.

Ivar felt something hard in his belly and looked down. Von Westarp was holding his snub-nosed revolver.

'I could not be caught with a Luger, now, could I?' he said.

'Wha — ? What am I — ?' Ivar tried, but he was too weak to complete his sentence, and still holding the water and bread, he started to half-walk, half-stumble where von Westarp pointed.

At the head of the mountain path down to Nærøysfjord, Ivar pocketed the remaining bread

429

and the canteen and started downward. His legs were as skinny, weak and brittle as dried twigs, and with every downhill step he felt as though the bones might snap. He fell twice, and each time von Westarp made him get to his feet and continue immediately. Only when they finally reached the river that fed into the fjord did the German allow Ivar a moment's respite.

Ivar waded into the water and allowed himself to sink beneath the surface. It was cold and invigorating and he realized his blood was running through his body again after the walk. Deprived of everything the sun gave the world for so long, he now felt as though strength was being fed back into his body merely by being in the presence of Nature. As though he was absorbing health through his skin. Stamina. Power. His country, its very nature, was feeding him strength, just as, through the bear, it had kept him going in his underground cell.

His face broke the surface of the water again, and he felt the sun upon him. He opened his eyes, looked up at the mountains, and watched as the last of the sun descended behind them. But it was summer, and the half-light would remain for pretty much the whole short night.

'There,' von Westarp said. He was pointing the revolver at a fishing dinghy with a small engine attached to it. Ivar recognized it as belonging to the Gulbrandsens.

'Heidi,' Ivar said, stepping through the water towards the boat. 'Johann.'

'The area was cleared of your co-conspirators once your deception was uncovered, Ivar,' von

Westarp said, himself moving along the shore to the boat. 'What did you expect?'

Ivar felt the returning sensation of anger, pushing his blood even faster around his body.

He turned in the water to face von Westarp.

'Why didn't you kill me?'

'I considered it. Believe me. But it would have been a mistake. In you get now.' Von Westarp had untied the boat and was wading through the water to it. He watched Ivar in and then stepped in himself. 'Start the engine.'

Ivar left the engine alone.

'Why would it have been a mistake?' he said. 'What are you planning? Why did you come back for me?'

'The time for planning has passed, I am afraid. I hope security will not be required, but if it is, you are it. Now get moving. We must meet those ships.'

Von Westarp flicked the barrel of the snub-nose at Ivar. Ivar pulled on the cord and the engine spluttered into life. He guided it out onto the water, and they began to wend their way along the fjord. The mountains stared down at them, the sky growing ever dimmer, Ivar at the tiller, von Westarp facing him, the revolver levelled.

The boat was not capable of great speed — ten knots at best — but as they progressed, the fjord gradually widened, and as it did so the boat felt more and more insignificant, just an anomalous scale on the skin of the giant snake of water. Ivar knew he did not have the strength to swim to the water's edge. If he was to escape, he would have to take control of the situation on the boat. But he was also too weak to fight the German. His only hope was to wait for the right moment. Then Ivar would yank on the tiller, swerve the boat, and hope the sudden movement threw von Westarp off balance. At the same time, he'd throw himself forward onto the German, and prise the gun from his hand. But von Westarp was staring right at him, all the time. He had to wait.

'You know, Ivar,' von Westarp said calmly. 'I am glad we have this time together. Because I want to tell you. I think you are remarkable. Truly remarkable.'

'Do you?' Ivar said.

The water ahead was calm for a hundred metres or so, but after a short peninsula the wind looked to be kicking up a bit of a current across the fjord. That would give Ivar a little more force for the swerve, when the time came.

'Yes. What you did was nothing short of heroic for one so young. But Arne and Sofie Stornes? Those who sent you — they are the savages of the piece. The villains. To do what they did to a child. To take his hate, his anguish, and use it against him — '

'Shit!' Ivar suddenly cried, looking behind von Westarp, pointing a finger. The German swung round to look without even thinking. Ivar threw the tiller away from him and leaped forward, grabbing hold of von Westarp's gun hand. The boat swung round in the water and Ivar landed on von Westarp, the inertia of the spin and his weight pushing the German over into the hull of the boat.

On top of him, Ivar kept a grasp of his wrist, shaking it, trying to free the pistol. Von Westarp grabbed at Ivar's face with his free hand, gouging at his eyes. He was heavier and stronger and von Westarp worked Ivar around until he was on top of him. He raised himself into a sitting position on top of the younger man.

He pushed Ivar's head down onto the hull with his free hand while pulling his other, holding the gun high into the air. Ivar could feel his grip on the man's wrist weakening. Von Westarp brought his hand away from Ivar's face, curled it into a fist, and hit him with all he had. Ivar's head was squashed between the impact of the fist and the wood of the hull, and his cheek sank under the sudden pressure, the bone fracturing.

Von Westarp tore his hand from Ivar's. In that jerking movement, his finger was pulled against the trigger and one bullet was fired into the deep blue sky. Von Westarp then brought the gun back down and pointed the barrel at Ivar.

'You attack a man of senior years from behind and lose. Thus you prove that you have neither honour nor intelligence.' He pulled back the hammer and placed the barrel of the revolver to Ivar's forehead.

'You say I don't have intelligence,' Ivar spat up at him. 'When you're about to shoot a bullet straight through my head and then through your own boat. Idiot. What happened to security?'

Von Westarp laughed, and pulled Ivar up by his shirt. 'We will meet the German *Kriegsmarine* just around the bend. You have strength and courage, I'll give you that. But I'm afraid that makes you no better than an African.' He said the word as though it tasted bad, and placed the gun to Ivar's forehead. 'Goodbye, Ivar Petersen.'

Ivar looked behind and above von Westarp, raising a finger. Pointing, his eyes widening.

'*Oh my God!*'

The German sounded merely bored. 'Do you really think I will fall for the very same trick a second time? You really do — '

But at that moment a sequence of big waves buffeted the boat, lifting and dropping it — the sort that could only come from the passage of a much larger vessel nearby; and then a brilliant light illuminated them.

'*Cut off your engine,*' a voice said in Norwegian over a loud speaker. It bounced off the mountains rising out of the fjord on either side of the water, booming and echoing from all directions, as though the light were in fact God come down from the heavens to speak to the pair in the boat. '*And put your hands in the air.*'

Von Westarp swung his head round to see a large deep-water fishing vessel ploughing through the water towards them. He turned back to Ivar and lowered the gun.

'What happened to the *Kriegsmarine?*' Ivar said.

'Ivar,' von Westarp said calmly, ignoring his words. 'Do you realize that I am the only person alive who knows that that is your real name?'

'There are records.'

'No. Stornes knew I would find them and had them destroyed. Without me you are and always will be Snorre Nilsen, a traitor who aided and

434

abetted the dreaded Teacher in his purging of the XU. All your co-conspirators are dead. Without me, your own people will think you worse than a German Nazi. I can tell them who you really are. I can tell them that you were working for the resistance all along. And I will. If you tell them I was working with you.'

'*What?*' Ivar said.

'That I have been feeding you information. I am a friend of the Norwegians, Ivar. You know this. Stornes fed a child on vengeance. He tried to create a cold-blooded monster. But I — I treated you as my own, I *exalted* you and nurtured you into manhood as a father would. Tell them. I saved your life, now save mine.'

'You didn't save my life,' Ivar said. 'You ruined it. Everything that I loved and valued, every person — you took. I have nothing.'

'Don't be a fool, Ivar. You have a child. And Eva. She waits for you. You are still young. You have your whole life ahead of you. Help me now and it can be a good life. A comfortable life for all three of you. If not, you will suffer needlessly. As will they.'

Ivar grabbed the gun from von Westarp's limp hand and pulled him forwards. Up close, Ivar saw it immediately. The man was terrified. He feared death as much as anyone. He must have seen something in Ivar's eyes, too, because with his next words his tone had completely changed.

'Please, Ivar,' he said. '*Please.*'

'You're going to pay for what you did,' Ivar said, pushing the German away so that he fell back in the boat. He raised the gun.

'*Put down the weapon*,' the voice boomed again.

'Understand that you will be punished if you do this, Ivar. They are executing us. You will be put before the firing squad. By the very people you fought to protect.'

'Then this whole thing will be history. Forgotten. That sounds just fine. I want to forget. Everything.'

'No, Ivar. Remember the children. My children. They will grow, and they will rise, and they will cleanse this world of all its filth. They will — '

'*We will fire. This is your final warning. Lower your weapon.*'

Ivar pulled back the hammer on the snub-nose.

'Please, Ivar,' von Westarp said. He was desperate now, begging. 'There's gold, lots of gold.'

'Gold?'

'Lots of gold. Here in Norway.' He reached out his hand. In it was a tiny nugget of gold, no more than a centimetre cubed. Ivar took it. As he did so, von Westarp took his hand, as though they were reconciled, the nugget between their palms.

'What is this?' Ivar said.

'You know what it is,' von Westarp said. 'And there are more. Thousands, millions more.'

Ivar pulled von Westarp closer, enjoying this single moment of power over the pathetic old man. He raised the gun to the German's cheek.

'If you want to know where it is, if you want to

be able to live with your head held high after this war is over, like a man, with your woman and child, then save me, and I will tell you where it is.'

Von Westarp saw his fate in Ivar's eyes.

'In my cabin on the ship I came in on — '

Von Westarp did not finish. The pistol jumped in Ivar's hand. Brain and skull flew out the back of von Westarp's head and splattered over the edge of the boat into the water, like gut-slop thrown off the back of a fishing boat. Ivar let the German slump backward into the boat. He was still holding his hand. The fingers ran through his and whacked on the wood.

'*Drop the weapon and get down on your knees or we will shoot.*'

Ivar did as the voice ordered. He heard sounds of men moving, orders flying, a motor starting and a boat approaching. Before the men boarded, Ivar opened his hand. The piece of gold was lying on his palm.

Ivar placed it in his mouth and watched the Norwegian men come aboard. And swallowed.

'Please,' he said, dropping to his knees and placing his hands on his head. 'I am a Norwegian.'

19

In the Big Horn steak house, Skarnes was nursing his second double, enjoying the air con and the cold of the iced glass on his palm.

'You must be Skarnes?' the Swedish barman said. He was holding a cordless phone out. Skarnes hadn't even heard it ring. He nodded and took the phone.

'Tobias?'

'My name is Ms Aamodt. I'm Mr Edinsen's personal secretary — '

'Herdis, right?' Disappointment bristled through Skarnes, a cooling sensation, surprisingly unpleasant in the air conditioning of the restaurant. His oldest friend — his only friend, if he was honest — and he couldn't even be bothered to make the call personally.

'I prefer Ms Aamodt, if you don't mind, Mr Skarnes. Aamodt if you're short of time.'

'Fine, Aamodt,' Skarnes responded. 'What have you got for me?'

'Mr Kim Larsen, of 280 Sognsveien; age thirty-nine; occupation farmer; political sympathies far-right; former member of formative black-metal band Chaos. One time Boot Boy, now NDL and Vigrid.'

All this painted a character, but it didn't explain why Bonde had been visiting him. If

438

anything it just made Bonde's presence there all the more strange.

'But he must have been arrested at some point.'

'I was coming to that. Arrested 1990, drunk and disorderly, warning; vandalism, 1992, fine; again in ninety-four. 1998, suspected burglary, 18 month suspended sentence for possession of stolen goods; 2000, suspected arson of stave church in Bergen; 2002, domestic possession of firearm without licence, 4,000 kroner fine; 2005, illegal possession of semi-automatic weapons, suspected intent to sell, five years, two served, remains on probation. Thought to have made extensive contacts with Blood & Honour on the inside. You bagged yourself a real beauty, Mr Skarnes.'

'He sells guns?'

'We think so.'

'Jesus!'

'It's a vicious world out there, Inspector.'

'You've found that, have you?'

Skarnes hung up before she could retort. But then he found himself staring at the keypad on the cordless. Bonde was into something serious, that much they now knew. If he was out of his depth he might feel the need for protection. And Hansen was out there tailing him solo. He had to get hold of her, and that was why he was staring at the numbers. He was willing himself to know her phone number, but he just plain didn't.

He drained his glass.

There was only one number he could call.

On his feet now, sweating again despite the air

con, padding up and down the bar, he punched
in the number.

'Crime Squad.'

'Agnes?'

'Yes?'

'This is Inspector Skarnes. I need — '

'Ole?'

'Yeah.'

'Ole *Skarnes*?'

'That's right. Listen, I — '

'What are you — '

'I need Hansen's number. Right now. Please.
It's important.'

'Ole, I — '

Skarnes heard some kind of exchange at the
other end, then another voice came on, thicker,
maler.

'Skarnes?'

'Who's this?'

'This is Halvorsen, you son of a bitch. Where
in hell is Hansen? And what the fuck are you
doing anywhere near her, you fucking drunk? I
thought you lived in a bottle these days.'

'Halvorsen, I need her number. Or I need you
to call her. Doesn't matter. She's tailing Bonde,
and — '

'Bonde? What the fuck?'

'Halvorsen, I don't care — '

'You keep away from her, Skarnes. You're out,
and good riddance to you. We don't want you
twisting the mind of that girl.'

'That's your job, right, you fucking monkey?'

Skarnes slammed the phone down on the bar.
Every pair of eyes in the place were on him. He

440

turned away from them and hammered his glass on the wood.

'Give me another.'

The barman stretched to fill the glass, trying to keep his body as far from the sweat-streaming maniac as possible. Skarnes downed it.

★   ★   ★

'Jones?'

'Sir?'

'There's a chap racing northwards in a red-and-black Zodiac. Be a good man and get on him, would you?'

'Yes, sir.'

'Oh, and Jones?'

'Sir?'

Henderson was sitting in an aluminium chair on the rear deck of the *Penguin II*, and had been speaking into the radio to the men on the Revenger. The *Penguin II* had pulled up and he was watching Bukhalov and de Veer drag Palmer out of the water as he spoke. The body slapped face down onto the plastic floor. Its eyes and mouth were open. The South African had been washed clean in the sea, and the wound in his neck, while still seeping blood, was gaping open and Henderson could make out the flesh and sinew beneath the skin.

'He's got our gold, so just see where he goes. Then report back, all right?'

'Very good, sir.'

Henderson heard the engine roar at the other end of the radio and hung up. Bukhalov and de

441

Veer were looking to him for further orders. On the other side of the deck, Broussard and Fallon sat wringing their hands. Looking at them, Henderson nodded at Palmer.

'What do you think, Georges?' he said, smirking. 'Should we report his passing and make sure his family receives the remains, give him a proper Christian burial?' Broussard looked at Henderson, helpless. He didn't have the stomach for this. 'Sink him, gentlemen,' Henderson said, and watched as Bukhalov and de Veer proceeded to thread a weighted dive belt around Palmer's waist, another around his neck and a third around his ankles.

As soon as Broussard had uttered the word *gold* over lunch in the Wolseley, Henderson had known he would be bringing a full complement of men and weaponry with him to Norway. Gold possesses a uniquely strong ability to infect people with greed, and as such nearly always leads to disagreement. Better to be the man holding the M240 than not. Besides, the gun-for-hire racket was a young-man's game. Like that other noble pugilistic sport men got paid for — boxing — mercenary history was littered with the corpses of men who had gone on too long. At forty-six, Henderson knew his working days were numbered. Yet he might well live forty more years. A retirement as long as that required funding, and an investment in gold had looked a good bet.

He hadn't expected the problem to come from the client himself, however, whom he understood to be a political animal of advanced years.

But that was the only explanation here: who else but the client could know so precisely what they were up to? It seemed plain to Henderson that the client had either decided he wanted to keep all the gold for himself (no matter that he was dealing with former elite marines), or he was a little wiser than Henderson initially gave him credit for, and realized that Henderson and co. would want to keep hold of the booty for themselves.

Either way, it was an entirely unacceptable route to have taken, and one no self-respecting mercenary could let stand. The client had to be shown he couldn't put one over Lieutenant Colonel Henry Percival Henderson. But unless he believed that his double-cross had been a success, this politician would likely panic and go to ground. To make sure he didn't, Henderson had to ask himself what he would have done had Jones not been out there right now pursuing the thief.

De Veer and Bukhalov slipped Palmer's body off the back of the deck. Henderson rose to his feet just in time to see the South African's face disappear. Then he turned to Broussard.

'Georges,' he said. 'I want to talk to the client.'

★   ★   ★

Bonde was still in the BMW. He'd been stuck in rush-hour traffic on the main road running east of the fjord for the last half hour. The longer he had remained crawling and stop-starting, the more animatedly irate he had become. The meet with Broussard was set for a barn outside Drøbak in less than an hour. He felt a physical relief when he finally got off onto the road to Drøbak. The traffic had thinned right down and he was gathering speed when his phone rang.

'I'm on my — ' was all he got out before the English voice started at the other end.

'You listen to me, Mr Bonde.'

'Who is this?' Bonde demanded.

'We got it up,' the Englishman said. 'And we want our pay.'

'What are you talking about?' Bonde said, a surge of concern stabbing his gut. 'Where's Broussard?'

'You will deal with me now, Mr Bonde, and if you prove reasonable, you will find that I can be, too. Should you prove otherwise, however, you will see just how *unreasonable* I can get. Do you understand?'

'What do you mean?' Bonde spat, his voice a little higher than usual as his trachea began to constrict. 'What has happened?'

Bonde heard a chuckle.

'Very good, Mr Bonde,' the man said calmly. 'Very good.'

'*Where is the gold?*' Bonde shouted into his phone.

'That is *just* what I wanted to ask you.'

'You've lost it, you mean?' The words came out of his mouth, his brain must have joined the dots, but his conscious mind could not grasp it. He suddenly felt light-headed, dizzy.

'We didn't lose it, Mr Bonde. It's been stolen.'

'*What?*'

444

'We did our job. The cargo surfaced, and we want to be paid for our work — as agreed.'

'You *lost* it? You fucking idiots. Do you know who that gold is *for*?'

'We didn't lose it, Mr Bonde. Your little black thief took it — come on, we're not fools. We want our pay, you bastard. You better be at the meet.'

'I was on my fucking way.'

'Of course you were, Mr Bonde. You just make sure you get there, or we'll — '

Bonde hung up and flung his phone onto the passenger seat.

His heart was pounding. He needed to think, he needed quiet, he needed *fuel*. Catching sight of a lay-by, he spun the wheel; the BMW billowed dirt and skidded to a halt. Waiting for the traffic to pass — first a Volvo, then a Lancia — Bonde put his hand in his pocket, pulled out his wrap of cocaine and opened it up. Having no inclination to cut the powder and roll a note, when the paper was fully unfolded, he threw the contents into his mouth wholesale, then licked the paper clean. Four-plus grams in one go; when the powder mixed with his saliva it formed a ball and he had to chew it like a wad of gum.

The gold was gone. The divers thought he had stolen it. They thought only he *could* have stolen it. They were wrong, of course.

Your little black thief.

When a black man had tried to take his briefcase that morning, he'd thought it was a random act.

That conniving old fucker.

445

Bonde grabbed his phone and punched in his office number. Eli picked up immediately.

'Eli, get me Superintendent Egeland on the line, right now.'

He punched the accelerator and started back towards Oslo.

★   ★   ★

If they were going to walk into town and find a pawnshop and hand over handfuls of gold, they would want to attract as little attention as possible. Blood-stained and in just his cargos and All Stars, carrying two sacks of gold, that wasn't going to happen. So Curt had two things to do before returning to the old man at Aker Brygge — he needed to stash the gold, and he needed a change of clothes. The latter was easy enough. He'd been squatting in a derelict City Port Authority store building on and off for the last few months, and he had a case of clothes there. Nothing special, but not covered in South African blood, either.

Stashing the gold wasn't so easy. Leaving two white plastic bags out in the open wasn't an option. He couldn't risk them attracting attention. But the divers would be looking for him. True, the dive boat wouldn't be nearly as fast as the Zodiac, but still he didn't have time to dig a hole to bury the bags, which is what he'd have liked to do, somewhere no one goes. Which meant he needed to hide them somewhere ready-made, but where no one would look — or at least where no one would notice. Somewhere like the back of a shed of a house down by the water. In weather like this everyone was on the water, but with the clouds gathering they'd be heading home sooner rather than later. He needed to act fast.

He spotted a candidate up ahead — a white timber structure on its own small island. The main house was a converted lighthouse. Behind it was a small hut with a round hole in the door, a renovated outhouse. There was no boat at its jetty. Approaching, Curt saw sun loungers and towels on the small brown lawn beyond the white picket fence. But no people.

Curt didn't want to have to go through the laborious start-up process if the residents returned, so he left the engine idling. Thinking it would be a bad idea to be spotted covered in the South African's blood here as well as in town, he gave himself a quick saltwater washdown, getting the worst off his chest and face. Then he tied off at the jetty and heaved the bags, one then the other, up onto the pontoon. From there he proceeded to move the first a little further up onto the island. Coming up the rock, he confirmed that the lighthouse doors were shut, and he saw no one in the windows. He went back for the second sack, left it with the first, then went to check the outhouse.

The door was unlocked. With the dawn of modern plumbing, the structure had been converted into a pump house. Half a dozen sacks of what looked like purification salts flanked a couple of insulated cylinders and an electrical pump bringing water up from the ground. His white bags would happily sit behind the sacks like cuckoo eggs — unnoticed until the cuckoo returned.

Curt returned to the Zodiac, pulled out a third, empty bag from the store, then carried the filled sacks one by one up to the pump house, and sat them in the shadows at the back behind the salts. He then opened one up and four times scooped a double-handful into the third bag. Once he had twisted up the slack, the package came to about the size of a bag of sugar.

* * *

'Fucking politicians!'

Superintendent Egeland was in his office at Grønland police station, and slammed down his phone into its cradle, once, twice, three times, then held it in midair for a second, composing himself. Letting out a deep breath that made the vein on his forehead recede, he placed the phone back to his ear and pressed 0.

'Vera,' he said. 'I need a line on that black vagrant Halvorsen and Hansen brought in this morning. Hangouts, associates, squats. Check the interview transcript, call his embassy. And make it snappy. And send Halvorsen in here, will you?'

* * *

Hansen couldn't swerve off into the lay-by where Bonde had skidded to a halt without revealing herself. She'd have pulled up right next to him, and he would have made her immediately. Instead, as she coasted onward, she depressed the brakes and watched him in the rear-view mirror, craning her neck to see beyond the car closing in behind her. The lay-by was situated on a straight, and before it was out of sight, she saw the BMW leave it again, taking off in the opposite direction. With the other car immediately behind her now, Hansen couldn't simply swing a u-turn, so she floored it and started looking for a place to pull over and turn. A little further on she crunched to a sudden stop in a gravel driveway on the right. The traffic passed, then she spun the wheel and pointed the Volvo back towards Oslo.

This was strange behaviour the politician was exhibiting. First he heads out to the north of town, then he makes south, and one-eighties again. Strange, but good, because it was the behaviour of a man with something to hide. She needed to know what that something was. If she came back empty handed, she knew from the insistence of Halvorsen's unanswered calls that there wouldn't be much to come back to.

Hansen floored the accelerator, giving the old Swede all the juice she had, hoping it was enough, urging her on with a shake of the wheel.

'Come on, baby,' she said, half-tender, half-fretful. '*Come on.*'

★ ★ ★

Skarnes was staring at the grain of the wooden bar, trying to think, trying to ignore all the eyes boring holes into his back. He had to get in touch with Hansen, he *had* to warn her of what she might be heading into. The whisky fizzling in his gut somehow delivered inspiration.

Of course.

He picked up the phone again and dialled a number.

'Backroom?' came the voice after the ringing.

'Hi there, how are you?' Skarnes said, his face setting into a manic grin. 'Listen, this is Halvorsen up in Crime Squad. My sister's been admitted to hospital. One of your boys is her man, but his phone's switched off. I've got to get a hold of him, thought you'd be the fastest route. Can you help?'

'Sorry to hear that, Inspector. I'll see what I can do, of course. What's the name?'

'Kobberrød. The name's Kobberrød.'

★ ★ ★

On the *Penguin II*, the radio had crackled to life.

'Jones?' Henderson said into it. 'What have you got?'

'He's stopped, sir,' came the reply. 'It looks like he's removing the cargo. Secreting it at an old lighthouse.'

'Very good, Jones. Leave the cargo, follow the thief.'

'You don't want the cargo, sir?'

'Send the coordinates over. We'll cover it. Maybe the secondary target will turn up there, or maybe the thief is meeting him to renegotiate the terms of their deal. So stay with him.'

Henderson returned the radio to its cradle.

'We have the gold, Henry,' Georges said. His tone suggested he was confused, but Henderson could tell from his troubled face that he already suspected the answer to his next question: 'Why do you need Bonde?'

Frowning at the Frenchman, Henderson leaned back in his wooden deckchair, the front feet lifting off the deck. Broussard wasn't to know that this was a signal known to all Henderson's men; nor did he pay any attention to the single backward step Bukhalov took from his side. At the same time, de Veer moved casually to the other side of the cylinder rack in the centre of the deck, and stood adjusting some equipment. Fallon was also on his feet now. Henderson's men watched his chair, waiting for the unspoken order.

★ ★ ★

'If my shit hits the fan with this, Lukas, I'm going to make sure the shower lands on you, you understand? So where is she?'

'I don't know, Uncle Lars. She's off the radar.'

'What do you mean, 'off the radar'?'

'She took off, and she's not answering her phone.' He hesitated, then added, 'She called in Skarnes.'

'*Skarnes?*'

'He rang trying to find her.'

'Jesus *fucking* Christ, Lukas — what are you doing? Find her, and find that fucking soldier, you understand me? And I don't want Skarnes

451

anywhere near them.'

'Okay, Uncle Lars. I'll see what I can do.'

'Don't fucking *see*, boy. *Do*.'

Just as Halvorsen closed the door, Egeland's phone rang.

'Mr Egeland?'

'What have you got, Vera?'

'I have an address in Bergen, and — '

'That's no good. What about here?'

'And he mentioned a squat in Sjursøya during the interview.'

'Better.'

'And a woman at the embassy remembered him, told me when they asked him for an address he said he called the City Port Authority home. That's the best I can do.'

'It's a start. Give it to Halvorsen, tell him to head there and check it out. And keep calling around. But first get me Henrik Bonde back on the line.'

★   ★   ★

When the female cop pulled off the two-lane in her Volvo, Wojciech passed on by. He saw her turning around in his rear-view and turned the Thema at the very next opportunity, about half a kilometre on.

With its Maranello firepower, it would have been easy for the Thema to catch the old Volvo from that distance. It would have taken a couple of seconds. Modern executive saloons were just as fast, but he liked the Thema because, to all but the most educated, it was an anonymous executive saloon, unfamiliar, yet instantly forget-table.

But this female cop could drive, so it was possible she knew cars and would ID his. More than that, Wojciech had been on her tail for hours now, and if he rode her again, chances were she'd notice, and whether she knew her Lancias or not, she would probably make the forgettable midnight blue saloon that had been behind her just a minute ago, when they'd both been going in the opposite direction.

So he hung back a kilometre or so, glimpsing the Volvo every now and then when the road opened up.

When they hit town, he'd move up.

★ ★ ★

When Curt got back to the Zodiac from the outhouse, another boat, with the word Revenger emblazoned up the side, was drawing close to the island. It held two men in swimming shorts. The lighthouse residents, he supposed.

Curt untied and stepped into the Zodiac, placing the package on the floor.

'The company sent me,' he called in English — they wouldn't expect a handyman to speak Norwegian. 'Just checking your levels. I topped you up. You shouldn't need any more for a month or so. You timed your return well.' Curt pointed at the sky. The cloud cover was almost complete, only great shards of God-light breaking through now. 'The rain's coming. Have a nice evening, gentlemen.' His teeth when he smiled were still stained bloody. The men on the Revenger just nodded and waved.

Curt pulled up the thrust lever and the engine growled, just as the first bolt of lightning lit the sky to the south. He started to count as the Zodiac bumped over the water. He reached eleven before the crack of thunder came.

His next stop was Sjursøya.

★ ★ ★

A bystander might have taken Bonde's sudden swerve off the main road onto a branch route for an overreaction to that same bolt of lightning. The move coincided with it perfectly. But in fact he was following directions. The sign pointed left towards the City Port Authority at Sjursøya.

Bonde could see from the snaking road leading down towards the water that the buildings and harbour a kilometre away were busy with traffic — human, wheeled and hulled. But closer, between the road and the water, lay a promontory as inactive as the CPA was busy. Heaps of industrial junk decorated the dusty scrub ground around an abandoned two-storey building.

The disused building looked as though it had grown weary of life. Its sheet metal roof had rusted, moss was growing from the gutters, the windows on the upper floor were nearly all broken, downstairs they were grilled, and the walls were smeared with weather, graffiti and bird shit.

Bonde wound the BMW down the road and

454

pulled off into the scrub outside the building.

Cutting the engine and releasing his seat belt, he leaned over and flipped open the glove compartment. Inside, sitting on the car manual, was Larsen's plastic bag. Bonde removed it, sat it on his lap and tugged out the contents. Larsen had told him the black metal handgun was a Heckler & Koch P30L, the weapon of the nation's armed police officers. This one was loaded with nine 19mm Parabellum cartridges, a bullet designed by Georg Luger himself. Larsen had told Bonde all this as he demonstrated cocking, aiming and flicking off the safety.

Bonde threw the empty bag back into the glove compartment and pushed the weapon into his jacket pocket. He had bought the gun in case he came across the man he'd met at the summer fair or one of his comrades, but it would do just as well against a thief.

Lightning flashed again as he climbed out of the car, and again. The sky darkening all the time, the flashing was beginning to resemble a defective strobe light. The next bolt carved the sky to the south just as the thunder sounded.

Bonde closed the BMW's door and made for the building.

★ ★ ★

'Georges,' Henderson said. 'I told you when we met in London that in hiring us you would be taking on more than mere divers. We also offer the best protection money can buy. Never mind that this man's actions have led to the killing of

455

one of my men. He has tried to *humiliate* us. Moreover, he has tried to humiliate *you*, Georges; he has sought to begrime your good name.'

Henderson was still leaning right back in his chair.

'What are you going to do to him?' Georges said, taking a step forward.

'Why, kill him of course, Georges,' Henderson said.

Georges took another step towards Henderson.

'Henrik Bonde is a public figure, Henry. One cannot just execute a European politician at will.'

Henderson smiled at the concern in those little French-peasant eyes.

'My dear fellow — of course one can. But if you do not have the stomach for it, you need not wield the knife, Georges. Probably best to leave it to a practised hand anyway. But Georges — ' Henderson leaned forward in his chair, all smiles gone. The front feet nearly touched the floor but then rose again to hover an inch off the deck. 'Nor must you get in our way.'

Georges looked back at Fallon.

'Georges, I don't think we should — ' Fallon said, sounding more willing to listen than his partner. But Georges was having none of it, and interrupted him.

'I have a family, Henry,' he said, turning back to Henderson. 'Pierre also. I must insist. We cannot be involved in any — '

Henderson exhaled in disappointment.

456

'Oh, Georges,' he said. 'You should listen to your partner more, you know. I do so hate it when people get insistent with me.' And he let his chair fall onto all four feet.

As soon as the front legs made contact with the deck, de Veer, in one sweeping movement, pulled his arm from a holdall and swung it at Fallon. Fallon did not even have time to flinch. His first reaction was to look down at his chest. The Dutchman was holding something flat against it. It took a second longer for Fallon to feel the six inches of steel that had penetrated his breastplate. He looked up at Georges. Bukhalov had his fist to Broussard's neck. When the Bulgarian moved it away, drawing a knife out of the Frenchman's jugular, blood spouted from the incision.

The Frenchmen both fell, their blood pulsating out onto the white plastic of the deck. Henderson stood.

'Knives?' he said. 'On a white deck? Really?' He shook his head. 'Sink them, and clear up this bloody mess.' Then he mounted the steps to the bridge.

★ ★ ★

'Inspector Halvorsen? Karin doesn't even have a brother. What's — '

The barman was holding the Red Label bottle over Skarnes's glass. Skarnes cut the air above it with his hand left to right and shook his head.

'It's Skarnes, Kobberrød.'

'Skarnes? What the f — '

457

'Don't ask. Listen, I need Hansen's number. You must have it on your phone, right? Give it to me, will you?'

Skarnes pinned the phone to his ear with his shoulder, grabbed a napkin from the stack on the bar and made a writing motion at the barman.

'Is everything all right?' Kobberrød said, a note of genuine concern in his voice.

'No. I need to find her. Give me the number, will you?'

Kobberrød was silent for a moment. The barman handed Skarnes a pen and he wrote down the number on the napkin as Kobberrød read it out.

'Thanks, Kobberrød,' he said. 'And sorry about the hospital bit.'

★ ★ ★

Hansen only spotted Bonde's BMW at the last second. She slammed on her brakes and the Volvo came to a halt just beyond the turn-off for the CPA. Bonde had already disappeared from sight. She considered driving down there, but she didn't want the Volvo's diesel announcing her arrival, so she got out of the car and pulled out her phone. She didn't want the sound of Halvorsen ringing to announce her presence, either, nor did she want the handset buzzing in her pocket and making her jump. She flipped the silent button on, tossed the handset onto the seat and started to proceed on foot.

★ ★ ★

When his call went to voicemail, Skarnes started whacking the restaurant's handset on the bar. The diners looked even more concerned at this latest outburst. The barman approached him.

'Sir? Mr Skarnes? I'm sorry, but — '

Skarnes stopped his abuse of the telephone, but not because of the barman's words. He didn't hear those at all. He was hearing what Hansen had said earlier.

'*The car may be a piece of crap, but the phone is state of the art. GPS.*'

He turned and walked through the restaurant to the exit. The barman looked relieved. He didn't care about the fact that Skarnes was taking the phone with him, dialling a number as he walked.

'Aamodt?'

'Yes?'

'This is Skarnes again.'

'Mr Skarnes, I don't — '

'I'm sorry about before. I'm sure you have a wonderful life. I'm just jealous. Is Tobias there?'

'He's a very busy man, Mr Skarnes.'

'I know. Please. Just one minute of his time.'

He got the hold tone and made his way outside. Even with the change in the weather the boardwalk was still busy, but now people were watching the lightning show. It was as though a mother ship was descending. The flashes were going off every few seconds, the thunder sounding like the sky was literally breaking. Skarnes was under the fake longhorn crown that marked the boundary between restaurant and boardwalk when Edinsen came on.

'Tobias? I need your help.'

'Again, Ole?'

'You can trace phones, right? I mean cellular ones.'

'If we have a court-signed warrant, sure.'

'Can you trace the location using the GPS chip?'

'Of course.'

'I need you to do that.'

'Ole, without a warrant, there's no way — '

'What if the phone belongs to a police officer?'

'That changes things, but not much. I still have to — '

'Come on, big shot — pull a few strings, will you?'

'What's going on, Ole?'

'You remember Kim Larsen, on Sognsveien?'

'I thought Herdis called you.'

'She did. He's a suspected gun-dealer. I think he sold a piece to a man Sergeant Hansen's following solo.'

'Is she Squad?'

'My replacement.'

'So call Egeland.'

'I've tried. They already closed down her investigation once. She's working with me, Tobias. She's off the leash. She set me to find out who Larsen was, but I can't get hold of her to tell her. She's not answering, or the phone's off or — or — She's out there alone, Tobias. We can't let her — '

Skarnes stopped dead, voice and body.

'Ole, I'll see what I can do,' Edinsen said. 'But these things take time. You on the same number?'

460

Skarnes started walking, staring straight ahead. 'Yeah,' he said, and the hand holding the phone dropped from his ear. He'd seen someone sitting on a bench on the boardwalk next to the ferry ticket office, where people were filing onto a boat. Skarnes broke into a run. It was Nilsen.

★ ★ ★

Wojciech brought the Thema to a halt next to the female cop's green Volvo at the turn-off to the CPA. Her car was empty. After a couple of seconds, he saw her making her way down on foot, half-crouching, her hands stroking along the dry scrub trying to keep herself low and hidden.

Below her, Bonde's BMW was parked outside a crappy building that reminded Wojciech of some of the military installations back in Bialystok. The BMW was empty and Bonde was gone from sight — presumably into the building. There wasn't anywhere else for him to go.

Wojciech watched the female cop making her way down and considered the situation.

Bonde was due to pay the Organization a hefty amount of money by midnight. He knew what the consequences would be if he didn't make the payment. Cezary Wonsowski could be a very descriptive fellow. Running all over town like this, the day before polling, Bonde had to be trying to get the cash together. Likely Bonde wouldn't be just drawing fifty million kroner out of his current account. So this was one of two things. Either Bonde doubled-back on himself in precaution and this was a meet at which he was going to take receipt of Cezary's cash. Or Bonde had made his tail, and was drawing the cop to a secluded spot where she could be dealt with.

Either way, the situation wasn't looking good for the cop.

As Wojciech saw it, she had two hopes, each depending on the nature of her character.

If this was a meet, then it looked like the rest of the party was yet to arrive. The cop's Volvo and Bonde's BMW were the only vehicles on the scene. There were no more cars, and no boats at the jetty beyond the building.

When the rest of the party did arrive, Wojciech would know what he had to do.

The best outcome would be that the new arrivals made the female cop feel outnumbered — she was one woman alone, after all, and unarmed, like all the rest of the cops in this innocent land. Maybe she'd retreat and go for reinforcements. Bonde would get his cash, make the payment to the Organization, and Wojciech would swallow the loss of Nygard.

But if she just called in for the cavalry, or if this wasn't a meet and Bonde had come out here to deal with her, then Wojciech would have to head down there.

If she turned out to be a regular cop, he'd explain that the Organization would pay her to leave Bonde alone on this. It would just be another envelope to another cop. The Organization already handed out plenty of those.

If she didn't retreat, or turned down the bribery option, Wojciech would have to consider

462

his hand forced. No one knew he was there, of course, but facilitating Cezary's deal had to take precedence. If it went through, the deal would make Cezary top of the candidates to take over in Oslo, and Wojciech could make sure Cezary knew it had only succeeded because of his intervention. That was too good an opportunity to miss, especially when the alternative was running the risk of Cezary finding out that Wojciech *hadn't* acted in his interests when he had the chance. It would be a pity. To rid the world of something beautiful always was — and this cop was certainly beautiful.

Of course, by the time any of this had been decided, the new arrivals would likely be spooked. But he wasn't too worried about that. Wojciech didn't too often feel outnumbered. He kept a subcompact Glock and a Fjällkniv hunting knife with a 20cm steel blade in the glove compartment of the Thema, plus a ten-metre rope and plastic cable ties in a bag in the boot. He'd make the new arrivals see that it was in their best interests to stick to their deal with Bonde. Failing that, if everything went tits up and Cezary's deal sank for whatever reason, he could always go to work on Bonde for Nygard. This was a good spot for it: pretty isolated, and any sounds the meeting happened to make would be carried away by the brewing storm and the industrial machinery at the port a little way down. And the weather meant activity on the water was thinning now, too.

★   ★   ★

463

The old man saw Skarnes coming right at the last moment. Skarnes raised a finger and pointed at him just before lifting him clean off his feet, carrying him backwards and ramming his puny frame against the glass wall of the ticket office. It was like lifting a polystyrene model of a man.

'Where are they?' Skarnes spat, after the first impact had jarred through the old man's body.

The old man looked scared, and searched the watching faces around them for aid.

An audible gasp of shock had rippled through the line of people shuffling towards the ferry and every one of them had stopped moving to look.

'Tell me where they are!' Skarnes rasped at the old man, jamming him against the glass again.

At last the old man looked at him, but before he could speak, a guy in a uniform stepped out of his booth to intervene.

'Hey,' Skarnes heard the man say from behind him. 'That's enough. Come on — leave the guy alone.' The ferry's horn sounded to speed up boarding. The rest of the crowd appeared in two minds as to whether they should watch, intervene or just pretend this wasn't happening and go on their merry way.

'I'm a police officer,' Skarnes threw over his shoulder, without taking his eyes off the old man. 'This man is a known criminal. Now tell me where they are, Nilsen.'

Still the old man said nothing.

'So arrest him,' came a female voice.

'Yeah,' a few more said.

'You police are all the same,' Skarnes heard another voice say, from the safety of the crowd, which had now begun to swell beyond those waiting for the ferry. The gravitational pull of the gathering was too much for idle passers-by to resist, but still no one intervened physically.

'I've got a young police officer out there who doesn't know what she's going into, so you fucking tell me. You understand me, you fucking Nazi?' His voice was cracking.

Skarnes shoved the old man back against the glass again. The old man winced, but still didn't answer. Skarnes rolled his head in an attempt to control his urge to batter the man into speaking. In doing so, he caught sight of the man from the ticket booth running off. Looking a little beyond, Skarnes saw where he was headed — a couple of uniformed beat constables.

'I won't let this happen. Tell me where they are. *Now.*' Skarnes yanked the old man forward so their noses almost touched. 'She's just a fucking child. Bonde's armed, you understand me? Don't you have any compassion left — ?'

He broke off because both his arms were grabbed. The cordless, still in his hand, went spinning to the ground.

★ ★ ★

Halvorsen had made his way down to the car pool and found the Octavia he'd got the key to. He was pissed off. He could feel the knots starting to tie in his shoulder muscles. He'd had to call Else and tell her he'd be late home. She hadn't sounded too angry. In fact she had sounded down right chirpy. 'Don't worry,

465

honey,' she'd said. 'I'm heading down to the gym anyway.' She'd never have said that five years ago. Five years ago she'd have sounded disappointed, told him she'd be waiting for him. Not any more.

On top of the suspicions that Else was getting her kicks with some prissy gym bunny, at work the mix of his uncle and Hansen was making everything so damned difficult.

And there he was in the middle of it all, the pressures stacking up all around. The knots in his shoulders. The rage rising. They all treated him like a moron. Well something was going to give, and he was going to duck out of the way of the fan, and still be there to mop up the mess when it was switched off.

He started up the Skoda and pulled out of the station car park, nice and slowly. He was in no rush to get to Sjursøya.

★ ★ ★

'Get your hands off me!' Skarnes shouted. 'I'm a cop, for God's sake.'

'You're a drunk,' one of the uniforms said in his ear. 'I could smell the liquor on you twenty metres away.'

The old man was clambering to his feet, aided by a number of people asking him if he was okay.

'She's just a child, Nilsen,' Skarnes said, his tone calmer now, more beseeching than demanding, on the verge of breaking. 'Come on. Don't you have any compassion left inside you at all?'

Just then, on the floor, the steak house's

cordless started to ring.

'Officer,' Skarnes said. 'You've got to let me answer that phone.'

The policeman gave Skarnes's arm a twist.

'I don't have to do shit,' he said.

'Then answer it yourself. It's Kripos. Ask them who I am.'

The policeman was hesitating.

'*Do it!*' Skarnes spat.

One of the policemen let go of him. Skarnes watched him pick up the phone and answer it.

'Hello . . . ?' he said. 'Edinsen? . . . Yes. I'm Constable Frei. I've got a man here.' He lowered the phone and said, 'What's your name?' to Skarnes.

'Skarnes.'

'Says his name's Skarnes . . . Uh-huh . . . Uh-huh. All right.'

The policeman looked at his partner and nodded reluctantly.

'Let him go.'

Skarnes shrugged off the second cop and took the phone from the first one.

'What have you got for me?'

'She's at Sjursøya.' It was Aamodt.

Skarnes started moving towards his car.

'Sjursøya? The port authority?'

'Nearly.'

The phone was beginning to crackle as it went out of range.

'And Skarnes?'

'What?'

'The phone's still active.'

'What does that mean?'

'It's still switched on, Skarnes.'

'So?'

'So either she's lost it, chose not to answer your calls, or . . . ' Aamodt trailed off, sounding apologetic.

'Or what, Aamodt?'

'Or she couldn't answer it.'

The phone died and he threw it aside as he broke into a run.

*   *   *

The old man watched Skarnes take off in his Mercedes.

All around, people were still watching the lightning. Even cars were pulling up now, the drivers getting out to stare up at the sky in awe. It was like a scene out of a sci-fi movie, an impression only amplified when a mechanical thunder started up behind the old man. It sounded like the mother ship coming in to land. In fact it was a De Havilland Otter floatplane taxi. The old man turned to see it just as it touched down on the water. He approached as it taxied, and when the pilot had seen the passengers off, the old man went up to him, hoping what he held in his hand would be enough to persuade him to go back up in this weather.

'Hey,' the old man shouted over the engine noise, holding out his debit card. 'You take plastic?'

20

All the other men in the back of the truck were German. Not many spoke. Those who did only whispered the question that was on all their minds: *Where are they taking us?*

Ivar had been in the prison camp for more than a month. It was the end of June 1945, and this morning they had been loaded onto the vehicle at gunpoint, with no hint as to their destination. The transport's tarpaulin had been pulled and tied as soon as they were all in, so they could not see where they were going. Cracks of light around the edge turned total darkness into a dark grey and showed the fearful eyes in the gloom. The only clue as to their final destination was the uneven terrain the vehicle's wheels were traversing, the bumps throwing them about, slamming their behinds into the wood of the benches, shooting pain up their spines. Wherever they were, this road was not metalled.

After a journey of some forty minutes, the vehicle jerked to a stop. They all heard the front doors of the truck open and shut, and the doors of other vehicles, too. The rope holding the darkness in was then loosened at one corner and the barrel of a rifle appeared, followed by two faces — British soldiers. The barrel pointed at

469

the prisoner closest to them.

'You,' the one holding the rifle said. 'Out.'

The German looked about at his compatriots. All eyes were upon him, but neither he nor anyone else said a word as he clambered out of the truck into the light. The tarpaulin was retied, and the eyes remaining exchanged more glances as they heard the English soldiers speak. The first words spoken were too quiet to hear, but then the volume increased.

'Move it,' one said, then, '*Schnell!*' and finally, 'Faster,' before a brief, sudden explosion sounded, followed by the patter of scattering debris, and after some applause and brief general discussion, the tarpaulin was drawn back once more.

'You,' the soldier said. 'Out.'

The process was repeated, and once more, there was an explosion. Nothing was seen or heard of the two men who had left the truck. Shortly afterwards the tarpaulin was pulled open.

'You. Out,' the soldier said. This time every man in the truck was staring at the floor, avoiding any form of eye-contact with the soldier.

'You, I said,' they heard again. 'Fucking look at me, boy.'

A couple in the truck dared to glance round, but Ivar continued to stare at the boards between his feet.

'Come on, Fritz, how about growing some balls here. You didn't mind shooting my pals, bombing my gran, did you? But now look at you,

you fucking Hun scum.'

Ivar raised his eyes a fraction and looked at the man opposite him. The man looked back, something more than fear in his eyes. Then Ivar noticed that the man next to that one was also looking his way. Ivar allowed his eyes to slowly pan across the line of men. Every one of them was looking at him. So was the Englishman, disgust filling his eyes.

'That's right, Jerry. On your feet now.'

Without asking his body to do so, fighting the motion even, but failing, Ivar felt his body rise and heard his shuffling feet carry him towards the light, into it, and he stumbled from the truck, landing face-down in the dirt at the edge of a ploughed field.

He twisted round. The soldier was standing over him, his outline broken by the glare of the sun behind him.

'On your feet now, chum,' he said.

Ivar rose onto his hands and knees. On a dust track ahead stood two more transport trucks and four personnel jeeps. Armed British soldiers were sitting in them, leaning against them, smoking and laughing with one another. Once again, all eyes were upon Ivar. Clambering to his feet, Ivar felt the soldier jab his back with the rifle.

'Now move,' the man said, nodding towards the field.

Something other than hunks of soil lay out there in the field, something glistening in the sun: material, wet, familiar. Ivar turned away in horror.

'What are you doing?' he said.

471

'Oh, speaky the English, do you?' said the soldier.

'Probably a fucking spy,' another one said.

'Out there are mines your lot laid, right? So now you're going to clear them, understand? You see that dead tree over there?' He pointed to the far side of the ploughed field. 'All you have to do is get to it, and get to it fast, all right? We haven't got all day.'

'But this is — '

'Stop the whinging and get moving, will you, Fritz?'

'But I'm not German,' Ivar stammered. 'I'm not a spy. I'm Norwegian. I'm on your side.'

'*Schnell*,' a third man said, stepping forward, but his accent was not German, or English. And his uniform was Norwegian.

'Please. I'm a Norwegian. You must help me. I'm not a spy, I was planted by the resist — '

'You're in the camp, you're a Nazi. So move it, or do you want me to shoot you?'

'No, don't shoot,' Ivar said. 'Please. Help me.' He could see his fellow countryman fighting something behind those eyes, the muscle in his jaw going off like a caught fish, but then the soldier shook his head and turned away.

'Maybe you'll get lucky, eh?' the English soldier said in his ear. 'And live to fight another day.'

Ivar watched the Norwegian retreat, then faced the field, and took a step forward, but did not go further. His footfall carried with it a hollowness that could not be boot on mud. He looked down. The toe of his boot was sitting on

472

the edge of a flat, shiny surface that was sticking up through the soil.

'I'll give you a hint,' the soldier said from behind him. 'Avoid metal. And long strides now. In exactly sixty seconds, Johnny here starts shooting.'

Ivar took a step to one side and dropped to his knees in the dirt.

'The bastard's begging!' one of the soldiers said, but Ivar did not look back. Rather, he raised his eyes to the tree on the other side of the field and braced his body.

'The Nazi does not fear death,' he whispered. 'The Nazi fears only his master.'

'No, lads. Look. He's in the blocks. He's going to — '

Before the soldier could complete his sentence, Ivar was sprinting, looking only at the tree, chanting the words . . .

'Only by making him fail his master, will I bring the Nazi to disaster. The Nazi does not fear death. The Nazi fears only his master. Only by making him — '

Before he had completed the mantra a second time, a noise had both deafened him and jolted him into the air simultaneously, hurling him head over heels before thudding him into the ground again a second later.

Ivar looked down. Only his left leg remained. Where his right had been was a mess of flesh, bone, blood, mud and clothing.

21

The female cop had stopped off at Bonde's BMW, parked up on the scrub outside the building. She was looking through the windows. Then she tried a door. It opened. She reached in under the console and popped the bonnet. Coming to the front, she pulled the bonnet up and leaned over the engine. Wojciech watched her arm disappear into a cavity around the engine. It was there a little while, then she yanked something a couple of times, her face twisting up with effort. Then she straightened, drawing her arm out. A couple of rubber tubes dripping liquid dangled from her fist like dead snakes. Probably the main fuel feed. Not only could she drive, she knew engines, too.

Wojciech smiled.

He was beginning to like this girl.

★ ★ ★

Curt dropped the empty jerry can on the floor of the Zodiac. That was the last of the fuel. He just had to hope it would take him far enough.

With the boat slowed and the rushing air no longer invigorating him, Curt noticed his body was beginning to feel the day's strain: the tension of the theft, the beating, the lack of food, the

474

dehydration. He was sweating again, too.

He shifted the thrust lever up and made for the bend towards the hook of the Oslofjord waterway to the south and east of the city. He was off the main channel there, but given enough time, the dive team would find him. He was still out in the open, and when the CPA came in view, the sky was looking truly angry and in addition to the thunder and lightning that was going off all the time, a wind was beginning to blow, churning the hot air, which wouldn't help his cause. It meant fewer boats out, which meant a red-and-black rubber hull would be easier to find.

Making his approach to Sjursøya, Curt did not pay much attention to the Volvo parked up the hill on the main road, nor to the midnight-blue saloon next to it. There were always cars parked around the CPA. And from his angle of approach, the BMW parked outside the building he'd been squatting in was hidden from view.

★ ★ ★

Even in the dying light, Wojciech recognized the person arriving at the jetty beyond the building in a black-and-red rubber-hulled boat with a sizeable outboard hanging off the back. The lightning lit up his shining black skin like a flashbulb. It was the young man he'd seen being arrested for approaching Bonde on the market square, and again fooling with an old white guy outside the police station.

Wojciech watched him tie off and then do

something with the engine at the back. After that the guy got out of the boat carrying a small plastic bag. The bag was about the size of a bag of sugar. The way he was carrying it up the jetty, though, it looked a lot heavier than something you got in a supermarket.

Wojciech figured the policewoman must have got involved where she wasn't wanted, that the black kid had been making a delivery to Bonde when she walked in on the game. Now they were meeting somewhere secluded where they wouldn't be disturbed. Which meant Bonde had not realized he was being tailed. Which meant the cop was about to mess it up again.

The cop was approaching the building now. Wojciech leaned over and popped the glovebox.

★   ★   ★

Crumbling and graffitied, with the doors and windows on the ground floor clad with grid metal, the CPA store reminded Curt of the blocks made ready for demolition on his council estate back home in Hackney. It was comforting, in a perverse sort of way. Nostalgic.

All the doors and windows were covered except for one of each. At the far end, next to the steel-framed window he'd uncovered, was his front door.

Curt entered through it. He'd only ripped the cladding off the one window, and the flashing slivers of lightning slicing through the sky outside clawed through the windows that remained grilled, breaking into smaller shards, scattering across the breezeblock walls and concrete floor like pieces of broken glass. There were two additional doors in the room. Curt had hidden three 200-kroner notes in a drawer in the cobwebby office through the green push-bar fire door to the right of the rain door; and the regular grey door to the left led to another room just the same as this one.

The room's contents were minimal, and just as he'd left them. In one corner was a small pile of building equipment that had been there when he arrived, which he'd used to get the window cladding off — a few rusty tools, a tarp, a couple of warped planks, some small cardboard boxes wilting in the damp. And in the opposite corner was the mattress he'd pulled out of the tip outside, with a blanket on it and his beaten up suitcase next to it.

He moved to the suitcase, unbuckled it, placed the gold sack inside, reclosed the suitcase, hooked it under his arm, then made for the green fire door.

★ ★ ★

Hansen arrived at the building just as Curt was coming up to the jetty in the Zodiac, but the thunder and the rising wind prevented the sound of the engine alerting her. She made her way to the only door she could see, paused outside it, listened, but heard nothing but the weather. The padlock on the door was rusted in place, but the wood into which the loop was screwed was rotten soft and she simply pulled it off, pretty much silently, before placing it on the ground and opening the door.

As she had expected, there was no one inside, just a dingy grey room, filthy with bird shit and dust, empty bookshelves, a desk, chairs. It had been an office. On the far wall to the left was another door, a green fire door like the one she had entered through. She crept round the desk, dodging the chairs, and put her ear to the closed door.

* * *

Curt was on the other side of that door, reaching out to push it open when he heard the crank of another door opening behind him. On the other side of the door Hansen couldn't make out the meaning of the words that followed, but for Curt they came through loud and clear.

'So, my little negro friend,' they said.

Curt whipped round. The voice was precise and sounded wrong, like a foreigner speaking a language he knows but doesn't feel; and it was coming out of the mouth of Bonde, who was standing in the doorway on the far side of the room.

'You are here.'

Bonde looked wired, strung out. His eyes were wide, his pupils dilated, he was sweating more than Curt and he couldn't keep his head still. It jerked about like it was on a spring as he inspected Curt.

'The fuck are you doing here?' Curt said.

'I'm here for my gold. So — where is it?' he said. 'Still in your boat?' He glanced over his

478

shoulder, through the window, but he looked back before Curt could make a move.

'It's not on the boat,' Curt said.

'Then where is it?' Bonde withdrew his hand from his jacket. It came out holding a Heckler. Curt felt the blood drain from his head and his suitcase dropped from his grip with a thud.

Indecision and light-headed fear flooded his mind, sending him straight back to Helmand. He was being ambushed all over again, and he was reacting just as he had back then.

'You have hidden it,' Bonde said.'

'Maybe,' Curt managed.

Talking was a start. In Helmand he hadn't even been able to do that. It had been like a scene from the westerns he'd watched as a kid with his grandfather, his unit moving on foot through a valley near Garmsir that was meant to be safe. But then the thunder started, out of a clear blue sky, from nowhere, and members of his unit had just started falling to the ground around him. The Taliban were shooting from the rocks like red Indians at a wagon train. Curt had just stood there, rooted to the spot as his friends and comrades burst red or ran for cover. Those that made it called for him to move, but he couldn't, he just stood there, untouched, unharmed, and watched and watched as the ground around him puffed with impacts and others crawled and shouted and bled.

The ISA forces had been forced to beat a retreat without him and he was taken. He had refused to make the video until his captors had sat him in front of the man he and his comrades had been trying to rescue that day — a Turkish corporal taken the week before.

They had shot the man's kneecaps off with a Kalashnikov, and that was enough. Curtis was all over You Tube for about eight hours before they closed the video down. After he made the film, they shot the Turk in the left temple and kept Curt alive, thinking a Brit was more valuable than a Turk. After that he was kept in a sealed cave for what felt like months, but was in fact only ten days. He was rescued on the eleventh.

With no family left in London, he got sent back to Freia, his NGO-employed girlfriend of five months, in her hometown of Bergen, Norway. Neither of them was equipped to deal with what trauma had turned him into. He was too far gone. One day, Curt found he had taken a train to Oslo and sold his passport, and was sleeping on a bench outside the station, then a derelict CPA store. Soon enough he realized life was done with him. He only needed the courage to end it.

Then the old man had appeared on the bridge and delivered him a chance — more than that, a reason for living.

Now at Sjursøya, he was in the moment of danger again, and all of a sudden this — this paralysis was coming over him again, just like it had in the valley near Garmsir, where the downward spiral had kicked off.

'Listen to me — Curtis, isn't it? Jeffrey?' Bonde said. 'I am a reasonable man. Not only that, I am an *influential* man. And I see that you are not a man to be dismissed lightly. So let me make a proposition. We will split the gold, you and I: half for you, half for me. And on top of that, I will see to it that you go home with your share safely. With the price of gold today, you will live like a king amongst your own people, for the rest of your life. We can be friends, you and I.'

* * *

After weaving his way through the narrow Old Town, Skarnes finally hit the coast road and opened the Mercedes right up, pushing it past all traffic, the lightning illuminating his way, the flashes melding pictures of Ida and Hansen in his mind. He couldn't let himself believe that anything had happened to her. He wouldn't let it. He couldn't.

He caught sight of a sign for the CPA blurring past. 10km.

* * *

While she could hear the voices clearly enough to identify their owners, from behind the door at Sjursøya Hansen couldn't make out the words. She had to move somewhere she could hear what Bonde and Curtis were up to.

* * *

Curt was staring at Bonde, his mind fighting his body.

The Taliban group had shouted unintelligibly

481

in his face, dragging him into their jeep, hooding him and taking him into some camp. But the language being spoken here was English, this was Europe, and the person he was dealing with wasn't a soldier — you could tell from Bonde's grip on the Heckler that he wasn't used to having a gun in his hand. If he was going to shoot he'd have done it already, winged Curt and started the torture. But he hadn't. Curt was in the driving seat here, he was the one with the training, and the one with the gold.

Curt forced himself to scan the room again. In the pile of rubbish ten feet away in the corner he spotted a length of two-by-four, a rusting claw hammer and an old adjustable spanner. He'd have to cover the distance to the tools and attack before Bonde could aim and shoot — and for that purpose the claw hammer was the clear winner. He'd leap over and grab it and swing round and swipe it into Bonde's neck, all in a single motion; let him bleed out. Alternatively, one direct hit with all he had would pierce Bonde's skull. He just had to time it right. And of course rediscover the ability to move his limbs.

'Mr Curtis, I do not want to have to use this gun. I am not by nature a man given to violence. But I will if I have to. My situation demands it.'

* * *

Hansen retraced her steps through the derelict office, and came out of the door into the weather. The wind blew her ponytail round her face, the lightning still coming, the thunder cracking. Keeping close to the wall, she moved along the outside of the building, towards the corner facing the water. She glanced round, seeing nothing, and was about to move, but stopped. The last crack of thunder was still sounding. That was more than ten seconds now, and it was growing, and growing. And it wasn't thunder any more. It was mechanical.

⋆ ⋆ ⋆

Wojciech had the Glock in his jacket pocket and the hunting knife in his hand and was out of the Thema. He was just about to shut his door and head down there, when something caught his eye. It was a phone, on the passenger seat of the Volvo, blinking a call. By the time he looked back down to the building, the policewoman had reappeared and was stalking around the building, looking to the sky like she was watching the weather.

Wojciech looked too. And saw what she saw.

⋆ ⋆ ⋆

The two men inside the building had become aware of the sound, too, both glancing towards the window, but their stand-off continued.

'Mr Curtis, the people I am dealing with will not accept failure to pay. They will kill me — they have made that perfectly clear. But I promise you that before they kill me, I will inform them of *why* I failed to pay them. And then they will be after you, too. On the other hand, in acknowledgement of your position of power here, if you show me where you have hidden the gold, I will let you keep half of it, and see you home with it. It is a very attractive offer.'

The sound had grown so loud now that Bonde had almost to shout. *'Tell me where it is!'*

'Fuck you,' Curt shouted back.

'I am going to count to five. If you don't tell me . . . '

Bonde raised the gun.

'One.'

Even inside the building the noise no longer sounded like thunder. It was an engine, but too loud for a car. Maybe a boat, a big one.

'Two.'

At that point, through the window, behind Bonde, Curt saw something move into view. The sound was an engine all right, but not on any boat.

'Three.'

It was a seaplane, already at the jetty, the props roaring. Curt shifted slightly to see the pilot alone inside.

'Four.'

Its passenger was already delivered. Its passenger was already inside the building.

'Five.'

It was the old man. On hearing his voice, Bonde jumped round in surprise. As soon as the gun was no longer pointed at him, Curt leapt. Hammer in hand, he twisted and brought it down on Bonde's wrist. But it was too late. The shot had been barely audible over the noise of the plane's engines. The old man crumpled. Bonde screamed. The gun clattered to the ground. Bonde was bent double, hugging his damaged arm as Curt grabbed the lapel of the politician's jacket with his left hand and looked across at the old man. He was on the floor, blood already seeping from his belly.

'You bastard,' Curt said down at Bonde, and raised the hammer over his head, every sinew in his skinny body tensed, the sweat rolling down his forehead stinging into his eyes, but he didn't blink. Bonde closed his eyes. Curt swung the hammer down.

'*No, Curt!*' the old man hissed.

Curt stopped the hammer an inch from Bonde's forehead.

'The police are on their way, Curt. If he is killed by a black man, he will become a martyr. Let them see what he has done.'

Bonde looked up.

'He called the police on you,' he said. 'Never trust an old Nazi, boy. And this one's the worst of them all. Say what you like about me, at least I love my country. Your partner here gave up his own people.'

The old man heaved himself up onto his feet.

'I was deceived, and my team, my family — people like you betrayed and killed them all. They took my identity and threw me away. I couldn't stand by and see Nazis walk free. Not after what they did. So I used my status as traitor to get close to them and — '

The pain was too much for him and he stumbled to the ground, grabbing his belly.

485

'Just like you're doing now. He's using you, Curtis, don't you see that?' Bonde spat at the floor before lowering his tone. 'He is the man they say he is, Curtis. Finish him off, and I promise you, you will escape a rich man.'

'I've already got the gold,' Curt said. He threw Bonde to the ground and moved to the old man's side, hooking a hand under his arm. 'Come on. Let's get out of here.'

The old man didn't move.

'We can get away from this,' Curt insisted. 'Up you get now.'

'I'm not exactly fleet of foot, remember?' the old man said, trying to smile.

'I can't leave you here.'

'Yes, you can.' Bonde spoke the words as he clambered to his feet. 'Because you're coming with me.' He was holding the Heckler.

★   ★   ★

Hansen did not hear the gunshot. All she could hear was the plane. When she got round to the back of the building, she saw it bobbing on the waves at the jetty. The propellers were winding down. There was one man inside, behind the controls.

He frowned at her.

She frowned at him.

When he made to open the door, she raised her hand. Seeing the badge in her hand, the pilot stopped. Hansen pointed at the door. The pilot nodded. Hansen raised one finger, frowning, trying to look like she was asking a question. Then two.

The pilot read her, and raised a single finger. One man had come off. And was inside.

Hansen showed the man her palm — stay where you are — and raised a finger to her lips — and keep quiet.

Then she moved to the door.

⋆ ⋆ ⋆

Wojciech was making his way through the tall dead grass on the hill the road wound down.

He had watched the plane coming in and that same old guy from outside the police station stepping out of it and then the female cop moving out of sight around the building. But since they had gone from view, there had been nothing to see, and he'd started moving, Glock in pocket and knife in hand.

Three possibilities. First, maybe the female cop was listening in to what was going on. Second, maybe she was making the arrest. Third, maybe they had her.

He threw the second option out immediately, because it would just lead to the third. The female cop had gone in there unarmed. The old man would be more or less useless, but if she tried to arrest the three of them, Bonde and the black guy would be able to overcome her easily. Maybe she was listening, but thinking about it, that just led to three, too, because if she was listening, she'd know she needed back-up and she'd need it to come before the three of them took off in the plane, so she should have been running back for her phone, but she wasn't. And if they had her, they would be spooked, which would mean they'd leave sooner rather than later. And they couldn't leave her behind to talk, so either they'd kill her or they'd take her with them. Both options would blow Cezary's deal out of the water, which was why Wojciech was moving.

He was a third of the way down when he heard a straining diesel. He dropped into the grass and looked up the road towards Oslo, and saw a speeding Mercedes approaching. When the whine of the engine eased and the car started slowing, Wojciech placed his hand in his pocket, took hold of the Glock and ducked down.

★ ★ ★

Skarnes spotted the green Volvo way before he reached the turn-off down to the CPA. It was sitting next to another blue car blocking half the entrance to the road. He had to slow right down to take the corner, and looked into the cars as he did. Both were empty. Down at the bottom of the turn-off, he could see a sleek BMW sitting outside an abandoned building. The door to the building stood open. There was no one in sight. Skarnes picked up speed down the road, but had to slow right down for the first tight pin turn. And there were five more of them to come.

★ ★ ★

The floatplane's propellers were nearly stopped. The engines were only whining now. The wind

488

was blowing up, rattling the grilles on the ground-floor windows, whistling through the broken panes on the upper floor. Hansen didn't hear a word of what was being said inside the building until she got to within a foot of the door. Even then she had to strain, but this time she heard.

*   *   *

'We are going to get in that plane and fly to the gold. Right now.' Bonde moved a little towards the window in order to have both men in his sights. Then flicked the Heckler's barrel. 'What are you waiting for, Curtis? Get moving.'

Curt was looking at the old man and didn't move.

'I said — '

Curt heard the ping of breaking glass and the rattle of shards falling to the floor.

He looked up. Bonde was falling towards him. As Bonde fell, Curt spotted a small round hole in the skin near his left temple. As Bonde twisted further and slumped, Curt saw the exit wound. Bonde's head was hollowed out, his brain, skull, skin and hair all mixed together in a wet mush.

Curt parried Bonde and let his body fall to the floor, looking out the window. In the distance, two hundred metres away, he spotted a boat, a big twin-engined speedster. It had Revenger emblazoned up the side.

*   *   *

On board, Harris was lining up his second shot. His sights showed the thief, Frank's killer. Jones was on the radio.

'Target down, sir.'

'Good job, Jones,' came Henderson's voice.

'And the thief, sir? We have him. Just say the word.'

*　*　*

The *Penguin II* was hanging in the water a couple of hundred metres off the lighthouse's island. Henderson looked down from the bridge to the dive deck where Bukhalov and de Veer were swabbing the Frenchmen's blood into the water. Curt's white poly bags were on the bench.

'We all have our jobs, Jones,' Henderson said into the radio. 'The thief was doing his. We've done ours. I'll see to it that Frank's family gets his share. Leave the thief and head back here for the divvy before this storm hits.'

*　*　*

Hansen saw immediately from the half pane remaining in the window frame what had caused it. The glass had shattered concentrically. That was a bullet hole. She listened for a moment, the first large warm drops of rain falling on her face. Hearing no more voices, she called out.

'This is the police. Is anyone hurt in there?'

Then she repeated it in English.

*　*　*

Curt recognized the voice and ducked instinctively, pulling the old man towards him.

'*Fuck!*' Curt said. 'We've lost the gold!'

The old man gurgled up a little laughter.

'Do you understand me? That was the divers that shot Bonde. They were at the lighthouse. I didn't make them — *idiot*. And now they have the rest of the gold. And the police are here. But there's some good news.'

The policewoman's voice came again.

'I'd recognize that voice anywhere. It's the policewoman who arrested me before. But she's just a junior. If there was a senior out there that's who'd be speaking. She must be on her own. We can get out of this. While she's dealing with Bonde we'll get away. *What the hell are you laughing at?*'

The old man shook his head.

'You couldn't keep it anyway.'

'What? What are you talking about?'

'The gold. It's not — clean.'

The man smiled, showing what teeth he had. There was a decent gap where his left first molar should have been.

Curt felt his gut flip as he understood — the nuggets with their ridges, and size, and irregular smoothness . . .

'They're — they're *teeth*?' he said, then looked at his suitcase. 'That's sick. What am I meant to do — '

Curt stopped when he felt the old man pull at his hand, place something in his palm and close his fingers around it. Curt looked. It was a piece of paper, folded many times until it was a thick wad only an inch square.

'What's that?' Curt said.

'The secret to the meaning of life,' the old man answered. 'My life.'

'Then why don't you use it?' Curt answered, puzzled. 'Come on, will you? We've got to get you to a hospital.'

'I'm an old man, Curt. I've already lived too long.'

Curt gathered up his suitcase and the Heckler and took the old man's hand in his. It was limp. The old man was losing strength fast.

'And I'm free,' the old man said.

Curt looked at him a second. The pool of blood was growing around his feeble, air-light frame, and Curt knew the old man was right. Moving him was hopeless. He'd be dead before they were out of the building.

Curt let go of the old man's hand. It slipped to the floor, landing with a faint slap in the blood. Curt rose and made his way to the fire door. He placed his hand against the pushbar, but paused before opening the door and looked back. The old man's eyes were half closed, sleepy.

'Hey, old man?' he said. 'You got a name?'

'Ivar,' the old man said, a whisper now. 'Ivar Petersen.'

Curt nodded. 'Goodbye, Ivar,' he said, then pushed through the door into the office.

* * *

Skarnes had taken the Mercedes down over the brush for the last two turns, jumping and bumping down the hill until he came to a stop

492

on the dirt. He was out and calling before the suspension stopped rocking.

'Hansen! Don't go in there! He's armed!'

★   ★   ★

Curt heard him first. He was in the derelict office taking his emergency six hundred kroner out of its drawer and he ducked under the desk, but when the voice moved around the building, he re-emerged and moved to the door Hansen had opened and stepped out. The rain was getting heavier, large drops splatting over his face. Curt opened his mouth, let a couple fall in and wet his tongue, then he moved.

★   ★   ★

Hansen heard Skarnes coming a few seconds later, just as she stepped over the threshold into the building.

Nilsen was lying on the ground, bleeding from the belly, next to Bonde, who was lying flat, his head half-missing. When Hansen came in, the old man looked up at her.

'What — I — What's gone on here?' was all she managed.

That was the moment Skarnes appeared, heaving in the doorway.

'Hansen! Bonde's — ' he spluttered, but then stopped dead. 'What the *hell?*'

Hansen didn't answer him.

'Mr Nilsen,' she said, 'Please. Where's the weapon?'

But over the rain drumming on the roof, she

493

heard the mechanical thunder of the seaplane's engines igniting, and she knew the answer.

★ ★ ★

The weapon was in Curt's hand. He had skirted the building, and was in the seaplane, wet with rain, holding it to the pilot's back, and the pilot was doing exactly as he was told — taking Curt and his suitcase out of there.

★ ★ ★

By the time Hansen and Skarnes got outside, the plane had taxied thirty metres from the jetty and was gathering speed. By the time it took to the sky, a Skoda Octavia had passed Hansen's Volvo and the midnight-blue saloon at the top of the road and had parked next to Bonde's BMW outside the building.

Halvorsen came up behind them as they watched the plane shrink into the distance.

'The hell's happened here, Hansen?'

They were the last words the old man heard before he closed his eyes and died.

★ ★ ★

A fourth set of eyes saw the seaplane depart.

Wojciech had seen the men in the Revenger, and he had seen the black guy getting into the plane, alone. Then the female cop and the man in the Merc, who seemed to be another cop, came out and watched the plane take off as the

494

Octavia driver joined them. Two of the people who had gone in to the building had not been accounted for. The police were not showing much interest in them. That could only mean one thing.

Wojciech scrambled back up to the Thema and sank into the luxury of its chocolate leather. He pulled out his phone and hit a number.

'Cezary?' he said. 'It's Wojciech.'

'So what?' Cezary said.

'So I'm hearing bad news, Cezary.'

'What sort of bad news?'

'About your guy. He's going to default on payment.'

'*What?* How the hell do you know that? He's — '

'He's dead, Cezary. There's no arguing with a high-velocity sniper round. But there's an angle here worth considering, and that's why I'm calling you and not your father.'

'What angle?'

'What if I could come up with another buyer for you?'

'By midnight?'

'By midnight.'

'I'd say do it.'

'We'll have to settle for payment by instalments, but the important thing is we get the photos, right? So you keep the meet, I'll send him along.'

'Just like that?'

'I can be very persuasive, Cezary.'

Wojciech hung up and typed in another number as he started up the Lancia. He slipped

495

her into gear and pulled out just as the call was answered.

'Hello?' a man said.

'Hello,' Wojciech said. 'Do you know who this is?'

'Yes, I do,' said Nygard. 'Is it done?'

Epilogue

May 1945 officially saw the end of hostilities in Europe.

The end did not come overnight, of course. In Norway, Soviet forces were fighting the Germans in the north from late in 1944. As they were forced south, the Nazis operated a scorched-earth policy, razing whole towns to the ground in order to leave nothing for the advancing Soviets.

Having hoped Norway would prove the last bastion of the Nazis, Terboven was dismissed as Reichskommissar *Norwegen* by Hitler's successor, Großadmiral Karl Dönitz. Dönitz himself was replaced by General Franz Böhme, who followed capitulation orders on 7 May. The next day, at Skaugum — home to the Crown Prince of Norway before and after the war, but Terboven's base during the war — Obergruppenführer Wilhelm Rediess, SS and Police Leader for the whole of the country, shot himself in the head. Soon after, Terboven himself lit the fuse on a stack of dynamite and blew himself to pieces.

It looked a lot like Hauptsturmführer Siegfried Wolfgang Fehmer had managed to escape in the chaos that followed surrender. He was searched for, but could not be found. He had vanished. One soldier, however — Sergeant John Maclean of British Military Intelligence — had the wit to intuit the Nazi's love of man's best friend, and by interrogating captured Gestapo officers discovered the location of Fehmer's German Shepherd. Maclean waited at the remote mountain cabin where the dog was being held and his hunch paid off. When the Gestapo man came for the animal, Maclean arrested him. The pair spent two days alone in the hut before reinforcements arrived.

Once the war ended, the vitriol began to flow. Women who had associated themselves with the occupying forces had their heads shaved and were placed in labour camps. Some were raped and beaten, made to walk the streets in processions of shame, the children they had borne to Nazi soldiers at their side. The Norwegian government did not know what to do. The women and children reminded everyone of the Nazis; they disgusted them. Should they send them to Australia? Reunite them with their Nazi men? It is a question that was never properly addressed and the bitterness and hurt — on both sides — extends into the twenty-first century.

No such problem presented itself when dealing with military and political issues. The organised resistance — the 40,000-strong *Milorg* — was ready and waiting for the Nazis to hit the ropes. The original government, who had fled on invasion and remained in exile until the war's end, on its return to Norway was ruled by the courts and parliament to have been the legitimate ruling force of the country all through the war years. This government had passed capital punishment into law in 1941, and deemed any person who operated in conjunction with Terboven or Quisling or *Nasjonal Samling* to be guilty: Norwegians of treason, Germans of war crimes. Whether you had tortured and killed fellow human beings or had simply been a member of the Fascist party, the charges were the same. In the immediate aftermath of the war nearly 30,000 arrests were made.

Of the 30,000 arrested, a total of thirty-seven were executed in a legal process that stretched from 1945 to 1948. Many Norwegians felt the number could, and should, have been far higher.

Twenty-five of the thirty-seven were Norwegians convicted of treason by the nation's High Court, a number that included Vidkun Quisling. Fehmer was one of twelve Germans found guilty of war crimes and put to death. He died by firing squad in Oslo in March 1948.

Others convicted in the legal purge after the war were imprisoned, fined or deprived of civil liberties. Some of these sentences were passed with due process, others without. Some of those arrested claimed to have been working as double agents for the XU. However, since the XU's files were classified, these assertions could not be proven. Such claims therefore fell on deaf ears. The XU's files were not declassified until the 1980s. When they were thrown open to the public, many who had been seen by their country as traitors for four decades had their names cleared, but due to the delay, this exoneration was often posthumous.

In light of the massive food shortage and enormous number of enemy soldiers surrendering, US President Eisenhower created a new prisoner designation in the aftermath of the war:

Disarmed Enemy Forces, designated by the British as Surrendered Enemy Personnel. This moniker was invented to sidestep the Third Geneva Convention, relative to the treatment of Prisoners of War, which states that captured enemy soldiers must be fed and housed humanely. However, much like the new category of Unlawful Enemy Combatants created following Al Qaeda's attacks on the United States in 2001, the reduction of human rights also led to more than mere negligence and deprivation.

It was as Surrendered Enemy Personnel that Snorre Nilsen, and others, were forced to clear one of the minefields the Nazis had laid as they retreated. The loss of his leg and the subsequent hospital treatment meant Nilson was not present at his trial. A statement — which had been taken during a break in his morphine treatment — was read out on his behalf in court. In it he claimed to be called Ivar Petersen and to have been working undercover for the resistance, that he had spent the last two years of the war held in solitary confinement. However, the tribunal deemed he had killed SS-Oberführer Gerhard von Westarp in an attempt to cover his complicity, and Snorre Nilsen was convicted on seven counts of treason. The judge called his deception and murder of Sofie Stornes, and his actions that led to the execution of the entire Stornes XU unit, the work of a particularly cruel and devious mind, but dismissed calls for a sentence of capital punishment. The trial had been delayed until after Nilsen's eighteenth birthday, however, in order that he could feel the

500

full brunt of the law. The judge decreed he serve forty years imprisonment, a term later increased when he murdered three other inmates. At the time of his original trial, while Nilsen would have been eighteen, Ivar Petersen was still only sixteen years old.

EGELAND OUT

It was a pretty unimaginative headline, even for *Aftenposten*, but the picture of Egeland staring out of the front page like a miserable sunburned toad was as good as anything they'd got for months. Skarnes turned to page two for the story:

Following a leak from the Oslo Police, Superintendent Lars Egeland of Crime Squad has been removed from his role and arrested. The leak suggests that the death of politician Henrik Bonde was not suicide, as previously reported, but murder, and that the judgement of suicide was settled upon by Egeland himself in an attempt to protect his misjudgement in releasing number one suspect, Jeffrey Curtis.
The Englishman, a former Corporal with the Royal British Engineers living rough in Oslo, was arrested for acting suspiciously around Bonde on the morning of 13 September. As the leaked documents show, Egeland personally signed Curtis's release, apparently in an attempt to reduce police workload, and against the wishes of Curtis's arresting officer, Inspector Halvorsen. Bonde was found

dead in a former City Port Authority building at Sjursøya later that day, having suffered a single bullet wound to the head. Previously reported to have gone there to take his own life, it is now thought Bonde's arrival startled Curtis, understood to have employed the building as a squat, who then killed the politician. Bonde's reasons for being there in the first place are now considered unknown.

Skarnes looked up when the pages were disturbed by the bar door being pushed open. Hansen was walking over in jeans and a sweater, a small rucksack over her shoulder. He hadn't seen her since Sjursøya. She had called him earlier today, said she had something to ask him that couldn't be said over the phone, so meet her after work here in Olympen. The place still had its 360° bar, but after the refurb that was about all that was left of the place he'd known. Certainly the clientele had changed. The two of them were the only police in there.

She sat down next to him at the bar. He slid the paper over.

'That's some leak, Inspector.'

She smirked and ordered a beer from the barman. 'You?' she said.

Skarnes shook his head, looking at the report again.

'You think you'll find him?'

'I hope not. He's no more guilty than you or me — you know that.'

'What about the manhunt?'

'An unfortunate bi-product of Egeland's

502

demise. It'll peter out. If we catch him, we'll ship him out. It's unlikely without a photo going out, though.'

Skarnes let Hansen pay for her drink, then said:

'I see Halvorsen made out all right.'

'I didn't do too badly myself.'

'The youngest inspector in force history.'

'Not bad after two months in the job. That's what I asked you here for, actually,' she said, taking a swig.

'What?'

'With Halvorsen making Super, I'm down a partner. How about it?'

'Me?' Skarnes nearly spat his cranberry all over the paper.

'Well?'

'Ingrid, I've already applied for my licence. My signatory would be very disappointed.'

'Edinsen?'

'It's a different world in the Squad now, Hansen. And it's your world, not mine. Besides, I have a habit of getting on the wrong side of people, and I've seen what you do to people who get on yours. As a private citizen, you won't be able to get at me. I'm grateful, Hansen, I am, but . . . *what?*' She was smiling and had pulled a gift-wrapped box out of her rucksack and sat it on the paper in front of Skarnes.

'I thought that's what you'd say. So I got you this.'

'What is it?'

'Open it.'

He did.

'It's a mobile telephone,' he said, puzzled.

'So next time you can call me.'

'Next time?'

'I figure with you out there as a private dick, you can do the things I can't. Be my outside man.'

'That's what you figured?'

'All on my own. I'm an inspector, you know?'

He inspected the box, slowly nodding.

'Not that there has to be a case for you to call me,' she added.

It was pity, Skarnes knew, but her pity he could use.

'Don't jinx me before I've started, *Inspector* Hansen. Now where was I? Ah, yes . . . '

'The death of Henrik Bonde is a grave and tragic result of one man's misjudgement,' said Chief Superintendent Klaus Beck in a press release. 'That man has been removed from his position and an inquest has been ordered to investigate the potential criminality of his actions. Make no mistake, we are taking the situation very seriously and if his misjudgement is found to have contravened laws, he will be charged and tried. Meanwhile we have instigated the largest manhunt in our country's history in an attempt to find Curtis and bring him to justice. At the same time, I would like to draw attention to the fine police work of Inspector Lukas Halvorsen and Sergeant Ingrid Hansen in doing their very best under what have been shown to be supremely trying circumstances. It is thus with great confidence that

I inform you of my decision to make Lukas Halvorsen Lars Egeland's replacement as Superintendent of Crime Squad, with immediate effect.'

Magnus Iversen, chief spokesperson for newly appointed Prime Minister Karl Nygard, leader of the Advance Party, under whom the police are set to see a 6 per cent rise in their annual budget, had this to say: 'Henrik Bonde was a fine man, a true Norwegian, and in his day, a formidable politician. Sadly, the mental disorder from which his doctor has revealed he suffered in his latter years resulted in him behaving in what can only be called an uncharacteristic manner in the lead up to the elections. Thankfully this did not affect results and we feel more than ever, with the full hideousness of this crime now coming to light, that the public chose wisely in selecting the Advance Party to lead their country. I would like to emphasise our stern promise to all Norwegians that the security of our country and its citizens is the number-one concern of their new government.'

When Wojciech read Norwegian he spoke it out loud without realizing. Having bought his paper from the stand next to the marble-columned station bar, he made his way to the left-luggage locker, reading all the way. He stopped at number D91, dropped the paper on the bench next to the rack, found a key on his keyring and opened the locker. Inside was a large manila envelope. He removed it, and checked the bills inside — a flick through confirmed it to contain approximately 500,000 kroner. A piece of paper was in there with them. He pulled it out. It was a piece of ruled A4, with an unsigned note written on it in generic block capitals. It said, 'Thank you.'

Wojciech had an empty leather satchel slung over his shoulder. He unbuckled it, placed the envelope inside, rebuckled it and slung it over his shoulder again. Then he closed and locked the locker and screwed the note into a ball. He threw the ball into a wastebin, but left the newspaper where he'd put it on the bench. He made his way back to the bar, went all the way through, and out to the car park beyond. Three rows out, he opened up the Thema, sank into the chocolate-leather upholstery, started her up, and drove home to Frogner, just another unidentifiable, instantly forgettable midnight-blue saloon in the traffic.

A little later, Wojciech's paper was picked up by another customer of the Central Station left-luggage lockers. The seaplane pilot told Curt he only had fuel enough for a twenty-minute journey, so Curt had him drop him off as near as he could get to the east of town: Grønland, the multicoloured, multicultural heart of the city, where Curt wasn't out of place — where plenty of people looked poor because plenty of people *were* poor, and plenty of the poor people there carried all kinds of bags full of all kinds of shit, and plenty wore mashed-up clothes, and plenty had black skin. Unlike anywhere else in the city,

Curt knew he could melt into the scenery in Grønland. But still, what he was carrying in his suitcase was gold, so he'd headed straight to the station, changed his clothes in the toilets, then left the gold and his suitcase in a luggage locker, keeping only a handful in his pocket.

After a week touring jewellers pawning individual teeth, he headed into an Internet café. Ten minutes later he headed to a hardware store and bought a heatproof mat, a kilo crucible mould, a tin of borax flux, a pair of tongs and a blowtorch with three canisters of fuel. Then he headed back to the station, collected his suitcase and checked into a dive hotel, into a room with a balcony, and got to work. Twenty-four hours later he had five one-kilo blocks of gold stacked on the table in front of him. He placed four of them in a bag, the fifth in his suitcase, and headed out. First he dropped the suitcase back in the luggage lockers at the station, then he headed to the east of town, to the address written on the old man's piece of paper.

The house was a crumby duplex, the paint on the wood cladding peeling, the stoop missing planks. Through the window, Curt saw some ginger-haired kids being put to bed in a cramped ground-floor bedroom. He placed the package on the doorstep, then pressed the bell under the name that matched the one on the old man's piece of paper. Then he headed back into town. Before he left the hotel the next morning, he flipped on the news and heard about the developments. The largest manhunt in history, but they weren't printing his picture.

He headed out, got himself a shave and a haircut, a suit and shirt, and a hat and shades. The paper he lifted from the bench after retrieving his suitcase from the luggage lockers was the final touch that saw him through the barrier and onto the Bergen train, ready to take what came. In his seat, as the train moved out under the bridge where he'd first met the old man, back when he thought life was done with him, Curt turned to page seven. He reread the story three or four times:

LUCKY DAY

A family in Manglerud opened their front door yesterday to find a paper bag on their doorstep. The bag contained four kilogram bars of gold.

'We can't believe it,' said Mikkel Langeland. 'It's as though we've been visited by a fairy godmother.'

The Langelands will not be splashing out, however. If police decide the gold can be kept, the pieces of metal, worth approximately $200,000, will be spent seeking justice. Mr Langeland is the son of a war child. His grandmother was Norwegian, his grandfather was a Nazi soldier.

'*Kriegsbarn* were treated horribly in the aftermath of the war,' he says. 'After my grandmother was killed, my father was sent to an asylum for no other reason than that the authorities did not know what to do with him. He was four years old. He suffered pain and humiliation, and did not emerge until his eighteenth birthday. We long fought for acknowledgement of this unspeakable treatment of children, and finally it came in 2000. My father is no longer with us, but still many *Kriegsbarn* remain too ashamed even to speak of this aspect of their lives. This gold will be used to establish a foundation in my father's name. The aim of that foundation will be to help, in any way required, those whose crime it was merely to have been born.'

Author's Note and Acknowledgements

The dedication at the beginning of this book says 'for Mona'. It could also have read 'from Mona', or 'because of Mona'. Mona is Norwegian and the only reason I was in an Oslo pub seven years ago. By going to the toilet and sending me to buy our drinks, Mona is the reason I got talking to a man of about sixty who was sitting alone at the bar. The conversation started innocuously enough: 'You're English, what brings you here?' But the next stage of the (apparently not internationally recognized) Rules of Conversation with Strangers was skipped, and within a minute of our first words this man was describing to me his childhood in an orphanage. The place held no record of his biological origins, and despite starting his hunt as soon as he left the institution, he didn't find out who his parents were until the files pertaining to something called the Lebensborn Program were made public in the mid 1980s, by which time he was nearly forty. His mother had been Norwegian and had died some years earlier. His father had been a Nazi soldier stationed in Norway during the war. He was still alive at the time, but the man at the bar did not seek him out and had struggled with being 'half Nazi', as he put it, ever since, and assured me he would continue to do so for the rest of his life.

Struck dumb by such spectacular personal revelations, when Mona reappeared, I managed to wish the man well and went to join her. At our table I regurgitated the story with great excitement, only to be informed that it was not especially unprecedented. Lebensborn's legacy is seared into the national consciousness. Its relevance to the Norway of today made the man's story, and that of Lebensborn itself, all the more fascinating, and is one of two reasons I settled upon writing this book.

An interest in Norway's wartime history inevitably leads one to the Resistance movement. Growing up, the French Resistance seemed to me a pretty good bet for the bravest, coolest people who ever existed. To some degree they remain so — the Norwegians didn't smoke Gitanes, after all, or speak French, but their courage was just as breathtaking, their achievements just as miraculous. By all accounts, both occupied countries were sinister, dangerous places, with trust in short supply and fear a way of life, and members of both movements deserve great respect and admiration. France, however, cannot match Norway for the incredible harshness of its natural environment. This is particularly true in winter, of course. Though the scenery is as spectacular as any in the world, survival in the wild in Norway would prove difficult at the best of times, even for the staggeringly adept and tough Norwegians. In war, fighting an enemy as ruthless as the Nazis, it can only have been possible with an unwavering unity of spirit, commitment and willingness to sacrifice, of which I am thoroughly in awe. The extreme

511

modesty of the subsequent personal accounts of the movement, the refusal of these men and women to consider themselves in any way exceptional, and how that lay with the ideas behind Lebensborn, is the second reason I wrote this book.

Seven years and two children after that evening in an Oslo pub, Mona is still on the other side of my table, overseeing the book's cultural, and where needed, linguistic veracity, acting as chief translator, whilst also holding down a job and being the best, most exuberant mother a pair of inordinately energetic four-year-old twin boys could ask for, all the while somehow retaining her patience and love for me. So while certainly it is because of her, and to some degree from her, first and foremost this book must be for her, with my eternal love and gratitude.

If a writer is nothing without his inspiration, a published writer, I have learned, is nothing without the team of people backing him up, making his work as good as it can be before sending it out to arrive in your hands. So thanks are due also to my agents Molly Stirling and Luigi Bonomi, who took me on and brought me to the attention of Simon & Schuster UK, where my editor, the ever-patient, encouraging and constructive Jessica Leeke, has proved a supportive joy to work with; and lastly thanks to Bruno Vincent and Will Atkins, for yet further improvements.

B.H. 2012

We do hope that you have enjoyed reading this large print book.

Did you know that all of our titles are available for purchase?

We publish a wide range of high quality large print books including:
Romances, Mysteries, Classics
General Fiction
Non Fiction and Westerns

Special interest titles available in large print are:
The Little Oxford Dictionary
Music Book
Song Book
Hymn Book
Service Book

Also available from us courtesy of Oxford University Press:
Young Readers' Dictionary
(large print edition)
Young Readers' Thesaurus
(large print edition)

For further information or a free brochure, please contact us at:
Ulverscroft Large Print Books Ltd.,
The Green, Bradgate Road, Anstey,
Leicester, LE7 7FU, England.
Tel: (00 44) 0116 236 4325
Fax: (00 44) 0116 234 0205

Other titles published by
The House of Ulverscroft:

DAY OF THE DEAD

Lisa Brackman

A holiday in Mexico is just what Michelle Mason needs after her husband dies, leaving behind a scandal and a pile of debt. On the beach, she meets a handsome American ex-pat — the margaritas have kicked in and she decides: why not? But their date ends horribly when Daniel is attacked by intruders in her hotel room. When Daniel disappears, Michelle is drawn into Mexico's dangerous underworld of corrupt policemen and powerful drug lords. What was a holiday romance suddenly becomes a matter of life or death. Can she trust Daniel — or is he responsible for the danger she is in?

FIFTEEN SECONDS

Andrew Gross

Dr. Henry Steadman has it all: a booming practice, a daughter he loves, and time to enjoy life. But while visiting north Florida, a police-stop ends in the shooting of a local cop — with Henry as the prime suspect. When he is framed for a second murder, this time of a close friend, Henry goes on the run. His only lifeline is community outreach worker Carrie Holmes, who believes in Henry's innocence. But they have no evidence, the police are closing in — and the real killer is still out there. Henry's nightmare is complete when his family is targeted. But now everything has been taken away from him, Henry has nothing left to lose . . .

BLOOD LOSS

Alex Barclay

When a teenage girl is beaten and raped, in the grounds of a derelict asylum, FBI agent Ren Bryce is called in to assist. But she is soon diverted to a missing person's case when an eleven-year-old girl and her teenage babysitter vanish without a trace from their hotel room. Faced with conflicting evidence and inconsistent witnesses, Ren works obsessively to unravel the dark family secrets at the heart of the case, before it's too late . . . Determined to uncover the truth, Ren's behaviour becomes increasingly reckless. Putting her own safety at risk, she enters a world where innocent lives are ruined for profit . . . and kidnap, rape and murder are all part of the deal.

CROSSBONES YARD

Kate Rhodes

Ray and Marie Benson killed thirteen women before they were caught, tried and imprisoned. Five of their victims were never found. Six years later, psychologist Alice Quentin discovers a woman's body on the waste ground at Crossbones Yard. The wounds are horrifyingly similar to the Bensons' signature style. But who would want to copy their crimes? When Alice is called in to consult, her first instinct is to say no. She wants to focus on treating her patients, not analysing the mind of a murderer. But the body at Crossbones Yard is just the start, and the killer may already be closer than Alice knows.

STRANDED

Emily Barr

When her marriage breaks down, Esther
Lomax needs to get away and hopes that
Malaysia's unspoilt shores will provide some
space and time alone. Sure enough, each
day of her holiday finds Esther beginning
to unwind and feel ready to face single
motherhood. However, a day's boat trip takes
a desperate turn when Esther and six other
holidaymakers are deposited on an uninhab-
ited island. Their guide, who had promised to
pick them up in an hour's time, fails to return
and the dreadful reality of the situation hits
the group. With no means of getting back to
the mainland and knowing nothing about
each other, tensions erupt — and time is
running out. Esther must ask herself the
ultimate question: will she leave the island
alive?